DAT
NIGHT
D0287538

ALSO BY SAMANTHA HAYES

The Reunion
Tell Me a Secret
The Liar's Wife

DATE NIGHT

SAMANTHA HAYES

bookouture

Published by Bookouture in 2018

An imprint of StoryFire Ltd.

Carmelite House
50 Victoria Embankment
London EC4Y 0DZ

www.bookouture.com

ISBN: 978-1-78681-766-2
eBook ISBN: 978-1-78681-765-5

PROLOGUE

Now

I stare at my hands, head hanging down, as I sit in the back of the police car. There's dried blood under my nails. Little dark crescents. I ball up my fingers, burying them in my lap with my wrists clamped together, glancing back at the cottage as the engine starts. An officer sits beside me.

Did I lock the door? Turn off the lights? Should I have left a note?

Back soon, darling. xx

Perhaps in twenty years.

'Belt on,' the officer beside me says, tugging on the strap. I nod, feeling like a naughty child. No, worse than that. *Way* worse. But how do I convince them that they're wrong about me?

I cover my face, screwing up my eyes. Then, without thinking, one of my fingers slips inside my mouth – a habit Sean chastises me about – with the other cuffed hand following. Our first Christmas together, he got me a voucher for a manicure at the salon in the expensive spa hotel nearby. A lovely thought, except he didn't hide his disappointment when I returned with beautifully filed and painted *short* nails. He'd been expecting – hoping for – acrylic talons. *Like Natalie*, I couldn't help thinking.

'But I can't work if they're long,' I'd told him, kissing him. He didn't complain after that.

I taste blood. Metallic and raw as the congealed crescent under my nail dissolves on my tongue. First finger, second finger, ring finger… I swallow down the retch, licking my lips, praying there's no trace on my mouth as the car bumps along the lane away from our cottage, past The Green with its stone memorial already adorned with an early poppy wreath. *More blood*, I think, as my eyes meet the stares of several locals huddled for a chat, the red a shocking flash behind them as they watch me pass. I recognise their faces, which isn't unusual in Great Lyne. Everyone knows everyone. The picture-perfect scenery blurs behind them as I stare at their faces – a mouth gaping, a neck craning, eyebrows raised that Libby Randell is being taken away in a police car, its yellow and blue neon markings bright in the half-light of the dreary day. Tongues will be wagging, gossip rife in the local pub, the village store, the primary school playground. An ending after the weeks of suspense.

Did she do it? What happened? Who'd have thought?…

It's what the village wanted, after all – a conclusion. The weight of not knowing had been pressing down like a looming storm these last few weeks, shrouding day-to-day life.

It was bound to break. Just not in the way anyone expected.

But relief is relief. People just want to get on with their lives, will accept whatever provides closure. And, of course, everyone had their suspicions – me included.

Perhaps she took off somewhere and killed herself – she always seemed unstable… Or the mother could be to blame, or her father (they were having problems, you know), or maybe she's run away and will turn up homeless in London. She could have had an accident and no one's found her body yet… Those poor parents. And poor Libby and Sean… Such a nice couple. Such a nice family.

And poor *Sasha*…

Everyone forgets poor Sasha.
No one knows what happened that night.

We're out of the village now. The comforting familiarity of its honey-stone cottages, the lanes where I've either walked or driven every day for the last seven years, is several miles behind us, replaced by fields and farm buildings and, soon enough, the A44. As I stare at a passing sign, I realise they're taking me to Oxford.

'Will I be gone long?' I ask the officer beside me. Her posture tells me she's poised, ready for action should I try to escape – her shoulders tensed, her left hand on the seat between us, her fingers splayed. I've seen her around these last few weeks, along with all the others – some in uniform, some not. The activity has come and gone in waves, the accompanying gossip trailing in the wake of the police presence. I'm hardly a flight risk, I think, in my mom jeans and one of Sean's old sweatshirts with stains down the front. I'd shoved my feet into my old gardening Crocs when they cuffed me and took me away – not fleeing-the-police footwear.

But then, I have nothing to flee from, I tell myself. We've all had to make statements over the last three weeks. I'll answer their questions (probably the same ones yet again), clear up any misunderstanding and ask them to let me go. I've only made a brief start on tonight's dinner party and probably won't be back in time to finish it now. I hang my head as I imagine my clients waiting for me later, their concern turning to disappointment and anger as they realise I've let them down.

'That depends,' the officer says, reminding me that I asked her a question.

I give a little nod, chewing on the fingers of my left hand now, sucking out the blood – gnawing, biting, cleaning. The officer driving, Detective Inspector Jones, is early-fifties, non-uniform, with a square, set jaw covered in a salt-and-pepper beard. His eyes flick to the rear-view mirror every few seconds – not so much checking the traffic behind, but rather checking me. I try not to meet his stares.

This is *me*! I want to scream. Just *me*! I'm a mum, a wife, a daughter-in-law, a best friend. Aged thirty-nine with a four-year-old child, a husband, my own business, a stepson and a cat. I've got good friends, I'm well liked, I do Pilates and pay my taxes on time. I keep our cottage nice, drive an average car, and sometimes we take weekend breaks to Polzeath because Sean and Dan – Sean's fifteen-year-old son, and the only reason he keeps in contact with Natalie, his first wife – like to surf together. My stomach lurches when I think of my husband's ex. Ever-present in our lives. Her demands affect all of us one way or another.

'Oh, *Alice*…' I whisper, suddenly remembering my daughter. My cuffed hands cover my face as I think where she is.

'Alice?' the officer beside me says.

'My… my little girl,' I reply, my voice wavering. My thoughts are all over the place. Finally, my head catches up with the panic in my heart. 'Marion…' I say, my lungs almost collapsing. *Thank God.*

'Marion?' the officer says again.

'My mother-in-law,' I add, knowing that Alice will be fine. Marion will bring her back home later. If she can't reach Sean or me, she'll get a little annoyed in that silent way of hers and go back to the farm, secretly pleased that she gets to spend more time with her granddaughter. Despite being tired these last few weeks, her health not the best, Marion will take delight in saving the day. And letting me know about it.

'Sorry,' I say, touching my forehead. 'I'm just a bit… thrown.' I glance across at the officer again, who stares ahead, a little pucker to her lips. 'It's just… it's just that I've never been arrested before.'

Let alone on suspicion of murder.

CHAPTER ONE

Before

'Come on, come *on*...' Libby said, her hand tapping the top of the kettle as she waited for it to boil on the hotplate. Sean passed behind her, his hands sliding across her waist as he reached down some mugs from the cupboard. Libby glanced at her watch.

'Mummy, can we get a kitten?' Alice asked, her feet kicking the table leg. 'And a tortoise?'

'A tortoise?' Libby replied with a smile, preoccupied with getting to the market early before all the good produce was gone. The new client was important and she needed to impress.

'No, Little Bean,' Sean added. 'We've got a cat already. And cats eat tortoises for breakfast, didn't you know?' He tickled her from behind, bending down to kiss her soft curls. 'Now, why don't you eat yours?'

'Because I don't like porridge. No one at playgroup has to eat it.'

'Here, have this, then,' Libby said, just wanting Alice to have something inside her before she went to Marion's. She slid her own untouched toast towards her and Alice leant forward, licking the jam and making an appreciative noise.

'What's the world coming to when a four-year-old turns her nose up at organic oats and honey, eh?' Sean said, laughing as he dragged a wooden chair out from under the table, its legs scraping on the quarry tiles. He sat down, taking the porridge for himself.

Libby laughed too, leaning against the worktop as she sipped her coffee, watching her little family – a look of disbelief in her eyes that they were actually hers. She was completely in love with them both. But her mind was really still on the lunch for twenty tomorrow. *A boardroom feast to impress* was the brief. She never usually got nervous, but this was a test run for a regular account. Weekly team meeting lunches, then, if that went well, catering for fifty at their monthly training events. She and Sean were OK for money – *just* – but she'd spent the best part of three years building up All Things Nice and wanted it to succeed. No, she *needed* it to succeed, what with the renovations having cost way more than anticipated. Besides, she liked that Sean was proud of her.

'Seeing as Mummy's a bit stressed today, Bean, why don't you paint her a picture at playgroup this afternoon?'

Libby made a noise in her throat, about to say something, but decided against it.

'I can paint at Nanny's house this morning,' Alice said matter-of-factly. 'She lets me make a mess anywhere I like and I don't even have to clear it up. *And* she gives me all the sweets that I want.' Her voice rose in a satisfied little squeak.

Sean and Libby caught each other's eyes. Libby was ever grateful to Marion, of course, for helping out – she couldn't manage without her. But sometimes Alice got away with things she didn't agree with. Libby knew biting her tongue was a small price to pay in return for free childcare.

'Are you on call tonight?' Libby asked. Sean had been doing more evening shifts lately.

''Fraid so,' he said. 'But I doubt it'll be busy.'

He'd said that last time but hadn't got in until after midnight. She decided not to say anything though, quickly loading the dishwasher with a few bits before dashing upstairs to gather Alice's stuff for the day. When she returned, she sent her daughter off to clean her teeth, straddling Sean's legs as he sat on the chair. He put his hands on her hips as she leant forward to kiss him.

'Mmm, the porridge *is* good today,' Libby said with a wink, planting her lips on his again. The kiss was deep enough to last the day, yet light enough for each of them to be left wanting more later. 'Let's hope it's a quiet night at the practice, then,' she said, feeling her body stirring. She fancied him more now than she did when she first set eyes on him six years ago. Both on the mend from failed relationships, they were each other's balm from that first clichéd look across the crowded bar. Except it wasn't particularly crowded and not really a bar – rather the half-empty local pub a couple of villages along from here where Libby was meeting some girlfriends. She'd recognised him from the gym at the hotel where she was working at the time.

'Right, you,' she said, standing up when Alice returned. 'Coat and shoes on, and into the car.' She glanced out of the cottage's leaded front window to the scene beyond. The village green sparkled with a light frost, the footprints of early-morning walkers tracking across it. 'Quick, quick now as I'll need to de-ice the car.'

Alice gave Sean a big hug, virtually climbing on his back as he shrugged into his waxed jacket and tied up his boots. 'Right, I'm off to work,' he said, easing Alice off him. 'I'll be getting a lift back with Archie later,' he told Libby. 'I'm dropping the Land Rover at the garage at lunchtime to get the brakes looked at. It might be in for a couple of days, depending what parts need ordering. I'll have to use yours if there are evening call-outs.'

'No problem,' Libby said.

Sean gave them both another quick kiss, grabbing the lunch Libby had made for him and closing the latched front door behind him in a waft of chilly air.

'Mummy, I need a wee,' Alice said, jumping up and down.

'Hurry up then, sweetie,' Libby said. 'I'll be outside scraping the ice off the car. Don't forget to wash your hands,' she called out as Alice trotted off. She pulled on her padded jacket, feeling in the pockets for her gloves. They weren't there so she went back upstairs to check another coat pocket. Warm clothes hadn't been necessary so far this autumn, but the last day or two the weather had been coming in from the north. She reckoned they'd have to start parking in the courtyard at the back of the cottage again. It was a squeeze to get both cars in, but at least it was sheltered from the weather and would make getting away in the mornings quicker.

Eventually she found her gloves and headed out to the car, seeing that Sean had already left. She plucked at the last one or two remaining geranium heads in the pots outside the front door, making a mental note to pick up some pansies or cyclamen at the fruit and veg market later.

Libby started the engine of the VW estate, turning up the fan and flicking on the heated rear window. She rummaged in the glove box, feeling around for the ice scraper, giving a quick glance to the open front door of the cottage for Alice. She gave a little smile – the thatched roof of the little porch canopy always reminded her of a neatly trimmed fringe and she and Alice had often joked about how the cottage had a friendly face. Sean hadn't long bought the place when they got together and they'd done lots to it over the last few years. It was definitely home. Definitely safe. The three of them. Maybe one day there would be four. She'd been dropping hints recently about trying for another.

'Come on, Bean,' Libby called out as she took to the windscreen with the scraper, stopping suddenly.

'Oh,' she said, noticing a piece of paper tucked beneath the driver's wiper. It wasn't a flyer or stuck down in the frost, so she assumed it must have been left some time this morning.

She pulled off her glove, lifting up the blade as the windscreen thawed from the heater. The paper was damp as she opened it – though she was more concerned with why Alice was taking so long inside than whatever had been left on her car.

'Alice? Chop-chop!' Libby called through the front door, putting the key in the lock. She opened up the piece of paper, seeing that there were just a few words written in blue biro, bleeding out from the damp.

She stared at it, her mouth opening, her eyes widening, unable to take in what she was reading. Then, when she glanced up at the door, her eyes grew even wider. The writing wasn't the only thing bleeding.

'Oh, *sweetie*,' Libby exclaimed when she saw Alice's nosebleed. Her lips and hands were scarlet. 'How did this happen?' She bent down, dropping the note to inspect her daughter.

She didn't know which was more disturbing – what was written on the paper or the sight of Alice's face.

As she pulled a tissue from her pocket, dabbing at the blood, she closed her eyes for a moment. But all she could see were those five words, etched into the back of her eyelids…

Sean is having an affair…

CHAPTER TWO

'Marion, I'm *so* sorry we're late,' Libby said, breathless. She'd had to rush back inside and wash Alice's face before leaving. And, while she wanted to laugh off the note, it had rattled her to the core. 'It's just been one of those mornings,' she sighed, going inside the farmhouse when Marion beckoned her in.

'Poor Mummy – eh, Alice?' Marion said with a virtually imperceptible raising of her eyebrows as she smiled at her granddaughter. She took Alice's backpack and coat. 'Don't worry, you're at Nanny's now and…' She paused, sucking in a breath. 'Oh *my*,' she said, flashing a glance at Libby. 'What on earth have you been up to, darling?' Marion bent down, tugging on Alice's previously clean sweatshirt, rubbing her hand over the brown stain, gently touching the traces of blood left around her neck.

'Dose beed,' Alice said, hamming it up for the reaction she knew she'd get as she tipped back her head to expose her nostrils, one of which was packed with cotton wool.

Marion stood up again, a hand touching her stomach as she winced, trying to hide the pain. If Libby ever mentioned her various ailments, asking if she was OK, Marion always brushed them off. 'Are you supposed to do that?' she said to Libby. 'Stuff things up there?'

'It wouldn't stop and we were in a hurry,' Libby replied, not having a clue if it was the right thing to do. All she knew was that it was gushing blood and, after the third plug, it seemed to slow down, not soaking through the cotton wool as fast.

Marion put her hand on Alice's shoulder, drawing her up against her legs. 'Well, there's no hurry now you're here, is there, sweetie?' she said. 'Your poor mum's always in one, though. Why don't you come in for a coffee, Libby? You look quite pale.'

'Thanks, but I—'

'Nonsense,' Marion said, turning and heading for the kitchen. 'I insist. You look as though you've seen a ghost.'

For a moment Libby thought about protesting, but she knew she was on a hiding to nothing. She could gulp it down, she supposed, and hopefully still catch the traders before the best produce was gone.

'Sure, thanks, Marion,' she said, unable to help shivering. She took off her gloves, stuffing them in her pocket, feeling the note that she'd put in there before she'd left home. She sat down at the kitchen table, her finger tracing the pattern on the tablecloth while Marion made the drinks.

'Does she get them often?' she asked when Alice was out of earshot.

'Sorry?' Libby replied.

'Nosebleeds.'

'Oh. No. Hardly ever,' she said, touching her forehead. The start of a migraine was all she needed. Or maybe she was coming down with something. There was a virus doing the rounds. 'I'm sure it's nothing. Alice said she bumped her nose on the basin when she bent down to pick up the hand towel.'

Marion gave a little nod, clasping her hands around her mug as she sat next to Libby. 'And Sean, how is he?' She took a long sip of her drink then pulled her thick cardigan around her, shuddering and briefly clutching at her stomach again, making another pained face. It was chilly in the kitchen, though Libby knew the coal fire would be going in the other room, that Alice would be warm in there. As long as she'd known her, Marion had chosen to live on the edge of discomfort – preferring blankets and a bedspread instead of an easy duvet, turning the heating off at night in winter, darning Fred's socks until they were more patching than sock, and the prospect of getting a dishwasher was remote.

Though, oddly, Marion had always been quite happy to advise – no, almost *insist* – that she and Sean decorate and furnish Chestnut Cottage sumptuously. Luxury by proxy, Libby mused, and she hadn't really minded Marion's input when they were renovating – what with her being so generous and helping them out financially with the decorating. They'd have been hard pushed to pay for everything otherwise. Marion had said they should look at it as another wedding present, though she'd implied it should stay secret from Fred. But they both knew Sean wasn't likely to talk to his father about Annie Sloan Chalk Paint, goose-down quilts and the benefits of underfloor heating anytime soon. So the secret was entirely safe.

'He's fine, but working as hard as ever. He's on call again tonight,' Libby replied, gazing out of the kitchen window. She saw a couple of farmhands shifting some bales on a trailer, likely for a local delivery, the tractor belching out smoke. It was a working farm, and if it wasn't for Marion's health, she'd be out there with Fred and the others, grafting until the light went. But as it was, she was happy to take care of Alice, helping her family in other ways. Marion, Libby knew, needed to be needed.

'He works *too* hard, I sometimes think,' Libby added. She took a large sip of coffee, burning her tongue as the sick feeling swept through her again.

Sean is having an affair…

She shook her head and blinked hard, trying to force the note from her mind. But it wasn't working. The handwriting in neat blue biro was getting more vivid by the minute.

'Are you worried about him?' Marion said, sounding concerned as she placed the biscuit tin in front of Libby. Almost as if she'd sniffed it out, despite the cotton wool in her nose, Alice appeared in the kitchen, shoving her hand in the tin. 'Just a couple, you monkey,' Marion told her. 'And go and look under the green sofa. There's a surprise for you.'

Alice gave a little gasp and trotted off again, each hand clutching a garibaldi.

'I'm waiting,' Marion prompted.

'Oh…' Libby forced a smile. 'He's just been on call a lot lately, that's all.' She sipped more coffee. 'But he's fine.'

'I mean I'm waiting for you to tell me what's *wrong* wrong.'

'Nothing's wrong,' she replied, far too quickly. She bit into a biscuit and swallowed, but her mouth was too dry to make it go down. 'Seriously, I'm fine. Just a bit stressed about getting to the market before they sell out.' Libby glanced at her watch but didn't really take notice of the time. 'I've a big job coming up.'

'Don't you burn yourself out too, Libby,' Marion said in that voice of hers. Somewhere between disapproval and knowing better. 'Surely you don't have to leave just yet?'

While Sean was a partner in a thriving vet's practice – the one he and Archie had set up twelve years ago – they still had to be careful with money, particularly after the financial hit Sean took in his divorce settlement. If they didn't have Libby's income each month, they'd have to budget a lot harder, especially with the cottage always needing something doing to it. As it was, they got by comfortably enough, but she certainly couldn't afford not to put in the hours. Besides, she'd worked hard to build up All Things Nice over the past three years and her reputation in the area was growing, with business really having taken off over the summer. She'd been calling on Sasha to help out more and more these last few months.

And anyway, she enjoyed cooking up a storm and serving it fresh in customers' houses. *The stress-free dinner party*, she called it on her website, with her regular clients needing no convincing that it was worth every penny to avoid the hassle of shopping, preparing, cooking and cleaning up – let alone any culinary disasters. Libby did everything – even decorating the table and providing dinnerware if needed – allowing her clients to enjoy their entertaining after a hard week's work. And there wasn't a shortage of such customers in the area – busy professionals living in beautiful country homes who, at the end of a long commute from London, were quite content to let Libby take over.

'Firstly, I do work hard. But secondly, I *love* it, Marion,' Libby said, finishing her drink and zipping up her jacket. She pulled her gloves from her pocket and was about to put them on, but the note fell out onto the floor. Libby went to pick it up, but Marion got to it first.

'Here you go,' she said, handing it back without looking. 'Just don't work yourself to the bone, OK? Sean and Alice need you.'

Sean and Alice need you rang in Libby's ears as she headed back to her car after saying goodbye to Alice. She waved at Fred across the farmyard as he chugged off in the tractor, the bales on the trailer bouncing behind. He gave a small nod back, as much as she'd ever expect from Fred, and she got in the car, sighing heavily as she started the engine. It would take her at least half an hour to get to the market, longer if she got stuck behind something slow.

Surely not Sean? she thought, driving off up the track, the note still playing on her mind. If her husband's name hadn't been written on it, she'd have said it was a case of mistaken identity or kids playing a practical joke.

Sean is having an affair…

No. No, he wasn't.

She absolutely refused to believe it.

CHAPTER THREE

The wholesale market was in an open-sided barn, slightly out of town. The small, muddy car park was almost full and Libby waved to several drivers who were leaving as she waited to enter through the gateway, their vans brimming with produce. She recognised them either from local hotels and restaurants, or the plethora of B & Bs that were dotted around. With the popular White House Barns Hotel and Spa at its core, the area attracted a lot of tourists and weekend money from London, not to mention corporate stays and conferences midweek. All good for business, Libby thought.

'Good for business if only I could get *in*...' she muttered, tapping her fingers on the steering wheel, relieved when Steffie from the flower shop in the next village finally let her pass through.

She pulled her phone from her bag and stared at the screen, her finger hovering over Sean's name. She knew he wouldn't appreciate her bothering him during surgery hours, not unless it was an emergency.

Was it an emergency?

It felt like it – that growing sense of unease bubbling in her gut. She just needed him to tell her not to be so stupid. That the note was a mistake. That everything was fine.

Instead, she dialled a different number, staring out of the window as it connected.

'Hey, you, what's up?' came the breathless voice at the other end. There was clattering and banging in the background.

'Oh, you know…' Libby replied. If anyone would understand, it was Fran.

The clattering sound stopped. 'Okaay,' she said slowly. 'You going to tell me what's up? I've got a chest of drawers perched at the top of the stairs and the bloody thing's about to topple back down if I don't…' Fran made a grunting sound. 'Hang on…' she said, panting. More noises and another bang, and she came back on the line. 'What's going on? You sound… odd.'

'I am odd,' Libby said, watching out of the window as people returned to their cars with trolleys of produce. 'What are you doing later?' she said, her voice flat.

'Badgering you to find out what's up, I imagine?' Fran replied.

'Seven o'clock at mine?'

'Yup. I'll bring the wine.'

'Thanks,' Libby said quietly, before hanging up.

An hour later, one of the market lads wheeled a barrow out to her car, dragging it through the muddy ruts, helping Libby pack the boxes of food into the back of her VW. 'Thanks, Stu,' she said, shutting the tailgate. Thankfully, she'd managed to find most of what she wanted, including the meat, which was what she'd most been concerned about. The best butcher only came twice a month to the market and today was one of his days. He'd been able to provide everything on her list, even supplying three dozen quails' eggs, which were to be part of a new recipe she was trying out. And she'd managed the entire task without thinking once about the note – until she got back in the car again. She sprayed her dirty windscreen with washer fluid before driving off, squinting through the smears into the bright autumn sun.

I could just throw it away, she said to herself, mulling it over on the way home, Radio 4 chattering quietly beneath her thoughts. *And not even mention it to Sean.* She turned off the main road towards Great Lyne, wondering if she should even bother mentioning it to Fran. Once it was 'out there', once people knew about it, it would seem more real. Even though it couldn't possibly be.

Could it?

She shook her head, retuned the radio to some upbeat music and made a pact with herself to get on with the day. It was more than likely that Sean would get called out for work later anyway, so at least she had an evening with her best friend to look forward to, whatever they ended up talking about. And whether it was them hoovering up chocolates in front of a movie, or putting the world to rights with their non-stop chatter, she felt lucky that Fran was in her life again. Even though Fran didn't have everything she wanted in hers any more.

'I mean, when would he even have time?' Libby said with a pained expression, her legs curled beneath her on the sofa. It had taken Libby several glasses of wine and much cajoling from Fran to even begin to speak about what was bothering her, and she was already having regrets. She felt stupid saying it out loud. Giving credence to the impossible. Airtime to someone else's malice. And she was also mindful that Sean could walk in the door at any moment, or Alice could wake up and come downstairs. This was definitely for Fran's ears only; by the end of the evening, she hoped to have had the whole thing prised out of her and her face aching from laughter for being so silly.

She and Sean loved each other and that was that.

'Well I did wonder that,' Fran replied. She'd just come back inside from smoking a cigarette – her third attempt at quitting this year having failed – and she hadn't commented much so far, just listened, a curious look on her face as Libby told her about the note. Fran had had her hair cut earlier in the day and the short blond crop accented her perfect cheekbones even more than usual, the highlights making her eyes appear azure. She had an unusual look, but a look that turned heads nonetheless, with no shortage of interested men giving her lingering stares. But either Fran didn't notice or wasn't ready to return the interest. Libby knew she was still grieving. What she'd been through took time, and it hadn't even been a year.

'He's either at work or with me and Alice. Or, if not that, he's just having a pint at the pub with the guys, or he's at his mum's. Plenty of people would confirm that, and it's not as if people don't talk around here. The community's far too tight for anyone to—'

'Have you got it?' Fran asked, her face deadpan. 'The note,' she added when she saw Libby's puzzled expression.

Libby got up and came back a moment later. After she'd returned with the grocery supplies earlier, unloading them into the courtyard barn – which had been converted into a catering kitchen over the summer – she'd taken the still slightly soggy note from her pocket and pressed it between the pages of a cookbook in the cottage kitchen. She knew Sean wouldn't find it there.

'Doesn't exactly give much away,' she said, handing it over to Fran. She poured more wine and sat down again, her feet curled up beneath her.

'And it was on your car this morning?' Fran turned the crinkly paper over, staring at the writing, frowning.

'Yep. It was probably just kids on their way to school, thinking it would be funny to cause a stir and put Sean's name on it. Or one of his mates having a laugh, perhaps? Maybe he upset someone without realising it and they thought they'd take a pop back at him. Though Sean would never upset anyone, of course. Would he? Or maybe it's not even meant for *my* Sean, and… and someone asked where "Sean" lived, meaning another person entirely and—'

'Libby,' Fran said seriously.

'What?'

'Stop it.'

'Stop what?'

'Overthinking this.'

Libby looked Fran in the eye. 'Really? Someone leaves this on my car and you expect me *not* to think about it?' She took a large sip of wine, feeling nauseous again.

'It's rotten for you, I know. But I'll tell you what you need to do…'

'And what's that?'

'Nothing. Absolutely nothing.'

'Oh. That's easy, then.' Libby rolled her eyes and went to take the note back, but Fran snatched it out of the way. She studied it again.

'Do you recognise the handwriting?'

'What, you mean the carefully printed capital letters with no identifying flourishes whatsoever?' Libby said. 'If Sean's name hadn't been on it, I probably wouldn't have given it a second glance, honestly. But—'

'I know, I know,' Fran said, reaching out and rubbing Libby's knee. 'But if this is all you've got to go on, it's going to do more harm than good to your relationship if you bring it up. How's Sean going to feel? Ask yourself that.'

Libby hadn't actually considered that. She'd only thought about how *she* was feeling – increasingly consumed by it as each hour of the day had passed. 'I suppose you're right,' she said, quietly.

'He's going to think you don't trust him, which is frankly awful, then he's going to start behaving differently, acting in a way that doesn't upset you or make you suspicious, even though he's got nothing to hide. Then the resentment will set in when he feels as though he's treading on eggshells around you. And that, ironically, is when he's more likely to have his head turned by someone else. When the trust is gone. It's a self-fulfilling prophecy.'

'And you'd know,' Libby said, thinking back. The two women had met in their early twenties soon after graduation, starting work at the same company. It was just some marketing and advertising agency – neither of their jobs were career-led or even to do with their degrees – but it was a case of needs must in those days, just getting by, seeing where life would take them. Within a month of meeting, they'd ended up sharing a flat together. It made perfect sense – they'd become close friends from the start and sharing was a way to save money. For four years they lived together, until life, loves and careers took them in different directions. But they'd always remained firm friends.

'And you want that for your marriage?' Fran replied, rolling her eyes.

Libby shook her head. She remembered Fran's disastrous love life when they were living together – sitting up countless nights consoling her sobbing friend when yet another guy had treated her badly. Her downfall was that she was simply too eager to please. Too desperate for a man. They smelt it a mile off.

'I wish I was you,' Fran had said to Libby after one particularly bad break-up. 'Then I'd never get dumped.' Fran had secretly coveted Libby's lifestyle since they met, including her boyfriends, her ambitions, her family – never more so than after the time she'd found the guy she believed was her 'forever man' in bed with another girl. Afterwards, she'd barely spoken to anyone, hardly eating or sleeping for months. But, gradually, something changed within her, as if she'd been cut to the very core, almost on a cellular level. Libby knew, from then on, that Fran would be OK – even if she spent the rest of her life alone.

Except, as it turned out, she didn't have to spend it alone. Through her and Sean, she met Chris. Her soulmate. And then he died.

'Stealth mode is what you want,' Fran said over the rim of her wine glass.

'Sorry, what?' Libby said, snapping out of the memories.

'If you want to know, and I mean *really* know if there's anything going on, then you don't confront him. You carry on exactly as normal. But you watch, you observe, and you check things out.'

'Check things out?' Libby's mind swam through the possibilities. Did she mean follow him? Spy on him? Rifle through his pockets? She didn't like the idea.

'There are ways,' Fran continued. 'You just have to be patient. And,' she said slowly, 'accept the consequences if you don't like what you find.'

'Find what, *where*?' Libby said, feeling tearful. But she fell silent when she heard the front door open and close from the hallway. A moment later, Sean was in the living room, shrugging out of his waxed jacket. Libby thought he looked cold and worn out.

'Hi, love,' he said, coming over and giving her a quick kiss on the head. 'Hello, Fran,' he said, adding a quick nod and the briefest of smiles.

Libby closed her eyes for a moment, breathing in the scent of the outdoors on her husband. When she opened them again, he was still looking at Fran.

'Nice haircut,' he said, chucking his coat on the back of a chair.

'A busy night after all, then?' Libby said before Fran could reply, unable to help the questioning inflection at the end. She'd meant it as a statement rather than a challenge.

'No, it wasn't actually.'

Libby looked at her watch, then at Sean again.

'I'm technically on call until seven in the morning.' Sean stretched out, his eyes switching between the two women, as if he sensed he was interrupting something. 'I was at the pub.'

'Drinking?' Libby said, realising that what she could smell wasn't the night air, but beer. 'What about the Land Rover?'

'It's outside,' Sean said. 'The parts are coming in a day or two, but Andy said it's fine to drive until then. Coffee anyone?'

'What, to sober up?' Libby said, instantly feeling bad.

'Er, no,' Sean replied slowly, looking from Libby to Fran and back again. 'I haven't had a drink. You know I wouldn't while working or driving.'

'Then why can I smell it on you?' Libby placed her own drink on the table, folding her arms as she stared up at him.

'The perils of drinking a pint of Coke in a small beery pub, I guess.' Sean's face broke into that smile of his, the one that always melted Libby from the inside out. She loved the way his eyes crinkled, how his mouth turned up more at one side than the other.

'I see,' was all she said, picking at her fingernail.

'OK, well…' Sean replied, shifting from one foot to the other. 'I'm going to get some sleep while I can. I'm half expecting the Fishers to call me out early about their stallion.'

Libby nodded, turning away as he left the room. 'Night,' she said as an afterthought.

Silence hung between the two women until it was clear that Sean had gone upstairs.

'I need a cigarette,' Fran said quietly, standing up and heading for the back door. 'And Libby,' she added, giving her a look, 'that's absolutely not the way you find out. Not if you *really* want to know the truth.'

CHAPTER FOUR

Libby tasted the sauce. It wasn't right. As she dug through the dozens of spice jars on the steel shelf, she knew there was a flavour missing. The barn kitchen was filled with classical music, as well as the scent of bramble and plum glaze that would be smothered on the venison before cooking. That was stage one of the main course she'd dreamt up for Saturday night's dinner – a seasonal four-course birthday meal for ten. She'd catered once before for the Hedges – a summer buffet party for thirty or so guests, where she'd set up the spread and left the hosts to it. It was such a success they'd rebooked her services again, this time for a sit-down meal for Michelle Hedge's fortieth.

Cinnamon, she decided, adding just a touch. She didn't want it to be overpowering, but something was needed to pick out the subtle blackberry undertones of the earthy yet mildly sweet glaze. Libby imagined the tender meat glistening with highlights of autumn as it rested, slicing it across the grain on a huge wooden board before serving with a medley of locally picked mushrooms.

'Ouch!' she said, dropping the spoon on the stainless-steel worktop. She clutched at her mouth as the end of her tongue burned. A few gulps of chilled water later and she stood at the back stable door of the barn, looking out through the glass panes into the cobbled courtyard behind Chestnut Cottage. Through the dusk and drizzle, she stared at Sean's empty parking space next to hers. There wasn't much room – just enough for both their vehicles, plus some turning space – with the barn sitting squarely behind the cottage and, behind that, the garden. Again, it wasn't huge but enough for a patch of lawn for Alice to have a swing and space to play, plus the overgrown area beyond where she'd begun preparations for a vegetable plot. Planting would begin in earnest in the spring, but for now she'd dug over a patch, got some onions in, rows of garlic bulbs and some winter greens. Her aim was to produce as much organic food on-site as she could.

My absolute perfect dream, was how she'd described Chestnut Cottage to Sean when he'd first brought her here. She smiled to herself, returning to the stove to check how much the glaze had reduced. Not enough, she thought, adjusting the heat. And it was true about the cottage being a dream – the kind of place she'd always pictured herself living. Though back then it had needed a lot of imagination and looked more like the stuff nightmares were made of: damp layered with rot and ancient, crumbling plaster, plus old, peeling wallpaper. The place hadn't been lived in for several years after the tenant had passed away and, with the leaking roof doing it no favours, the property manager of the large local estate that owned it was only too willing to let Sean have it at a knock-down price for cash. It was the same estate that owned the White House Barns and Spa, along with many of the cottages in the area.

Libby had never worked out how Sean had heard about it before it went to open market, and she didn't like to pry, but together they'd taken out the biggest mortgage they could afford for the renovations and, with the extra financial help from Marion, they'd moved in within a couple of years. Camping out in the static caravan up at Sean's parents' farm had been an adventure at the start, but with Alice being a toddler at the time, a particularly fierce winter had driven them into the spare room in the farmhouse. Of course, Marion was in her element looking after them – though Libby never told Sean that she often felt stifled and smothered by her. She knew Marion was only trying to help.

Libby jumped as her phone rang, smiling when she saw it was Sean. Then her stomach knotted. Even if the words on the note had faded from her mind this last day or so, she'd not been able to get what Fran said out of her head: *Not if you really want to know the truth…*

'Hi, darling,' Libby said. 'You OK?'

She could tell he was driving, the phone on hands-free with the rattle of the diesel engine almost as loud as his voice.

'All good,' he said. 'Just on my way to the last call-out then I'll be home. Need anything from Stow while I'm passing?'

Libby thought, though not about what they might need. 'Where's your appointment?' she asked, her voice wavering. It was a normal question, one she regularly asked without thinking. Except now she *was* thinking about it, wondering where he was going.

There was a small silence before Sean replied. 'The Drakes' place,' he said. 'It's one of their horses.'

'Oh, OK,' Libby replied, vaguely knowing the Drakes. While they weren't professional breeders, they 'dabbled', as Sean had once put it, and turned out some nice animals. They also took in rescue horses, which was likely what Sean's visit was about. 'But isn't their place east of here? Why would you be passing through Stow?'

Another silence, filled with the sound of gears crunching. Libby thought she heard Sean swear. 'Did I say Stow? Sorry, love. I just meant the local Spar on the way back. Anything we need? Do we have more coffee in the cupboard or should I get some?'

'We have coffee,' Libby said slowly. Her stomach cramped again. 'There's nothing we need. I've made a lasagne for tonight and I'll be fetching Alice soon.' Libby looked at her watch. 'How long will you be?'

'Should be back by half past five, easily,' he said. 'Righto, love. See you soon. I'm turning down their drive now.'

He said goodbye and hung up, leaving Libby staring at her phone screen. Then, on a whim, she opened up the Google

Maps app, tapping in the address of the vet's practice, then the Drakes' farm. 'If he left the surgery at three,' Libby said aloud, knowing that's when the afternoon clinic ended, and factoring in the seventeen minutes the app said the journey would take, 'then he should have got there way before now.' But of course, she supposed, he could have got delayed in clinic or had notes or other jobs to do before he left. She pretty much knew what his working day entailed. At least she thought she did.

But she couldn't help calling the vet's reception anyway. As ever, Jean answered. She was Archie's wife and had worked at the practice for as long as Libby had known Sean.

'Hi, Jean, it's Libby,' she said.

'Hello, Libby,' she replied and they exchanged a few pleasantries. 'Anyway, Sean's not here, I'm afraid. Have you tried his mobile?'

It wasn't uncommon for Libby to call the practice to get a message to her husband. Mobile signal was poor at the surgery as well as patchy generally in the area.

'It's not connecting,' she said, hating that she'd lied. 'Do you know what time he left?'

'Ooh, now there's a question I can answer,' Jean said, laughing. 'It was two o'clock on the dot. I always make a cuppa at two and asked if he wanted one. But he'd got his coat on, his bag and keys in his hand.'

'I see,' Libby replied, looking at her watch again. It was just after four now. What had he been doing for nearly two hours?

'Did he have a call-out just after two, then?' Libby asked.

'Well, I know he had to go to the Drakes' at some point. They've just taken in a new rescue. Lame, apparently. But…' Libby heard Jean clicking her mouse then flipping through the pages of her diary. 'I don't think we've had any other call-outs this afternoon, not for Sean.'

'OK, thanks, Jean. No problem.' Libby's mouth was dry as she hung up, wondering where Sean had been, what he'd been doing.

She screwed up her eyes before turning back to the stove. When she stirred the glaze, it made a sticking sound, peeling away from the edges of the pan. 'Damn,' she said, turning off the flame. Taking a fresh spoon, she tasted the sauce, being careful to blow on it a few times first. 'Damn, damn, *damn*…' she cursed, dropping the spoon into the washing-up sink. There was no mistaking the bitter, nutty taste of burnt fruit.

But Libby was too distracted to think about a culinary rescue mission. Instead, she took off her butcher's apron, double-checked the gas was off and headed across the courtyard back to the cottage. Her face was wet from the drizzle as she dashed over the cobblestones, going in through the back door to the boot room. The house seemed cool in comparison to the catering kitchen. Cold and empty without the three of them in there, Libby thought, as she stood staring around the unlit kitchen. For a moment, she imagined herself and Sean chattering, laughing, telling each other tales of their days, while Alice sat at the table colouring or playing a game on one of their phones. *My perfect dream…*

She shook her head, trying to convince herself that it still was a dream and she was living it, that she was the luckiest woman alive to be married to Sean, to have dear little Alice as their daughter – not to mention living in such a beautiful home in a friendly village. But, for now, she knew she had a small window of time to, to…

Libby hung her head. 'Time to *what*?' she said aloud, annoyed with herself as she went through the kitchen. She glanced out of the front window as she headed into the hallway, just checking that Sean wasn't pulling down the lane. But all she could see were the usual cars belonging to the neighbours, the woman who ran the post office walking her Jack Russell, and someone she didn't recognise cycling past.

Libby went up the narrow, creaky staircase and into her and Sean's bedroom. She flicked on the light, breathing in the scent of fresh bedding. They'd chosen a calming grey colour to go on the walls and, with the white linen, the wooden boards adorned with soft fur rugs and the antique mirrors making the low-ceilinged room seem more spacious than it really was, the bedroom was her and Sean's oasis of calm.

Now, as she opened the door to Sean's wardrobe, she felt as though she were tainting it, adding an ingredient of suspicion and mistrust where none was warranted. Would he be able to tell, she wondered, as she walked her fingers through the shirts and jackets hanging up there.

She started with his jackets. He didn't own that many, wearing either his scrubs in clinic or, usually, jeans and a shirt with a sweater, and his waxed jacket in the winter, keeping work boots and a spare set of clothes in the Land Rover in case things got messy on a call-out. At home, jeans, polo shirts and his favourite sports jacket were mainly what he wore, sometimes putting on a smart shirt if they went out to lunch at the weekend or were visiting friends. Sean was as laid-back and easy-going with his choice of clothes as he was in himself. And that's what had drawn Libby to him in the first place – no fuss, no self-consciousness, making him even more attractive.

Libby pulled a tissue out of the sports jacket pocket. She was about to throw it in the bin but thought better of it. He might remember it was in there, wonder where it had gone. In the same pocket were a few folded receipts, looking as though they'd been there a while. Indeed, the date on them confirmed they were from a shopping trip they'd taken together to Oxford, on one of his days off, to find Alice a birthday present. The receipt for the bicycle they'd bought her was there, plus another for the coffees they'd grabbed mid-morning, and the bistro lunch they'd decided upon on a whim when the rain had started. Her heart skipped for a moment when she saw the lingerie shop receipt – the £45.99 spent on 'sexy push-up/panty set'. But then she relaxed as she remembered the pair of them walking past the boutique, the displays catching Sean's eye, making him squeeze her arm as he'd stopped her.

'Want to take a look?' he'd asked, that smile of his breaking. He knew she loved pretty things. So they'd gone in, picked through the racks of lingerie that were far from everyday.

'For our *special* nights,' Libby had said with a twinkle in her eye. They regularly put time aside for themselves, with Marion taking Alice overnight.

'No,' Sean had replied. 'You should wear stuff like this whenever you want, not just for me. Then I can imagine you in it as you're slaving over a hot stove,' he'd laughed as they'd left with the smart perfumed shopping bag tied up with ribbon, their fingers tightly clasped.

Libby sighed, tucking the receipt back in Sean's pocket. She closed her eyes for a moment, hating herself for what she was doing. What was she expecting to find – a phone number written down? Love notes? Condoms? A secret mobile phone?

Libby put the jacket back on its hanger and closed the wardrobe door, flopping back onto the bed. Her head sank into the soft pillows and a waft of lavender rose up around her, calming her anxious thoughts. *Suspicion is not a part of my life*, she thought, closing her eyes, wishing she could convince herself that she meant it.

CHAPTER FIVE

Sean was nearly two hours late. Earlier, Libby had fetched Alice from Marion's and brought her home, promising her that Daddy wouldn't be long, that they could all eat dinner together then watch an episode of the nature programme Alice loved so much. After that, she would have a warm bath and a story from Daddy if he wasn't too tired.

Too tired from what? Libby wondered bitterly, sipping on her gin and tonic alone as she sat on the kitchen window seat, staring out into the lane for signs of Sean's car. With Alice hungry and restless, Libby had already fed and bathed her, settling her in front of the TV in her pyjamas. She refused to go up to bed until she'd seen her dad. *Understandable*, Libby thought, taking another sip of the sloe gin she'd made the year before. Ice cubes tinkled in her glass as she swirled it round, peering out into the night whenever a car cruised slowly past the house.

Fifteen minutes earlier a small silver Honda had driven down the narrow lane, almost coming to a stop outside the cottage. With the lights off in the kitchen, the street lighting gave off just enough of a glow to show a blond-haired woman driving, peering out of the passenger side window as though she was looking for somewhere. Or some*one*, Libby thought. Then, five minutes later, the same car had driven back again, having looped around the village, making Libby's skin prickle. The woman seemed to be taking an unusual interest in Chestnut Cottage, Libby thought. But then she exhaled with relief as the woman finally parked and went into a house a couple of doors down. None of the properties along their lane had numbers – just names, and some of the signs were faded. Cheshunt House, where the woman had gone, often got their mail and vice versa.

Libby got up and poured herself another gin and tonic, looking out of the rear window above the sink just as the Land Rover's lights arced around the backyard, illuminating the barn for a few seconds before dazzling her as she sipped. She wanted to smile, to feel warm inside – relieved that Sean was home – but, because he was so late and hadn't called (nor indeed answered her calls or texts) – she felt sick.

All because of the note.

'God, I need one of those,' Sean said as he came in from the boot room, dumping down his stuff and eyeing Libby's drink. He shrugged off his coat and came over to kiss her.

'Sure, I'll make you one,' she said, quickly ducking aside before his lips met hers. He stood motionless for a second or two, before going back to hang up his jacket. He returned, hand outstretched to take the drink, but she put it down on the kitchen table instead.

'Good day?' he asked, pulling out a chair and sitting down.

It was written all over his face that he'd had a bad one – or at least a bad afternoon. Libby knew the signs – a frown set deep between his thick eyebrows, lips pursed in puzzlement as though he'd not been able to help an animal, perhaps ending in euthanasia, and his big fingers pressing against his temples to fend off the growing headache. But today, she felt something was different. Did he appear so stressed because he was *guilty*?

'Do you *have* to do that every time?' she said, glaring at him as she sat back on the window seat. It was one of her favourite places to sit – usually with a cup of tea and a book, glancing up to wave as people passed by in the lane. But now, the little seat served as a way to not sit too close to Sean.

'Do what?'

'Scrape the chair. Every time you sit down, you drag it instead of lifting it out. It makes a terrible noise.'

'I didn't even notice,' Sean said slowly, his frown deepening. 'I'm sorry.'

Libby looked away, staring out of the window at the silver Honda that was parked across the road on the edge of The Green, shuddering as she remembered the stories she'd read on an Internet forum earlier, written by betrayed wives. Some were heartbroken, some consumed with anger, some wanting revenge, while others were intent on forgiveness and reconciliation at any cost – even if the price was their own self-respect. Libby wasn't sure which camp she'd fall into if the unthinkable happened to her. Or *was* happening to her. Probably all of those emotions, she'd decided, before shutting down her computer and snapping the lid closed. She couldn't bear to read any more posts.

'Have you eaten?' Sean asked, pulling Libby out of her thoughts.

'Oh, no, not yet…' She was about to add *I wanted to wait and eat with you*, but instead she said, 'I'm not hungry,' and looked away again.

Suddenly, there was a hand on her shoulder. She tensed.

'What's wrong, love? You seem… upset?'

Libby shrugged and sipped her drink.

'Talk to me,' Sean said, crouching down beside her. 'Did something happen?'

Libby got a faint waft of his body wash, a trace of aftershave as well as the usual farm smells that often accompanied him home. *A good sign*, she thought, if he'd really been to the Drakes' place. *But why did he take so long, and what did he do between leaving the surgery and calling her?*

'Nothing's wrong,' she said, finally looking at him. If she went too silent, too moody, then she'd never get answers. She remembered what Fran had said – *act normal.*

Libby stood up, slipping past Sean as he reached out to embrace her. She turned on the oven to heat up the lasagne again, taking some lettuce from the fridge. Making a quick green salad would distract her.

'Well, you could have fooled me,' Sean said, sitting down at the table again. When Libby glanced up, she saw he had his phone in his hand and was scrolling through something as he sipped his drink. She knew he disliked social media and wasn't one for texting much either. Occasionally, the vets took turns to post on the practice's Facebook page about interesting cases or uplifting stories, as well as different topics relating to pet welfare and care. But that was as deep as Sean's interest in Facebook went. As far as she knew.

'Everything OK at the Drakes' place?' Libby asked, glancing up. He was engrossed in whatever was on his phone, the flicker of a small smile on his face. He didn't reply. Libby hacked at the romaine lettuce more forcefully than was required.

'Sorry – what, love?' he said, putting his phone down on the table face up. But then he changed his mind and slipped it into his pocket.

'I asked how it went at the Drakes'. The call-out. Remember?' She couldn't help pulling a tight smile.

'Laminitis on a rescue mare. She was in a bad way. It took longer than I thought.'

'Oh. I see.'

'I had to wait for the farrier to come and he was held up. There was no way I could leave before we'd got a wooden clog on.'

'OK.'

'Then Sally Drake made me a cup of tea and insisted on me trying the cake she'd made and…' Sean trailed off when he saw Libby's face. She'd stopped chopping the lettuce and was staring at him, the knife held above the wooden board, its tip pointing in his direction. 'Libby, for God's sake, tell me what's wrong. You're upset about something and I don't like it. Maybe I can help.'

Sean got up and went over to his wife, removing the knife from her hand and wrapping his strong arms around her. He was a big man – tall and well built, though not overweight. And while his size commanded attention in any room, his easy manner often drawing people to him, Libby was now wondering who else he had attracted.

He kissed her neck, sweeping aside her hair as his lips brushed over her skin. She closed her eyes, torn between wanting to turn around and kiss him back, and pushing him away.

'Sean…' she said, knowing her body was tense, not melting into his shape as she would normally.

He stopped, holding her around the waist still, breathing in her scent. 'What, love?'

'Something happened yesterday morning. Something… unsettling.'

Libby held her breath, instantly wishing she'd kept quiet. Before Sean could even ask what she was talking about, she slid out of his embrace and took one of her many cookbooks down from the shelf. She flipped through the pages, the book falling open where she'd tucked in the note. She took it out, her hands shaking as she placed it on the worktop.

She said nothing. Just stared at him as he glanced at the folded paper, then up at her again. Eventually he picked it up and opened it, biting his lip as he read the five words that had haunted Libby since she'd found it.

'What the hell…?' he said, turning it over. His chest puffed out, his shoulders drawing up into an overstated shrug. 'Well this is ridiculous,' he said calmly, reassuringly. He laughed then, flicking the note back onto the worktop with disdain. 'Is this why you're being so… odd?' Sean popped the stopper from the sloe gin bottle and sloshed some more into his glass. 'For heaven's sake, Libby,' he added when she said nothing.

'Well, how would you feel if *my* name was on there instead?' she replied, fighting back the tears. She returned to the salad, tossing the leaves into a glass bowl before throwing in some cress.

'Where did it come from?' Sean asked, casting another dismissive look over it.

'I found it stuck under my car windscreen wiper when I was taking Alice to your mum's yesterday morning.'

'Yesterday morning?' he said thoughtfully, glancing out of the front window. He paused a moment. 'Kids, most likely,' he said, rolling his eyes and going over to the bin, lifting the lid to throw it away.

'No,' Libby said, snatching it from him. 'Don't.' Their eyes locked as they each held on to the paper, the upsetting words sitting between their fingers. Sean let go before it tore, then Libby slipped it in her back pocket. 'Is it true?' she said, still staring at him, her face deadpan. She wanted to see his reaction, read every flicker of his eyes, every unconscious movement, gauge every nervous twitch. Did he touch his nose? Run his fingers through his hair? Look away or instantly deny everything?

Sean held Libby's gaze, his eyes drawing her in. His face radiated a blend of hurt, compassion and a deep need to reassure his wife. 'Oh, *love*,' he said, drawing her close again, overriding her resistance. 'Do I even need to answer that?'

'Yes. Yes, you do,' Libby replied, hating how frosty she sounded, hating that she'd actually confronted him. But she couldn't help it.

Sean looked her in the eye, everything about him reasonable and concerned. 'No,' he replied softly. 'It's not true. And while I don't like that you even had to ask, I do understand,' he said, kissing her forehead softly. 'In fact, I almost *like* it that you had to question me, that you got upset.'

'How come?' Libby said, feeling the first wave of reassurance and relief wash through her.

'Because it means you care,' Sean added, pulling her close. 'I'd be more worried if you didn't.' And this time when he hugged her, Libby allowed her body to meld into the shape of him.

CHAPTER SIX

Now

Detective Inspector Doug Jones drops down through the gears, slowing the car. He turns left at a junction just south of the city centre onto a narrow cut-through before pulling out onto a wider road in front of the police station. I'm not familiar with the area – though on the way here we passed several places where Sean and I have spent many happy Sundays, browsing quaint boutiques, antique shops and second-hand bookshops before a lazy meal at our favourite French place. Since Alice came along we still sometimes visit the city, of course, but our mission is very different – usually centring around entertaining our daughter, hopping between parks, toy shops and public toilets.

I stare out of the window, up at the police building – the facade made of soft, sand-coloured stone, austere in appearance yet somehow filled with a resigned wisdom, as if the building has seen it all over the years, looking as if it might heave a sigh at any moment, rolling any one of its many window-eyes in exasperation as it squarely faces the grand building opposite. My heart thumps as I catch sight of 'Crown Court' set into the portico across the road from the police station, my neck straining so I can see it as we turn slowly down a ramp taking us into an underground area, disappearing into the darkness. When my eyes grow accustomed to it, I see we're in a secure parking area.

The car pulls up by a door, and the detective stops the engine. He gets out and comes around to my side of the car, shrugging into his jacket. Only when he's blocking my way does the female officer get out and join him, each of them flanking me as I ease my body out of the vehicle. My legs feel like jelly, barely able to hold my weight.

'Mind your head,' the detective says, lightly taking hold of my cuff-bound wrists.

'Will I be able to call my husband?' I ask as I'm led through a heavy steel door. My voice doesn't sound like me. It's shaking and about an octave higher – nothing like the happy, content woman I was three weeks ago. Several other officers are waiting inside, closing around me as if they're expecting a kickboxer to be brought in, not an eight-and-a-half-stone mum from Great Lyne wearing Crocs and an old sweatshirt with cooking stains down the front.

'Custody sergeant will sort all that out,' someone says, though I'm not sure who. I'm feeling light-headed as I'm taken along a series of white corridors, the shiny grey lino flooring making it seem as if I'm walking on water, with some kind of shimmery blue lighting running the length of the wall as we pass. I could be in a fairy grotto or… or… on my way to hell. That seems more likely. My entire body aches from fear and stress.

I've done nothing wrong…

'You'll have to wait here in the holding cell until the sarge is available,' the female officer says, standing in the doorway – one of many leading off the corridor.

Cell, I think, staring into the small, blank room beyond. Yes. The same as hell.

I feel numb as I go inside. The officer's face is deadpan, even when I pass by her, imploring her with my eyes as I stand in the middle of the cell, searching for some kind of female connection, trying to ground myself. *Have you got kids?* I want to ask. *Maybe a daughter, like Alice?* Out of her uniform, she could be any other mum at the nursery, perhaps someone I'd get chatting to at the park. My eyes beg her, trying to ignite a spark of solidarity – woman to woman – that, surely, they must know they've got it wrong. Horribly, *horribly* wrong.

But her expression remains blank.

Nervously, I look about, taking in my new surroundings. It's about the same size as the small box bedroom at Chestnut Cottage, though without any of the homely touches – the little desk I picked up at a flea market, sanded and covered in white chalk paint before waxing. The watercolour paintings of the local countryside, the handwoven rug part-covering the wide oak boards, the way the door lintel dips down at one side, with the middle part gnarly from old woodworm. No, this is nothing like Chestnut Cottage. It's the antithesis, in fact. There's a low, single bunk built into one wall with a bright-blue plastic mattress on top, a grey blanket folded at one end, and nothing else apart from a stainless-steel toilet bowl plumbed into the corner and a built-in hand washer and dryer beside it. The walls are painted a white brighter than any white I've seen – with a patch of grubby hand marks around the bunk – and the ceiling is higher than normal, presumably so no one can hang themselves. As I gaze up, I spot the black circle of a CCTV camera looming down. Watching. Judging.

Guilty or not?

Then that giddy feeling again, with a rising sickness. I can't take it all in. What it all means. The gravity of my situation. I know Sean will be here soon to take me home, to tell them they've made a terrible mistake. I'll fall into his arms and he'll make everything OK, as he always does. As he has done since that terrible night.

I turn and stare at the officers.

I am arresting you on suspicion of the murder of Sasha Long. You do not have to say anything…

'You can sit down if you like. I don't know how long you'll have to wait,' the woman says, glancing at her watch.

I nod, going over to the narrow bunk, tentatively lowering myself onto it. The plastic mattress wheezes out a sigh. If I don't speak, then what can they do? I'm not admitting to something I haven't done.

The smell of microwaved food winds its way down the corridor and into the cell through the open door. The officers block the exit, the detective inspector leaning on the frame, glancing at his watch, peering down the corridor to see what's going on. The other officer stands slightly closer, looking bored, her arms folded, occasionally glancing down at me. They make some brief joke between them, talking in almost-code, like they perhaps would on the radios clamped to their shoulders. The sudden smile on the female officer's face make her seem human for a moment, as if she has a life like me – a home, a family. Though whereas she knows she will see hers at the end of her shift, I can't be sure I'll ever see mine again. My mouth is so dry. Parched. My tongue sticking to the roof. Perhaps I should bite it off. Then I can't say a word.

'I'm thirsty,' I whisper.

'We'll get you booked in. Then you can have water, something to eat if you're hungry.'

The smell of reheated food hits my nose again, conjuring up some kind of bland sauce with lumps of meat floating in it. I'm reminded of my kitchen, the food I was forcing myself to prepare for the function I'd reluctantly agreed to do tonight. I shudder as I think how I'll be letting down my clients, how word will soon spread about why I didn't turn up.

'You need to get back to normal, Lib,' Sean had said, telling me I couldn't carry on like this forever. 'Apart from anything, you've let yourself go. People will talk.' While he knew I'd taken it hard – as had everyone in the area – he was getting impatient with me and, rightly, he just wanted our lives to get back on track. He was affected too – of *course* he was – and those first few days he was gripped by shock just as much as me. It happened on our watch. The guilt was unbearable.

I am arresting you on suspicion of the murder of Sasha Long…

She must be dead, then, I'd thought as I'd heard the word *murder*, screwed up my eyes, wondering if they'd finally found a body. Updates have been scarce the last week or so, almost as if the search has been scaled down, abandoned. As if Sasha had never existed.

A shiver runs through me as I put my fingers to my nose, hoping to breathe in the scent of garlic from when I was chopping it earlier, or maybe the heady rush of rosemary or thyme, or even the bleach I used to scrub out the washing-up sink. Anything to remind myself of normality. But all I can smell is the rusty stench of blood under my nails.

'It's your lucky day,' DI Jones finally says from the doorway, beckoning me with his head. 'Follow me.'

Slowly I stand up, holding his gaze. When I falter, nearly stumbling back down onto the bunk, the female officer takes my arm, guiding me towards the cell door.

'Watch your step,' she says, leading me out of the cell and down a corridor, eventually reaching a wider area with a counter to one side, screened off by a glass partition. There's a man standing behind it, watching as we approach – his look pitying, as if he knows what I've got coming when I don't.

The detective explains briefly to the sergeant what happened, why I've been arrested, what will happen now. Then the desk sergeant asks me if I understand why I'm here, why I've been arrested, repeating it back to me.

I nod, barely perceptibly, staring at my feet, even though I don't understand at all.

I haven't done anything wrong! I want to yell over and over, but remember that I can choose to say nothing, that I can just keep quiet. I imagine what Sean would tell me if he were here, watching as my handcuffs are removed.

We've been through that night a thousand times, love… Just tell it like it is…

I stretch out my arms, rotating my hands before cupping my aching skull. I drop forward onto the desk, my forehead banging down heavily, a sob coming out.

'Stand up, please,' someone says.

Quickly, I do as I'm told.

Empty your pockets, please. Take off your belt… have you had any alcohol in the last twenty-four hours? Are you under the influence of non-prescription drugs? Do you take any medication? Who's your next of kin?

The questions go on and on, and, while I can answer these without much thought, I know they're only going to get harder.

'Who is your next of kin, please?' the custody sergeant repeats, tapping the counter.

'We only went out for a meal,' I whisper, tears in my eyes. 'It… it was meant to make things better. Clear the air.'

And suddenly I'm back there. In the pub restaurant, the fire blazing, our smiles burning even hotter between us as we ripped open the warm focaccia to share, a bottle of red wine half gone already, our eyes not letting go of each other, knowing that when we got back to the cottage later we'd be tearing our clothes off, making love as if we were the only two people left in the world. The note completely forgotten. Never mentioned again, and all it took was a night out.

Except that's not what happened. Not even close.

'Sean Randell,' I say quietly. 'My husband,' I add, as if I'm convincing myself who he is, not them.

CHAPTER SEVEN

Before

'You look stunning,' Sean said, coming up behind Libby, running his hands down her waist and onto her bottom. He gave her a light smack and kissed her neck. Libby watched them both in the full-length mirror in the bedroom, wrapping her hand up around his neck as his body melded against hers. They'd always been a good fit.

'Why, thank you, Mr Randell. You don't look half bad yourself.' She gave him a kiss, tasting the wine they'd opened while they got ready. But then she stopped, not wanting to smudge her make-up. She'd made an extra special effort for tonight, knowing that the evening wasn't all about Sean doing the right thing – him putting her mind at rest about the note. It was also about them reconnecting, taking time out for themselves. Since she'd confronted him about it, things had been tense on and off, mainly because of her, she realised. Insecurities that she'd thought were long buried had reared up. It had been a long time since she'd thought of David, all the turmoil he'd brought into her life.

'What time is Sasha due?' Sean said, glancing at his watch. He'd booked the table for eight but they were going to have a cocktail in the bar first. Something they used to do regularly before Alice came along.

Libby was about to reply 'any minute now', when they heard a knock at the front door.

'Speak of the devil,' Sean said, grabbing their empty glasses and heading downstairs to let their babysitter in.

Libby doused on some perfume and quickly sprayed her hair again, running her fingers through the long dark strands. She grabbed her jacket – a favourite deep-indigo fake-fur find from the dress agency in Chipping Norton – slipping it on over the above-the-knee black dress she'd bought last year but only worn a couple of times. She knew Sean loved her in it, the way it clung to her body – not in an obvious way, but just enough to show off what lay beneath. With knee-length boots and a scarf loosely draped around her neck, Libby gave one last glance in the mirror before she went downstairs. She reckoned she looked good, conscious that they'd likely bump into a few people they knew, and conscious, too, of wanting to look her very best, to show the world that she was Sean's woman, that she was attractive, desirable, sexy. Just in case the *other woman*, if there even was one, was watching.

The barmaid, the waitress, someone else's wife...

If anyone was making a play for Sean, she wasn't about to take it lying down. She would be quite clear that she belonged to Sean and he belonged to her. That they were a team and nothing would come between them. Not even a stupid anonymous note.

It was when Sean had found Libby crying in the barn kitchen, blindly chopping up bundles of fresh herbs, a couple of days earlier, that he'd suggested a meal out. He'd taken her by the shoulders, wiping her face.

'Hey,' he'd said softly. 'You've got nothing to worry about, OK?' Then he suggested they had a special night together, just the two of them at their favourite place. It would be romantic, he said. Just what they needed. And something to put a big full stop at the end of this nonsense.

'Nothing's going on, I promise,' he'd said a thousand times, cupping her face. 'You're the only woman in my life.'

In return, she'd stared up at him, her eyes blurry from tears, trying to read what was behind his, searching for the truth and looking for lies. But all she saw was the man she loved. Just as she always had.

'I know,' she'd replied, sniffing and kissing him back. 'I know.'

'Hey, Sash,' Libby said when she went down into the living room. 'How are things with you? It seems like ages since I last saw you.' In reality, it was only just over a week ago when Sasha had helped serve a dinner for a group of bankers up at the big house between their village and Chipping Norton. Sasha had never once let her down, with her polite, careful and efficient manner winning over the clients as well as being invaluable to Libby. She'd tried out other local girls, and a couple of boys, who wanted part-time jobs, but no one worked as hard or competently as Sasha. And, being a student, the hourly rate was affordable for Libby, though she always made sure Sasha got a cut of any tips from the customers.

'Hi,' Sasha said back, glancing up from the sofa before turning away again. 'You look nice.' She'd already taken out a couple of college books from her backpack, spreading them out on the wooden table in front of the log burner. It wasn't a huge living room – only space for one comfy sofa and an armchair, plus the little table and a small TV beside the inglenook, but it was perfect for the three of them.

'Thanks,' Libby replied, grinning and giving a little twirl. 'A much-needed date night,' she half-whispered with a wink, expecting Sasha to play along. When they worked together, they often enjoyed silly banter and chatting, including topics such as boyfriends, clothes and, even once or twice, sex when Sasha had needed advice. Libby hoped that her relationship with Sasha was how it would be with Alice when she was a teenager – honest and open between mother and daughter. She knew that Sasha's mum had had a few problems lately and wasn't always there for her. While Libby didn't want to stick her nose in, she felt that Sasha occasionally looked to her for advice that should have come from Jan. Libby wasn't sure how much Sasha knew about her mum's situation and hoped that any gossip going around the village hadn't got back to her daughter.

Sasha stared at Libby. Her face was blank, with no silly comment back about the 'date night' or even any of the teasing she would have expected from her. Sasha might only be seventeen, nearly eighteen, but she was going on forty when it came to conversation.

'Sash?'

'Cool,' she replied quietly, taking her pencil case from her backpack.

Libby paused, wondering if things had perhaps got more tense at home. She thought Sasha looked a bit pale, tired almost, and hoped she wouldn't fall asleep while looking after Alice. Her daughter had been prone to coming downstairs lately, asking for water or milk or just wanting attention, and would be more likely to get up if she knew Sasha was there. She was like a big sister to her, and loved it when Sasha came over if Marion was unavailable.

Sasha tapped a pen on her teeth as she opened a maths textbook, staring into space.

'Much college work to do?' Libby asked. She knew she wanted to go to university to be an engineer.

'Yup,' Sasha replied, looking at her book.

'Sash,' Libby continued, sitting on the arm of the sofa. She placed a hand on the girl's back. 'Is everything OK? You seem a bit…' Libby wasn't sure how to describe it, just that she sensed something was wrong.

Sasha slowly turned and looked up at Libby, her eyes drawing together in a frown. She was just about to say something when a car hooted outside. She snapped her mouth closed.

'That'll be the taxi,' Libby said. '*Sean?*' she called out in the direction of the kitchen. 'Cab's here, hurry up.' Sean had offered to drive – the Land Rover was back from the garage now – but Libby had insisted that they both relax and share a bottle of wine.

No reply. She knew he was in there. She could hear him clattering about as if he'd just come in from the back and was now doing something at the fridge. She heard the rattle of bottles as he closed the door. Libby was just about to call out again when he came into the living room from the kitchen.

'Taxi's here, love,' she said.

'All ready?' Sean replied, coat on, house keys to hand. He patted his pocket, took out his phone, checked it and tucked it away again. Then he took out some cash from his inside jacket pocket. 'Put this in your purse, will you, love?'

'Yes, yes I'm ready,' Libby replied, standing, not taking her eyes off Sasha until she had to. She took the money from Sean, putting it away safely. 'Any problems, give me a call,' Libby said, giving Sasha's shoulder a little stroke. 'I've left some food for you in the fridge. It's in the labelled plastic container.'

Sasha nodded and watched as they left, Libby noticing how Sean gave her a last glance over his shoulder before he closed the door behind him.

CHAPTER EIGHT

'I'd forgotten how much I bloody love this place,' Sean said, his face breaking into a smile as they paid the taxi driver and went inside the Old Fox. Chalwell was only a couple of miles from Great Lyne, but too far to walk on a night out, especially in heeled boots. *Well*, Libby thought, as she mulled over what Sean had just said. *It's too far for me to walk, but clearly not him.* She knew Sean had stumbled back across the fields more than once recently after meeting his mates for a few pints. It wasn't something he did often, and Libby didn't mind in the least, but something was off about what he'd just said.

'I thought you were here only last week?' she said, tapping the low beam on the way to the bar, reminding Sean to duck his head. 'Hardly enough time to forget you like the place, is it?' She hesitated, watching him as he drew up to the bar, suddenly feeling light-headed, unsure if it was from the heat of the blazing log fire or the warm, beery smell that seemed to have soaked into the very fabric of the building. While there was usually something comforting about it, tonight she almost felt repulsed by it, as if it was the stench of something she wasn't a part of, rather than the familiar smell of everything (and everyone) local she'd grown to love these last few years.

'Was it only last week?' Sean said, turning to the bar. He clearly wasn't expecting a reply, but Libby gave him one anyway.

'Yes, yes it was,' she said, but he pretended not to hear. Instead, he passed her a cocktail menu and ordered a pint of Hooky for himself. While the Old Fox was as typical a Cotswolds pub as they came – a mellow ginger-stone building with a low part-thatched, part-tiled roof, beamed ceilings and open fires – the owner liked to cater for all, tourists included, and regularly put on tapas nights, cocktail evenings, live music, barbecues in the summer and even hosted the occasional wedding reception if there was a ceremony in the village church.

'Just a glass of white wine for me please, Mick,' Libby said to the landlord, placing the menu down on the bar. She suddenly didn't feel in the mood for cocktails.

'Sure?' Sean said, leaning on the bar. He frowned when Libby nodded. They went and sat at a small table near the fire, the heat of it warming one side of Libby's face as they sipped their drinks. She stared around, giving a quick wave to a couple they knew a few tables away and mouthing 'hello' to a farmer she recognised from Great Lyne. Several other familiar faces were dotted around, the man from another couple giving Sean a pat on the back as they passed, exchanging a few words about a livestock case he'd dealt with.

'Well,' Libby said when they were alone again. 'This is nice, isn't it?' She didn't mean for it to come out as it did – her words terse her voice even more strained as she sat up straight on her stool, her legs crossed. She sipped her wine, thinking she perhaps *should* have chosen one of the amusingly named cocktails on the menu to get in the mood. But even her favourite at the Old Fox – the Cotswolds Cosmo – didn't tempt her right now. Despite her best efforts to keep it in check, her mood had been up and down since she'd received the note.

'It's perfect,' Sean replied warmly, his eyes narrowing as he reached out and took her hand. She squeezed his fingers back. 'Everything OK with Sasha just now?' he asked, nodding at the lad who worked at the garage as he passed them, heading for the toilets.

'I think so,' Libby replied. 'Though she did seem a bit… I dunno, out of sorts. A bit quiet and thoughtful. Did you notice?'

Sean swallowed, even though he hadn't taken a sip. 'Not especially. Does she have exams looming?'

'Not until next year, as far as I know,' Libby said, shifting her stool away from the fire, moving closer to Sean. He smiled, encasing her hand tighter within his big palm.

'Well, you know what teenage girls are like, eh?' he replied.

'Yeah,' she said, giving him a smile. 'I do.' Though she couldn't help noticing how he kept pulling his hand away to touch his nose. And his eyes were anywhere but on hers.

'All right, mate?' Sean said as someone Libby vaguely recognised sat down in the window seat near them. His wife joined them, bending down to give Sean a kiss on each cheek.

'Long time no see, Seany,' she said, her bright-red lips flashing a broad smile at him. She glanced quickly at Libby, who was about to smile and say hello, but the woman turned to Sean again. 'Missed you last week, you know. The team wasn't the same without you. I need those quick wits on my side next time, OK?'

Seany…

Libby felt something stirring inside as the woman's low-cut top revealed her bra as she leant down close to Sean. She felt her shoulders tensing, and tried to think of something witty to say that would end what the woman seemed to think was an intimate moment with her husband.

'Leave the poor chap alone, will you, Di?' the man she was with called over from the window seat, saving Libby the trouble. He rolled his eyes and grinned at Sean. 'Can't take her anywhere, can I?' he joked.

Libby forced a laugh, catching the woman's eye again, which was accompanied by a small smile. Almost pitying, Libby thought.

'Don't be a stranger, Seany,' the woman said, giving Sean's shoulder a squeeze before joining her husband.

Libby stared at Sean for a moment, not even feeling the flicker of a smile that would normally have accompanied such an encounter. It might once have been funny, but since the note it just left her feeling sick. She leant forward and wiped her thumb across each of Sean's cheeks.

'Lipstick,' she said quietly, cleaning her thumb on a paper napkin. She sipped her drink, noticing how her hand shook as she held her glass. *Don't ruin the night*, she told herself. *He's trying to make everything OK. Why would he even bother taking me out if there was any truth to the note?* This final thought had only just occurred to Libby but, as she listened to Sean telling her about his day, she realised it was true. Surely any man who wasn't invested in his wife, who had lost interest, wouldn't be hell-bent on making her feel secure and wanted? If it were the other way around, she'd certainly be doing the same.

As Sean went into detail about an operation he'd performed earlier, Libby finally felt herself relaxing. Perhaps it was the wine, or maybe the warmth of the fire and the familiar faces offering welcoming waves and smiles across the low-beamed bar, or perhaps simply being in the presence of her husband. Either way, she decided she would forget about the note and concentrate on the man she loved deeply – the man she knew loved her back just as much.

'Your table is ready,' a young waitress in a white shirt and short black skirt said, drawing up beside them. Libby couldn't help giving her a quick look up and down. She wasn't much more than sixteen, a little younger than Sasha. She'd got a rip in her black tights and she kept trying to wriggle her clingy short skirt down to cover it up, but it kept riding up again. 'Shall I carry your drinks through?' she added.

'Thank you,' Sean replied, gathering his and Libby's coats. He watched as the girl walked off, leading the way to the restaurant at the rear of the pub. As surreptitiously as she could, Libby tracked where Sean's gaze fell and it certainly wasn't on the girl's legs, even though she was pretty and attracting stares from several young guys who'd come in for a pint.

'This is lovely,' Libby said, once they'd settled down at the table. 'I'm starving.'

'Me too,' Sean said, rubbing his foot against Libby's leg. 'I'm so glad we've found the time to do this.'

'It's been all work a bit lately, hasn't it?'

Sean nodded, agreeing. 'I'm so proud of what you're doing with the business,' he said, taking a menu from the waitress. 'But I don't want you burning yourself out.'

'I'm fine,' Libby said, though she felt her heart skip a little when she thought of all the extra work she'd taken on lately. 'Though I do worry about Alice, and if I'm spending enough time with her.'

'She loves it up at Mum's, you know that. But it's you I'm more concerned about. Why don't you see if Sasha can do more hours at the weekend, a bit of donkey work in the kitchen while you have some time to yourself? I'll be around to keep an eye on her.'

Libby thought about this. 'It's a possibility, I suppose. Anyway, you can talk, with all the extra hours you've put in lately.' She nudged him playfully with her foot.

It was true. Sean had been on call a lot these last few months, and had been asked to cover extra clinic shifts too. Though it was hardly his fault that they'd had several junior vets come and go recently and, with another partner recuperating after an operation, it had been every man on deck. *And woman*, Libby thought, knowing the practice wasn't an all-male environment. Her heart skipped again.

Sean studied the wine menu and ordered a bottle of Rioja he knew Libby loved, plus some focaccia and olives to share while they decided what to eat. A few minutes later they were ripping into the rosemary-and-garlic-infused bread and sipping on plummy wine. Libby felt a warm glow winding through her veins.

'I'm so glad you suggested this,' she said, licking her finger. 'You know, after everything…' She hesitated, not even wanting to say the word.

'You've nothing to worry about, you know, Lib,' Sean replied. 'I love you. And just so you know, tonight isn't me trying to cover up my guilt. There isn't any. I just wanted to spend time with my beautiful wife. So let's not mention the you-know-what.'

They both laughed then, with Libby changing the subject and recounting a story Alice had told at playgroup about a 'you-know-what', Libby said, trying not to spray out her wine. 'Mrs Ludlow said it was her duty to inform me about Alice's "inappropriate vocabulary".' Libby covered her mouth, trying not to spray out food. 'You should have seen her face when I told her that I was certain Alice would have used the correct term, penis, rather than a euphemism.' Libby shuddered with laughter, biting her lip. 'But don't worry, I convinced her that it was entirely innocent, that you're a vet and Alice asks questions about animals' anatomy.'

For the next ten minutes the pair laughed and chatted, with one story or anecdote leading to another. Their hands joined across the table and it seemed like they'd not talked properly in ages. The waitress came and took their orders – a seafood platter to share for starters, followed by lamb shanks with celeriac for Sean and mushroom and truffle risotto for Libby – and then their conversation kicked off again, ranging from booking a holiday for next Easter, to Christmas plans as well as Sean offering up ideas on how Libby could promote All Things Nice.

'I definitely think you should ask Sasha for more hours. She could probably do with the extra money,' Sean said, cracking open a lobster claw. He dunked it in a garlic sauce and popped the pinky-white meat in his mouth.

'Do you think I ought to check in at home, make sure everything's OK?'

Sean shrugged, shaking his head. 'No need. She'll call us if there's anything wrong.'

'She just seemed a bit… quiet earlier.' Libby pulled her phone from her bag. 'And the phone signal's patchy here.'

'Voicemail comes through eventually,' Sean replied. 'Anyway, I'm on Wi-Fi so she can always WhatsApp me. She's not stupid.'

Libby paused. 'Oh, I didn't realise she had your number.' She set her phone down on the table and took a prawn from the seafood platter, picking it open. 'That's good,' she added, knowing that, indeed, Sasha wasn't stupid. Far from it, in fact. There was something about the girl that was beyond her years, the way she confidently dealt with her dinner clients without being intrusive. And she oozed common sense, having helped Libby out of a couple of culinary scrapes in the past.

'Was that you or me?' she said a few moments later, wiping her fingers before turning over her phone. She'd heard a buzz, felt the vibration in her wrist through the table. But there were no notifications on her screen.

'Relax,' Sean said, squeezing her hand. He briefly checked his phone, his eyes lingering on the screen for a second or two, before putting it in his top pocket. 'You worry too much.'

'You're right,' Libby agreed, resolving to get on with enjoying the evening. It might be another couple of months before they'd be able to go out alone again.

It was only when Libby saw what must have been the fifth alert on Sean's phone – his lit-up screen clearly visible through the cotton fabric of his shirt – that she couldn't hold it in any longer.

'Are you going to reply to your girlfriend's texts or what?' she said, instantly regretting it when she saw the look on Sean's face. 'God, I… I'm *so* sorry,' she said, staring down at the table. She took another gulp of wine – she was on her third glass now – downing the remainder in one. She poured more for both of them. 'It's just that I can see your phone's going off and you're not checking it. What if it's Sasha?'

'Libby…' Sean said, retrieving his phone from his pocket. He glanced at the screen, thumbed it a couple of times before putting it inside his jacket pocket on the back of the chair. His jaw tensed and his fingers knotted as he took a couple of deep breaths, his eyes filled with what looked, to Libby, like panic. 'Will you just let this go, OK? I can take it because I love you, but you're doing bad things to yourself, obsessing over everything I do. I can see it… and I know it's all because of that damned note.'

Libby stayed silent, digging her fingernails into her palms under the table. She'd always sworn she wouldn't be *that* woman – insecure, needy, mistrustful.

'Will you please believe me that the only women in my life are you and Alice, OK?' He grabbed both of her hands then, squeezing her fingers before twiddling her wedding band and engagement ring. He brought her left hand to his mouth and kissed them. 'I gave you these for a reason, OK?'

'OK,' Libby said, feeling about three inches tall. 'And anyway, there *is* another woman in your life.' She suppressed the smile.

'Who?' Sean said, peeling a large prawn.

'Your mother, of course,' she replied with a laugh, muffled only by Sean popping the prawn between her lips.

CHAPTER NINE

Ten minutes later, Sean's phone rang.

Libby stared at him, a forkful of risotto halfway to her mouth. Sean stared back, his blue eyes seeming to turn icy grey, and the colour draining from his cheeks.

After a few moments, the phone finally stopped buzzing.

'Who was that?' Libby said, dropping her fork down on the dish with a clatter. It bounced off the plate and onto the floor. She left it there, swiping the spilt rice off her dress.

Sean said nothing.

'Go on, call her back, will you? In fact, give me your phone and *I'll* call whoever-she-is back. How about that?' Libby half stood up to retrieve the fork but the waitress got there first, swapping it with a clean one. Libby ignored her. 'In fact, why don't you invite her to join us for dinner? She might as well be here, seeing as she's taken up most of your attention tonight anyway.' She bowed her head and covered her face with her hands briefly, hating what the note had done to her, to *them*. But she couldn't help how she felt.

'Libby, stop…' Sean's voice was on the cusp of anger and sadness – angry that his wife was causing a scene, her voice raised while he kept his low, other diners looking their way; and sad that it had come to this – their romantic evening together ruined by Libby's jealousy.

'I'll stop when *you* stop,' she said, changing to a terse whisper as she eyed the people staring at her, some of whom she knew.

There was even one of her clients sitting on the other side of the dining room, though she didn't think he'd heard.

'I'm going to the gents,' Sean said, folding his napkin and placing it on the table. Libby couldn't help noticing the tremor in his hand as he pulled his phone from his jacket pocket. 'Perhaps you'll have cooled down when I get back.'

She said nothing, watching as he strode off to the toilets. 'Christ,' she said under her breath, hanging her head again. She took a few more large sips of wine before pouring another glass. They were already over halfway through a second bottle. What the hell was she thinking, losing it like that?

She fiddled with her nails under the table as she waited for Sean to come back, hating that she was seeing a side of herself that she thought she'd moved on from since her split with David – the man who had sucked her in, literally making her believe she was going mad with his lies and deceit. She tried to convince herself that what she was feeling now was a product of how much she adored her husband, brought about entirely by the note, rather than old emotions resurfacing.

But the note had substance. The note was *real*. And someone had taken the trouble to write it and leave it on her car. How could she let it go? She needed more than a meal out and being snapped at by Sean to make her feel OK about this.

Libby watched as Sean came back to the table and sat down, brushing his mop of sandy hair from his forehead. Libby turned away, unable to look at him for fear of melting into an apology. She loved him so much, it was killing her to feel like this. She felt something warm on her hand. Sean's fingers clasping hers.

'Libby…'

She faced him, desperately wanting to clutch his fingers back. But she didn't. She just stared at him with a blank expression. 'Sean,' she said slowly. 'Is there another woman? Look me in the eye and tell me the truth.'

He stared back, not taking his eyes off her as he took a sip of wine. Libby thought she felt a tiny tremor in his hand.

'No,' he said after a few moments' pause, as if he were measuring the depth of her madness for thinking such a thing. 'There isn't.' He sipped more wine as Libby pulled her hand away.

'Then who were all those calls from? And the texts?' She stared at him but he remained silent. 'Fine. Will you show me your phone?'

Sean shrugged and took it from his pocket, handing it over. When Libby looked at the missed calls list, there were no recent numbers showing as incoming. The last call he'd made was to the vet's practice earlier that afternoon, with a couple of calls coming in from her around the same time.

'You've deleted them,' she said, switching to his texts. The last messages were from his mother earlier that day, so she didn't bother to look. 'And you've deleted whoever texted you too,' she said, unable to find anything received in the last hour. WhatsApp was the same, with only a couple of mates messaging him in the last few days.

'I didn't delete anything, for Christ's sake, Libby.'

'Then why isn't that call showing on your list? And all those texts?'

Sean shrugged. 'I have no idea. The only thing I have any idea about right now is your paranoia. And it's not attractive, frankly. If it makes any difference, it was my mother phoning me, though I don't see why I should have to justify that or be made to feel guilty.'

Libby checked herself as she felt another, bigger, outburst brewing. 'You're sweating,' she said quietly, the calmness of her voice terrifying her more than her welling anger. 'And shaking,' she added, seeing his hand as it rested on the table.

'So would you be if you were getting the third degree,' he said, trying to add a laugh but failing. He threw down his knife and fork. 'You know what, Libby? I've tried to make this OK. I've tried to reassure you but I can't do any more than I already have and—'

'But if it was just your mother calling, then why didn't you answer?' Libby persisted.

'You know what she's like, Lib. I didn't want to be chatting to her now and spoiling our evening, but that backfired, didn't it? I called her back from the toilet. She said she felt bad she couldn't look after Alice tonight and was checking that we'd found a sitter. She wished us a lovely time. Satisfied?'

Libby watched as Sean's jaw tensed. It still didn't explain the unlogged call or lack of messages on his phone.

'You know what she's like as well as I do, love,' he added. 'Always checking up on me.'

Indeed, Libby did know what Marion was like. While she tolerated her mother-in-law's involvement in their family life, sometimes it felt stifling – not simply interfering as such, but something deeper than that. As if she had a burning need to know everything, be involved in every aspect of their lives – especially Sean's. 'So your mother really *is* the other woman?' she said, spitting out the last couple of words.

'As ever,' Sean said, cutting up some lamb, chewing it slowly, a smile spreading.

'I don't believe you,' Libby said after a moment.

That was all it took. Sean stood up, grabbing his jacket from the back of the chair, slinging it on and swiping his phone from the table. He stared at Libby for what seemed like an age before turning to go. 'Enjoy the rest of your meal,' he said, briefly turning back. 'I've had enough.' And he strode out of the dining area towards the bar, the limp he'd always had suddenly becoming more pronounced. Libby knew that when he was stressed his right knee gave him trouble.

She desperately wanted to call out, tell him to wait, to come back, but she didn't. Instead, when he was out of sight, she swigged down the last of her wine, pushed her plate aside and slowly slipped on her coat, trying to ignore the stares of the other diners as she tracked the same path between the tables that Sean had taken. There was no sign of him in the pub lounge so she went to the bar to settle the bill.

'Everything all right with your meal, Libby?' Mick, the landlord, asked, looking concerned.

'It was lovely, thanks,' she replied. 'Sean's not feeling a hundred per cent so we thought we'd head home. Food was delicious though,' she added, even though she wanted to be sick. 'Can I settle up?' She held out her card.

'Machine's not working, I'm afraid,' he replied. 'But don't worry—'

'That's fine,' Libby said, glancing at the bill. She pulled out some notes from her purse – from the money Sean had given her earlier – and handed them over. Thankfully, she had just enough, including a tip.

Outside, the parking area was dark, with only one street light on the lane. But the glow from the pub windows allowed her to scan around and finally spot Sean standing over by some cars, his back to her, his phone pressed to his ear. Slowly she approached him, trying not to let the gravel crunch beneath her feet. But as she drew up, he turned, immediately ending the call and slipping his phone into his jacket pocket.

'Taxi's on its way,' he said. 'And that's who I was calling, before you grill me.'

'Sean…' Libby reached out and touched his arm. He flinched. 'I can't believe the night has ended this way. How did some random idiot playing a joke get us in this mess?' She wished he'd look at her, but he didn't. And she couldn't know for sure that the note was a prank.

'Because you don't believe me, that's why,' he said sourly as she came around to stand in front of him. She was shivering, though not from the cold.

'I don't know what to believe any more,' Libby said. 'If it were the other way around…' She hesitated, trying to imagine the situation in reverse. 'Will you have a thought for how I feel, Sean? It's unsettling.'

Sean stared out into the night before walking a few paces out of the car park and onto the village lane, looking each way for signs of the taxi. Libby came up to his side.

'You know what I don't like about this?' Sean suddenly said, turning to face her. Beyond his shoulder in the distance, Libby saw the cones of car headlights approaching.

She shook her head slowly, staring up at him.

'It smacks too much of Natalie.'

'You think *she* wrote the note?' Libby said, without thinking or realising what he meant. It was a possibility, she supposed.

'No, of course not,' Sean said. 'I mean your behaviour. I didn't think you had it in you, Libby, but frankly it's…' He paused as the taxi drew up beside them, the passenger window lowering and the driver peering out at them. 'Frankly it's too much like her,' he added, opening the car door. When Libby just stood there, her mouth hanging open, Sean got in.

Natalie… she thought, her heart thumping. Sean's first wife. The woman who had caused him nothing but grief and heartache during their marriage and now continued to do so, using their teenage son, Dan, as a pawn.

Libby got into the car and, once they were out of the village, away from the lights, she allowed the tears to pour down her face.

CHAPTER TEN

Now

This cell is slightly different to the last one. Mainly because the blanket is blue rather than grey, and the plastic mattress looks more worn, dirty at one end, narrower. As the officer accompanies me inside, I look at up him, imploring him with my eyes to make him see sense, to let me go, for him to tell me there's been a terrible mistake. But he doesn't. He just instructs me to sit and wait and that I'll be interviewed in due course. 'The duty solicitor will be along soon,' he says in a voice that betrays weariness; it's probably the end of his shift. He just wants to go home. And so do I.

When the custody sergeant had asked for my next of kin's number, I gave him Sean's, explaining he was a vet and might be in surgery or out on a call, but he didn't seem to care. In fact, when he put it in the system, he asked for another number, so I reluctantly gave him Fran's mobile as a backup. I didn't want to worry Marion. Then he'd pressed on through a checklist of things he had to do before they could lock me up. I was searched and photographed, swabbed and fingerprinted, and they took everything out of my pockets – which consisted of a tissue, my house keys, and the sweets I took off Alice last night when she refused to clean her teeth. Now my jeans are hanging low on my waist because they took my belt too.

The door bangs closed behind me. I'm shaking. Standing alone in the middle of the small cell, the black lens of the camera above watching me, scrutinising my fear, tuning in to my thoughts. I'm too scared to even cry. Slowly, as though my legs aren't my own, I take a few steps towards the bunk. I need to sit. To lie. That, or I'll pass out. I wonder if they've called Sean, if he's on his way here now, going to give them hell at the custody desk and insist they release me, let me go. Sean will sort everything out, I tell myself. He always does.

'Se-*eaaan*!' I scream, turning suddenly and lunging at the door. I thump my fists on it over and over until I'm scared my bones will break. Hair flies across my face, getting caught in my mouth, sticking to my lips as I yell his name over and over.

Then I fall silent, exhausted, terrified of what will happen to me. Someone from down the corridor kicks off in response, shouting obscenities and for me to shut up. A prisoner. *Another* prisoner. Like me.

I walk slowly back to the bunk and flop down, my head resting flat on the plastic. Using my feet, I pull up the blanket, spreading it over me as best I can. I'm shaking. Freezing. Now they'll think I'm guilty for sure.

'I've done nothing wrong,' I whisper, my words caught up in short sharp breaths. I go over what they said would happen to me, trying to remember. That I was going to be questioned, possibly be detained for up to twenty-four hours, that I could have a solicitor if I wanted. I'd just nodded, positioning my feet on the stick-on footprints on the lino floor as they instructed, shaking as I was photographed.

Smile!

I cover my face, trying to block out the fluorescent lights above, but all I can see behind my eyelids is Sasha's sweet face, that look she used to give me when we were clearing up after a busy night, just wanting to get out, get home, having a laugh about anything and everything as we unloaded my car into the barn kitchen ready to wash all the dirty dishes and pans. After we'd finished, she'd peel off the latex gloves she always wore when working, especially when helping me cook, and I'd give her an envelope of cash, sometimes some leftover food to take home for her mum, before driving her back. I always treated her well.

'Oh, *Sasha*…' I whisper, forcing the tears to come. But none do. My eyes stay dry – unlike when I was in the taxi home after that disastrous meal with Sean at the Old Fox. Where it all began. What I wouldn't do to be back there again, sitting next to my husband as we bumped along the country lanes, me feeling nauseous, though not from the twisting and winding road, but rather because Sean didn't say a single word to me all the way home. Even when I reached out and took his hand he withdrew it, folding his arms across his chest and staring out of the window. I'd gone too far.

'Love,' I'd said quietly. The taxi driver was vaguely familiar and I didn't want him knowing all our business. People talk to each other in the villages. 'Please… Look, I'm sorry.' There. I'd said it. I'd apologised and was hoping for the same in return. I'd make it up to him somehow – perhaps cook a special meal for us the following evening when Alice was in bed, put some music on, candles, spend the evening talking. Though not about the note. I'd vowed that when I got home, I would rip it up and burn it. Never mention it again. I wanted the damn thing out of my home and out of my life. I wanted things back to normal.

When the taxi pulled up outside our cottage, I heard Sean curse under his breath, half turning to me, giving me a glare. The driver was tapping his fingers on the wheel to some tune or other on the radio. I was hoping Sean would break the silence, even if it was just a perfunctory 'Have you got the cash?' but he didn't. He just got out of the car, his knee almost giving way as he stood up. I heard him gasp; though, as always, he tried to hide the pain.

I rummaged in my bag for my purse. 'Do you take cards?' I asked the driver, having spent most of the cash in the pub, wanting to keep some back to pay Sasha. He nodded, taking out his machine. The transaction went through and I slipped a couple of pounds into his hand. 'Thanks,' I said, getting out and joining Sean at our front door. We'd only brought one set of keys with us and I had them. It was as I was fishing them out of my handbag that I realised I'd left my scarf in the taxi. I turned to flag the driver down, waving frantically, but he didn't see, his red tail lights disappearing around the corner at the end of our lane.

'I'll have to phone the company tomorrow to get it back,' I said to Sean. 'I don't want to lose it. You gave it to me, remember?'

He didn't reply, just waited for me to get the key in the lock and the door open. I felt my eyes fill up with tears again, especially as I was going to feel foolish explaining to Sasha why we were back so early. It was only just gone nine. I'd still pay her for the whole evening, of course, and take care of her cab fare home. Even though she only lived a mile or two away in the next village, Little Radwell, there was no way she was walking home alone in the dark.

I opened the door and went into the hall, slipping off my jacket and hanging it on the hooks opposite the front door. Sean went straight past me and on into the kitchen. I heard him running the tap and clattering about as I went through to the living room, wanting to speak to Sasha before Sean did. The television was chattering quietly in the background, the light from it casting a golden flicker around the room.

'Hi, Sash, we're back a bit early. How's Alice been?' I'd said, spotting her books lying open on the coffee table, a couple on the sofa. But I stopped dead in my tracks…

Outside my cell I hear a noise, as if someone's about to come in. I sit bolt upright, clutching the blanket to my chest, trying to force my breathing into a steady rhythm instead of the shallow rasping breaths that are coming out of my mouth. But all I end up doing is holding it, waiting for my fate, hoping that, if I'm lucky, I'll pass out and never wake up.

CHAPTER ELEVEN

Before

'Sasha?' Libby said again, as she glanced around the living room. She froze – aware that the television was still on – an episode of *Friends* was playing quietly in the background – and that Sasha's college books were still spread out. But she couldn't take in what she was seeing. Sasha was... well, she was *gone*. Her heart thumped, immediately thinking of Alice, that she'd been left with no one to care for her if she'd woken up.

She'd already yelled out her name several times – *Sasha!* – but there'd been no reply.

Sean came rushing in from the kitchen.

'Oh *Christ*,' he said. 'Get upstairs now and check on Alice. Hurry!'

'Yes, *yes*,' Libby replied, hardly able to breathe as she dashed up the stairs, her legs weak. She paused for a second on the landing, her nails digging into the banister rail as she gathered herself, hardly daring to go in. When she slowly opened Alice's bedroom door, spilling soft light across the room, Libby saw her daughter curled up on her side soundly asleep, breathing softly. Her furry dog was tucked under her chin. She sighed out in relief, shaking, stifling a cry as her eyes drank in her beautiful daughter.

Libby pulled the door shut again and peeked into her own room to check if Sasha had been in there to borrow something, or, maybe, to use her en-suite bathroom. Right now, she didn't know what to think. But everything looked undisturbed. When she went down to the kitchen, it was empty, as was the back hall and toilet, with both sets of lights off.

'Alice is fine, thank God,' Libby said, still shaking. Sean was sitting on the arm of the sofa, surrounded by Sasha's belongings. 'What the hell do we do now?' she added, fighting back the tears as her arms hung limply by her sides.

Sean's eyes locked onto hers, his head shaking slowly, accusingly, as if he was trying to convey something to her. 'What do you mean by *that*?' He had the TV remote control in his hand, tapping it repeatedly against his other palm. She could tell his mind was whirring.

'She… she's *gone*, Sean.'

'Well that's bloody obvious,' Sean spat back, making Libby flinch. She knew there was a deeper meaning, that right now he must hate every fibre of her being. 'Let's think about this carefully,' he said, sighing out. 'She must be somewhere, right?' he added, looking at her intently as he stood up. Libby hated that he sounded so cold and accusing, as if it were all somehow her fault – though she knew, deep down, that it was – but she also knew that he was in control, as always, and that he would make everything better. At this moment, dealing with Sasha and whatever had happened was more important than anything else going on between them.

'Maybe she'd gone out to the barn kitchen and something happened,' Libby suggested, knowing it wasn't helpful. Sasha had no reason to go out there. But when Sean gave her a slow nod, she knew what to do, that she still needed to check. She headed back through the kitchen, grabbing the key off the hook in the rear hall and crossing the cobbled yard, lit only by the light coming from the kitchen windows.

But the barn was deserted and there was no sign of Sasha.

'Sash?' she called out as she headed back to the house. 'Are you out here?'

Silence, apart from a couple of cars cruising slowly along the lane and an owl hooting in the field behind. Libby covered her face briefly, before finding some strength and going back inside.

Sean was in the kitchen again, his face ashen. He took her by the shoulders, gave her that look again. She knew what it meant. 'I don't understand,' he said, his voice on a precipice. 'I just don't under*stand*…'

'No…' Libby said, shaking her head, holding his gaze, feeling as if she was in a trance. She was shaking. 'It's not like her. Just not like her at all to be so *stupid*.'

'We need to think about this. You should give her a call.'

Libby nodded furiously, knowing he was right, and also relieved that he was speaking to her again, albeit only because of the situation they were now in. She fetched her phone and dialled Sasha's number but, a moment later, they heard a phone ringing in their living room. When they went back in, Sasha's phone was on the coffee table, glowing and vibrating with 'Libby' displayed on the screen.

'Great,' Sean said, picking it up. He put it straight back down again in exactly the same place. 'At least we tried.'

'*Tried?*' Libby said, trying to stay calm, though her voice was wavering. 'Thing is, she's usually glued to the thing. If she'd gone off somewhere, she'd have taken it with her. Especially since…' She trailed off, not wanting to betray Sasha's confidence. She'd told Libby about the troubles between her and Matt, her boyfriend – how, since things had broken down between her mum and dad, she wondered if she'd ever be able to trust a boy. Libby had listened to her, consoled her, and while she desperately wanted to tell her that in ten, maybe twenty years' time she'd look back on her first relationship fondly, but with a little roll of her eyes, she didn't. Sasha wouldn't believe her anyway. Libby knew that Matt hadn't exactly been kind to her lately, ignoring her calls, breaking dates at the last minute. Not a great boyfriend by all accounts.

'Since what?' Sean said, pacing about. He peered out of the front window.

Libby shook her head. 'It's nothing. Just something she said. Not relevant.' Libby went to the bottom of the stairs again, listening. The last thing she needed was Alice waking up. She returned, shaking, wishing tonight had never happened. 'What do we do now?'

Sean sat down again, but in the armchair by the fire, not on the sofa where Sasha had been studying. He leant forward, elbows on knees, tapping his fingers together, glancing at his watch. 'Let me think, for Christ's sake, Libby. I'm in shock, plus anything could have happened to Alice left alone.'

'I know… I know… But what about Sasha?' Libby said. To Sean, the girl was just their babysitter, but Libby had grown fond of her over the last year or so. And she trusted her with Alice one hundred per cent.

'It's not our fault,' he said, suddenly standing up. '*Whatever* has happened to her,' he added as an afterthought.

Libby felt her cheeks colour. 'She didn't do much college work tonight, look,' she said, pointing at her books. 'She's only got through a few of these maths problems.'

'Good point,' Sean said, mulling over possibilities. 'What if a friend had called round earlier and she went off with them? If she's not here, that seems a likely explanation.'

Then Matt was on Libby's mind again, and so was that time Sasha had turned up for work with streaks of mascara on her cheeks. She'd pretended she had something in her eye but later confessed it was because Matt had hung up on her, that he didn't think they could keep seeing each other. Libby knew how much Sasha adored him. They'd been seeing each other since school.

'I suppose. But she's not irresponsible. She wouldn't just leave Alice alone, even for a few minutes. It's not right, Sean.'

'No, it's not right,' he said, dragging his hands down his face. 'It's not right at all.'

The couple sat waiting, wishing that Sasha would burst into the living room at any moment, full of excuses, embarrassed by whatever had happened, that Alice wasn't being cared for. Unspoken tension hung between them, growing ever bigger as the minutes passed. And Sasha didn't come bursting in from anywhere.

To pass the time, until they figured out a plan, Sean stoked the fire, chucking on a couple of logs, while Libby went to the kitchen to make tea. When she placed the mug in front of Sean, he ignored it and went to the drinks cabinet in the corner to pour himself a whisky.

'Want one?' he said, holding up a glass. Libby shook her head, staring at the flames.

'I'm going to check on Alice again,' she said, standing, unable to settle for more than a few minutes.

'No, you already know she's fine. Just let me think, for Christ's sake.'

Libby sighed, keeping her gaze fixed on Sean. 'What if one of us goes out to look around the village,' Libby said. 'Would that help? At least we'd be doing something rather than just sitting here fretting.'

Sean frowned, glancing at his watch. 'We probably should. It's been a while since we got back.'

Libby hung her head. What she wouldn't give for Sasha to just walk in the front door all bright-eyed and apologetic.

'I'll have a drive around,' Sean said, knocking back his whisky, glaring at Libby.

'You can't go, you've been drinking. I've had less, so I'll do it.'

It wasn't entirely true that she'd had less alcohol, though the implications of Sean losing his licence were way worse than for her. Surely she'd be fine for a slow loop around the village? She'd take it steady, and it had to be done. Anyone would.

'Be careful, OK?' Sean said, taking her by the shoulders as she was getting her coat on. 'Have you got your phone?'

'Yeah,' Libby said, feeling a wash of relief at his touch, even though his hands were shaking. 'I won't be long. I'll go up Hunter's Lane and around that way. Let me know what happens here.'

'Of course,' Sean said, kissing her head. 'Everything will be OK, right?'

Libby held his gaze for a moment, smelling the whisky on his breath, before nodding and heading out to her car. It didn't feel as if everything would be OK at all.

CHAPTER TWELVE

Libby struggled to put the key in the ignition. She started the VW and reversed around in the tight space of the courtyard, watching the front wing as she manoeuvred behind Sean's four-wheel drive.

'It *must* be my fault,' she whispered over and over as she pulled out onto the lane, turning on the fan as her window misted up. 'If I hadn't gone on and on about the note then we'd never have gone for a meal to make up and… and…' She let out a little sob, but then forced herself to get a grip. She couldn't lose it now. She shivered at the thought of Sasha. It was a cold night and she hated the idea of her being out in it. She simply couldn't understand what had happened. It just wasn't like her to do something so silly. She was always so sensible and careful. She played out the situation in her mind as she headed up the lane, trying, too, to convince herself that it wasn't her fault, knowing that they'd have to call someone soon – her mother, her father, perhaps Matt.

She couldn't quite bring herself to say *the police*.

Libby followed Hunter's Lane around the village, driving cautiously, until it merged with Drover's Way. She kept to second gear, sometimes first as she edged between parked cars on either side of the narrow road. Stone cottages with low thatch brows flanked either side of the lane, looking as if they'd huddled up for the night. So far she'd not seen anyone out and about as she peered out each side of the car but, up ahead, she thought she saw a figure standing, perhaps with a dog on a lead. She drew up slowly, lowering the window. It was Eric, who lived a few doors down from them. He had Maisy, his spaniel, on a lead and was clearing up after her, slowly bending down. Even at eighty-two, he didn't let minor ailments stop him.

'Hi, Eric,' Libby said out of the window as the car idled. 'How are you?' She hated that her voice shook.

Eric turned, his hand in the small of his back. When he saw it was Libby, a broad smile broke out on his weathered face. Tufts of white-grey hair poked out from beneath his cap. 'Libby, m'dear,' he said in that way of his. He held up the plastic bag, chuckling. 'You caught me getting my hands dirty,' he said, coughing as he laughed.

'You haven't seen a young girl around, have you?' Libby asked, unsure if he knew Sasha. 'Sasha Long from over in Little Radwell,' she added when Eric frowned. 'Phil and Jan's daughter. She has blond hair down to here, is about my height, a pretty girl. She's seventeen.'

Eric made a rasping noise, followed by his trademark laugh again. 'Ah yes, Phil's lass,' he said, coughing and nodding. 'But it's been a while since I went looking for a young lady, I'll have you know.' His arm extended as Maisy strained on her leash. But then his expression turned serious when he saw how worried Libby looked. 'Nothing wrong, is there?'

'Oh, well…' Libby said, swallowing, hesitating. Though she was thankful she'd spotted someone to ask. Sean had said it was important she should stop if she saw anyone, find out if they'd seen her. It was a tight community and the locals would be concerned. 'She was babysitting for us but when we got home she…' Libby trailed off again. It made it all too real, too *serious*, if she said the actual words. But she knew she had to say something. 'I was wondering if she'd popped out. If anyone had seen her.'

Eric straightened his back, pulling a face. 'Not seen no one out tonight, love,' he said, rubbing his weathered hand over several days' worth of stubble. 'But that's a bit strange, I'll grant. If I see her, I'll tell her to get in touch. I might stop for a late one at The Falconer's on the way home, so I'll ask in there too.' He waved his hand in the direction of the pub.

Libby glanced at the car clock. It was almost closing time but she knew they did lock-ins for locals like Eric. A tap on the window was all it would take for him and Maisy to find a spot by the fire.

'Night then, Eric,' Libby said. 'And look after that back.' She gave him a quick wave and wound the window up again, putting the car into gear and driving on down the lane, scanning each side of the road as she went. But there was no one else around.

As she turned onto Drover's Way, she tapped the brake suddenly, her eyes straining in the dark. She swore she saw something – movement, perhaps pale skin or light-coloured hair behind a parked car. Libby waited a moment, but there was nothing. It was probably her imagination. She gripped the wheel tightly, concentrating as she drove, even though she was only going about fifteen miles per hour. Her knuckles turned white and her hands trembled as she stared at the road ahead, while keeping on the lookout.

'God, God, *God*,' she muttered under her breath, glancing at the controls to turn up the fan. The windscreen was misting up again. At the same moment, her phone rang so she quickly looked down to see who it was. Sean's name and picture were on her screen.

'*Oh…!*' she cried out as her head suddenly lurched forward. For a second, she didn't know what had happened. She was stunned and, quite literally, knocked sideways as the car jolted and stalled. When she peered out of the window, she realised that she'd scraped the rear end of a parked car that she simply hadn't seen. Everything was misting up and, after the wine, her judgement wasn't its best.

Her phone stopped ringing but immediately began again as she was restarting the engine. She answered it on speaker and pulled forward, stopping just in front of the car she'd hit. She ought to get out, see if there was much damage, but her breathing was getting faster, her chest tight and painful – almost to the point of not being able to take another breath. She prayed there wasn't any damage. Sean would be so cross with her. This wasn't what he'd sent her to do.

'Libby?' came Sean's voice. 'You there? What's going on – Libby?'

For a moment she couldn't speak. Her vision blurred and she was suddenly freezing cold. 'Sean…?' she whispered. 'Are you home? Is there news?' Her words were breathy and thin.

'Libby?' Sean said again, as the line broke up. 'Can you hear me?'

'Yes, I can now,' she replied, touching the side of her head. 'I think I've just hit a car. I don't know if there's any damage.' All Libby knew was that she shouldn't be behind a wheel with this much alcohol in her. If the police found her now, they'd smell it on her breath and certainly test her. She knew she was way over the limit. She couldn't stand the shame. *This wasn't her! This wasn't her life!*

There was a tap on the window.

'Sean, I'll call you back,' she said, hanging up. A woman was standing beside her car, mouthing something through the glass. She couldn't tell if she was angry.

'I'm sorry,' Libby mouthed back as she fumbled for the window button. 'God,' she said. 'I misjudged. I'm so sorry… I… didn't mean to…'

'Are you OK?' the woman replied, a concerned look on her face.

'Yes, yes, I'm fine.' Libby touched her head again. It took a moment before she realised it was Cath, the woman from the post office. She'd only moved to the village eighteen months ago with her husband and had saved the little shop from closing down.

'Don't worry, it's not my car you hit. I was just walking home and thought I heard a noise.' Cath went around to the front of Libby's car, making a surprised face in the headlights. She folded her arms as she looked at the other car. Libby thought it best she got out, though she staggered a little as she stood up. She held on to the roof. 'I feel terrible. I've never done anything like this before.' It was true, she hadn't.

The woman paused, pulling her coat around her. 'You look quite pale… Liz, isn't it? Are you OK?'

'It's Libby, and I'm fine. Just stupid misjudgement. I'll leave my number and come back tomorrow to find the owner. I'm only down the way in Chestnut Cottage.' Libby fought to control her breathing, especially when her phone began to ring again.

Cath stood still for a moment, staring at her, then back at the cars. Libby prayed she couldn't smell wine on her breath. 'Fair enough,' she said finally. 'And not too much harm done anyway,' she added, running her hand along the other car's bumper. 'It's only a small scratch. Good night, Libby,' she said, before walking off, glancing back a couple of times.

Libby lunged back inside, grabbing her phone as it rang again. But she was too late. The call had ended. She sat there for a moment, her head leaning back against the seat rest, wondering how her evening with Sean had transformed from romantic dinner into a nightmare. Her head thrummed as she stared ahead at the lit-up tower of the church at the end of the lane – the church where she and Sean had been married five years ago. She remembered walking through the village in her vintage lace dress, a broad smile set on her face for the entire day as all their friends and family watched on. She'd not wanted to be driven to church as it was such a short distance and the middle of summer, but mostly it was because she wanted everyone to see her and her bridesmaids – wanted everyone to know that she was the woman marrying Sean.

It was the most perfect day of her life. She'd met the man of her dreams and, shortly after they were married, she'd fallen pregnant with Alice. The only downside to the day was seeing Natalie, Sean's first wife, lurking outside the church after the ceremony – her face blotchy and tear streaked, watching on as the newlyweds were showered with confetti, the bells ringing.

Neither of them had said anything to her, and she'd soon scurried off through the gravestones, disappearing around the back of the church – but Libby knew she'd snapped a few pictures before she'd left. When they discussed it later, Sean put her mind at rest, telling her that she'd taken their divorce eighteen months before badly, and that she still wasn't over it. Thankfully, Dan, who was only ten at the time, hadn't spotted his mum as he'd followed them out of the church.

Libby jumped as her phone rang again. 'Hi,' she said, sniffing into the handset. 'Yeah, I'm OK. What about Sasha?' she said, wanting to know if there was news. 'Where are you? What's happened?' But Sean just told her to come home, that she'd been gone ages and they needed to do something different now. Reluctantly, Libby agreed and headed back, driving extra carefully as she looped the remainder of the village, all the while scanning around for Sasha. But there was no sign of the girl at all.

CHAPTER THIRTEEN

Libby took off her coat and perched on the edge of the armchair. She stared up at Sean, who was pacing about holding another tumbler of whisky. 'Do you really need to drink quite so much?' Libby asked, shaking her head.

'Well, you know, it's been such a fun night so far, I couldn't resist.' Sean raised his glass at her, his expression blank. 'Sorry,' he added, shaking his head.

Libby stared at him. He looked exhausted, stressed and out of breath. He still had his coat on and, even though it was a chilly night, he had a skim of sweat on his face. She reached up and wiped a dirty mark off his cheek, making him shy away. As she sat staring at Sasha's stuff strewn about, seeing the empty space where she'd been sitting earlier, she couldn't stop shaking.

'It's time to make some calls, isn't it?' she said, glancing at her watch. They both knew that made it all the more real: telling people. 'I can't bear the thought of worrying Jan just yet,' she added. 'The poor woman has had enough on her plate lately. But how can we not phone her mother?'

'We have to,' Sean said, making a concerned face. Neither of them knew Jan Long particularly well, and Sean knew her even less than Libby, though he knew Phil Long through the pheasant shoots on the estate, as well as from the local pub. Libby had heard snippets of gossip going around that the couple were having troubles, that there was possibly another man involved and that's why Phil had moved out. But she'd kept out of it, avoided the rumour mill. She was more interested in Sasha's welfare, how she was coping if it were true.

'How about we contact her boyfriend first? If you reckon there's been a bit of drama there, it's not unreasonable to think she's gone to see him, to sort things out?' Sean suggested.

'Good idea,' Libby said. 'He lives between here and Little Radwell – you know, the row of cottages by the bridge?'

'Do you have his number?'

'Possibly,' Libby said, thumbing through her calls list. 'Sash rang me from his phone once. That was a couple of months ago though.' Libby bit on her lip as she searched. 'Damn. Incoming calls don't stay logged that far back. I'll look on Facebook.'

Within a minute, Libby had found Matt's profile via Sasha's and sent him a message. They weren't friends, but she knew it would get through.

'Kids these days are always online, aren't they? Hopefully he'll see it soon enough,' Sean said, dragging his hands down his face.

'We can't just sit around and do nothing though, can we?' Libby went to the front window, peering out, up and down the lane. There was no sign of anyone. She glanced at her watch. 'Who should we contact next?'

'Maybe send the same Facebook message to a few of her close girlfriends? Do you know their names?'

'A couple,' Libby said, engrossed in her phone again. 'But I'm not sure what good it's going to do. We need to actually speak to someone, surely? And then we'll need to call the…' Libby trailed off. Neither of them wanted to go that route, but it was looking all the more likely that the police would have to become involved.

'Look,' Sean said. 'I can only imagine the worry we'll cause, but I do think it's time to call her mother. She'll be expecting her home soon anyway.'

Libby stared at him, her heart thumping, trying to imagine the future and Alice babysitting for a local family. How would she react if she received such a call? What would she do? All she knew was that her heart would be on fire and she'd immediately call the police. 'She'll come straight round here, you realise?' Libby said. 'I know I would.'

'Unless she just assumes Sasha is still on her way home,' Sean said, swirling his tumbler before finishing the last dregs. He raised his eyebrows and Libby nodded, knowing they were thinking the same.

'She'd have taken her stuff with her though, right? And let us know that she'd left. Or, maybe she has texted me but it hasn't delivered yet. You know how unreliable texts are around here.'

'I'd thought of that while you were out. I tried to get into her phone but it's code locked and fingerprint protected.'

Libby stared at him, a cold shudder running the length of her spine. Sean stared back as she tried to read his eyes, but they were bloodshot – probably from too much whisky – and expressionless. Like her, he was worried and fearful. But they couldn't sit around and do nothing. They'd be accused of impeding an enquiry if things got that far.

'Call Jan,' Sean said. 'It's time, Libby.'

Libby nodded and dialled the Longs' landline. She didn't have Jan's mobile. 'It's ringing,' she whispered. She stiffened when it was answered, heard a woman's breathy voice.

'Sash?' she said.

'Hi, is that you, Mrs Long? It's Libby Randell here, from Great Lyne. Sasha was babysitting for us tonight.'

'Oh… hello. Sorry, I thought it might be Sash calling on someone else's phone for a lift.'

Libby sensed the tinge of disappointment in the woman's voice. She also sounded exhausted.

'She said she might call me for a ride home, you see. And I'm waiting to go to bed.' She added a little laugh.

'I see,' Libby said, making a face at Sean. She didn't feel real. 'We're back from our meal now and, well, we were actually wondering if Sasha had come home already?'

'Home?' the other woman said. 'No, she hasn't. That's why I was expecting her call. She mentioned not wanting to waste anyone's money on a taxi and she and Matt… well, he wasn't going to give her a lift tonight, so I said I'd wait up.' Jan sighed. 'I hope she isn't walking home. What did she tell you when she left?'

'That's the thing,' Libby went on, feeling a sweat break out on her face. 'She wasn't here when we got back. We haven't seen her since we left for the pub earlier, actually. And she'd left Alice alone.'

'*What?*' Jan said, her voice ending in a squeak. 'What do you mean, she wasn't there when you got back?'

'Just that, really,' Libby said, her voice wavering. 'She's not here.' She glanced around the living room, as if to convince herself. 'It's so unlike Sasha. I wanted to check she'd made it home safely.'

'No, no she hasn't. Not yet.'

Libby heard the other woman scrabbling around in the background, the jangling of keys.

'I'm going to go out in the car and look for her between here and yours,' Jan said, trying to hide her concern. 'She'll no doubt be lugging that heavy backpack of hers along the lane, wishing she'd called me. And, knowing her, her phone will be out of battery.' She laughed but it came out too loud, hysterical almost.

'Thing is,' Libby went on, 'she's left all her stuff here—' She stopped as the line went dead, staring at her phone before placing it back to her ear again. 'Jan?' she said, just to make sure. 'She hung up,' Libby said to Sean. 'She's going out to look for Sasha along the lane between there and here.'

'I'll get the kettle on, then,' Sean said, looking around at Sasha's stuff. 'Should we pack it up so it's not too distressing for Jan?'

'Good point,' Libby said, reaching out for a couple of Sasha's books, sidestepping round everything. 'But… but what if…?' They stared at each other, both thinking the same – that the police, if they had to call them, wouldn't want anything disturbed.

'Maybe leave it, then,' Sean said, heading out to the kitchen. Libby followed him. He filled the kettle and put it on the hotplate. 'How bad was it?' he said, leaning on the kitchen sink and peering out at Libby's car, trying to see any damage after she'd told him what had happened.

'Not too bad,' she said finally. 'I was in such a panic, I didn't really look at the other car. Cath from the post office saw the scrape and is bound to tell someone. I don't want to fall out with anyone in the village.'

'I know,' Sean replied. 'But you didn't mean to do it. I don't think you need to tell anyone.' He put his arms around her, pulling her close. Libby melded into him as he stroked her hair and kissed the top of her head, grateful the tension from before seemed to have been forgotten. 'And please try not to worry about Sasha,' he added. 'It's all going to be OK, you'll see.'

'I just can't stand to think of her out there alone, freezing. It's so cold tonight.' Libby shuddered in Sean's arms.

'I know, I know,' he said. 'I don't like it either. But focus on Alice being left alone. That can't be ignored.'

'You're right,' Libby whispered into Sean's shoulder. 'About everything.' She didn't think she ever wanted to move again as she stood there, pressed against him, his scent calming her as she breathed him in. 'I love you,' she said, looking up at him. 'And I'm truly sorry about earlier. About the note. I promise I'll never mention it again.'

Sean nodded before kissing her. And afterwards he put his finger gently over her lips.

CHAPTER FOURTEEN

Libby and Sean stared at each other as they heard the knock. It was Sean who got up to answer the door, with Libby straining to hear if it had woken Alice. But all she could hear was Jan Long's voice at the door, getting louder as Sean brought her through the hallway and into the living room. Libby stood up, her legs feeling as though they were about to give way.

'Jan, hello,' she said, pulling a concerned face. She noticed the woman scanning Sasha's things. 'Did you find her?' Libby already knew the answer to that – Jan wouldn't be here if she had.

'No, not yet,' she replied, sounding a little calmer. 'Bloody kids,' she added, rolling her eyes.

'Where did you look?' Sean asked, indicating she should sit down.

'Just the route between my place and here,' Jan said. 'I stopped at Matt's house on the way but there was no one home. His parents have gone away for the weekend and I think Matt was out with his mates tonight. The place was in darkness.'

Sean and Libby nodded, neither of them knowing what to say.

'Is this like her?' Sean asked, although Libby knew it wasn't. 'To just take off without telling anyone?'

Sasha was the most responsible young person Libby knew, seemingly in all areas of her life. When Libby's business began to take off, she'd put a couple of adverts in the local shops for help. Half a dozen college students had applied, wanting the extra cash, and Libby had interviewed them all. But Sasha stood out a mile and, after giving several of them a trial run, she was the only one obviously up to the job. She was polite, hard-working, showed initiative, plus she had a genuine interest in food, confiding to Libby after a couple of weeks that she'd always been watchful of what she ate.

'I'm so careful what I put in my body,' she told her as they were packing up the car with crockery. Libby remembered the event well as there were two vegans attending as well as a guest with coeliac disease; she was quite used to catering for all types of dietary needs. But Libby couldn't help wondering if Sasha may have, or was heading in the direction of, an eating disorder. She was so thin and obsessed with running too, plus she rarely accepted food while working for her. She thought she'd keep an eye on things, say something if she was worried. But she wasn't sure if that should be to Sasha or to her mum.

'No, it's not like her at all,' Jan said, jangling her keys as she sat perched forward on the edge of the armchair. 'Well, a couple of times she's gone off without letting me know where she is. Turned out she was with Matt – he's got a car, you see – and they once decided to go off for the weekend on a whim. She didn't have a phone charger with her and was basically having so much fun that she forgot to let me or Phil know.' Jan rolled her eyes and gave a half-smile, as if this recollection made the current situation not so bad.

'So do you think she might have gone off with Matt now?' Sean asked, looking hopeful. 'If his house was deserted and his parents away, maybe they've gone somewhere together? Or perhaps gone out for the evening and will go back to his later?'

Libby knew he was casting about for possibilities.

'They've been having problems,' Jan said, making an exasperated face. 'As much as you can have relationship problems at their age.'

Libby nodded. This fitted with what she knew too, from when she and Sasha had chatted.

'Matt's been messing her about lately,' Jan went on. 'Going off with his mates more than usual, and she's been feeling a bit ignored.' She exhaled then, her face telling of something else on her mind. She wondered how much Jan was overlaying this situation on top of her own, if indeed the rumours were true. But Libby wasn't about to pry. The woman looked exhausted and, while she was undeniably pretty – her thick hair framing her face, her slim fingers ending with perfectly painted nails – woman to woman, Libby could tell she looked as though she'd had enough. And, if they hadn't been in this situation, then she'd have poured a glass of wine for each of them and chatted it out.

'Sash told me once she thought Matt might have someone else – you know, another girl,' Jan said.

'That sounds tough,' Libby said, making a face. 'I know how much she likes Matt. She often talks about him.'

'Yeah, she likes him all right. But, as her mother, I've sometimes wanted to step in, take her by the shoulders and tell her to end it. He's not always treated her right.' She looked down then, fiddling with the keys. 'Anyway…' she finished, looking embarrassed.

'Would you like a cup of tea while we wait?' Sean said. 'Unless you think we should go out and look around the village again?'

'*Wait?*' Jan said. 'I think it's past just waiting now, isn't it?' She looked at her watch and took her phone from her coat pocket. 'I'm going to make a few calls to her friends,' she said. 'And her father, of course. I'd be grateful for a cuppa, thank you.'

Sean nodded and went to the kitchen.

'I sent Matt a Facebook message earlier,' Libby said. She checked her phone for the hundredth time. 'But he hasn't read it or replied yet. I didn't have his phone number, but I do think it's worth you calling him.'

Jan already had her phone to her ear. 'Matt, yes it's Jan, hi,' she said. 'I'm OK, thanks. You?' She stared at Libby and made a face. Libby could hear the boy's voice on the other end of the line and thought he sounded as though he was slurring, plus there was loud music in the background, as if he was in a bar or club.

'I'm just a bit concerned about Sash,' Jan went on. 'Can you hear me? Is she with you, Matt?' She held her breath then her shoulders fell. 'Oh, OK, that's a shame. When did you last hear from her?' Jan held the phone away from her ear and checked the signal. 'Hello?' She shook her head as the line went dead, calling him straight back, but Libby heard it divert to voicemail. Jan tried a couple more times before she left a message, urging Matt to call her back as soon as he could.

'No luck, I take it?' Libby said, just as Sean came back in carrying a tray of mugs. He was about to put it on the coffee table and slide the books out of the way, but thought better of it and set it on a side table instead.

'No,' Jan said thoughtfully, taking the cup of tea from Sean. 'He sounded a bit… drunk,' she added.

'Well, he's eighteen and it's Friday night,' Sean said, sitting down again. 'Have you tried Sasha's other friends?'

'I think it's her dad I need to call next,' Jan confessed quietly. Sean and Libby didn't say anything. 'He's not been spending much time at home at the moment, you see. She may have gone to him or even his parents. She's close to her dad.'

'Ah, OK,' Libby said, not wanting to pry too much. 'Perhaps he came to pick her up?'

'Yes, that's what I'm hoping,' she replied, dialling and waiting again.

Libby and Sean exchanged glances. It was getting more and more likely that the police would have to be involved, but neither of them wanted to suggest it. That was Jan's decision to make, though they were aware that time was of the essence if something bad had happened.

'He's not answering,' Jan said, ending the call. 'Probably because he saw my number come up.'

'Can you text him?' Sean suggested.

Jan was already tapping at her screen, and followed up by messaging a few of Sasha's girlfriends. 'How long do you think I should leave it before I call the police?' she asked, looking at her watch. 'It's after midnight now. This really isn't like her. And I know she'd never abandon your daughter on purpose. I'm so sorry she did that. Something bad must have happened. *Oh…*' Jan covered her face, a couple of sobs bursting between her fingers. Then she sat forward and grabbed Sasha's phone off the table. 'And she'd never leave *this* behind. She's glued to it.'

Jan pressed the iPhone's home button before entering the passcode. 'She always uses the same code and we sometimes use each other's phones if one is out of charge,' she said, thumbing through a few apps, checking call logs and messages.

'Yes, we do the same,' Libby said, glancing at Sean. Though she couldn't deny that, over the last few weeks, he'd been more protective of his phone. She thought she'd try his passcode later, if she got the chance, just to see if he'd changed it.

'There's only a call from you showing, Libby,' Jan said, putting the phone back on the table. 'Nothing else recent.'

'Look, Jan, I'm not trying to worry you but I think it's really time to call the police now,' Sean said. They both knew this would mean their involvement, maybe giving statements. 'If nothing else, just to ask for their advice perhaps?'

Jan nodded slowly, sniffing back tears. 'Yes, you're right. I just keep hoping she'll call me from someone else's phone, or walk in the door at any moment, all apologetic and ashamed that she left Alice.' Jan spread her hands wide, allowing them to fall down on her lap.

Sean googled a number for Jan to call. Time was ticking on and, while no one liked to acknowledge it, a teenage girl disappearing in this way was concerning, and every minute now counted.

Jan jumped as her phone rang, answering it immediately. 'Phil, hi, thanks for calling back,' she said quietly. 'Yes, I can talk.' She paused, listening. 'Oh, OK. Well that's a worry. When did you last see her?' Another pause. 'No, I'm not saying that, I simply asked when you'd seen her, not who *else* you'd seen. You have to turn things round all the time, don't you, as if it's all about you? And *I'm* not the one doing the accusing, remember?' Jan sighed, biting on her lip.

Libby made eye contact with Sean, each of them wondering what Jan meant. Then she got up to look out of the front window in case there was any sign of Sasha, while Sean went upstairs to check Alice was still sleeping.

'*No*,' Jan said loudly, making Libby jump. 'I haven't been out tonight and no one's been round to the house, for God's sake, Phil. And what the hell's that got to do with finding Sash, anyway? I'm glad you're so concerned about our daughter…'

Libby sat back down again, perched on the arm of the sofa, sipping her tea while Jan finished the call.

'Look, just let me know if you hear anything from her, OK? And if you can be bothered, or aren't too pissed, then getting in your car and driving around the area looking for her might be a help.' She gave an apologetic look to Libby, rolling her eyes. 'Yes, goodbye.' And she hung up, dropping her phone back into her bag at her feet, letting out a big sigh. 'Men,' she whispered just before Sean came back into the room. 'He's not seen Sasha since earlier in the week. He has no idea where she is, though was more interested in what I'd been up to.' She added the last bit under her breath, making Sean and Libby exchange glances again.

'It's 101 you need to call,' Sean said, showing her the police information page he'd found. 'I think it's worth reporting this now, Jan. I'm really sorry.'

Jan nodded. 'You're right, I know. It just seems so… *real* once I do that.'

'Shouldn't she call 999?' Libby asked, feeling sick at the thought. 'Isn't 101 for non-emergencies?'

'I'm sure they'll redirect Jan if they think it warrants it,' Sean said. 'It's a start and we don't want to waste their time.'

'True,' Jan said as she grabbed her phone and dialled, waiting for the line to connect. Within a few rings it answered, and Jan described the situation to the call handler, giving out details of what she knew. Which wasn't much at all.

CHAPTER FIFTEEN

'I've got an incident number,' Jan said, hanging up. Her face indicated that she didn't really know what that meant, except it sounded serious. 'They're... well, they're sending someone out.' She bit on a nail. 'They thought it best,' she added.

'That's a good thing,' Sean said, reaching over and touching Jan's hand as it lay on her lap. He gave it a squeeze.

'It really is,' Libby said, noticing. 'They have resources, stuff we can't access. They'll find out where she is in no time, you'll see.' She swallowed, looked away.

Jan nodded. 'They said I should wait here. I'm so sorry if I'm keeping you up. But when I explained how she'd disappeared, how old she is, how out of character this is for her, they said they wanted to come out and talk to us tonight. I suppose I could ask them to do it at my place, if you prefer?'

'Don't be silly,' Sean said, with Libby echoing agreement. 'There'll be questions that need answering and we're happy to help.' He gave a decisive nod.

'Truth is, I don't really want to be alone. Nathan, Sash's little brother, is sleeping over at a friend's house tonight so I don't have to worry about him. He went to the cinema with his mate's family.' She forced a small smile, knowing that at least one half of her offspring was safe.

'Can I get you anything?' Libby asked. 'Food, water? A drink, perhaps, to settle your nerves?'

Jan thought for a second. 'A small drink might help, thank you. I sometimes do.' Her expression revealed that things hadn't been easy for her lately.

Sean went to the drinks cabinet, pouring Jan a small whisky. 'Here,' he said, handing her the glass.

'Thanks,' she said. 'Though I must stay clear-headed. I want to go out and look for her in the car again.' She half covered her face with one hand, hanging her head. 'In fact, what am I even thinking, sitting here doing nothing?' She put down her drink, got up and dashed to the front window, peering up and down the lane. A fine rain was dribbling down the panes, making the view obscure. 'My daughter's out there somewhere and I'm sitting here with a drink.' She reached for her coat, was about to put it on, but Libby put a hand on her arm.

'Jan, I think it's best if you stay here for now and wait for the police. Do you know how long they'll be?'

'Not long, I don't think,' Jan said, dropping her coat and sitting down again. Her shoulders were hunched and her face crumpled from worry. 'They asked if she was vulnerable in any way and, when I said I didn't think she was but that this was totally out of character, that she's only seventeen and was meant to be babysitting, that's when they said they'd come out. As though…' Jan pulled her cardigan around her, showing off just how thin she was. Just like her daughter, Libby thought. 'As though they already *knew* it was bad,' she whispered, knocking back half of her drink anyway.

'Look,' Sean said, 'it's common knowledge that most people who seem to be missing aren't actually. There'll be some story behind this that you had no idea about. You know what teenagers are like,' he added. 'Kids get up to all sorts of things behind your back that most parents would be horrified about. Sometimes it's best that we don't know.'

Libby looked at him, tried to signal for him to be quiet, but he didn't see. Instead, he left her wondering if he was speaking more from past experience than the current situation, given that Alice was only four and Dan, aged fifteen, had been a model son so far.

Forty-five minutes later a police car pulled up in front of the cottage, its lights illuminating the lane, followed shortly by a knock at the door. Sean went to answer, while Libby continued to comfort Jan, who hadn't had any luck phoning around Sasha's friends. A couple of them had replied by text, but just to say that they'd heard she was babysitting tonight or hadn't been in touch. It only added to the frustration.

'Jan,' Sean said, leading a tall man into the living room. 'The police are here.'

The plain-clothes officer ducked his head as he entered, his eyes scanning around as soon as he came in. Behind him, a female officer in uniform followed, removing her hat as she stood behind her colleague. Libby wasn't sure which was more intimidating – the deep furrows on the man's brow, his dewy beard and moustache glistening from the drizzle outside and the steely, unreadable look on his face, or the younger officer's uniform and radio that crackled at her shoulder, the bright yellow of her jacket. Libby decided it was the uniform, and the kit attached to her, that made everything seem unbearable.

'Please, take a seat,' Sean said to the two officers, gesturing to the sofa. 'I'm sorry there's not much space. And just so you know, this is just how we found Sasha's stuff, so if you'd rather I brought in chairs from the kitchen or we sat elsewhere, that's fine.' Libby knew he didn't want to imply that they may want the sofa undisturbed, therefore suggesting that something bad had happened on it, but didn't want to be the cause of contamination either.

'Detective Inspector Doug Jones,' the man said, holding out his hand to Jan. His voice was deep and slow, and oddly reassuring, as if he'd done this a hundred times before and would suddenly make Sasha reappear at any moment. 'And this is PC Watts,' he added. 'And, agreed, let's go elsewhere, please.'

A moment later they were all seated around the pine kitchen table with the kettle boiling. It almost felt to Libby as if they'd got a few friends around for a drink, that they should put some music on or get the cards out for a game. The detective, who at first seemed unapproachable, gruff and the type to take no nonsense, had soon put them all at ease and was chatting with Jan as he waited for his drink, a comforting smile breaking through the thickness of his beard and moustache. He turned to Sean and Libby when Jan mentioned that Sasha had been babysitting for them.

'It's just so out of character for her to take off like this,' Jan went on. 'I'm so sorry you've been bothered. Friday must be a really busy night for you.'

The detective didn't say anything, rather listened and scratched his beard – a mix of black and grey. A pale-blue shirt, dark jacket and jeans made him seem approachable yet entirely capable.

'Not at all,' he replied, stirring his coffee. 'It's what we're here for. So your daughter Sasha was babysitting here from what time?' he said, looking between Jan, Libby and Sean.

'She arrived about—'

'Seven thirty,' Sean said, interrupting Libby. PC Watts had a notebook and was jotting everything down, silencing her radio as the chatter continued at her shoulder. 'Our table was booked for eight, though they don't mind fifteen minutes either way, and we wanted to have a drink in the bar first. It's only a short taxi ride from here.'

Libby nodded, confirming everything Sean was saying.

'So what time did Sasha leave home?' DI Jones said to Jan.

Jan looked puzzled for a second. 'That's the thing,' she said. 'She went straight from college to a friend's house for some food then came here. I think her mate's mum must have dropped her off. Is that right?' Jan looked embarrassed at having to ask Libby and Sean about her daughter's movements.

'She was alone when I answered the door,' Sean said. 'I didn't see a car and didn't ask how she got here. I didn't think to.'

The detective nodded. 'And how did she seem when she arrived?'

'Fine,' Sean said immediately. 'We'd just finished getting ready and I came down to answer the door. She had her backpack of college books with her and went straight into the living room. Alice was already in bed.'

Libby looked at Sean, thinking she should add something. 'I got my coat, came down and said hi to her. As Sean said, she seemed…' Libby hesitated, 'absolutely fine. She'd got out some of her books to study. Maths, by the looks of it. They're still in the living room.'

The PC made notes, occasionally glancing up.

'Sash told me I looked nice and I mentioned that Sean and I were having a "date night". I think she thought that was a bit, I dunno, silly perhaps. At our age. We must seem ancient to her.' Libby added a little laugh, but it seemed out of place so she cleared her throat instead. 'We left shortly after that as the taxi arrived.'

'And before this, when was the last time you saw her?' the detective asked. His hands were clasped in front of him, resting on the table, one finger tapping on the opposite knuckle.

'About a week ago,' Libby replied. 'She sometimes helps me out with my business. I cook – private dining for local corporate clients, dinner parties and stuff like that. Sasha had helped me serve for a bankers' dinner. She seemed fine then too. Nothing unusual.'

'And the last time I'd have seen her was…' Sean thought for a moment. 'Well, either when she last babysat for us, maybe a month ago, or possibly if she was in the barn kitchen helping Libby. She's often popping in and out so I couldn't say exactly.' He glanced at Libby.

'We converted the little barn out the back into a catering kitchen,' Libby added when the detective seemed puzzled. 'It's easier from a hygiene point of view than using the cottage kitchen. Certificates and such like,' Libby said, wanting the officers to know she did everything right.

He nodded, seemingly appreciating the detail they were giving. 'So you went out for your meal at…?'

'The Old Fox in Chalwell,' Sean said.

'And tell me about when you came back – what happened when you realised Sasha wasn't here?'

Libby expected Sean to answer but, when he didn't say anything, she stepped in. 'We took a taxi home from the pub and, when we came in, Sasha just wasn't here. Of course, we didn't realise to begin with, as that's not what you're expecting – your babysitter gone. At first I thought she was either upstairs with Alice or maybe in the toilet.' Libby gestured towards the back hallway off the kitchen. 'But she wasn't anywhere. We looked all around, even in the barn kitchen and the garden,' Libby added. 'It's just so weird.' She felt her voice tightening around the words as she replayed the scene in her mind.

'Has she ever done anything like this before when she's babysat for you? Or ever let you down when she's worked in your catering business, Libby?'

'No, not at all,' was her quick reply. 'Which is why this is so odd.'

'Sash is a good girl, Detective,' Jan chipped in. 'She's reliable, works hard at college, always keeps me posted where she is – well, usually,' she added.

'Usually?'

'There have been a couple of times when she's forgotten to let me know she's OK or has had a change of plan. But that's because her phone was out of battery or she'd got caught up in the excitement of things. Once was with Matt, her boyfriend. And I've already checked with him tonight. He's not heard from her.'

'So she's left all her college books and phone behind,' the detective said. 'Which would indicate that she either intended to come back or…'

They all waited for him to finish, but he didn't and, instead, Jan, Libby and Sean each played out in their own minds what the detective was implying.

Or she's been taken against her will…

'After it became clear that she wasn't here,' Libby said, 'we knew we had to make some calls.' She prayed the detective wouldn't ask how much alcohol they'd had, think they'd somehow been irresponsible.

'And what time was this?' DI Jones asked.

Libby stared at the ceiling. 'Some time after eleven, I suppose?' she said, glancing at Sean for confirmation.

'That's about right,' he added. 'We hoped that Sasha would turn up of her own accord so didn't panic immediately, though we were nonplussed that she'd just taken off and left Alice.'

Jan bowed her head briefly, covering her face. Libby reached out and touched her arm.

'We were hoping she'd turn up but when she didn't, that's when I messaged Matt, her boyfriend. After that, we knew we had to call Jan. We were hoping Sasha had made her own way home and perhaps just forgotten her backpack.'

'Can I take a look at her belongings, please?' the detective said, nodding and standing. 'Then we'll decide what resources we need to put in place, how we're going to move forward.' He offered a comforting smile, though no one felt particularly reassured.

In the living room, they showed the detective Sasha's things. Despite their own caution at touching anything, the detective didn't seem too concerned about picking up one or two items.

'What's she studying?' he asked Jan, who stood behind him, arms clamped across her chest.

'A levels,' she said quietly. 'Maths, physics and chemistry. She wants to go to university, to do engineering.'

The detective nodded, clearing his throat as he flipped to the cover of a textbook. 'Advanced mathematics,' he read out loud. 'Clever girl, is she?'

'Very,' Jan replied. 'She takes after her dad.'

'And where's Dad right now?' DI Jones asked, picking up Sasha's A4 pad. He scanned down her jottings and crossings out, turning through the pages.

'We recently separated,' Jan said. 'He's staying in one of the empty estate cottages for the time being. I'm guessing he was out at the pub tonight. He usually is,' she added quietly. Then she burst into tears, dropping down into the armchair.

'Oh, Jan, try not to get too upset,' Libby said, stroking her shoulder.

'What I don't understand is why she would leave all her stuff behind,' Sean said. 'Especially her phone.'

'Exactly,' DI Jones said. 'Is she or are any of her friends in any kind of trouble, do you know, Mrs Long? Does she have anything going on that would require her to just drop everything and leave, whether it was alone or with someone? Have a good think, however insignificant it may seem.'

'No, none at all that I know of,' she replied. 'I… I just don't understand.'

'When you came back, was there any sign of forced entry at all, front or back?' he asked Sean and Libby.

'No,' Libby replied quickly. 'I didn't notice anything like a break-in when we got home.'

'Right,' the detective said. 'It's time for me to make a few calls, see if we can't find this young lady before morning.'

CHAPTER SIXTEEN

'I can't just do *nothing*,' Sean said, sitting on the bed, watching as Libby threw a few random things into a holdall. The expression on her face – teary eyes, lips parted, cheeks drained of blood – told him she wasn't thinking straight, couldn't care less what they took with them. She went into the adjoining bathroom and returned, chucking their toothbrushes and a tube of paste into the bag, not bothering with any of her cosmetics. A couple of pairs of socks, some underwear, a sweater each and a hairbrush, and Libby zipped up the holdall.

'I need to sort some stuff for Alice,' she said, not looking at Sean. He grabbed her wrist as she passed by the bed.

'I'll take you both up to Mum's then I'm going out to search.'

'What's the point?' she replied, her eyes brimming with tears again as he held on to her. Jan was still downstairs with PC Watts. 'The police are on it now. There's nothing you can do.'

'It can't hurt, surely?' he said, releasing her.

'Anyway, I don't think we should wake your mum at this hour,' Libby said, glancing at her watch. She hadn't failed to notice how tired Marion had seemed lately. All she knew was that DI Jones had told them to get a few things together, that they'd need to vacate the cottage as he'd likely need to call in a forensics team. And he had no idea how long that would take. Meantime, he didn't want anyone in the living room and, ideally, any of the other rooms either.

'She won't mind,' Sean said. 'You know how she likes to help.'

Libby nodded. That much was true. 'Surely we can just stay upstairs here until they're ready to... *do* stuff,' Libby added, not knowing what it was they were going to do. In her mind, she had an image of white-suited police officers going over every inch of their house, pulling it apart, finding out more about their lives than just the couple of hours Sasha had spent here.

'We'd better just do as we're told, love,' Sean said, standing up and wrapping his arms around her. It was Libby's favourite place in the whole world, being held by her husband. She suddenly had an overwhelming urge to wake her daughter, press her between them and never let her go. 'Even if that means sitting in the car for a few hours until morning. It's awful, horrific, but it is what it is.'

It is what it is...

It's what Sean said to her the first time she encountered Natalie, his ex-wife. She and Sean had been seeing each other for six months when Sean had felt it was time to introduce her to Dan, his son. It soon became clear to Libby that the lad had coped with his parents' break-up just fine – even preferring them apart, as he once confided in Libby. *At least I don't have to listen to them rowing all the time*, he'd said, though Libby had never asked what about. Natalie, however, hadn't taken things so well, and even now, years later, she was unable to accept that Sean had remarried. Not only had she turned their divorce into a three-year legal battle, with solicitors' costs wiping out a chunk of the money at stake anyway, but she'd used Dan as a pawn – a pawn in proceedings, but also when a contact order was put in place for Sean to see him. He loved his son dearly and it broke his heart to see him being used in this way. Whatever Natalie wanted, she usually got – whether it was more maintenance, a new car, or help with her mortgage. If he refused, Sean didn't get to see Dan, and back to court they had to go.

It was for this reason that Sean was always friendly towards Natalie, giving her whatever she wanted, being courteous and kind – almost to the point that Libby wondered if he still had feelings for her.

'It is what it is with Natalie,' he'd told her the first time he'd spoken in depth about his ex-wife to Libby. They'd known each other a couple of months by that point and, previously, neither had really felt it necessary to discuss their past loves. They'd been too busy concentrating on each other and the excitement of a new relationship. Of course, Libby had known Sean was separated, still technically married at the time, though he'd been living with his parents since the split, saving a deposit for a new place of his own as well as waiting for the marital finances to be sorted. Meantime, he'd thrown himself into his work and his son's well-being.

'Nat's been having trouble accepting…' He'd paused then, pulling on his hair, which, Libby later came to know, was a sign of stress. That, as well as his limp becoming more pronounced. '… accepting that things between us are over. I just don't think she ever expected me to find someone else. Especially a woman like you.'

'She knows about me?'

Sean had looked away then, his face colouring under the soft lights of the pub. Or it could have been the glow from the fire, Libby thought. But either way, she could tell he was unsure how to answer. In the end, he just came out with it.

'She found out for herself,' he said, taking Libby's hand, softening the blow.

'Oh. Wait, *what*?'

'What you have to understand with Natalie is…' He'd trailed off then, thinking. 'Is that she can't stand not to know everything. It's probably a control thing, I dunno. I'm not her shrink.' He'd laughed then, trying to allay the concern on Libby's face.

'Found out for herself?' Libby repeated, trying to sound light and breezy about it. But she wanted to know. 'Has she been watching us? Watching *me*?'

'That's Nat for you,' Sean said with another laugh, though less convincing. 'Like I said, it is what it is.'

*

Libby was snapped out of the memory by the bedroom door slowly opening. At first, she thought it would be DI Jones – she knew he was still in the cottage, and the PC too. But then Alice shuffled in, rubbing her eyes as she stood there in her pink nightdress.

'Hello, darling,' Libby said, easing out of Sean's arms. She bent down to her daughter, scooping her up and settling her on her hip.

'Can't sleep,' Alice said, looking around, blinking. 'There's too much noise in my head.'

Libby looked at Sean.

'Oh, Little Bean,' he said, taking her from Libby. 'Come here and have a Daddy cuddle. Don't you worry about the noise, sweetness. It was probably just a bad dream.'

Alice buried her face in her father's neck and shoulder, easing her thumb into her mouth while she twiddled her hair, curling her legs around his waist. But then she pulled back, holding on to his shoulders. 'No it wasn't a dream, Daddy. There was big bangs downstairs and it woke me up. Was there a burger?'

'Burglar, you mean?' Sean said, gently touching her under the chin. 'And no, there wasn't. Don't you worry. Perhaps it was just someone outside in the lane, parking a car or something.'

Alice frowned, her pale eyebrows pulling together as she bit on the fullness of her bottom lip. 'Wasn't a car. It was in the house and… and… and I didn't like it so I got Mr Flumps to save me. We made a tent under the duvet so we couldn't hear it.'

Libby caught Sean's eye again.

'When did you hear the noises, sweetie?' Libby asked, stroking Alice's foot.

'That tickles,' she said, snatching her leg away. 'This last night,' she added, looking confused. 'They were big giant noises.'

'Don't worry,' Sean said. 'Mummy and Daddy are home now and there's nothing to be scared of. In fact,' he said, taking a deep breath, 'how would you like to go and see Nanny for breakfast? She can make you pancakes or perhaps you can go with her to collect fresh eggs from the henhouse.'

Alice buried her face in Sean's shoulder again, nodding. 'Yes, please,' she said, sounding muffled.

What do we do? Libby mouthed at Sean. He shrugged in reply.

'How about I tuck you back into bed for a little while and, when we're ready, we'll wake you to go to Nanny's? You can stay in your nightie, if you like.'

Another nod from Alice, who was already half asleep again. But as soon as he went to carry her back to her own room, she stiffened and squealed.

'*Your* bed, Daddy,' she whined.

'OK, OK,' Sean said, pulling back their duvet and laying her down. 'You can sleep in here.' He tucked her in and flicked off the lamp, beckoning Libby out onto the landing.

'Now what?' Libby whispered, folding her arms. 'Should we tell the detective?'

'No need,' Sean said, rubbing his face. 'It's hardly important. Alice had a bad dream, that's all.'

Libby nodded. 'I suppose. But think about it. What if someone *was* in the house and hurt Sasha? God, and with Alice upstairs.' She shook her head, trying to rid her mind of the image. 'I just can't stand to think of it,' she whispered, eyeing her husband, wondering if he agreed.

'The detective didn't mention signs of a struggle when he looked round,' Sean said, glancing down the stairs. He lowered his voice. 'I'm not sure putting Alice through a grilling is in her best interests.'

'If you're sure,' Libby said, glancing at their bedroom door.

'I am,' Sean said, just as the PC came up the stairs, her hand on the banister rail as she turned the corner. They both stared at her, aware that their bedroom door was opening behind them. They heard Alice's sniffles as she came close.

'Mr and Mrs Rand—'

'Mummy, *Mummy*, I can't get to sleep,' Alice wailed, her sobs increasing as she ran up and hugged Libby's leg. She was almost squealing as she stared up at the officer. 'I'm… I'm scared that bad lady is going to come back…' And, before Libby could pick her up again, Alice had dropped to the floor and covered her head with her arms, her shoulders shaking in time with her sobs.

CHAPTER SEVENTEEN

Now

The solicitor is smart, slim and younger than me. I've stared at her for the last fifteen minutes without saying a word, just concentrating on her bright eyes, her long lashes and dark, flawless skin. She doesn't look as though she's on my side, even though she said, several times, that she's here to help and advise me. But she doesn't seem to understand that I shouldn't be here, that there's been a terrible mistake. She has no clue about my life, my home, Alice, Sean, the village, my business, Marion, the farm and everything else that makes up me. It's simple really. Yet how do I tell her? How do I explain and untangle everything so she, and the police, will see that I'm innocent?

I open my mouth to say something, but think better of it and close it again.

'If you won't speak, Libby, it's hard for me to advise you,' she says. Her lips are full and glossed, while her hair is sleek and pulled back in a thick black ponytail. Bright eyes stare at me, the intelligence behind them scaring me, making me think I'll say the wrong thing before I've even said it.

She's on my side…

'Libby?' Her voice is crisp and precise, like the rest of her. My eyes flick down to her hands, pen in the right one poised above a notepad. The same kind of A4 ruled book that Sasha had been using that night.

Everything always comes back to Sasha.

'OK.' She lets out a small sigh. 'Do you understand that you're going to be questioned about the murder of Sasha Long?'

I give a little nod, the first sign I've given since I was shown into the interview room. It's a grey place, reflective of the landscape in my mind. Desolate and empty.

'I've met with the arresting officer handling the case and he's presented me with some evidence. I should stress the word *some* here, as it's rare, especially in a case such as this, for them to reveal everything they have at this point. But I'd like to hear your side, have you tell me what happened. Then we can decide where to go from here. Does that sound OK, Libby?'

I nod again.

The solicitor – Claire something, I think they said she was called – looks at me, leaning forward slightly. I smell her perfume – sweet and flowery with a hint of something else. Something strong and dark. Like her. 'And there *will* be more evidence, Libby, please be assured of that. They'll likely lay their best cards on the table towards the end of the interview, trying to wrong-foot you, trip you up over what you've already said – if you say anything at all. You've been arrested for a reason, and the alleged crime is serious. *Very* serious, Libby, so if you're innocent and want to walk out of here later with no further action, you need to completely refute what they're saying by giving your version of events.' She pauses for a moment. 'Or, of course, if it's appropriate, I can advise you how to make a confession.'

She sits back in her chair, her nude-coloured blouse falling open a little at the front so I can just make out the edge of her pale bra. Her black pencil skirt and court shoes, her subtle yet flawless make-up, her hands that don't look as though they've ever seen a washing-up bowl, are a stark contrast to my current state.

Unwashed, unmade-up, exhausted and terrified. Shaking from the inside out, I am the opposite of the woman sitting across from me.

'Of course, you have the right to remain silent and say "no comment" to everything you're asked in interview. But please do keep in mind that if this case goes to court and you later wish to rely on evidence there that you don't provide now, it's not going to help your cause. Not at all.'

'But *what* evidence?' I say, my thoughts coming out as actual words. Tiny, barely audible words. 'They're saying I did something and I *didn't*.' I cover my face, not wanting her to see my tears. 'It was only a meal. A meal in a pub and then all this happens. A living nightmare. And poor Sasha... *gone*.' I try to sniff back the sobs but can't hold them in any longer. My head drops to the table. 'I can't stand the thought of what Jan and her family are going through, and I hate that this has happened to them and to Sasha. But how can my life go from perfectly normal, perfectly wonderful, to this? I didn't *do* anything wrong. I *swear* I didn't.' I look up, snivelling, wiping my nose across the back of my sweatshirt sleeve. 'We just went out for a meal.'

'OK,' Claire says, taking a clean tissue from a pack in her handbag and passing it to me. 'That's a start. Now, why don't you tell me everything about that night...' She glances down at her papers. 'The night Sasha Long went missing.'

'You never know what you're going to need to remember,' I say after blowing my nose, wiping my face and having a few sips of water. When they question me, I just need to tell them what happened. Exactly the same as Sean and I have done all along.

Sean, I think, picturing my husband's face as I stare at the solicitor. He's smiling, standing in front of me with his big hands planted firmly on my shoulders and he's looking me squarely in the eyes. I see his mouth moving, telling me something, overlaid on top of Claire's face as she sits opposite. As ever, I know he's got my back, that he's by my side, telling me that we'll get through this together, that none of it is our fault, that we'll one day look back and know it made us stronger, closer, more in love than ever. I try to lip-read what he's telling me, wanting nothing more than to hear *I'll get you out of there, Lib, don't you worry…* but all I can see are his lips saying *It is what it is…* over and over.

'Sean and I went out on a "date night",' I tell her, sniffing. 'Sounds silly, I know, but… but something had happened in the few days before to make me feel a bit, well, insecure. It was stupid of me, I now realise, and completely unjustified. Sean knew I was upset so he suggested a meal out on the Friday night, at the Old Fox in Chalwell. We'd both been working hard and needed some time out together.'

'Can you tell me more about what it was that had made you feel insecure?' Claire asked, making notes at the same time. 'Am I right in thinking it was perhaps a… trust thing between you?'

I pause, thinking of Sean again, trying to read his lips, what he's telling me to say. 'It's not really relevant,' I reply. 'But it's the reason we went out that night.'

Claire's face softens slightly – eyes narrowing just a touch so the tiniest of lines appear at the corners, her lips pursing, not in pity but rather in understanding, empathy. As if she knows exactly how I felt that night.

'It was just a stupid misunderstanding really. And trust was at the core of it, yes. It's the reason Sean booked the table. To make things better between us.'

'You said something had happened in the few days before the meal? Can you tell me about that?'

'Do I need to?'

'Libby, the detective is going to be asking you all kinds of questions. And he's not going to be gentle like me. You don't have to answer, like I said, but it's hard for me to advise you if I don't have the full picture.' Claire turns her wrist, glances at her watch. 'I'm conscious of time too.'

'OK,' I say, my heart juddering. 'I'd got reason to believe Sean might be having an affair. Stupid, I know. And he's not, but something had got to me, made me have doubts.'

'What had got to you?'

'A note,' I say, half rolling my eyes, shrugging. 'Someone left a note under my car windscreen wiper saying that Sean was having an affair.' There. It's out.

'I'm sorry to hear that, Libby. Did you mention this in your previous police statements?' Claire shuffles through some papers, scanning the documents in front of her.

'No,' I say, saving her the trouble. 'I didn't think I needed to.'

She stops, looks up at me, then makes some more notes on her pad. 'So you'd gone out for a meal to patch things up after getting the note?'

'Yes.'

She's silent for a moment, her eyes lingering on my face for a few seconds before turning back to her papers. She taps her pen on her lip as she reads, running her finger down the lines, turning pages.

'And when you came back from the pub, Sasha wasn't in your house. Alice, your four-year-old daughter was asleep upstairs. You went out in the car looking for Sasha…' She makes a noise as she speed-reads further into the papers, her finger quickly tracking the words. 'Then you contacted Sasha's boyfriend, some friends, her mum, then the police were called… investigation… um… OK, Libby…' she mumbles, flicking to another document beside her.

She looks up, laying down her pen and leaning forward on her arms. 'Part of the police evidence relates to disparities and contradictions between your and your husband's statements, Libby. Some things don't match up.'

'*What?*' I choke on the water I'm sipping, coughing. 'What do you mean, disparities?' I say, covering my mouth briefly. 'We both know exactly what happened. We were both there.'

'Tell me about your husband's relationship with Sasha, Libby? How well did they know each other, for instance?'

I sit there, staring at her, my mouth open and my eyes even wider. 'Why do you keep saying my name?' I ask, feeling dizzy, sick, as if I'm not real. 'Over and over, you keep saying it. Like you're trying to trick me. Or make me go mad.' I half stand up, leaning forward on the table. My arms are shaking, my eyes bulging wide. I sit down again when Claire recoils. 'You're not on my side at all, are you?' I whisper, sweating. 'You're just trying to catch me out.'

'Libby, I'm not and it's a simple question. And one the detective will undoubtedly ask you.' The solicitor taps her pen on the edge of the table, her eyes fixed on mine. Tap, tap, tap… 'Your husband. Sasha. And you. The jealous wife.' She tilts her head to one side.

'For *fuck's* sake,' I say, getting up and going over to the wall, standing there with my back to her. 'You have no idea what you're talking about. Sasha and *Sean*?' I swing around, my arms clamped across my chest, the long sweatshirt sleeves pulled over my hands. *Sean's* sweatshirt. I feel his arms holding me, giving me strength like he always has. 'She's our babysitter, for God's sake. And she sometimes helps me out in my business. She's a student and *only seventeen*.'

'And she could also be dead, Libby,' Claire says, making me feel as though the floor has disappeared from beneath me. 'It may well be that they've found a body.'

CHAPTER EIGHTEEN

Before

Marion stared at them, a bottle of pills in her hand, as they stood in the doorway. Alice was perched on Sean's hip with her arms slung around his neck. It was only a few minutes' drive to the farm, just a couple of miles outside Great Lyne, but Alice had fallen asleep almost as soon as Sean had started the engine of Libby's car.

'Oh my goodness, is everything OK?' Marion said as she tucked the pills in her pocket. Libby thought that they must look like refugees – Alice still in her nightie and wrapped up in a dressing gown and coat, with Libby in old tracksuit bottoms and a baggy cardigan over a T-shirt, the first things she could find when it became clear they had to leave the cottage. She'd wanted to change out of her dress. Her hair was messy and last night's make-up was still smudged under her eyes. It was 5.40 a.m. and neither of them had been to bed, with Sean not looking much better, having also changed out of what he was wearing last night. In a fit of distraction, Libby had put a load of washing on, trying to keep herself busy with menial tasks. It hadn't worked.

'Mum, I'm so sorry to disturb you at this hour. Can we come in?'

'Yes, yes of *course*,' Marion said, her face crumpling with concern as she stepped aside. Libby had been due to drop Alice off with Marion at nine o'clock anyway, while she got on with preparations for that evening's dinner party and Sean worked a morning surgery, but the three of them arriving at this hour was not what she was expecting. 'It's fine, it's fine. You know I'm up early anyway,' she added, rubbing Alice's back as Sean passed through into the kitchen. 'You both look as white as sheets and done in. Tell me, what's going on?' She pulled out a couple of chairs from the big kitchen table, pushing aside some papers and other clutter that had accumulated at one end. 'I'll put the kettle on.'

'Thanks, Mum,' Sean said, lowering himself into the chair, trying not to wake Alice. Libby remained silent, wondering how Sean was going to break the news that Sasha was missing and their cottage was soon to be filled with a police forensics team.

'How was your meal at the Fox?' Marion asked, reaching down some mugs. 'You can't have stayed out very late if you're up this early.'

'It was lovely, thanks, Marion. Just what we needed and the food's always good,' Libby said when Sean didn't answer.

'Well you know us, we're not exactly party animals any more,' Sean said, giving Libby a look. 'But something a bit odd has happened, Mum, which is why we're here.'

'Oh?' Marion said, pausing what she was doing. 'That sounds ominous. Firstly, tell me – are the three of you OK? You're not ill or in any kind of danger?' Usually cool-headed and stoic, Libby saw the look in Marion's eyes, the way they latched onto Sean's.

'We're fine, Mum. But like I said, something happened last night.' Sean waited until Marion had made a pot of tea and sat down. Her hands shook as she poured it. She then went to the fridge for a carton of juice for Alice, who had woken and was grumbling on Sean's knee.

'Alice, darling, do you want to watch some telly while we chat to Nanny?' Libby said, scooping up her daughter. Alice kicked her legs against Libby for a moment, whining, but the promise of breakfast biscuits and cartoons won her over.

'I'll get straight to the point, Mum,' Libby heard Sean explain as she sat back down at the table. 'When we came home from the pub, Sasha was gone.'

'Oh, *goodness*,' Marion said, covering her mouth for a second. 'When you say "gone", do you mean, literally gone?'

'Yes,' Sean said. 'She just wasn't there.'

'We looked everywhere, of course,' Libby added. 'Alice was on her own upstairs. Asleep, thank heavens.'

'So, what… the girl had just abandoned her? Where did she go? Has she apologised yet?'

'That's the thing, Mum,' Sean went on. 'We still don't know where she is. No one's seen her. Jan, her mum, came over immediately and, in the end, we had to call the police.'

'The *police*?' Marion said. Her mug quivered as she brought it to her mouth slowly, eyeing her son over the rim.

'It's why we're here,' Libby said. 'They need to…'

'They need to look over the cottage,' Sean finished when Libby's voice wavered.

'I just can't believe any of this is happening,' Libby said, glancing out of the kitchen window, across the farmyard. The first flecks of red were vaguely visible above the furthest barn.

'Well, I'm shocked at how irresponsible she's been,' Marion said, shaking her head. 'There's no excuse for leaving a four-year-old alone. You must both be livid.'

'I think it's past being angry with her,' Libby said. 'It's completely out of character. I know Sasha pretty well and she wouldn't do something like this without a good reason.'

'Or,' Sean added, 'without coercion.'

'I don't know what to say.' Marion added more sugar to her tea, stirring it longer than was necessary. 'I *knew* I should have cancelled my church meeting last night to babysit for you. We were only setting some rotas. Frankly, they could have done without me and then none of this would have happened. I feel terrible.'

'It's not your fault, Mum,' Sean said. 'I'm going out to search soon,' he continued. 'I'll get some of the shooting guys together to scour the area. If she's wandered off in the dark, anything could have happened. She might be lying in a ditch with a broken ankle for all we know. And no one knows the countryside around here like the beaters.'

Marion nodded, staring at Sean, her eyes wide and incredulous, but also with a tinge of adoration for her son. 'Meantime, you and Alice stay right here with me, OK?' she said to Libby. 'Stay as long as you need.'

'Thanks,' Libby said, wondering how on earth she was going to cater for the dinner she'd committed to tonight or, worse, break it to her clients that she would most likely have to cancel.

It was light and Sean had been gone nearly two hours and, having forgotten to bring her charger and mindful of preserving her battery, Libby hadn't texted or called to see if there was news. Marion didn't have an iPhone cable, preferring to stick with her old flip phone. Besides, she knew Sean would call her if there was anything to report.

As Libby half-heartedly entertained a grumpy, sleepy Alice on the sofa, she imagined Sean rallying a couple of the local farmers and their workers to help, perhaps some of them out on quad bikes, covering more distance quickly. Sean had made several calls before he left, telling a couple of the guys he went shooting with what had happened. As the under-keeper on the local estate, Sasha's dad, Phil, was of course involved. Pheasant season hadn't long started and, between them, they had five or six eager spaniels who would instinctively pick up a trail. The regular beaters would scour the land on foot, familiar with every inch of it from flushing out the birds on shoots, the gun dogs following on. And, with Phil being a key participant, support for finding Sasha would be high. If anyone could find her, they would.

'As long as it doesn't interfere with the police's plan,' Libby had said to Sean as he pulled on his heavy jacket ready to leave. A hard frost had formed overnight, everything encrusted white with an eerie silence hanging over the farmyard as Sean opened the back door. 'They mentioned about getting a dog handler in,' she'd reminded him. 'We don't want to get in the way.'

'Trust me, we won't,' Sean had replied, staring at her, his eyes boring into hers as she balanced Alice on her hip. She pulled her fluffy gown around her, shivering. Then he'd leant down and kissed her, squeezing her hand. 'Everything will be OK,' he'd said, punctuating each syllable with a nod, before turning and leaving.

'Marion, is that you?' Libby suddenly called out from the sofa, hearing a noise, wondering if it was Sean back already. She looked at her watch. It was nearly 10 a.m. and she'd been dozing by the fire in the living room with Alice snuggled up against her, cartoons on the TV in the background.

But Marion didn't reply. Then the noise again. A knock – someone at the door, sounding like it was at the back door that led into the kitchen. Marion had probably ventured out on the farm, helping out when she felt able, even if it was just cleaning out the henhouse or sorting out Fred's tool shed. Libby knew her health issues slowed her down, though Marion was the type never to discuss such things, believing that if she didn't acknowledge her ailments, they'd go away. Libby had offered to go with her to her hospital appointments, but she'd flatly refused the support, not even confiding in Sean.

'Just sit up a moment, sweetie,' she said to Alice, sliding out from underneath her daughter. 'I'd better see who it is.'

Libby's heart raced as she headed for the door – her next thought that it was the police with news of Sasha. But when she answered the back door it took her a few moments to realise who it actually was standing there. And it certainly wasn't the police.

'Oh. Hello, Libby,' the woman said. The corners of her mouth lifted and her eyes shone with one-upmanship as she hitched up the strap of her smart bag, hung over the immaculate tan wool coat she wore flapping open over skinny jeans. Her black leather boots seemed endless on her long legs. 'I didn't realise you'd be here.'

Libby stared at her. 'Natalie,' she said finally, her voice cracking under the weight of her name. She was the last person she wanted to be dealing with right now. 'How… how are you?'

'It's Marion I came to see, actually,' she said, stepping inside without being asked. 'Did you have a rough night?' she continued, casting a look up and down Libby. Her long blond hair swished around her shoulders as she put her bag on the kitchen table, removing her huge owly sunglasses. She forked them on her head, revealing glittery blue eyes – highlighted and shaded under perfect brows. Effortless beauty, as ever, Libby found herself thinking, though it was the least of her concerns. Natalie flouncing around was, in the scheme of things, unimportant.

'Marion is about somewhere, though I'm not sure where,' she said. She had no idea what Sean's ex-wife could possibly want with her ex-mother-in-law. Though she'd always had a hunch that Marion still favoured the woman, having gleaned that it was Marion who set Sean and her up in the first place many years ago. Sean had never divulged the full story, but Libby knew that Natalie's parents, also farmers and local landowners, were good friends with Marion and Fred. They also took it hard when Sean filed for divorce.

'I'll wait here for her, then. She won't mind.' Natalie took off her coat, revealing a white chiffon blouse tucked in at the front of her jeans, showing off her slim hips and flat stomach. Then she pulled out a chair and sat down, crossing her impossibly long legs.

Libby cleared her throat. 'Coffee?' she said, hitching up her tracksuit bottoms. While she just wished the woman would go, she didn't want to be rude. She was the mother of Sean's son, after all, and was always going to be in their lives in some way. They may as well try to get along.

'Espresso, please,' she said.

'I'm afraid it's instant granules only here,' Libby said, filling the kettle and dropping it on the hotplate harder than she intended. 'The only actual choice you have is milk and/or sugar.' Her heart thumped as she folded her arms, leaning against the rail of the cooking range. She couldn't stand it if Natalie saw how much she was shaking – through lack of sleep and the woman's sheer brazenness. They rarely encountered each other, with Sean usually stuck in the middle when it was time to take Dan home or pick him up, or attend a school play or carol service. Or deal with solicitors. But Libby had never been alone with her before. It didn't help that she looked awful and had had no sleep, while Natalie may as well have stepped from the pages of a fashion magazine.

'Black, no sugar, thank you,' Natalie said, checking her phone quickly. 'Oh, and I passed Sean on my way here,' she added in what Libby could only describe as a taunting voice. 'We stopped for a chat. He… he also looked worn out.'

Libby froze. Was there news? Anything could have happened since he left. She gave a brief nod in reply, in case Natalie was referring to something else.

'Plus there were police everywhere in the village.'

She wasn't.

'Tell me to mind my own business, Libby,' she went on, 'but is everything OK with you and Sean? I got the impression that maybe…' Natalie flicked back her hair and stuck out her chin, highlighting her angular jawbone even more. 'That things are… perhaps difficult between you?'

'Everything's fine, thank you,' Libby replied, wiping her hands down her face. She didn't care any more about the smudged mascara, the dark circles under her eyes. And she wanted nothing more than to tell Natalie to mind her own business and leave, but she bit her tongue. 'We've both been work—'

'Mum*my*...' Alice said, suddenly running in from the other room and lunging at Libby's legs. She stared at Natalie before making a whimpering sound and burying her face in Libby's old cardigan, mumbling again something about bad dreams and monsters in the house.

'Oh, haven't you got the same curly hair as your daddy,' Natalie said in a baby voice, tilting her head to the side. 'What a cutie you're turning into!'

Alice peeked up briefly, before running off again when Natalie made a comment about how she looked so similar to her big half-brother, Dan, at that age. Libby had never been so grateful to see Fred, her father-in-law, kick off his boots at the back door as she was then. A waft of freezing air accompanied him inside.

'Hello, *Nat*,' he boomed in that voice of his, except, unusually, it was accompanied by a broad smile, exposing several missing teeth. Libby tried not to care that he'd completely ignored her and gone straight over to Natalie to deliver a hug – he'd got her off the hook, after all, and she was grateful for that. 'Sorry I stink a bit,' he continued, laughing. 'Been fixing the muck spreader.' He wiped his big hands down his overalls, turning to Libby. 'Coffee on the go?' he said, without even greeting her. She'd not seen him yet this morning as he was out working when they'd arrived. While Fred was cool and distant with most people – it was just his way – she wasn't too worried as she knew he had a soft spot for her. But, it seemed right now, that his spot was even softer for Natalie.

'Of course, Fred,' Libby replied quietly, thankful that Marion also came back into the kitchen and, after she'd handed out coffees, she made her excuses and slipped away to find Alice.

Libby closed the living room door behind her, settling back onto the sofa, wishing that Sean was there, wishing that she could rewind time to this time yesterday – *no*, to this time a week ago, and just have life back to normal.

'Mummy, why is that lady here? I don't like her. She's scary,' Alice said, snuggling up against her.

'That's Dan's mummy, Natalie,' she said vaguely, staring at her phone, wondering what to do. 'You know that.'

'She's a bad lady, isn't she? She scareded me last night when you and Daddy went out.'

'Sorry, sweetie?' Libby looked at her daughter, frowning as she suddenly realised what she'd said. But Alice didn't seem willing to engage further and was engrossed in the television again.

Libby tipped back her head and stared at the ceiling, sighing as she heard laughter and chatter from the kitchen, Natalie's shrill voice ringing out. In the end, she sent a quick text to Sean.

News?

Then, when there was no reply, she texted Fran.

I need to see you… xx

CHAPTER NINETEEN

'Please, Lib,' Sean said, pacing about. 'It's only for a night or two. Why do you have to make this hard?'

'Wait… *what*?' Libby stared at him, hands on hips, her mouth hanging open. 'Maybe it's because something terrible has happened to Sasha, I've had to move out of my house so the police can tear it apart, my daughter is exhausted and upset by something, none of us has had any sleep, I've had to cancel tonight's dinner event, and your ex-wife has been swanning around telling me we've got marital problems while loving every second of me looking like ten tons of shit. Do you think maybe *that's* why it's hard?'

'Libby,' Sean said, shaking his head. 'You're stressed. Calm down. And you honestly care about what you look like at a time like this?' He bent down and fiddled with the radiator under the small paned window of the back bedroom – his old room when he was a child – trying to turn on the stiff valve. They were both freezing.

'No, of course I don't care what I look like, but it felt as though she was looking down on me and I really don't need—'

'Libby,' Sean repeated calmly. 'I told you. If you get stressed and lose it, that's not going to help anyone. Especially *you*. Alice needs you to be strong. *I* need you to be strong. Don't fall apart, love. Have you thought about how Jan must be feeling right now? Her daughter has seemingly vanished off the face of the earth.'

Libby halted herself, her shoulders slumping forward. 'Sorry, you're right,' she said, dropping down on the bed. It was hard and lumpy and the eiderdown had a musty smell. But Marion had been kind enough to let them stay for a couple of days or however long the police needed to be at the cottage, so she could hardly grumble. 'I should give Jan a call, see if there's anything I can do to help. Even if it's just taking her some food. I've got plenty of frozen dishes.'

'That's better,' Sean said, standing above her and cupping her face. 'And you really didn't need to cancel the event tonight, did you? Surely carrying on as normal is better all round? Plus we can't really afford for you to lose business.'

Libby stared at the floor, her eyes tracking the green and red cabbage roses in the pattern, imagining Sean playing with his cars on it as a little boy. He'd told her the room hadn't changed at all in the couple of decades since he'd left. By all accounts, and there weren't many, Marion had found it hard to let her only son go, even though he'd been twenty-three when he'd finally gone off to train as a vet. Libby knew that something had happened to Sean during the time between leaving school and deciding on a life path, she just wasn't sure what. If she ever brought it up, he glossed over that period as if it was never talked about.

'I know, you're right. But I don't think I can do a good job for my client on no sleep and with this mess hanging over us. I should be getting on with food preparation now but can't even think about it, let alone do it. Anyway, the police are probably swarming all over our house as we speak.' Libby fell backwards onto the pillow. 'I told them I'd do another dinner for them at no charge in the future. They were quite understanding, but it's not going to help business.'

Sean stared at her for a moment before nodding, biting his lip, looking thoughtful. 'There's something I need to tell you, Libby,' he said, his voice low.

'Oh?' Libby replied, sitting up again.

'Mack found a shoe when we were out searching earlier,' he said, hanging his head briefly. He went over to the window and stared out, leaning his head against a glazing bar.

Libby hadn't had a chance to ask when he returned as she was still reeling from Natalie's presence. It was Sean, thankfully, who'd finally encouraged his ex-wife to leave.

'Oh my *God*,' Libby said, getting up off the bed. 'That must have been awful.'

'It was,' Sean replied after a long pause. He turned around slowly, silhouetted against the low sun in the bright morning sky. 'And it wasn't where you'd expect it.'

'I see,' Libby whispered, coming up close. She hardly dared think what it might mean. 'It… it was Sasha's, I take it?'

'They don't know officially yet. When we came back into the village, Mack handed it over to an officer who was outside our cottage. He's marked where he found it with his scarf, tying it round a fence post so they can go back and look. It was up near Blake's Hill.' Sean's voice was grave.

'No, *no*… Christ.' Libby looked up, staring into Sean's eyes. 'Was it just one shoe? I mean, who loses one shoe, Sean? What colour was it?' She thought back, trying to remember what Sasha had been wearing last night. Jeans, her favourite sweatshirt and her parka coat, though that was still slung over the back of the sofa.

'It was a white trainer,' Sean said. 'Size five. And yes, it was just the one shoe.' The look he gave Libby betrayed that he was thinking the same as her: that it wasn't good news. Though neither of them said a word.

DI Jones commanded a large presence in the low-ceilinged farmhouse kitchen. As ever, Marion was fussing around with tea and biscuits, complaining that if she'd known she'd have all these visitors, she'd have got something better in than just plain digestives.

'Mum, it's fine. I don't think the detective is bothered about biscuits.' Sean shook Doug Jones's hand and briefly introduced him to Marion. 'Is there news?' he asked, turning his back to the room, trying to say it in a way that Marion wouldn't hear above the noise of the kettle and the clattering of cups as she set things out on a tray.

'Is there somewhere private we can talk?' the detective said. 'You and your wife?'

'Of course,' Sean replied, looking over his shoulder for Libby. She'd been there a moment ago, trying to amuse Alice, but there was no sign of her now. 'Mum, I'm going to have a chat with the officer in Dad's study, if that's OK.'

'Yes, feel free,' Marion said, pulling back her long grey hair into a ponytail and securing it with a band. Her eyes flicked between Sean and the detective. 'I'll bring in some tea.'

'Sean?' Libby said, halting suddenly as she saw him and the detective in the front hallway. She took hold of his arm. 'What's happening?' She squeezed him, bracing herself for them having found a body. Since last night, she'd had terrible thoughts and images in her head that she couldn't shake. They switched between Sasha lying dead in a ditch somewhere remote – her skin pale and cold, her eyes staring blankly at the night sky, her tongue lolling out of her open mouth – and that of the poor girl being forcibly dragged and manhandled out of Chestnut Cottage, her belongings abandoned as she was carted off to her fate. Each option made her shudder.

'The detective wants to have a chat with us, love,' Sean told her. 'Just to go over what we know.'

Libby swallowed. 'Of course,' she said, hugging her cardigan around her as Sean led the way. She'd only been in Fred's study a couple of times previously and thought 'study' was misleading, given the boxes of papers stacked up, the general clutter of the small room. Despite the mess, the three of them found somewhere to sit – Libby and Sean on an old sagging chesterfield, with DI Jones perched on a wonky captain's chair in front of Fred's rolltop desk.

'As you've probably guessed, no one has heard from Sasha yet,' DI Jones said. Libby thought his voice was rather matter-of-fact given the circumstances. He took a pen from his jacket pocket and balanced a clipboard on his knee. A few papers were pinned to it and, as he was talking, he was filling out details and writing notes. 'So, naturally, given the circumstances surrounding Sasha's disappearance, we're taking this matter very seriously. We've opened an official missing person investigation.'

Libby leant closer to Sean – an attempt at calming herself. 'I just can't believe this,' she said. 'It's just so awful. *Unthinkable*. I mean, Sash was all set to help me with a dinner party tonight. I've cancelled, of course, but… I just don't understand how…'

The detective looked up from his notes. 'I know there's a lot going through your mind, Mrs Randell, but perhaps we can take it one step at a time?'

Libby nodded, trying to make her thoughts stay on track and not leap ahead as they had a habit of doing. Not think the worst. She was reminded of the time Sean hadn't come home from work a couple of years ago, how she'd phoned and texted him and watched and waited until she could do no more. When calls to Marion and a couple of his mates proved fruitless, she'd risked embarrassing herself by calling his boss, several work colleagues and, eventually, a couple of local hospitals in case he'd been in an accident. It was as if he'd disappeared off the face of the earth, and Libby was beside herself with worry. In the past, if he was going to be late, he'd always let her know.

It was 2 a.m. when Libby heard thumping on the front door of the cottage. She hadn't been able to sleep and was sitting bolt upright on the sofa, her phone in hand and the television playing something mindless on low volume in the background. She'd leapt up, praying it was Sean come home and, when she saw him standing there, leaning against the door frame, barely able to keep himself upright, her heart had almost disintegrated from relief.

She'd helped him in as he'd staggered inside. 'Sean, what the *hell…?*'

'Libby, don't… I don't need this, I was just… it's OK, for fuck's sake give me a break. I was… I'm fine, I love you, I just need to get some sleep and I'll be fine just let me…'

He bumped past her, his hands sliding along the wall as he tripped over the uneven flagstones. In the kitchen, he ran the tap, ducking his head to drink directly from it but getting it all over his face and hair instead. Libby had never seen him like this before.

'Sean, where have you *been*? You're… you're drunk. What's going on?'

Of course, in the four or five years they'd known each other they'd indulged in a few boozy nights with friends, perhaps gone a little too far and regretted it the next morning, but Libby had never encountered Sean – an upstanding man with a responsible career and commitments – behave like *this*. This was a deep-down, purposeful kind of drunk. The kind that was self-inflicted, as though he'd wanted to escape his feelings. As if he was a different man entirely to the one she knew.

'I'm fine, just need to go to bed…'

'So that's it?' Libby had said. 'Like, no explanation as to where you were or why you didn't call me? I've been worried sick, Sean.'

He'd looked at her then, almost as if she were a stranger. There was something in his eyes that didn't belong to him, as if he didn't want to *be* him. At that moment, she didn't recognise the man she knew and loved. The memory of that evening had stuck with her, but it was the way he'd looked *through* her, rather than *at* her, that had disturbed her the most.

As if he were with someone else instead.

CHAPTER TWENTY

DI Jones was patiently writing down everything that Sean and Libby remembered from the previous night, pausing to listen, to clarify if either of them garbled or stumbled over their words. While they were conscious of getting their story straight, Libby was also conscious, and worried, that with each retelling of events she'd either forget something important or add something in that she'd unwittingly dreamt up in an attempt to make the whole thing seem less serious than it actually was. It was, she realised, a kind of denial that any of this had happened.

And she couldn't stop shivering.

'So, before you left, you told Sasha that you would be home around eleven?' DI Jones said.

'Yes,' Sean confirmed.

'Was that the usual sort of time you'd return when Sasha's babysat for you in the past?'

Libby nodded. 'Sometimes it's been a bit later if we've gone to a party or into Oxford with friends, maybe getting back at one or two a.m., but we've always said she can stay over if that happens. And that was only ever on a weekend, never a college night.'

'So you didn't ask her to stay over last night?' DI Jones leant forward, elbows on his jeans, his forearms exposed from under his turned-up cuffs.

'We knew we wouldn't be very late back so it didn't seem necessary,' Sean said. 'Sometimes Matt, her boyfriend, picks her up and they go to his place. It's not far. Other times we'll put her in a taxi or, depending on whether we've had a drink, one of us will run her home. It's never been a problem before.'

The detective didn't say anything as he jotted down more notes.

'I just don't get why she left all her stuff,' Libby said as tears filled her eyes.

'So what time did you get home last night?' the detective asked, glancing between the two of them. 'I need to know exactly.'

'Hard to say *exactly*,' Sean said. 'But I suppose it wasn't long before we started contacting people. Lib, have you got your phone on you? You can check the time we made the calls.'

Libby nodded and pulled her phone from the front pocket of her cardigan. She forced her fingers to stop shaking as she brought up the Messenger message she'd sent to Matt. 'Eleven twenty-seven,' she said, looking at Sean. 'Then I made a call to Jan, Sasha's mum, at eleven thirty-two. See?' She held out her phone to the detective, who gave it a quick glance.

'And that was after you realised that Sasha wasn't in the cottage or on your property?'

'Yes,' Sean said. 'It's not a huge house, so it didn't take us long to figure out she wasn't in it. We thought she may have popped into the village to meet a friend or something, that she'd be back at any moment looking sheepish when she realised we were back, but no…' He closed his eyes briefly.

'Did you go out and look around the village?' DI Jones asked, tapping his pen on the clipboard.

'No,' Sean said immediately. Libby gave him a look.

'Actually,' Libby said, hesitating. 'Um, yes we… *I* did that. You remember, Sean? I thought it was worth a quick drive around just in case.'

The detective stared at them, mainly at Sean.

'Sorry, yes, Libby's right. I'd forgotten.' Sean touched his forehead. 'But you were only gone a few minutes at most, love.'

He shrugged as he glanced at her. 'Anyway, I'd had a couple of drinks by then so I stayed home.'

'Meaning… that the alcohol made you forget your wife went out in the car to look for Sasha, or that you couldn't do it yourself because you'd had a drink?'

'Well, both really,' Sean replied, giving a small laugh, the kind that was just still appropriate under the circumstances.

'And had you had a drink too, Mrs Randell?' DI Jones asked Libby.

'Just a glass of wine or two early on in the evening. By the time I got in the car, I'd have been fine.' Libby thought of the car she'd scraped – and Cath. She swallowed. 'Apart from Eric walking his dog, I didn't see anyone. And he'd not seen Sasha either.' She remembered coming home, finding Sean in the hallway, his coat on, breathless, ruddy-faced from the cold air.

'OK,' DI Jones said, sitting back in the chair, making an uncomfortable face as he stretched his back. 'I've got a forensics team up at your cottage now. Naturally, they're going to want to go over everything thoroughly – we only get one chance at this – so I can't give you any guarantee of timescales. I'm hoping you'll be able to go back home tomorrow. Monday at the worst.'

'Not today?' Sean said, rather more gruffly than was warranted.

'Unlikely,' the detective replied. 'If there's anything you need, let me know where it is and I'll have one of the officers bring it outside for you to collect.'

'Thanks,' Libby said, her stomach churning. 'Just do what you need to do.'

'What I'd like to do is speak to your daughter, Alice,' he said, looking at each of them in turn.

'You contradicted me,' Sean said. They were out in the farmyard, taking Alice for a walk to see the ducks and hens. They all needed the fresh air. 'Nice work, Lib.'

'You wanted me to *lie* to the police about going out in the car?' Libby replied, shaking her head. 'I couldn't do it, Sean.'

'Well, you lied about the number of drinks you'd had,' he replied. Alice skipped on ahead, her curls bouncing on her shoulders. Despite her tiredness, she'd perked up after Marion had made her a good breakfast, and she thankfully seemed unaffected by her brief meeting with DI Jones, who, despite his best efforts, couldn't eke a single word out of her.

'That's different,' Libby said. 'I didn't want to tell a cop that I'd driven my car after a bottle of wine. I thought I was doing the right thing. Anyway, you didn't mention what Alice said when she refused to speak.' She hung her head, wondering what kind of mess they were getting into. Seeing her daughter bury her face in the crook of Sean's shoulder, squirming and curling up her legs when the detective asked her a few simple questions, broke Libby's heart. No four-year-old should have to be subjected to that. But she was grateful that DI Jones didn't push things and suggested that, if it came to it, an officer who specialised in dealing with children would be called in.

'I think Alice saw Natalie in the cottage last night, Sean,' Libby said, staring up at him.

'Natalie?' he said, sighing heavily. 'Alice had a bad dream, that's all. There's no point subjecting her to a grilling by the police.'

'But—'

'I tried to cover up for you because you hit a car. *Drunk*. You didn't find Sasha so it was irrelevant if you went out or not. I was trying to save your skin, Lib.'

'I… I just thought it would be helpful to mention that I'd asked Eric if he'd seen Sasha, like you said. You know, to confirm everything?' Libby watched him, her mouth hanging open. She'd never seen Sean like this before – his jaw clenched defiantly, his eyes almost bursting from pressure. He strode on, his hands thrust deep inside his pockets.

Then the tears came. She couldn't help herself. Stopping in her tracks, Libby turned her back and covered her face, not wanting Alice to see, but the way her body lurched forward – a deep ache squeezing her heart, wringing out every bad emotion she'd ever felt – it took all her strength to keep upright. She felt her knees buckling beneath her.

And she would have gone down if it hadn't been for the strong hands under her armpits from behind, keeping her upright.

'Hey,' Sean said, pushing his face into her neck. 'C'mon, you. I know it's awful but we'll get through this, OK?'

Libby stared up at him. 'How can you *say* that?' she said, tears pouring down her face. 'It's all my fault – it must be. If only… if only…'

'Easily,' he replied, pulling her in for a hug. 'But I need you to stay strong. The whole family needs you, Libby. Don't lose it. Think of poor Sasha.'

'That's… that's *all* I'm thinking of,' Libby said, sniffing and scanning behind Sean to check where Alice was. She spotted her standing at the duck pond, the pink wellies that Marion had bought for her to keep at the farm half submerged in the muddy bog at the water's edge. She was tearing up slices of stale bread, chucking them into the water for the birds.

'Be careful, Alice,' Libby called out, her voice choked from tears. She searched in her pockets for a tissue, eventually wiping her face on her sleeve.

Sean was shaking his head. 'Look, love, it's not even been twenty-four hours and you're a mess. Repeat after me: "It's not our fault. It could have happened to anybody".'

'Sean, don't…' Libby said, shrugging out of his grip. She stared up at him. 'I knew her pretty well, OK? She was a sweet girl with her whole life ahead of her and now… now this has happened. In *our* house.'

'You *know* her pretty well, Libby. Not *knew*. And she *is* a sweet girl. Present tense, love, OK? Think positively. They've not found a body yet.'

But, as her eyes flashed over to the pond, Libby didn't care about semantics and tenses.

Alice wasn't there any more.

Stumbling and slipping, Libby charged over towards the pond, ducks and geese flapping and honking as she approached, yelling out.

'Alice? *Alice*... where are you?'

She cast around frantically, trying to take in as much of the farm as she could. Alice wasn't by the pond, or running through the clump of trees or climbing on the old gate half hanging off its hinges, nor was she on or hiding under the flatbed trailer... She wasn't anywhere...

'Al-*ice*...!'

This time, Libby's knees did give way and she dropped to the ground, clutching her face, a stone digging into her kneecap. She didn't care as the tears started up again. She was shaking from the inside out.

'Lib, Lib, darling... you've got to stop this. You're a nervous wreck and that's not like you.'

When she glanced up, Sean was standing above her, Alice sitting happily on his hip, kicking her muddy boots against his jeans.

Libby made a noise somewhere between rage and relief, screwing up her eyes as she dragged her fingers down her face. Behind her eyelids, all she could see was Sasha – alone, terrified, being dragged out of the cottage by a monster and, worse, all with Alice upstairs asleep. Anything could have happened.

Anything *did* happen.

'Why don't you go and play on the tree swing, darling?' Sean said, sliding Alice to the ground and steering her in the direction of the ropes Fred had slung over a branch last summer for his granddaughter, replacing the rotten old swing he used to play on as a child. Alice ran off excitedly.

Sean crouched down to Libby, who was kneeling in the mud. He touched her shoulder. She flinched.

'She was behind the henhouse looking for eggs, that's all.' He paused, waiting for her to say something, but she didn't. Just sobs choking up her throat. 'I'm worried about you, Lib. If this is how you are now… Well, we don't know how long all this will go on for, do we?'

Libby wanted to scream even more, but managed to check herself. 'You're right. It's just that anything could have happened to Alice last night and… and…' She broke down again. 'And just now too…'

'Look, love… I'm not the only one to notice that you're on edge,' Sean added. 'Natalie said she's concerned about you, that you didn't seem yourself.'

Libby hoisted herself to her feet, stumbling again. 'I know, I know. You're right.' She sighed. 'Though I'm not sure what any of this has got to do with Natalie,' she said, feeling wretched, the tears still streaming.

'She was only trying to help and…' He glanced over Libby's shoulder, his expression changing as he trailed off.

'*She* sent the note, didn't she?' Libby snapped, her eyes growing wide. She put her hand up over her forehead, shielding the glare as the autumn sun suddenly broke from behind a cloud. 'It *was* Natalie, wasn't it?'

But Sean didn't reply. He walked off to where Alice was playing, shaking his head in disbelief. As she watched him, Libby saw that Marion had come out. She was standing close behind Alice, stopped in her tracks and her mouth hanging open as her eyes danced between the pair of them.

CHAPTER TWENTY-ONE

From the outside, it didn't much look like Chestnut Cottage any more. Not the home Libby knew, anyway. Three marked police cars filled the spaces outside the little row of thatched cottages and a uniformed officer was standing beside the latch and braced door, his head almost reaching the low brow of the porch canopy.

Libby watched, car keys in hand, wondering if they were tearing things apart inside – given the white-suited figures she could just make out through the leaded front windows. She'd only driven down to the village out of curiosity, but now she was here she had an overwhelming urge to run inside, yell at everyone to get out, to leave their things alone, to make everything go back to how it was before.

She glanced at her watch. Twenty past four. This time yesterday she was thinking about what to wear for the meal, if she'd have time to wash her hair, believing that a night out would repair the damage she'd done between her and Sean. She'd resolved that by the time they got home from the pub, everything would be fine between them and the air would be cleared. She hated that her insecurities had made him feel so wretched.

'Hello,' Libby said, tentatively approaching the officer. 'Are they…' She glanced at the front window, pointing nervously. 'Are they really busy in there, or am I allowed in to get a couple of things? I'm Libby Randell, by the way. I live here.'

'Mrs Randell,' the officer said, nodding. 'I'd need to get clearance from the SIO for that. Forensics are underway.'

'SIO?'

'Senior investigating officer,' he explained.

Libby shuddered, assuming that would be DI Jones. When he'd left Fred and Marion's farm a few hours ago she hoped she'd never have to see him again. 'DI Jones said we could get a couple of things if needed. We had to leave in a bit of a rush. I've got a four-year-old, you see, and there are some things she wants.'

'Of course. I'll make sure the request is passed on, Mrs Randell, and someone will be in touch.'

Libby nodded, a sinking feeling growing inside. Then the front door opened and a woman in a white paper suit came out, a large black camera slung around her neck. She pulled off her face mask and said something to the officer at the door before stretching and catching sight of Libby. She snapped off her latex gloves and removed her shoe covers, dropping them into a box beside the door. Then she ambled down the front path and over to an unmarked car parked on the lane. Libby watched as she pulled out a silver flask and poured herself a hot drink.

'Leaving that lot to it for a while,' she said to the officer as she came back up the front path. 'Not much to go on but they're picking through and marking up. I'm off out tonight so I hope they get a move on.' She eyed Libby again, clearly wondering who she was and why she was loitering at the garden gate.

'Any idea how long it will take?' Libby asked, thinking she'd take another chance. She stepped from one foot to the other, a pained expression on her face as she clamped her arms around her body. She wondered what they had found that warranted taking pictures.

'Mrs Randell lives here,' the officer explained to the woman. 'She needs a couple of things from inside.'

'Oh, right,' she replied. 'Maybe I can grab something for you? What is it you need?'

Libby felt her cheeks flush. 'Oh, well, my iPhone charger would be useful. It's plugged in beside my bed in the main bedroom. And there's a make-up bag on the bathroom shelf I could really use. I'd say that's pretty urgent,' she said, laughing and pointing at her face. 'Oh, and it sounds silly but there's a recipe book in the kitchen I was going to get. I'm a chef, you see, and have to plan for a couple of menus. I don't want to let clients down.' She smiled quickly. 'You'll find it on the shelves at the end of the kitchen cupboards. It's the one with a green spine.'

'Sure, I'll see what I can do,' the woman said.

'Didn't you say you wanted something for your child, too?' the other officer said.

'Oh, yes. Yes, I did. If you see a shaggy brown dog, about this big with a blue velvet nose, you'd make a four-year-old girl very happy,' Libby said. 'He's probably on her bed. She can't sleep without him.'

The woman gave a little nod before slipping on a pair of fresh shoe covers from a container beside the door. Then she disappeared inside the cottage, returning five minutes later with a carrier bag of items. Libby went over to her to save her removing the covers again.

'Thank you so much,' she said quietly, glancing inside the bag, noticing the cookbook was there. She turned to go and, as she was heading back to her car, her phone rang.

'Fran,' she said, getting into the driver's seat, fighting the urge to break down in tears and blurt out everything to her best friend. Instead, she shut the door and reclined her head, her voice choked. 'Yes, yes, I'd really like to see you too, thank you,' she replied, sniffing, grateful for a glimmer of normality. And, just as they said goodbye, her battery finally ran out and the tears came again.

Libby stared out at the fields surrounding her. The rolling countryside she'd grown to know and love had taken on a different hue, as if it had been painted in a colour palette normally invisible to the human eye. *Her* eye, anyway. Everything had a strange and dark tinge to it – as if she were viewing the world through a filter. Through *sadness*. She put the window down to check if the sounds were the same. She needed grounding, somehow convincing that there was a way out of the flat spin her life had become.

Silence.

Not even the song of a bird or the clop of a passing horse's hooves. No breath of wind or the sound of a tractor rumbling in a distant field. Even the nearby main road, sometimes audible up here on the hill, was silent and eerie, as if the land knew something bad had happened.

She was only a mile or so out of Great Lyne, parked up in a gateway – the place where she and Sean often ambled up to, taking a long Sunday walk together if Marion came round to look after Alice yet again.

'Don't begrudge her,' Sean had said once. 'Not many grandparents would help out as much as she does. We need her, Lib. We're lucky.'

But Libby couldn't help wondering if it was really Alice she'd come to see, or if she was checking up on *her* – making sure she was taking care of Sean, the house, holding things together.

'So what if I don't use the same fabric conditioner as she does,' Libby had complained to Sean after Marion had made a comment. 'Knowing your mum, I'm surprised she doesn't use pure bleach to do her wash anyway. And as for having a dig at the lunches I make for you, well…' Libby had literally bitten her tongue until she'd tasted blood at that remark.

'Lib,' Sean had said, cupping her face. His smile sent shots of warmth through her, neutralising Marion's latest round of comments. 'She wasn't having a dig. The lunches you give me are the envy of everyone at work. No one else brings in gourmet leftovers from dinner parties, right?' He'd squeezed her cheeks then, kissing her lightly. 'And my clothes are soft enough for a baby to wear, so stop fretting. You know what Mum's like.' He'd laughed then, though Libby wasn't sure if it was at his mother or at her.

'I know,' she'd said, backing down. 'And I'm sorry. But I'm a grown woman and perfectly capable of managing my own—'

'Do you remember what I told you way back?'

Libby rolled her eyes, trying to hide her smile. 'How could I forget?' She'd grinned at him then, always feeling a little bit special when she recalled what he'd told her, as though she'd somehow passed a test.

'Look, I'm a bit wary about you meeting her, OK?' Sean had admitted, about three months after they'd started seeing each other. He had an embarrassed grin on his face.

'*Wary*?' Libby laughed. 'But she's just your mum, Sean. She sounds lovely.'

He'd made a face then, half serious, half jokey. 'Well…'

'Well, *what*?' Libby had snuggled closer to him, crossing her legs over his as they lay on the sofa at her place – the little one-bedroom cottage that came with the position she'd taken at the White House Barns Hotel. The job was the reason she'd moved to the area and also where she'd first spotted Sean. They'd both given each other tentative glances while working out in the gym and, when they saw each other again in a local pub, Sean had approached her.

'It's just that…'

Libby had grinned and poked him in the ribs, pouring more wine. The fire was flickering in the grate – a couple of logs with dancing flames wrapped around them. It was Christmas and the tree lights twinkled, reflecting in Sean's eyes. *Watery eyes*, she remembered thinking, wondering why he was so emotional about the prospect of her meeting his family.

'It's just that, in the past, if I've introduced anyone to Mum…'

'As in a girlfriend?'

Sean shrugged, looked away.

'Go on…'

'Well, they usually…' He forced a smile. Libby knew he was trying to make light of it but could see the thread of pain. 'They usually find a reason to end things shortly afterwards.' He laughed, taking a large mouthful of beer, grabbing the TV remote control and searching for something to watch.

'You think if I meet your mum I'll break up with you?' Libby said, hand on his wrist.

'Yup.'

'That's ridiculous. Don't be so silly.'

Sean had stared at her, almost as if he was trying to convey a secret message – a warning. Though Libby wasn't sure what. All she did know was that, whatever his mother was like, she would not break up with him because of meeting her.

'What about your ex-wife?' Libby suddenly asked, having mulled it over for a moment. '*She* must have met your mother?'

Sean was thoughtful. 'Yes, yes of course,' he admitted, flicking through the channels and settling on the news. 'But in that case, it was Mum who introduced me to Natalie. She said we'd be perfect for each other. That Natalie was different.'

*

Libby put the window up and stared across the countryside, resting her head sideways on the glass. Sean was probably trying to reach her, wondering where she was. But, with her phone dead, she was grateful for the few minutes' solitude, especially after seeing her home swarming with police. A moment up here was time out, and it was almost easy to pretend that what had happened actually hadn't. That she was just on her way home from the market and, when she got back, everything would be back to normal.

'*Normal*,' Libby whispered to herself, steaming up the glass. She took a breath and shook her head, reaching for the keys in the ignition. But then she saw the plastic bag of items on the passenger seat, the blue nose of Alice's precious dog poking out. She reached across and took out the cookbook, flipping through to the page where she'd hidden the note. She wanted to read it one last time before ripping it up and burning it. It had done enough damage.

But the note wasn't between the middle pages where she thought she'd tucked it away. In fact, as she riffled through the rest of book, she realised it wasn't between *any* of the pages. She turned it upside down, shaking it out frantically before dropping her head down onto the steering wheel and sobbing for all she was worth. It was only when a passer-by tapped on her window to see if she was OK that she realised the horn was blaring, that the sound of her crying had drowned out the noise completely.

CHAPTER TWENTY-TWO

'Libby!'

Before she knew what was happening, Libby felt a pair of arms slung around her from behind, almost knocking her over. She stumbled, catching her breath.

'It's *so* good to see you. You've not been up here in bloody ages!'

When she finally managed to turn around, wriggling in the vice-like grip, she saw it was Trish, her old boss, with a beaming smile on her face, her long hair yet another vibrant shade of blue. She'd been through an entire rainbow of dyes in the time Libby had known her.

'Hello, Trish,' Libby replied, pulling away and wrapping her coat around her. She folded her arms across her chest. 'Lovely to see you too. I've just been so busy… you know how it is.' She bowed her head. 'But Fran insisted I come up for a quick coffee.' She glanced at her watch then, not wanting to be rude but also not wanting to engage in chit-chat.

'We sodding well miss you here, you know, woman,' Trish said loudly, punctuating the words with several emphatic nods. The spacious open-plan foyer of the White House Barns carried her voice, convincing Libby that everyone could hear. She glanced around – spotting a few regular customers and familiar faces. A fire was roaring in the fireplace, with clients relaxing on the chesterfields, drinking coffee or pre-lunch cocktails.

The place had once been a huge part of Libby's life and the reason she moved to the area. In her time as head chef, the White

House had been her home for several years. And the reason she and Sean got together. They'd even had their wedding reception here.

'If you ever want to come back, you know there's always a job for you, my love,' Trish said, pulling her large tunic top down lower over her middle.

'Don't tempt me,' Libby replied without thinking. The regular income would take a lot of pressure off her and Sean and, she had to admit, she missed the place. She'd brought a fresh approach to the hotel's menus, using only locally sourced produce. The already thriving business had gone from strength to strength, even opening an organic produce shop and deli on the premises for local suppliers to sell their wares. It was all Libby's doing and she'd achieved a lot in just a couple of years.

'But it's hard with Sean on call and Alice,' Libby added wistfully, knowing Marion's health wasn't up to the antisocial hours for childcare. 'I can choose the evenings I work now,' she said, thinking that one day soon they'd also want more children. 'I couldn't do those long shifts again.'

Trish narrowed her eyes. 'I'll get you back in my kitchen if it's the last thing I do. Even if I have to split you and Sean up so I can have you all to myself,' she said, letting out a huge belly laugh that turned a few heads.

Libby gave a small smile, only hearing *split you and Sean up* echoing around the barn's vaulted interior. 'Well,' she said after a moment. 'I'd better go and find Fran. She'll wonder where I've got to.' She touched Trish's arm. 'Lovely to see you,' she said before heading off to the orangery.

'God, you look dreadful,' Fran said after she'd poured Libby some tea. She'd not long arrived herself and had ordered a pot of Earl Grey as well as some cakes. She knew what Libby liked. 'What the hell's been going on, Lib?' She slid the cup and saucer across the table before offering her the plate of macaroons and carrot cake squares.

Libby put her hand up, refusing the cake. She angled her head away slightly. 'Maybe I'll have one in a minute. I feel… I feel a bit sick right now.'

'You're not pregnant, are you?' The tone of Fran's voice lifted. 'Remember how nauseous you were with Alice?'

But Libby was already shaking her head. 'No, no I'm not pregnant.'

Fran narrowed her eyes. 'It's that bloody note, isn't it? I hope you've seen sense and chucked it away.'

'Well, to start with, that "bloody note" has gone, yes.'

'Good,' Fran said, sipping her tea. Her cheeks were tinged with a soft peach blush, highlighted by the light in the orangery – the complete opposite to Libby's wan appearance. 'So you threw it out?'

Libby shook her head, also sipping tea. 'Nope. It's just disappeared.'

'Oh. That's odd,' Fran replied, staring at Libby, cup halfway to her mouth. 'Did you check the other cookbooks? You may have put it in the wrong one. Or hidden it somewhere else entirely?'

Libby glanced out across the parkland at the rear of the orangery, watching as a few deer trotted briskly between some trees in the distance. 'How did you know I put the note in a cookbook?' she asked, turning back to Fran. Her heart thumped and her cheeks flushed – nothing like the soft, purposeful glow of Fran's made-up face. Libby's was now burning scarlet.

'I saw you hide it away, silly. Or perhaps you told me where you'd put it. One or the other, I can't remember.' Fran bit into a macaroon, chewing and watching Libby before swallowing drily. She sipped on her tea again, washing it down. 'You didn't want Sean to find it, remember?' Fran paused, waiting for a reply, but when there was none she reached out for Libby's hand. 'You look so upset, Lib. What's wrong?'

Libby pulled her hand away. 'No, no you *didn't* see where I put the note, Fran. And I didn't tell you, either.'

'Libby, you're stressing yourself out again.' Fran tipped her head to one side.

'Just before you left my place, you gave me back the note and I put it in my jeans pocket. I hid it again later.'

Fran gave Libby a pitying look. 'Then I must have seen where you got it from when you first showed me,' she said, her voice becoming impatient. 'It's not a big deal, Lib. What's more of a big deal is the state you're in about it. What's going on?'

'You've not heard?'

'No. What?' Fran frowned, shaking her head.

Libby took a deep breath. 'Sasha Long, you know, the girl who sometimes works for me…? She… she went missing on Friday night.' She closed her eyes for a moment, took another breath. 'She was babysitting Alice, and when we came home she wasn't there. No one's seen her since.'

'Oh my God, that's *awful*,' Fran said, taking in what Libby had said.

'I'm surprised you've not heard. Or seen all the police cars in Great Lyne. Sean said it'll probably be on the news tonight. It's been on local radio briefly but I've not been able to listen. It's too awful.'

'You've had all this going on and not called me? I'm *so* sorry you're going through this. I mean… what about Alice, did she see anything? Jesus…' She took a moment to think as the implications sank in. 'Have the police got any idea what happened? God, her poor parents. I know you hear of people going missing, but when it's on your doorstep…' Fran blew out between her teeth. 'Shocking.'

'Sean and I had to move out. They've been searching our house. God knows what for. Sasha obviously isn't there.' A shudder swept through her as she broke out in goosebumps. 'I'm not sure I can ever face going back.'

'I don't blame you,' Fran said.

'I suppose they're looking for signs of a break-in or intruders, trying to piece together a trail of Sasha's movements in the house while we were out. Or worse…'

'It's amazing what the police can do now with all that forensic stuff,' Fran said. 'My boss's wife is a cop. The stories he tells about how they find something out of nothing are incredible. No one can get away with anything these days.'

Libby stared at her. 'Really?' She paused, blinking. 'Let's hope so in this case, then,' she said, deciding to take a slice of cake after all. 'Sasha's poor mum and dad were going through a rough time already. This is all they need.'

'That's true,' Fran said. 'I know her dad, Phil Long. I have a friend who works on the estate with him. He's…' Fran trailed off.

'He's what?'

'He's a good guy, you know. Been through a hard time. I'm not saying Sasha's mum isn't a good woman – I barely know her. But by all accounts…' She stopped, holding up her hand. 'Look, it doesn't matter. I'm not a gossip.'

'What, Fran? You can't say that then not tell me the rest.'

She sighed, making a face. 'For a start, Phil told me that…'

'Told you about Jan…?'

Fran nodded. 'He said that she's borderline alcoholic, really hard to live with. Though Phil's hardly squeaky clean himself. He smokes weed and…'

Libby hadn't known any of this, but it wasn't for her to judge either of them – especially not at a time like this.

'Anyway,' Fran went on. 'Let's just say that, according to Phil, there have been three people in their marriage for quite a while.' She stared at Libby, biting her lip. 'Though it's probably paranoia talking. You know what smoking that stuff does to you.'

Libby suddenly went cold, her body shuddering from the inside out. She frowned, touching her forehead. 'No, no I don't know. I've never touched the stuff.'

Sean is having an affair…

'And now they've got this with Sasha to deal with,' Fran said, making a sympathetic face.

Libby made a noise – a mix of agreement and deep thought. 'Fran, you don't think that Jan and Sean…?' Libby checked herself by shoving the last of her carrot cake into her mouth. But it was too late. She and Fran had known each other long enough to almost mind-read.

'No, Lib. I *don't* think that. And neither should you.' She stood up, rummaging in her bag. 'Anyway, there are far bigger things going on now with poor Sasha.' She checked her pocket for her lighter. 'Won't be long. Addiction calls.'

Libby nodded, feeling ashamed for even thinking that way, watching as Fran went out through the glass doors, heading for the smoking area. She sat back in her chair, staring out of the large orangery windows as she finished her tea. A fine drizzle had started up, smudging out the area of park where she'd spotted the deer. Fran was right, of course. She was being selfish, and blaming Sean for her own insecurities when there were greater things to be concerned about. It wasn't as if he…

Her thoughts trailed off as she heard a phone vibrating. She checked her bag, but it wasn't hers. Then she saw Fran had left her phone on the table beside the teapot. Libby idly peered at the screen, but before she could get a proper look Fran had returned, swiping it up.

'I'm always leaving the damn thing lying about,' she said, smiling.

But Libby didn't reply. She just stared at Fran then down at the phone in her hand again. No number had appeared on the screen, and not a full name either. Though Libby could swear, as she looked back out across the parkland, that she'd seen the initials 'SR' flash up as the caller's ID.

CHAPTER TWENTY-THREE

Now

The solicitor's words hit me hard.

'You think they've found a body? Is it Sasha? Have they told you?' I grip the edge of the table.

'The fact is, I don't know,' Claire replies. 'But there's a chance.' She makes that face again – part pity, part disbelief. I wonder if she mistrusts all her clients, views them as guilty until they prove otherwise. 'But DI Jones isn't going to tell me everything,' she continues. 'Not yet. He's known for keeping his powder dry. And there doesn't need to be a body to make an arrest if there's other compelling evidence.'

'They *can't* have found her body. Is that why they've brought me in, really? Please, dear God, no.' I shake my head. Keep shaking it faster and faster until my brain hurts. Hair flies across my face and my vision goes blurry, the bland grey and beige colours of the room blending into streaks, the fluorescent strip light above flickering and buzzing.

But Claire's face stays sharp as I fix my stare on her – her bright eyes, the compassionate pucker of her lips. She's here to help me, I tell myself. She'll make them believe I'm innocent and then I can just go home. Home to Sean and Alice. Pretend none of it ever happened.

I drop my head down onto the table, pressing my forehead against the cold grey surface. '*Nooo…*' I wail, sobbing hysterically.

'Dear God, *no*. Not Sasha.' I claw at the tabletop, my fingers falling on Claire's paperwork. She tries to pull it out of my way, but I grip on tightly, pulling it between my fingers, scrunching a few pages up in my fist.

'Libby, stop. You really can't do—'

'Don't tell me to stop!' I yell, lifting my head. My hair is swept across my eyes and stuck to my wet face as I bare my teeth. I can tell by the look on her face that she thinks I'm demented, that I'm a threat to her. She glances at the door. Looks nervous.

Just tell it like it is, love. Just tell them what happened...

'Sean?' I say, swinging round. 'Sean?' I stand up, looking behind me, watching the door as if he's just come in. But my legs give way, my lungs burning from my short, sharp breaths, and I slump down again. 'Sean, is that you?'

'Mrs Randell. Libby, calm down, please or I'll have to call someone. I can't help you if you—'

'But I just heard Sean's voice in here, I swear. He came in, didn't he? Has he come to get me?'

'No, Libby, he hasn't. No one's come in.'

I dive under the table, looking to see if he's there. Then I twist round in my chair again, making sure he's not crept up behind me, about to plant his hands on my shoulders, tell me it's time to go home, that there's been a terrible mistake and Sasha's not dead and we're going out for a nice meal tonight, and Marion is going to babysit for us and... and...

'What did they tell you?' I say, imagining that they've found her, what she must have looked like – pale and cold, her face sweet and still. Was she naked? Hurt? Was she hidden in a bush or left for dead out in the open?

'I have no specific details yet, I'm afraid. But I'm assuming there's significant evidence, given your reason for arrest.' Claire picks up her pen. 'Look, I have to ask you something, and I don't want you to take this the wrong way, Libby, but I need to check regarding your mental health. Do you often hear voices when there's no one there? Have you ever been diagnosed with a mental illness?'

'*What?*' I say. The ridiculousness of her question gives me a moment's clarity. 'No, of course not. There's nothing wrong with me. I just… I just thought I heard…' I shake my head. 'Look, I've been under a lot of stress these last few weeks. Everyone in the village has felt it one way or another. Jan, Sasha's mum, has completely fallen apart. Phil, her dad, too. Sean and I just feel… so *guilty*. We've been going through our own kind of hell. Do you understand that? The poor girl was in our house when whatever happened to her happened.'

Claire nods, adopts a sympathetic tone. 'I understand. When you're interviewed by the detective, if you have nothing you want to say or can't answer a question, I'd recommend not reacting like that though.' The solicitor pulls a face. 'It's not going to do you any favours.'

I feel like I'm being told off. The naughty schoolgirl. 'OK,' I say quietly. 'Sorry.'

'This note you mentioned before, Libby. The one you found on your car. Do you know who sent it?'

'No,' I say, wondering whether I should tell her about the *second* note. That one disappeared too. 'Someone just trying to cause trouble, I suppose.' Then Natalie is on my mind – standing in front of me wearing one of her perfectly coordinated outfits, looking down on me. Her hair glossy, nails immaculately painted. 'I really don't see the relevance.'

'Who would want to cause trouble, do you think?'

I stare at the ceiling. Sean and I talked about this, of course, going over a thousand times who might have left it. Correction – *I* went over it a thousand times. 'It's unrelated to Sasha,' I say.

'But Libby, receiving that note caused you to have a night out with your husband, which resulted in Sasha babysitting and then going missing. I'd say the detective will think it's very relevant. It's unusual. Or do you get these sorts of notes all the time?'

'Of course not.' I bite my lip. 'Look, Sean's been married once before. To Natalie, the mother of his son, Dan. They split up a few years ago but she's never got over him leaving. And she hates that he married me and that we have a child of our own.'

Claire looks at me, her face unreadable. Yet in its blankness I manage to see her disdain, her pity, thanking her lucky stars that she's not me.

'I suspect it was Natalie who wrote the note, but of course I can't say for sure. I've hinted to Sean about it, but I don't want to be *that* woman. The jealous wife. I've given him a hard enough time as it is. Anyway, having a meal out with Sean was meant to put any ill feeling behind us. *My* ill feeling.'

'And what did the note actually say?' Claire asks.

'To tell you the truth, I can't really remember,' I say, the five words emblazoned on my mind.

Everything will be OK, Sean had told me, his hands on my shoulders in that way of his. I nodded, agreeing with him. *And don't confuse things. Stick to the relevant facts. Remember, we want Sasha found alive as quickly as possible too, OK? Like everyone does.*

I'd trusted him completely, thanking God we were in this together. We'd already made one lengthy statement to the detective but he kept coming back, asking new questions. *Just an informal chat*, he'd told us. We answered everything, of course, sometimes separately. No one wanted Sasha back alive more than us.

'You can't recall the words of the note that caused you so much upset?' Claire says.

'I've tried to forget it. It just implied that Sean was… well, up to no good. But he's a good man and would never hurt me,' I say, shrugging. 'Not my finest moment.'

'And where is the note now, Libby?' Claire taps her pen on the table. 'These are all things you're likely to get asked. If they haven't already got it, the detective may ask you for it.'

'I threw it away. Hardly a keepsake, right?'

'I understand,' Claire says after a pause, reading through her notes again. She puts down her pen, leans back in her seat. 'If you're innocent, just tell things as they are. However, if you're not sure, if you're going to tie yourself in knots, then it's best to say "no comment". But not if you want to mention something as part of your defence in court. *If* you go to court, I should add.'

'OK,' I say, closing my eyes. But all I can see is Sean, his face up close, his eyes boring into mine when we came home from the pub that Friday night. He was angry, making it hard to understand what he was saying. And then his hand came out of nowhere.

I'd reeled, staggering backwards against the wall, my cheek stinging, smarting, feeling as if my teeth had been knocked out. I cupped my cheek where he'd slapped me.

'Sean?' I'd said, fighting back the tears. 'Sean, *please*...' He'd gone to sit on the arm of the sofa, his head hanging down. I couldn't feel my face and one eye was watering. He'd never laid a finger on me before. When he looked up, his eyes were watering too. I went over to him.

'What did you *do*?' he'd said, staring up at me. There was hate in his eyes. I didn't understand why.

'What do you mean, what did *I* do?' I'd been going to embrace him, try to take away the pain I knew he was feeling, but I halted. 'You just *slapped* me.'

'You were hysterical. I had to shut you up. Don't twist this back on me.' He'd turned away then, shaking his head. In fact, his entire body was shaking. Looking back, I felt the same – out of control. Yet, as ever, Sean was one step ahead of me. Generally, this never mattered. In fact, it's one of the things I've always loved most about him. His intelligence, his ability to pace out the next steps with ease

– like a real-life chess game, always thinking six moves ahead. It made me feel secure, as though he was watching out for us. His family.

'I'm sorry,' I'd said, hanging my head, knowing I deserved it.

Then I'd caught sight of it, lying on the floor, half underneath the sofa. At first I didn't realise what it was, but as I drew close and bent down to pick it up, it was unmistakable.

'This is Natalie's, isn't it?' I'd said, holding up the silver bracelet. It was dripping with charms. 'I swear it's hers. I've seen her wearing it.' Over the years, each sighting of Natalie had left me with a lasting impression. She was one of those rare people who left an indelible mark, especially on other women.

Sean had leapt up off the sofa then, snatching the bracelet from me. 'Give it to me,' he'd said. He turned it around between his fingers. 'I don't know whose it is,' he said. 'Probably Sasha's.' He dropped it down onto the coffee table then, along with all Sasha's other stuff, as if it were infected.

'No, no it's not hers,' I replied. 'I've never seen her wearing it.' It was true, plus it certainly didn't look like something she'd wear, or be able to afford. 'But I do remember it on Natalie and—'

'No, Libby. You *don't*. You're wrong, OK?' Sean's eyes fixed on me. Then he came close, making me flinch when he raised his hand. But it was only to push it through his hair. I noticed the sweat on his forehead, his top lip. 'Go out and look in the barn for Sasha,' he said, his voice calmer now.

'But…' I was going to protest but knew he was right. 'OK,' I said, heading out to the kitchen. I took the key from the hook in the back hallway and went out, stumbling across the cobbles. The wine had gone to my head, making my thoughts muzzy.

It was dark outside, the courtyard lit only by a square of light coming from the cottage window. 'Sash?' I made sure to call out, opening the barn door and going inside. 'Are you here?'

It was silent apart from a couple of cars cruising past on the lane, an owl hooting in a tree behind the barn. Shivers ran down my spine.

And then I heard a noise. 'Hello?' I called out, staring back out into the courtyard. I shrugged and switched on the lights, going over to the pantry, leaving the door open. I'd left her a meal in the cottage fridge, telling her to help herself, so she had no need to come out here. I locked up the barn again. Of course Sasha wasn't in there.

That noise again. An outside light coming on next door.

'Who's there?' someone called out. Our neighbour, Arn, was hot on security ever since his garage had been broken into last year. All his tools had been taken.

'It's just me, Arn,' I called back. 'Libby. Sorry to have disturbed you.'

'Everything OK?' he said, his head appearing over the stone wall. He wasn't a tall man but often popped up for a chat if he heard me outside hanging out the washing or playing with Alice.

'Everything's fine,' I said. What if he'd seen Sasha earlier? What if he knew something? I should have asked him but didn't. I wasn't thinking straight. 'Night then, Arn,' I said, hurrying back to the cottage. As I locked the back door, I saw him disappear again and his outside light go off.

'Did you look properly?' Sean said, leaning against the kitchen sink. 'Move stuff about in case she was hiding?'

'Obviously,' I replied, shivering.

He nodded. 'I checked upstairs again. I even went through the built-in cupboards in case she was hiding in there. I made a bit of a mess.'

'OK, good,' I said, thinking a mess was the least of our worries.

We'd gone back into the living room then and Sean had stoked the fire, peering into it for ages. I remember wondering how he could do something so trivial at a time like this. But then I went to make some tea – equally unimportant, though somehow comforting as the situation grew more serious. When I came back, Sean was drinking whisky. He offered me one, ignoring the tea. I took it gratefully and knocked it back in one go.

'I'm going up to check on Alice again,' I said, but Sean stopped me, telling me I was being obsessive. 'I think one of us should go out and look around the village,' I suggested, already reading Sean's train of thought. I glanced at my watch. 'It's ages since we got back. I'll go. I've drunk way less than you.'

Then he turned his back on me, made some comment about being driven to drink after an evening like we'd had. I couldn't help the tears welling up in my eyes then. I just wanted to get out of the cottage, have time to think. To work out how to make things right again. Though they seemed so very far from that.

'Be careful, OK?' Sean said, grabbing my shoulders as I was putting on my coat. I flinched again as he shrugged into his own jacket. 'Have you got your phone?'

'Yes,' I said, nodding. Then I told him where I'd go, just a quick spin around the village. 'And if I see anyone, I'll make sure to ask if they've seen her,' I added, repeating his instructions. I felt Sean's hands shaking on my shoulders, in time with my own tremors.

*

'I didn't mean to,' I say, gripping the edge of the table.

The solicitor stops, tipping her head to one side. She's been talking and I've not been listening – my mind filled with thoughts of that night.

'Sorry, Libby?' she says. 'You didn't mean to do what?'

I stare at her, the scene still playing out. Driving down the lane, peering out of the car windows. Sasha was everywhere I looked – her face imprinted on my mind as I tormented myself – yet she was nowhere to be seen. I was sweating, my vision skewed from the wine, the alcohol taking hold of my senses.

'The lane narrowed,' I went on, shaking my head. 'It was dark. The windows were fogged up. It was just an accident.'

Be careful, you've been drinking too, Sean had said before I left. Then he whispered something else in my ear and I'd nodded.

'Accident?' Claire says, her voice coaxing and earnest. 'What kind of accident?'

I look at her, knowing I'm going to disappoint her, that what she wants is an easy afternoon, not to be kept late, to go home. She doesn't really care if I'm charged or not, just wants to make sure I go through the process fairly with my rights intact and she gets paid for it.

'Have you got a husband?' I ask her. 'Or a partner. Girlfriend, boyfriend?'

The solicitor's eyes narrow. I hate her. Want to punch her. She can walk out of here. I can't.

'It's not me we're here to talk about,' she says. 'Did you accidentally hurt Sasha? Is that what you're telling me?'

'*No*,' I say, wondering whether to mention bumping the car. 'Of course not. Is this what you do? Make people say things to suit your version of events?'

'No, Libby. But you're not helping me or yourself here. It's hard for me to advise you.'

'Sorry,' I say quickly, just like I'd said to Sean a thousand times that night. I'd turned into a mess, wasn't coping. 'I haven't done anything wrong. I swear,' I add as Claire slowly turns up the sleeves of her blouse, exposing a pretty silver bracelet with a heart charm on it. I stare at it, wondering what happened to Natalie's bracelet that night, if Sean ever gave it back.

CHAPTER TWENTY-FOUR

Before

'Are you sure this is a good idea?' Libby said, balancing the dish on her palms. Her bag kept slipping off her shoulder and her hair was billowing in her face, getting in her mouth. She blew it out, looking up at Sean.

'Of course,' he replied, staring straight ahead. He rang the bell again. 'It's absolutely the right thing to do. Would you want to think no one cared about us if Alice had gone missing?'

'Sean, don't,' Libby said, shuddering at the thought. She screwed up her eyes to get it out of her mind. But all she could see was Sasha's face – her mind in overdrive as she imagined her dead, her skin blue-grey, lying somewhere alone. She let out a little sob.

'And try not to cry,' Sean said. 'This isn't about you. It's about the poor people inside this house.'

'*People?*' Libby said, finally hearing a noise inside, as if someone was coming. 'I thought they'd separated?'

Sean glanced back. Jan's car was on the drive, but there were a few others parked on the street. 'That's Phil's van over there.'

'Oh, OK…' But Libby stopped, turning back to the door as she heard the chain slide, the key turn. 'Jan,' she said, making a sympathetic face as soon as she saw her. Jan was wearing a faded blue towelling robe, hanging open over an old T-shirt and leggings.

Her feet were bare and her hair was unbrushed, pulled back in a ponytail that was coming undone.

'Libby,' she said, her voice not much more than a croak. She dragged her gaze up to Sean, one eyebrow flickering as he also greeted her. 'I thought you might be the police. You know. News.'

'Sorry,' Libby said. 'We brought you… you and Phil some food. We didn't think you'd feel like cooking.' Libby held out the terracotta dish covered in foil. It was a Moroccan lamb tagine that she'd had in the freezer, left over from a dinner party.

'Thanks,' she said, turning to go back inside, leaving the door open. Libby looked at Sean, who cocked his head, as if to say *follow her in*. Libby trod nervously over the threshold of the 1970s semi, stepping into the hallway. There were a couple of streets in Little Radwell built around that time, Mason Close being one of them, but the rest of the village was classic Cotswolds stone cottages. Sasha had grown up here, attended the local primary school, then the high school before going on to the nearby sixth-form college. Libby stopped, staring around, seeing the coats hanging on the hooks, the pairs of shoes on the rack underneath, some of them looking like Sasha's – white trainers, Converse, Adidas, Nike. She shuddered as she recognised a couple of Sasha's coats and a scarf.

'Come through,' Jan said, leading the way past the stairs and into the small front room. Floral curtains hung at an aluminium window and a gas fire flickered in the pale brick surround. The brown carpet was worn in the doorway with a burgundy patterned rug taking up most of the floor space between the green velour sofas. There were several scented candles burning on the coffee table, alongside some incense. Almost shrine-like, Libby thought. 'Please, have a seat.'

Sean and Libby sat down beside each other, Libby still holding the dish. 'Here,' she said, rising briefly again. 'Shall I put this in the fridge? You might be glad of it later.'

'I'll do it,' Jan said, taking the food and disappearing into the kitchen, returning a moment later. 'That was thoughtful, Libby. Thank you.'

Libby nodded. 'We're just so sorry that Sasha hasn't come back yet,' she said. 'We wanted to let you know that we'll help in any way we can, *do* anything we can, and obviously cooperate with the police as much as they need. We feel utterly wretched.'

'Don't,' a voice said from behind. Libby and Sean turned to see Phil standing there. Libby knew him, though not particularly well. Just from a few occasions in the pub over the years, or when he'd called by to fetch Sean for a shoot. He was a tall, broad man but today he looked half his size. Broken.

'Hello, Phil,' Libby said, standing up. She went to give him a hug but he just stood there, letting her give him a squeeze around the shoulders. Libby did the same to Jan too, realising she'd not greeted her properly yet. At a time like this, they needed to know people had got their backs, that they had support. 'I'm so sorry about what's happened. And of course, no one feels as wretched as you two must. Do they, Sean?' she added, turning to him. 'It's unthinkable, and we all just want Sasha to be found safe and well.'

Sean's head was down and he was leaning forward, forearms on his thighs, staring at the carpet. Libby was babbling, she knew, but it was hard to know what to say. And Sean was saying nothing.

'Thanks, Libby,' Phil said, his voice deep yet fragile. 'We're just waiting for news. It's agony. We feel so helpless. I've been out searching, of course, checking in with all her friends – anyone really. It's not like her. Not like her at all and it's been four days now.'

'Tell me again how she seemed on Friday evening, Libby,' Jan said, her face crumpled with worry lines. Her hands were bony and thin, her collarbones protruding through the T-shirt where her robe had fallen open. 'You were the last ones to see her. What was her mood like? What did she say? Has she ever mentioned any problems? I know she's very fond of you.' She spoke fast, her words tumbling out.

'Honestly, she seemed fine,' Libby replied. 'She arrived on time and we'd lit the fire for her. She got her books out straight away and got on with her studies. She was doing maths, I think, and she seemed in a cheerful mood. We told her when we'd be back and then…' Libby stopped. They didn't need to hear about what happened when they arrived home.

'Sean, *look*,' Libby had said that night, rifling through the contents of Sasha's backpack, most of which had been tipped out on the floor. She held up a packet of tobacco and some cigarette papers. 'I had no idea,' she'd said, shaking her head. They'd gathered up some of her stuff then, putting it back – purse, college lanyard, make-up bag – unzipped with the contents spilt out too. There was a ruler, a couple of pens, some tissues and a tattered copy of *Take a Break* magazine, folded open at the puzzle page. It looked as though someone – *Sasha?* – had been looking for something in a hurry.

'Teenagers sometimes sneak a smoke, Lib,' Sean had said, helping to shove her stuff away. 'It's perfectly normal. There's probably a bag of weed in there too if you look,' he'd added, dropping the pack on the sofa again.

'Have the police got any leads yet?' Sean said to Jan, giving Phil a quick look too. Sasha's parents were sitting in opposite armchairs.

'Not really,' Phil said flatly before Jan could speak. 'Just the shoe found on Saturday morning. It sounds bad, but she has that many pairs of trainers, neither Jan nor I can say if it's definitely hers. It's being tested. We've got a… what's she called, Jan? That officer who comes up to tell us what's going on?'

'A liaison officer,' Jan replied. '*Family* liaison officer. Ironic,' she added, her jaw tense.

'They're still partly working on the assumption that she left of her own free will,' Phil added, ignoring Jan's comment. 'Though they were looking for signs of a struggle too.'

'Well, surely that's a good thing?' Libby said, eyeing Sean. 'If she left of her own accord?'

'I suppose they were looking for blood,' Jan said. 'And they've grilled us a dozen times already, can you believe?'

'Jan…' Phil said in a warning tone. 'Don't.'

'Someone told the cops we've got *troubles*; isn't that right, Phil?' she went on, ignoring him. 'As though that makes us suspects.'

'I think it's normal to question everyone close to Sasha,' Sean said before Phil could reply. 'They've done the same to us, so try not to worry.'

Phil shook his head, blowing out a sigh. He pushed up the sleeves of his denim shirt and Libby noticed the lines of dirt on his rough hands. *Big* hands, she thought, watching as his fingers fidgeted, his head bowed as he leant forward, forearms on his knees. He'd worked outdoors most of his life, farm labouring and now managing the game on the land owned by the big local estate. Sasha had once told Libby that her dad had always dreamt of owning his own farm, but could never afford the prices in the area.

'Let's just pray that she had a wobble and ran off to a friend's place for a few days,' Phil said, looking up. 'Dear God, let that be the case…' He pressed his fist against his heart, dropping his head down again, his large shoulders jumping up and down in time with his sobs. Sean was closest and made a move to comfort him, but then thought better of it. When Jan didn't do anything, Libby leant over and offered him a hand to hold as well as passing him a tissue.

'Sorry, sorry,' he said, his face red and crumpled, squeezing Libby's fingers. 'I just can't deal with this. Can't deal with the *not knowing*. It's the worst kind of agony.'

'I know,' Libby said, catching her breath as she saw a marked police car pull up outside the house. A female officer in uniform got out and came up the path. The doorbell rang. 'Maybe it's time for us to go?' Libby said to Sean. 'Let's leave Jan and Phil to talk to the officer.'

'Of course,' Sean said, standing up as Jan went to answer the door. 'Take it easy, mate,' Sean said to Phil, giving him a tentative pat on the shoulder. 'Let us know if there's anything we can do.'

Phil nodded without looking up. Libby and Sean turned to leave and, as they were going, they passed the officer in the doorway. Her face was deadly serious.

CHAPTER TWENTY-FIVE

'Sit, do nothing,' Marion ordered when Sean had taken Alice upstairs for a bath. Libby didn't need telling twice and dragged out a chair at the kitchen table, watching as Marion cleared away the plates. While they were out visiting Jan and Phil, she'd made macaroni cheese – knowing it was Alice's favourite – and served them each a portion when they'd returned. Libby had pushed hers around her plate, not feeling hungry, but had tried to eat something so as not to seem ungrateful. What she really wanted was a large drink. Nothing less would slow the rampant thud of her heart. She didn't think she'd ever wipe Jan's desolate expression from her mind. The poor woman looked... *dead* inside.

'We really appreciate this, Marion,' she said. 'Staying here, you looking after us, taking care of Alice.'

The older woman turned from the sink, her hands still plunged deep in dishwater. She gave a nod, a small smile appearing within the lines around her mouth. Libby knew she was in her element.

'Don't even mention it,' she said, rinsing plate after plate. 'It's a terrible time.'

Unusually, Marion had turned up the heating at the farm, wanting them all to feel comfortable. Word from the police was that they were free to return to the cottage now, and could have done yesterday, but Marion had insisted they stay at least until tomorrow, as if having the three of them there had given her renewed purpose, a feeling of usefulness.

'Terrible business all round,' she said, drying the cutlery and dropping it into the big dresser drawer. 'That poor girl. You hear of these things but never expect them to happen on your doorstep.'

'Exactly,' Libby said, sipping on the mug of tea Marion had made her. She winced at the sugar but didn't say anything.

'Takes me back though, having Sean here, in his old room,' she said with another, bigger smile. 'Is it warm enough up there, love? I don't want you to be cold. I know this old place isn't exactly the Hilton but—'

'It's fine,' Libby said as she spotted Marion's eyes glistening.

'I just can't help blaming myself about it all,' she went on, abandoning the washing-up and pulling out a chair next to Libby.

'Don't be silly,' she said. 'No one's to blame.'

Marion reached out and took her hand. Libby noticed her papery skin, the age spots and brittle nails, clipped as short as possible. She was a grafter, always had been, and Libby sensed that she had a need to constantly rescue people, as though without her input or care, things would fall apart. While she was grateful for her help with Alice, she couldn't help thinking it was to satisfy her own needs more than theirs. Or rather, she corrected herself as she watched Marion pour herself some tea, *Sean's* needs. It seemed Marion had never quite let go – as though there was something inside him she felt she needed to fix.

'I… I drove past your place that night, you know,' Marion said, looking at Libby over the rim of her mug as she took nervous little sips. 'On Friday.'

'Oh?'

'There was nothing untoward going on that I could see. That's what I told the police, anyway. Like everyone else, I just want to help, to do something useful.'

'Well you are helping, Marion,' Libby replied. 'By looking after us.'

Truth was, even though they could go home, Libby didn't want to. What if the forensics team *had* found signs of a struggle – some of Sasha's hair caught in a door hinge or traces of her blood on the carpet as she'd been dragged out? She'd seen some of those shows on TV, knew how experts could piece together what had happened just from the tiniest fragments of evidence. She prayed that they wouldn't find anything at Chestnut Cottage, hoped to God that there was nothing to suggest anything other than Sasha going off in a teenage strop. And she couldn't get the family liaison officer's expression out of her mind either, when they'd left Jan and Phil's. She hadn't heard a word since and wasn't sure whether to text to find out.

'It's a pleasure to have you here, love,' Marion replied, unusually affectionately. 'Life's far too short, you know, and I feel blessed to have little Alice running about, enjoying the space. It only feels like yesterday since Fred put up that swing for Sean. He had to repair it for Alice to use. It was rotten through.' Marion gave a little laugh, wiping a finger under her eye. 'Sean loved going on it. He once said he was going to swing so high that he'd be able to kick the clouds and make it rain.'

Libby smiled. 'That sounds like my Sean,' she said. 'Soft on the inside, though he doesn't like to show it.' She laughed, forgetting everything for just a couple of moments.

Marion didn't often speak about the past, when Sean was growing up, what he was like as a kid. Or, if she did, it was an equally truncated version of snippets Libby had heard from Sean. Like the time Marion told her he'd punched a boy on the nose on his first day at high school – the only time he'd ever retaliated. Libby had never found out why, and when she pressed Sean for details he just said that his mother was exaggerating, that he'd accidentally bumped into one of the so-called tough kids in the corridor and got called names for a couple of days.

'Oh, well you say that,' Marion added with a chuckle. 'He never *used* to hide it. He was so kind to everyone too. When he was on the swing, he said he was trying to make the clouds rain on the bad people because he couldn't stand to punch them back, like his dad had told him to do. But then…' She trailed off.

'Really?' Libby said. 'That's so funny.'

Marion nodded. 'You wouldn't think it looking at the size of him now, but he was a sensitive lad. Always felt things differently to other people. *Saw* things differently too.'

'I see it in him. I do understand. And he adores animals so much. Probably more than he enjoys human company sometimes. Though he's a pushover with Alice. And of course, he'd do anything for you,' she added, wondering where, exactly, *she* fell in the list of important things in Sean's life. She'd never once have questioned that she was up there, top of the list with Alice – and she tried to convince herself that she wasn't questioning it now. But she couldn't help thinking that the hard time she'd given him about the note had knocked her off pole position.

'Mothers and their sons,' Marion said, eyeing Libby.

Libby smiled back. 'Perhaps I'll know what that's like one day. We don't want Alice to be an only child.'

It was the look on Marion's face that made her toes dig into the soles of her trainers, her nails clench hard against her palms. Sean had once said that his mother had wanted a houseful of children, but that it wasn't to be. It was just him.

'It's hard bringing up just the one child,' Marion went on, pretending the comment hadn't got to her. 'As a mum, I felt… I felt almost inadequate. That he didn't have that sibling rivalry to shape him, to spar against, to have as a role model or be a role model *to*.' Marion sighed then, taking a tissue from under the cuff of her sweater and blowing her nose. 'It was Fred who said that, actually. That if there'd been two of them… a brother to model himself on, then…' She trailed off, shaking her head, a deep frown forming. 'What I'm trying to say, love, is that I think I overcompensated. Somehow felt like a failure for not being able to have another baby. That what happened was all my fault.' Marion shook her head and turned away, as though she'd said too much.

'Oh, Marion,' Libby said, taking her hand again. 'You're nowhere near a failure. If it makes you feel any better, I'm fumbling in the dark most of the time when it comes to parenting Alice.' She nudged her mother-in-law then, giving her a wry smile. Marion showing anything apart from a pair of broad shoulders whatever life threw at her – let alone getting emotional about it – well, it was… unusual.

'I remember feeling like the worst mother ever when he—' Marion stopped, getting up and going into the pantry. She returned with a small bottle. 'For emergencies,' she said, grabbing a couple of glasses and pouring some out. 'I'm not supposed to have any with the medication I'm on, but surely one won't hurt?'

Libby took it gratefully, sipping the whisky slowly while Marion knocked hers back. She sat toying with the empty glass.

'It's funny. I can still sense it even now when Sean…' She poured out another measure for herself. '… when he's… *hurting*.'

'Really?' Libby said, taking another sip. The drink seared the back of her throat, making her cough. 'Mother's intuition?' she said, noticing Marion's faraway look, as though she'd gone back in time.

'It was ever since that day,' she went on. 'I should have been there, somehow stopped the accident. But I wasn't. And ever after, I swear I've done everything I could to make things right, but sometimes…' She trailed off again, glancing towards the boot room as if she'd heard something. 'Sometimes everything isn't enough,' she added in a whisper.

Libby swung round when she saw Marion's expression change, her mouth gape open. Her eyes had grown wide and glassy. She felt a rush of cold air on her back.

'Oh, hello, Fred,' Libby said as her father-in-law stood there in his work jacket, sizing up the situation. 'You must be exhausted.' Libby stood up, grabbing an oven glove and going to the cooking range. 'We saved you some food.' She raised a hand to halt Marion. 'No, I've got it. You've done enough.' She took the remaining macaroni cheese from the oven and served some up. 'We were just discussing old times,' she told Fred as he shrugged off his jacket and sat down. 'About when Sean was little and… and…' She stopped when she got no response, grateful to see Sean now standing in the doorway with Alice's dirty jeans in his hand.

'Fat lot of use mother's intuition has been for that poor lass who's gone missing,' Fred finally said, glaring at his son, showing he'd been listening to Libby and Marion's conversation for longer than they'd realised. He paused before squirting on a load of ketchup and shovelling the food into his mouth.

'I'll go and put these in the wash, then,' Sean said quietly, clearing his throat, the two men staring at each other as he walked off.

CHAPTER TWENTY-SIX

'I'm freezing,' Libby said, draping herself around Sean. The blankets and eiderdown gave off a musty smell as she turned onto her side, wrapped up in her pyjamas and a cardigan. Sean was wearing only a T-shirt and boxers, which she was grateful for as she could soak up his body heat.

'Softie,' Sean said, sliding his arm around her shoulders. He pulled her close. 'You're not used to the hard life.'

'Funny,' Libby replied. 'That's what your mum said about you earlier. That you're a big softie.'

'No wonder my ears were burning.'

Libby snuggled closer, breathing in the scent of his day – the familiar smell of his body wash caught up with the tang of something else. She thought she recognised it.

Fear.

'What was Mum saying?'

Libby thought she felt him tense a little, the curve of his shoulder twitching beneath her.

'Just that really. That when you were a kid you were the sensitive type.' Libby waited for Sean to add something, but he didn't. 'It was weird, but I think your mum felt, well, as though she let you down in some way. Though I don't know what she meant exactly.'

'That's Mum for you.' Sean let out a little cough, turned to check the time on his phone. 'It's late. Let's get some sleep.'

Libby pressed against him more, if that was possible, while he wrapped his free arm across her front, kissing her head. The room was dark, with only the moonlight bleeding in through a chink in the curtains, illuminating the Anaglypta wallpaper, daubed in a nondescript shade of blue, cobwebs in the corners. She closed her eyes, knowing she was far from sleep. All she could see behind her eyelids were the ghostlike figures of the police forensics team picking over their house, her fingers peeling the note off her frozen windscreen and various images of poor Sasha, wherever she was.

'Marion mentioned about your accident,' Libby whispered, conscious they may be overheard. 'How old were you?' She was desperate to know more.

Sean groaned. 'It's late, Lib.'

'But I want to know about it,' she continued. 'Can't you tell me quickly what happened?'

Libby knew the rhythm of Sean's breathing – that moment between wakefulness and sleep. How his quiet, measured breaths soon turned into relaxed and unselfconscious rasps and, sometimes, a gentle snore. She was always comforted by him letting go. Once, when she'd gently complained about his louder snoring, he'd told her that it wasn't snoring, rather it was him protecting her, scaring off anyone who might hurt her in the night. 'It's a growl, Lib, to keep you safe, to keep the bad guys away.' She couldn't help smiling, couldn't help loving him more.

But right now, Libby could tell Sean wasn't at that point of sleep at all. Even though she saw his eyes were closed in the moonlight, she knew he was very much awake and alert, his mind working hard, reflected in his breathing. Steady with a slight sigh out every other breath. Things on his mind.

'What's up?' she said, nudging him gently.

'Nothing.'

'Seriously, I can tell you're thinking.'

'I'm tired.'

'You can't just block it all out, you know. It doesn't work like that,' Libby said softly.

Neither of them moved a muscle, though Libby was aware of the tension in Sean's body – right through from his shoulders and arms, down through his middle and ending up in his calves and feet, where Libby had hers entwined.

'The accident,' she pressed on. 'Tell me.'

'Fuck's sake, Libby,' Sean said, pulling his arm out from beneath her. 'I don't know. I probably fell over and grazed my knee or something. You know what Mum's like.'

'No, no I don't,' Libby went on. 'I saw a side of her tonight I didn't recognise. Something… different. Tender, even.'

Sean let out a little snort.

'You're pretty disparaging of her when, really, all she wants to do is look after you, take care of you.'

'I'm forty-two. I don't need taking care of.'

Libby sighed as Sean switched over onto his other side. She was faced with the expanse of his back, covered in T-shirt, and ran her fingers down his spine, working her way back up again to massage the base of his neck, the tense muscles in his shoulders. He couldn't help the involuntary shudders, the gentle moan, his hand slipping behind him onto Libby's thigh.

'It was nothing,' he mumbled. 'Just a farm accident. Mum felt guilty, that's all.'

'I'm sorry to hear that,' Libby whispered, reaching up to kiss his neck. Another moan. She decided not to press further as he clearly didn't want to talk about it, but there was something on her mind that she *did* want to talk about, even if they were both exhausted.

Libby pressed herself as tightly as she could against his back.

'Sean,' she whispered, swallowing. Her mouth was dry.

'Love, I'm tired, OK?'

'I know, but… but I went to get some stuff from the cottage the other day, not long after the forensics team had arrived. I wasn't sure how long they'd be there and I needed my phone charger.'

'Mmm…' Sean said. 'OK, Lib. Night.'

'It's the note,' she went on, trying to hold her breath as she was speaking. 'I mean… I needed the cookbook, I really did. For that dinner next week. I'm so behind with everything. I'd shoved the stupid thing inside the pages last week but when I flipped through it, it wasn't there. I have no idea what happened to it and I'm wondering if the police—'

Sean hurled himself over through a hundred and eighty degrees to face Libby. She winced as his arm flung over her head. He was a big man, and always watched out for her when he turned. But not this time. She touched her temple where the side of his hand had accidentally caught her.

'Are you *still* going on about that?' he said. 'After everything?' He propped himself up on one elbow, looming down over her. His lips were tight and pursed, his eyes narrowed to slits looking almost demonic in the moonlight.

'I just thought it was odd that it had gone. Did you take it? Chuck it out, maybe?' Libby felt herself shaking.

'It's where it belongs,' Sean went on. 'In the bin. Along with this conversation.'

Libby hesitated 'Why are you so defensive all the time? Can't you see how it's affecting me? With everything else that's happened, you could be a bit more sympathetic, Sean. I'm your wife, for God's sake. I'd quite like it if you put my feelings first. To me, all I hear is you protecting someone *else's* feelings. Whoever she is.'

Libby screwed up her eyes, trying not to cry. She felt Sean's breath on her check, then the jolt of the bed as he flipped round and dropped his head back onto the pillow.

'You're not thinking straight,' he said. 'Please, get a grip.'

'Who were you talking to earlier?' Libby said, knowing she was pushing it. Fact was, she didn't care any more. She felt the sting of hot tears burn the inside of her eyelids.

'*What?*' Sean let out a huge sigh. It signalled something, though Libby wasn't sure what. All she knew was that she couldn't let it lie, as though a switch had flicked.

'Who were you talking to on the phone? You hung up as soon as I came into the room.'

'I did not.'

'You *did*.'

'I'm not having this conversation, Libby. Not when the police are out looking for Sasha.'

'And what happens when they find her?' Libby pressed on. 'Will you answer my questions then?'

'*If* they find her,' Sean added, his voice slowing. It was what everyone was worried about.

'They will,' she said. 'It's just when and where.' Libby reached over to her bedside table for her glass of water. 'And then there was the call from that other number. Before we ate dinner, when you had Alice on your lap. You rejected it. You never reject calls.'

'I do if it's from someone I don't want to speak to,' Sean said.

'That's not true. Even if it looks like a nuisance call, you answer it. I know you, Sean Randell. Why did you reject it? It was from a number not in your contacts. And then you had another landline call you cancelled—'

Libby gasped, stifling the scream as the glass flew out of her hand. It took her a moment to realise that Sean had swiped at her, sending it flying, shattering against the wall opposite.

Neither of them said a word. Just breathing. Short and sharp, out of rhythm. Their hearts pounding. Libby listened out for Alice, who was in the next room. And Fred and Marion, who occupied each of the front bedrooms. They'd not shared a bed for years.

'I can't take it, Libby,' Sean said, seething.

'Me neither,' Libby replied through shallow breaths, her body fixed in the same position, her hand up as if she was still holding the glass. Her heart was on fire. 'Was it *her*?' Libby said, her voice strangely calm, even though the rest of her wasn't. She'd overstepped the mark again, couldn't make things worse if she tried.

'*Who*, for God's sake?'

'The woman you're having an affair with. The woman who wrote the note. Is that who you were talking to?'

Libby gasped as she felt the weight of her husband suddenly lying on top of her, expelling the breath from her lungs. His face was close – his eyes wide and bulging with something that she'd never seen before. His arms were pinned either side of her, clamping her down. She wasn't sure if it was hate, love or regret in his eyes. All she knew was that she couldn't move.

'There is no other woman,' he said flatly. 'When will you realise this?' Beside her, Sean's fingers gripped the sheet, twisting it into a knot, pulling it tight around Libby's shoulders. 'I don't know how you can be so selfish at a time like this.'

And, when Libby said nothing, Sean pressed his mouth against hers, kissing her passionately – his tongue probing her mouth more deeply than she'd ever felt before, his hands cupping her face so hard she thought her skull might split, breaking only to tear off her pyjamas. And, eventually, she succumbed, allowing her body to give back what she was receiving, equally as urgently.

After they'd finished, when they'd dropped back onto their pillows, exhausted, sweating, neither of them saying a word, Libby lay awake for most of the night wondering what it was her husband was trying to hide. Or, more importantly, *who*.

CHAPTER TWENTY-SEVEN

Libby stared at Chestnut Cottage from The Green, remembering the first time she'd ever seen the place. It had been snowing, and Sean had held her mittened hand, so excited to be showing her his project.

'It's uninhabitable,' he'd said when he first told her about it. 'And I got it for a song because of all the rot, the roof, the everything. But nothing a few years of hard graft and three times the planned budget won't sort out,' he'd joked.

Libby had seen it in his eyes – the passion for the listed building, wanting to care for it almost as much as he cared for each and every one of his animal patients. Sean had a knack for seeing the life in things, even if there wasn't much of it left. She wondered if that's what he'd noticed in her when their eyes first met in that most clichéd of circumstances across the pub bar. She was down, yes, still feeling bereft after the bad break-up with David a few months earlier, but she'd been determined to dust herself off from his controlling and toxic ways, not allow it to taint her future. Sean had come along at just the right time. Besides, she couldn't deny the attraction she felt for the man she remembered from the gym.

'It's so beautiful,' she'd said that snowy day. She'd literally not been able to close her mouth in awe – not because of the cold or the snowflakes that were landing on her nose, but because the face of the thatched cottage almost seemed to be winking at her, encouraging her inside – the way one end of the thatched roof hung low over one window 'eye' of an upstairs room. 'How did you even find such a place?'

'Ah…' he said in a teasing, drawn-out voice. 'I have friends in the right places,' he went on. 'Property in Great Lyne rarely comes on the open market. It's all about who you know around here.' He'd tapped the side of his nose.

'I'm impressed,' she replied, gazing around the picture-perfect village green with its ginger-stone pub and little school opposite built in the same soft and irregular hunks that looked more like honeycomb toffee than anything. 'So who is it you know?' She gave him one of her smiles – the type he said had attracted him to her in the first place.

'If I told you, I'd have to kill you,' he joked, squeezing her hand and taking her over The Green and up to the front door. 'Seriously though, it's estate people. The big landowner around here owns most of the village properties and occasionally sells off the odd one here and there. Many are rented out by the estate, but this is freehold and she's all mine. A beauty, eh?'

Libby looked up at him, beaming. She couldn't have been more in love. Every minute with Sean had been perfect, but seeing the cottage… well, that symbolised a future. A *perfect* future. Together.

'All *ours*, I should say,' Sean corrected. 'Here… you do the honours.' He handed Libby a set of keys.

'Really?' she said, taking them from him, unable to feel any more special. Snowflakes settled on her eyelashes as she edged the big key into the lock and turned it, her hands fumbling within her mittens. She felt every old lever in the lock give before she pressed down on the latch and opened the door, but before she could even see what was behind it, Sean had scooped her up and carried her over the threshold.

Libby couldn't help squealing and laughing as they ducked their heads to get inside. As she looked around, her nose picked up the smell of damp and rot, though that was quickly overshadowed by the potential. Everything was pretty much as it would have been a hundred years ago – the black cooking range in the kitchen fireplace, complete with its working oven to the side, the original stone sink with a single cold tap above that didn't look as though it had been used in decades. White, furry damp patches effervesced the blood-coloured pamment floor tiles, while the walls were covered in peeling wallpaper. Libby remembered brushing cobwebs off her face, losing her footing as they trod the rickety staircase to find what would be their bedroom, and their delight when they discovered another secret room behind it, which eventually became their en-suite bathroom.

'*Christ*,' Libby said now, clenching her fists and screwing up her eyes, treading the exact same path across The Green towards the front door of Chestnut Cottage. She'd not been able to park directly outside. Not because of police cars this time, but because all the spaces had been taken – and she hadn't wanted to park in the courtyard either. That would have felt too much like 'going home', and she wasn't ready for that yet.

She shuddered as she unlocked the front door, using the same old key as Sean had handed her the first time she'd ever seen the place. Except nowadays they'd got a much newer Yale lock as well.

Libby shrugged off her coat and hung it on one of the hooks in the hallway. She noticed that Alice's little pink denim jacket was on a different peg from usual – the first sign that things had been moved.

In the living room, Libby looked around. She stared at the sofa and table where Sasha's belongings had been left – though they were gone now. She supposed they should have told the police that they'd gathered them up, shoved them in her college backpack. But, in hindsight, as long as they were all there for the police to see and inspect, she didn't think it really mattered.

The cottage felt cold, unloved. The fireplace was still filled with ash – the remains of last Friday's fire. Although, judging by the state of the hearth, it looked as though the police had been through it, picking amongst the embers. Libby reached for the poker, scraping through the mess, finding nothing but ash and a few charred remains of wood. She stared at it, frowning, before scanning around the rest of the room. She couldn't see that anything obvious was missing at first glance – apart from Sasha's stuff, of course.

Libby went through to the kitchen and put on the lights. It felt cold in here too, even though she could hear the tick-tick of the central heating pipes, the soft purr of the boiler in the cupboard in the boot room. She stopped, almost sensing the police's presence – invisible fragments of whatever they'd done still lingering in the cottage. She didn't like it.

'Fu—*uck*...!' she suddenly screamed, tearing at her hair, gripping fistfuls of it, pulling hard. She screwed up her eyes as a deep growl travelled up her throat, resonating around the low-beamed room. Without even knowing what she was doing, she swiped at a couple of dirty glasses left on the kitchen table, sending them skidding off and smashing onto the floor. Glittery shards spread about as she covered her mouth, seeing what she'd done. A broken piece of wine glass with her lipstick still on the rim settled by the fridge – a reminder of the quick drink she and Sean had had before they'd gone out on Friday night.

Libby thumped her fist down on the table, making the flower vase – stuffed with a dying spray of autumn colour – jump and wobble.

'No, no, no, no, *noooo*,' she wailed. 'I can't stand it. I can't *stand* it.' She paced about, trailing her hands over everything – the worktops, the walls, the range cooker – the kitchen that had seen her prepare and cook hundreds of meals for her, Sean and Alice. What she hated the most was that the place she'd called home for the last three years suddenly didn't seem in the *least* like home any more. It felt stripped of its soul. Every ounce of *them* gone.

Libby fell to her knees at the end of the kitchen cupboards. The shelves were crammed with cookbooks, some of which she'd had since she was seventeen years old. She pulled them off, one by one, before flinging the rest to the floor. She grabbed several of them by the spines, letting the pages fall open as she shook them, watching for anything fluttering out in case she was mistaken about where she'd hidden the note. Then she went through them again, her fingers frantically flipping through the pages, pulling out old bookmarks and cut-out recipes flattened from years stuck inside the hardbacks.

Nothing.

She pulled herself to her feet – her knees aching from the cold floor, her entire body shaking. There were only two things on her mind: Sasha, and whoever left that note on her car. And, because both were filling her brain equally, Libby couldn't help but think they were one and the same problem. That they were somehow connected.

'Oh God!' she cried, leaning on the worktop, clutching her head. She knocked a packet of biscuits onto the floor – the ones she'd bought for Sasha to help herself to on Friday night, knowing she would only eat that particular brand. As she picked them up, she saw they were untouched. Then she pulled open the refrigerator door to see what was in there. Just the usual – salad stuff in the crisper drawer, cheese, eggs, a home-baked ham that she thinly sliced each morning for Sean's sandwiches. A few vegetables, including an aubergine she'd been intending to griddle with the steaks that were still wrapped up on the bottom shelf. Saturday night's dinner. Untouched. Of course, the food she'd left for Sasha had gone.

Libby pulled out the steaks along with a few vegetables that had turned mouldy. She wrapped them all up in newspaper and went out to chuck them in the dustbin before dragging it out to the street. She'd forgotten to put it out for the last collection and it was almost overflowing.

She headed back inside to the little room she and Sean used as a study. It was mostly Sean's space for any work he brought home – usually papers he was writing for various publications. Several times lately she'd found him hunched over his laptop in the early hours, the glow of his screen lighting up his tired face. But now she was wondering what else he was doing on his computer late at night. Who he was talking to.

She opened up the laptop and went to log in. They both knew the other's passwords, PINs for phones, social media logins – always had done. But, tapping in the familiar password, Libby realised on the third try that it wasn't her mistyping that was preventing her logging in – it was because the password had been changed. She stared at the screensaver – a group selfie of Alice, Sean and her on the beach at Rock last summer. She screwed up her eyes and slammed the lid closed.

CHAPTER TWENTY-EIGHT

Now

'You didn't tell me if you have a husband,' I whisper to Claire as we're escorted to an interview room. It's something to distract me, to make-believe everything's normal even though my legs feel as though they're about to give way.

After I'd spoken to Claire they'd taken me back to my cell for an hour, maybe more, and I drifted in and out of sleep, my back aching as I lay on the thin plastic mattress, staring up at the camera in the corner. Then they said I was going to be interviewed by the detectives, that my solicitor would be there with me. *Good*, I'd thought, thinking that I'd soon be able to go home, once they realised I hadn't done anything wrong.

'I'm not married,' Claire says quietly, shuffling some papers around once we're seated. I know she's only answering to be polite, that I'm just another face in custody. Perhaps a little different to most – middle-class mother with her own business, a cute little daughter, a professional husband. But, in her eyes, still a potential criminal. A murderer.

I give Claire a look, as though we're best buddies already, that we have a connection even though we've only known each other for less than an hour. But she's all I've got right now. I wonder if Sean has had a phone call yet, knows where I am, if he's outside right this minute trying to arrange my release. I know he'll be doing all he can, frantic with worry.

'Have you ever been in love, then?' I ask her, hearing voices outside in the corridor, layered over the occasional drunken shrieks from the cells further down. I have no idea what time it is, and there are no windows, but it must be late. Is that their tactic – wait until I'm too exhausted and disorientated to answer coherently? I don't even know how long I've been here.

Claire lets out a little laugh. 'Of course,' she says. 'But sometimes love isn't enough.'

I think about this, wondering what else would make it enough. Loyalty, commitment, honesty, trust… *fidelity*?

'Maybe you're right,' I whisper as the guarding officer opens the interview room door. Claire clears her throat and stands up. DI Jones strides in, his big hands wrapped around yet more paperwork, his shirtsleeves rolled up over thick forearms. The edge of a faded greeny-blue tattoo pokes out from beneath the scrunched-up cuff. I recognise the woman with him from when they came to the cottage together. She's also in plain clothes – black tapered trousers, wide at the top to accommodate her middle, and a tucked-in white shirt with a grey tank top underneath. Her dark hair is pulled back in a tight ponytail, a few wisps escaping at the sides, grey roots appearing at her temples. Thick fingers, stocky limbs, eyes that latch on to me as soon as she comes in and sits down, plus a tight mouth that looks as though it would spit bullets. I wouldn't want to mess with her. I *won't* mess with her.

Oh, Sean, I cry in my head, conjuring up an image of him next to me, holding my hand, guiding me through what to say. I wish he was here and, even though he's not, I sense he's close, thinking of me too.

'Detectives,' Claire says, briefly shaking hands with them as they sit down. I don't move. *Can't* move. I hang my head, staring at my lap, hoping I'll wake up at any minute.

'Mrs Randell,' DI Jones says. He's always called me Libby before.

'Sir,' I say, hardly daring to look up, wondering if that's what I should call him.

'As you already know, this is DC McCaulay,' he goes on. 'Do you want to start the recording, please?' he says to her. When the device is active, he states where we are, the time – it turns out it's only twenty past eight in the evening – and then he gives his name and his number, getting the other detective to do the same. 'Also present is…' He looks at my solicitor.

'Claire Swithland, solicitor with Raby, Swithland and Stone,' she says.

'Would you please state your full name and date of birth, Libby,' he says, reverting to my first name.

'Elizabeth Mary Randell, twenty-fourth of February 1979.'

'Thank you. You're under arrest on suspicion of the murder of Sasha Long and we're going to be interviewing you in relation to that. We're going to make sure you know all your rights and ask you some questions, do you understand?'

I nod, staring at my fingers, turning my wedding band around and around, allowing the detective's words to flow through me as he tells me what to expect, what I'm entitled to, repeating that he will be recording the entire interview.

'OK. Let's make a start.' He looks through some papers. 'Tell me about your relationship with your husband, Libby,' he says, leaning back in his chair. It's the first time I've seen that he's got a beer belly. Not a huge one, but the way he's sitting – hands clasped across his chest, legs slightly apart, chair tipped back – shows it straining at his shirt buttons.

I look him in the eye, trying to smile. Sean said it was important to be polite and friendly whenever we dealt with the police. 'What would you like to know?'

'Oh, you know. Day-to-day stuff, how you both rub along, if there are any arguments or maybe you're the perfect dream team?' DI Jones gives a creased smile back.

'We're just normal, I suppose,' I say, wanting to ask why this is even relevant. But I need to stay calm, on track, listen out for questions I don't want to answer. I glance across at Claire and she gives me a little nod, reassuring me. 'Like any married couple.'

'So you have your ups and downs?' DI Jones goes on.

'Of course,' I say. 'It's normal. *We're* normal.'

'Who would you say wears the trousers in the household? You or your husband?' DC McCaulay chips in.

'What?'

'As in who's the boss? There's always one a bit more dominant, wouldn't you say?'

I wrinkle up my nose, looking at each of them before turning to Claire. She gives me another nod. 'I don't know,' I reply. 'Both of us?'

'We're the ones asking the questions, if that's OK with you,' DC McCaulay says.

'Both of us,' I repeat, without the inflection. 'We're equals. We make decisions together and parent Alice together. We both work hard and share all responsibilities.' Sweat breaks out on my back as my heart speeds up. But, of course, that's what they want. I take a breath.

'Have you ever had an affair, Libby?' DC McCaulay continues.

'*What?*'

'An extramarital affair. Have you ever had one?'

'No!' I say, wondering if I should have added 'comment' afterwards.

'How long have you and Sean been married?'

'Nearly five years, and together for going on seven,' I say.

'And were you married before that?'

'No, Sean is my first husband. I was in a relationship for a few years before I met him, but it didn't… it didn't work out.'

'Can you tell us why?' DC McCaulay asks, looking up from notes she's taking.

I swallow, looking at Claire. She mumbles something but DI Jones talks over her. ‘Did you have an affair, Libby?’ He brushes his hand across his nose. ‘Is that why your previous relationship ended?’

I stare at him, my thoughts dragging back to when I was with David, when I met him, how, within a matter of weeks, we knew we wanted to be together forever. We just ‘fitted’ – our bodies and minds slotting together, literally as though we'd been made for each other. That's what David said anyway, on our first date. Then, within three months, he'd convinced me to give up my flat, move in with him, and it wasn't long after that when it all began – him getting upset if I went out with my friends, checking through my phone, following me to work, phoning me about fifty times a day. He was convinced I was having an affair.

‘No,’ I say flatly as old feelings course through me. The familiar denial, making me wonder if I was going mad, if perhaps I'd given the wrong signals to a guy at work and I *was* actually having an affair without even realising it. Sometimes I'd thought it would be easier to say I was, just to stop David going on about it. He'd have thrown me out, at least. Because there was no way he was letting me go otherwise.

‘Does the name David Toft ring any bells?’

‘Yes, he's the person I lived with before I met Sean. I don't see how ’

‘David Toft says you had an affair,’ DC McCaulay chips in. ‘And that's why you split up.’

‘No!’ I cover my face, dropping my head down. ‘You've spoken to him? He's ancient history as far as I'm concerned. He doesn't even know Sasha. He was a controlling—’ I halt myself just in time, but can't help my cheeks colouring, my shoulders tensing, the adrenalin racing through me. ‘Look,’ I say, trying to stop my voice shaking, knowing they want me to lose my cool. ‘David was convinced I was. But I wasn't.’

Claire leans over to me, whispers something in my ear.

'Did you write the note that was left on your car windscreen, Libby?' DI Jones says.

'*What?*' I say, my head spinning as I wonder how they even know about the note. Sean and I agreed not to mention it, deciding that it was irrelevant and, *frankly embarrassing*, he'd said. But perhaps he'd changed his mind. 'Why would I do that?' I sound breathy, panicked.

Stay calm, Lib, Sean told me after the police had left Marion's after yet another visit for what DI Jones described as an informal chat. They'd been to see Jan and Phil too, plus a couple of others in the village. Word got around. Tongues wagged.

'I'll ask you again. Did you write the note that you found on your car windscreen stating that your husband was having an affair?'

Claire leans in again, whispers something.

'No comment,' I say reluctantly, wanting to scream.

'Can you tell me who Angus Prior is?' DC McCaulay asks.

My eyes flip between the two detectives, each of them staring at me.

'I…' My mouth is almost too dry to get the words out. 'I suppose David told you about him too, right? Well, contrary to what you'll have no doubt heard, Angus was a friend. A *good* friend, but that's all. He got me out of a… a bad place.' I don't know why they're mixing up past and present.

'Did David Toft ever have an affair, to your knowledge?'

My heart hurts – a twinge of pain as it clenches and unclenches. 'Almost certainly,' I say. 'Practise what you preach, don't they say? And he was always preaching to me about being unfaithful. But I still don't see what…' I shake my head. I mustn't be argumentative. Just play their game. 'Yes, I believe he did.' The red flags were there but I chose to ignore them. I'll never forgive myself for that.

'So it's fair to say that you were very hurt by the experience, that you'd naturally be wary, even suspicious, of partners in the future?'

'I guess,' I say. 'But I trust Sean.'

'You trust him, or you *trusted* him?'

I shake my head, upturning my palms. 'I trust him.' Then I clench my fists, trying to hide the sweat.

'Is this your handwriting, Libby?' DC McCaulay asks, producing a clear plastic sleeve with half a sheet of slightly crumpled A4 paper in it. She slides it in front of me and, as I lean over, I see it's a shopping list.

'Yes, it is,' I say, only needing to take a glance. Sean always joked about how careful I was with my writing, how it was so different to his scrawl.

'And this?' she continues, producing another piece of paper in a similar sleeve. It's a letter I began writing to my aunt, but never got around to finishing or posting. She loves getting news updates and a couple of photos of Alice in the post. They must have found it in the study.

'Yes, I wrote that too.'

'And did you write this?' the detective asks, passing across yet another piece of paper.

I stare at it, not knowing what to think. 'I… I…' I reach out for the plastic sleeve, picking it up, my eyes scanning over the words.

I'm warning you again about your husband. He's having an affair.

The second note.

'Did you write it?' DI Jones says, echoing his colleague.

My cheeks burn. 'This is not the note I found on my car. I… I don't understand.'

'Please answer the question, Libby. Did you write this? Is it your handwriting?'

I swallow. 'No… no comment,' I say quietly, my head hanging low as I recall hiding it among the other papers on my desk, intending to burn it later. I'd decided not to mention it to Sean – knowing it would do more harm than good – but when I came to destroy it, it had disappeared. Just like the first note. I can't stand to think that Sean took it, but there's no other explanation. And if he's given this note to the police, then why not the first?

Everything will be OK… Just do as I say…

'You seemed pretty certain about the other two handwriting samples. But uncertain about this one.' DI Jones lines up all the samples to face me.

'No comment,' I reply.

'The thing is, Libby, our experts say that the same person wrote all of these samples. Without exception. How do you explain that? I suspect you're not telling me the truth here and that's very serious. Do you know why?'

I give a tiny shake of my head, my shoulders drawn together.

'I'll tell you,' he says, leaning across the table. 'Because it makes me wonder what else you're lying about.' He speaks to me like I'm a child, each word deliberate and drawn out.

I look at them all again. 'But the writing looks different to mine,' I whisper, pointing to the plain block capitals on the note. 'The "I" is leaning the opposite way here, look,' I say quietly, touching my shopping list. 'And the "g" isn't the same. Plus my writing is much smaller. I don't think they look the same at all. I'm sorry, I can't explain it.'

'I think I'll take my handwriting expert's word for it, if that's all the same to you, Libby,' DI Jones says, pausing. 'Were you trying to disguise your handwriting, Libby? Make it look as though it was written by someone else?'

I shake my head. 'No comment.' Then I close my eyes, but all I see is David's face up close to mine, accusing me over and over and over of sleeping with other men… secretly messaging other men… going out for drinks with other men… even looking at other men on television or in the street.

'Is this the note you found on your car, Libby?'

'No.'

'So where is the note that you found on your car and what did it say?'

'What does it have to do with Sasha? I thought *that* was why I'm here, not because of some stupid note.' I half stand up, my fingers gripping the table, but I quickly sit down again when DC McCaulay makes a move. I cover my face, choking back a sob.

'Answer the question, please,' he says.

'It… it said "Sean is having an affair". Or something like that.' Even though the words on the note were emblazoned on my mind from the moment I saw it, it's almost as though it never existed, as though I'd dreamt it all up. 'And I don't know where it is.'

'Let's try this another way,' DI Jones went on. 'Would it be fair to say that whoever wrote the note you say you originally found on your car, also wrote this one?'

'I don't know,' I say. 'No comment.' I hear Claire sighing and fidgeting beside me.

'So where did you find this, what appears to be a second note, Libby?'

'Nowhere,' I say. 'I've never… It wasn't…' I fall silent as I remember the pen shaking in my hand as I tried to disguise my writing. 'No comment.'

'Let's move on for a moment,' DI Jones says, gathering up the plastic sleeves. 'You went out for a meal with your husband on Friday the nineteenth of October at the Old Fox pub in Chalwell, is that correct?'

'Yes.'

You already know this a thousand times over, I want to yell.

'Was there any particular reason for the meal out?'

You know this too!

'It was to clear the air.'

'Meaning what?' DC McCaulay asks.

I sigh. 'I'd got upset about finding the note on my car.'

'And did it clear the air?'

'Yes,' I say, forcing a tiny smile so I don't betray the truth – that going out made things a hundred times worse. A *million* times worse.

'Can you recall what you had to eat that night?'

'Yes, we had a seafood sharing platter to start with – prawns, a couple of oysters each, some deep-fried squid, scallops and some crab claws. Then I had a mushroom and truffle risotto while Sean ordered the lamb shanks.'

'Did you have any wine?'

'Yes, a little,' I say, feeling the colour rise in my cheeks again.

'Did you have dessert?' DC McCaulay asks, fiddling with her pen.

'We were too full for dessert,' I say. 'The main courses were generous.'

'What time would you say you left the Old Fox pub?'

I stare at the ceiling. I've already told him this several times before, too. 'It's hard to say exactly to the minute. We chatted to some friends in the bar first, then ate our meal slowly, lingering between courses. Then we sat and talked for ages afterwards. I'd say it was just before eleven. Maybe a bit after,' I add, hearing Sean's voice in my head.

'You seem very certain about what you ate, yet rather unclear about the time you left.'

'That's as precise as I can be.'

'How did you pay the bill?'

'Is this relevant?' I ask, wishing I hadn't. 'Is it helping to finding Sasha? If it is, I don't mind but I don't see—'

'How did you pay the bill?' the detective repeats.

'Cash,' I say. 'It was quicker.'

'You were in a hurry?' McCaulay asks. 'Why?'

'Actually, no, I remember now. The card machine wasn't working when I went to the bar to pay. That's why I used cash. I wasn't in a hurry.'

'You went to the bar to pay the bill? Don't you usually pay at the table there? Last time I took the missus to the Old Fox, that's how it worked.'

I shake my head, shrugging. 'I think service was a bit slow. I can't remember. I probably thought it would be best to pay at the bar.'

'In cash.'

'Yes.'

'How did you get home?' DC McCaulay asks.

'In a taxi.' I clasp my fingers together, to stop my hands shaking. It doesn't work.

'How did you pay for the taxi?'

'Oh…' I think, remembering Sean getting out of the car, leaving me to sort out the fare, the tension hanging thick between us. 'I can't recall. It was late. Probably cash too. Maybe Sean took care of it.'

'Do you recognise this?' DC McCaulay says, sliding across another plastic sleeve with a photograph inside.

'Yes, I think so,' I say. 'Is that my scarf?'

'Perhaps *you* can tell us that,' she goes on.

'I think it is, yes.' I take a closer look. 'Yes, it's definitely my scarf. I thought it was lost.'

'You left it in the taxi,' DI Jones says. I'm just about to thank them for finding it but my mouth snaps closed. 'The taxi your husband phoned for at 9.12 that evening, and the taxi you paid for at 9.32 on your Lloyds debit card ending 4803.'

I stare at the wall behind the detective. It's like a cinema screen, playing everything out as I remember following Sean into the house after the taxi dropped us home, him storming off inside as I called out to Sasha, telling her we were home early, asking if Alice had been OK. I jolt as I remember how, a short while later, he'd grabbed me, how I'd screamed, how he'd yelled at me in the living room when I broke down. And then he'd slapped me.

'Libby?' DI Jones says.

I give him a look, touching my cheek, almost still feeling the sting.

'I think it's time you told us the truth,' he says, his head tipped to one side, his arms clamped across his chest as he leans back. 'Don't you?'

'No comment,' I reply, staring at the wall again.

CHAPTER TWENTY-NINE

Before

Libby sat back in Sean's chair in the study. What was she *doing*, trying to get into his computer? Every suspicious thought she had about him was destroying her trust, tearing their marriage apart. She stared at Alice's little face on a photograph on the mantelpiece. She remembered taking it, snapping it just as her daughter's mouth opened to take a lick at the strawberry ice cream she was holding. Her face and shoulders were sandy from falling off the body board Sean had been teaching her how to use, and her hair was ratty and wet, straggling around her neck.

Libby took a breath and stood up. Enough was enough. Things had to get back to normal some time, though she admitted that life up at Marion's had been a kind of refuge – something she never thought she'd say. All she knew was that she wasn't relishing the idea of moving back into the cottage. She'd barely got dressed for days but, with a little coaxing from Marion, something had made her shower, put on some clothes, brush her hair and drag herself down to see what state the cottage was in. If she didn't at least try to make it their home again, she wasn't sure she'd ever be able to come back.

In the kitchen, she swept up the broken glass and wiped down every surface with disinfectant, spraying frantically as she went. She even cleaned all the doorknobs and anything else the police were likely to have touched – as if they themselves were infected. As she went meticulously around the room, she found more and more smears of what looked like black powder – fingerprinting residue, she supposed. As she rubbed hard at the door paintwork, the front of the fridge, she wondered what, if anything, they'd found.

In the living room, Libby cleaned out the fireplace, taking the ash out to the dustbin on the street, squashing it down until a cloud of dust billowed up in her face. Back inside, she plumped up all the sofa cushions, dusted and polished the furniture and vacuumed the floor.

Upstairs, Libby stood in Alice's bedroom doorway, her heart sinking at the mess. She was sure that her daughter's bedroom had been reasonably neat, but now it looked as though Alice had got most of her toys out as well as all her clothes. Every drawer in the chest was open, with little T-shirts spilling out, and the wardrobe was the same, with clothes fallen off their hangers. As she'd done downstairs, she set to and tidied it up, making sure every surface was polished and the floor clean.

And her and Sean's room was no better. Even the bed had had its sheets stripped and taken away. Libby cringed as she saw that the bedside table drawers had been left half open, but the personal stuff she and Sean kept there was thankfully just as they'd left it.

'I don't understand why they'd want to go through our clothes,' Libby said to herself, sighing as she hung up dropped blouses and shirts. The cupboard above the wardrobe had had a particularly good going-through, it seemed, and some items had fallen out. Libby kept some handbags up there, a few belts and a couple of hats, while Sean had some hand weights shoved at the back. There was also a shoebox filled with things Alice had made or drawn for them that they hadn't had the heart to throw out.

Libby dragged a chair across, grabbing some stuff off the floor and shoving it back in the top cupboard. She tried to push the doors closed, but they wouldn't click shut and kept popping open.

A couple of items fell to the floor, so she tried again, rearranging things until a sweat was breaking out on her face – not from exertion as such, but more frustration at having to do this in the first place.

'*Damn*,' she said, when something else dropped out, almost hitting her in the face. When she got down to retrieve it, she saw it was a small gift bag with a tag attached. Inside, something was wrapped up in gold and black foil paper – only small, about the size of the mini-cereal packets Alice liked.

Libby sat on the bed and looked at the tag. The words 'with love x' were written on it, nothing else – no name. She recognised Sean's handwriting – his oversized and messy scrawl, as though his hand wasn't a part of him whenever he held a pen. Her breathing quickened and her hands shook as she took out the wrapped item. Had Sean bought her a present and hidden it away? She had no idea why he would. It wasn't her birthday for a few months yet, or Mother's Day or an anniversary of any kind. Knowing how last-minute he was, it was too early for him to be thinking about Christmas presents. He was very much a two-days-before man, and other family members' presents usually fell to her to buy.

'Perhaps he just wanted to buy me something nice for the hell of it,' she whispered to herself, her heart slowing a little. Maybe to help make amends after everything, she thought. She even managed a small smile at the thought of his random kindness, felt guilty for having found it, even if it was by accident. Though if she was honest, Sean had always been more a bunch of flowers man – though never petrol station chrysanthemums. He'd sometimes dive into the florist's near the vet's practice at lunchtime and surprise her with a handmade bouquet when he came home.

'Unless it's not for *me*,' she added, turning the present over and over in her hands. Without opening it, there was no way to tell. It didn't rattle or smell of anything, and there was nothing to glean by feeling its shape. It was just a rectangular box.

Was this gift for *her*? Libby wondered. The other woman? The thought made her want to throw it across the room. She picked at one end of the neatly stuck-on Sellotape, seeing if it would peel off cleanly, but the paper began to tear. If she unwrapped it, there was not much chance of making good again. Sean would know it had been opened.

In an impulsive moment and not caring about the consequences, Libby pulled off the paper, revealing a black and gold box, similar in style to the paper. Whatever it was, she could tell it was good quality just from the box itself and, as she lifted the lid, it took her a moment to realise what was inside. The silver lighter was bedded into a grey satin interior and, as she took it out, she saw it was an old-fashioned flip-style one with an engraving in a panel on the side. It looked expensive.

Libby turned it over in her hands, knowing immediately that it couldn't possibly be for her. She had never smoked a cigarette in her life.

She stared at the symbol or whatever it was engraved into its side, tears collecting in her eyes. She had no idea what it meant, though it reminded her of something – she just couldn't place what. It looked for all the world like a tall letter M but with a little arrow pointing downwards on the longer right-hand stroke.

'Maybe it's a present for Fred,' Libby whispered hopefully. But she'd only ever seen Fred smoke a cigar once or twice at Christmas. And besides, he and Sean didn't have the type of relationship where they exchanged gifts. She stared at the symbol, thinking perhaps she was mistaken, that it was in fact an N not an M, but whichever way she looked at it, it was making her feel sick.

Why had Sean bought someone a lighter? Even if he was a smoker, she knew he wouldn't have bought it for himself – and he wouldn't have written a gift tag either, let alone write 'with love'.

No, this gift was for someone else. Someone *special*.

Libby's hands were shaking. She didn't know whether to wrap it up again and put it back, or shove it in Sean's face and confront him. In the end, she did neither. She just stood there, almost in tears, as she heard the front door opening – the familiar click of the old latch downstairs.

'Sean?' she called out, quickly shoving the gift bag and lighter under the duvet. She would have to wrap it up properly again later. 'Is that you?' But no one called back a reply.

CHAPTER THIRTY

'*Jan…*' Libby gasped, standing in the living room doorway, after creeping downstairs. She let out the deep breath she'd been holding. 'You scared the life out of me.' Already on edge, Libby was shaking, but mainly from relief. When Sean hadn't replied, she'd assumed the worst – an intruder. She was annoyed with herself for not locking the front door, but the poor woman was distraught.

Jan stared up at her from where she was kneeling on the floor, her face streaked with tears. Her hands were spread flat on the sofa cushions and her head dropped back down onto the seat. Libby saw the gentle juddering of her shoulders as she began to cry again.

'Oh, *Jan*,' she said, going up to her. 'I know… I *know*.' She hated that she was suffering so much.

'I'm sorry, I should have knocked. I wasn't thinking,' she said, lifting her head, sniffing. 'But I just wanted to be close to where she last was,' Jan said. 'Or, at least, where she was last seen. Connect with her somehow. Do you understand that?'

'Of *course*,' she said, rubbing her back. 'Would you like some tea?'

Jan shook her head. 'What happened, Libby? Where *is* she? I can't stand it!' She was suddenly on her feet, her face twisted with worry. 'And where's all her stuff gone? What's happened to it?' Then there was anger in her voice, her arms gesturing wildly. She wasn't thinking straight.

'The police have taken it,' Libby said. 'I'm sure they'll give you it back when they're finished with it.'

'You mean when they find a *body*. Is that what you're saying?' She got up and strode to the leaded front window, staring out, palms pressed against the glass. 'And what the hell does *he* want?' she said, leaning forward, straining her neck to see up the street. Her breath fogged the panes.

'Who?' Libby came up beside her.

'Phil, just now. He was walking past, looking in,' she said. 'He's probably following me, wanting to know where I am. We're supposed to be separated, for God's sake, but I can't take his paranoia and suspicion any more. I just can't… not now.' Jan broke down in tears again and, as Libby pulled her close and hugged her, all she could see was David's snarling face from years ago, accusing her, wearing her down until she didn't know which way up she was.

'Thanks for saving me earlier,' Libby said to Sean. 'Jan was in a state.' There wasn't much conviction in her voice but it was true – Sean had come along at just the right moment to quell Jan's increasingly agitated mood, especially after she'd seen Phil lurking outside.

Libby and Sean were at the farmhouse, sitting at the kitchen table while Marion read Alice a bedtime story. Fred was out at the pub – his usual place on a Friday night – and wouldn't be back until later. Libby lifted the hem of her T-shirt and wiped her nose on it, making a face back when Sean gave her a look. She didn't care if he thought she was disgusting. Things had gone beyond that.

'Thanks for saving you *again*, you mean?' His tone was sour, like the whisky they were sharing. Unusually for Sean, he'd come home with a bottle earlier and already Libby felt drunk – not the pleasant kind of light-headedness she sometimes enjoyed after a couple of glasses of wine. More a roaring burn ripping through her brain, disorientating her, obliterating what was on her mind.

She stared at him, ignoring his comment. 'I don't think I can ever go home, you know. It's just not the same.'

'Don't be ridiculous.' Sean sloshed more whisky into their glasses. 'We have to.'

Libby wondered how she would ever see Chestnut Cottage in the same light again – especially since finding the lighter. Her shoulders tensed as she remembered the little tag… *with love x*. He'd chosen to write those words, had consciously made the decision to buy a gift for someone, wrap it and label it, intending to give it with love. All Libby knew for sure was that it wasn't for her.

'Give me your phone,' Libby suddenly said, quite calmly, holding out her hand.

'What?'

'I want to see who you've been calling and messaging. Give me your phone.'

'Oh for Christ's sake,' Sean said, standing up. 'Not this again, Lib. Don't you think there's actually a shedload of bigger stuff going on right now?' He pushed his face up close to hers so she could smell his whisky breath. Then he paced about the kitchen, glaring at her every time he passed. He swiped up his drink and drank it down in one go.

Libby bit her lip, trying to stop herself blurting out about the gift. She knew he'd deny it, that he'd already have a cover story concocted – that he was looking after it for a mate, or that it wasn't his and he'd just found it somewhere, or that he'd bought it as a gift for someone long before they met and forgotten about it. He'd convince her she was going crazy, that she was mad, paranoid, not thinking straight. And perhaps she was.

Without saying a word, Libby took herself off into the downstairs toilet and leant on the vanity unit, staring into the mirror. She saw a gaunt, tired woman staring back – a woman she barely recognised. Food had been the last thing on her mind this past week and sleep was something that came in fits and starts. If she did drop off, she'd wake in a panic, thoughts screaming through her mind, her body drenched in sweat. Her face was pale, with dark circles under her eyes.

As for taking care of Alice in the way she normally would, she shuddered at the thought of how she'd allowed Marion to do everything. But that was Marion's way. At least this time, Libby was grateful for her doing things her way, even if it did make her feel like less of a mother.

As Libby splashed cold water on her face, she realised life as she knew it was falling apart. *Had* fallen apart. Against Sean's advice, she'd cancelled this week's dinner clients – despite needing the money – barely even finding the willpower to clean her teeth, let alone cater for dozens of people. She'd only made it up to the cottage earlier after a good talking-to from Marion. It was the shock of seeing the place in disarray after the forensics team had been in that prompted her to tackle a tidy-up – but then that had ended on finding the gift. The thought of moving back, after everything, was unthinkable. Home was tainted, stained with indelible memories.

Libby dried her face on the hand towel and went back into the kitchen.

'Oh – hello, Dan,' she said, stopping in her tracks.

Sean's son stood there, his school bag slung over his shoulder, his fringe spiked with some kind of gel. Libby clamped her arms around her body, suddenly feeling freezing cold.

'Hi, Libby. Mum dropped me off,' he said, but Libby didn't get a chance to reply as Sean came back into the room. Natalie was following close behind.

When Libby saw the lipstick mark on Sean's cheek, she forced herself to bite her lip yet again.

'Is Marion here?' Natalie said cheerfully, dumping her peach-coloured slouchy bag on the table. It bumped against Libby's whisky glass, nearly knocking it onto the floor. Libby lunged for the drink, getting a glimpse of the bag's contents: make-up pouch, the bristles of a hairbrush poking out from beneath. A matching leather purse. A packet of cigarettes. Libby gripped the whisky tumbler in both hands, afraid it might crack from the pressure. Natalie was certainly the type to use – no, *demand* – an expensive lighter. 'How did her hospital appointment go?' she asked, staring directly at Libby.

'Appointment?' she replied, hating that Natalie knew more than her. She glanced at Sean. 'Yes, yes, fine, I think,' she said, swallowing.

'Mum's around somewhere,' Sean said, sliding a hand around his ex-wife's waist so he could squeeze past. 'Fancy a drink, Nat?'

Natalie stared at Libby – a look on her face that showed she was trying not to sweep her eyes up and down her. Rather she took her in in one pitying glance. 'No… no thanks,' she said slowly. 'I can't stay long. Looks like someone's started early, though.' She stared at the glass in Libby's hands.

'Well, we both have, actually,' Libby replied, but when she looked for Sean's glass, it was gone. 'It's been a tough few days,' she added, knocking back a large swig, trying not to choke.

'Ah, there you are, Mum,' Sean said, glancing behind Libby almost as if she wasn't there. 'Nat's here. You didn't find a bracelet, did you? You know, the one with all the silver charms?'

Libby glared at Sean, feeling her stomach knot. What was he *doing*? Dan pulled out a chair at the table as his grandmother greeted him, planting a kiss on his head. *The perfect family*, she thought to herself, staring at the four of them, not feeling a part of any family at all, let alone a perfect one. Then her eyes were drawn to Dan's schoolbooks – an exercise book in particular. She stared down at his neat print, her mind trying to catch up with her racing heart as she sidled round, trying to get a better look.

'Oh no, don't tell me you've lost your lovely bracelet, Nat?' Marion said, frowning. 'It's full of such wonderful memories.'

'I know, I'm gutted, Marion. The catch has always been a bit loose and I've been meaning to get it repaired. I have no idea when or where I might have lost it, which doesn't help. I'm checking everywhere I've been.'

'Oh dear, I'm so sorry,' Marion said, glancing at Sean a couple of times. 'But of course, if it turns up, I'll let you know.'

Libby looked from Sean to Marion to Natalie and back to Dan and his schoolbooks, her entire body tense. To stop herself saying anything else she'd regret for the third time in less than an hour, she downed the rest of her whisky and excused herself, fighting back the tears as she went upstairs to run herself a bath.

Ten minutes later, as she sank down into the water, she wondered if she was going mad – seeing things that weren't there. Seeing what she *wanted* to see – anything to make reality different. Unsure what to believe, Libby allowed herself to slide further down into the water, her hair billowing out as she submerged, praying that when she resurfaced, everything bad would be washed away.

CHAPTER THIRTY-ONE

'Here,' Marion said, handing Libby a cup of chamomile tea. After Natalie had left, Sean had decided to go down to the local for a couple of pints. Libby doubted he'd talk with his father – each man preferring to sit at opposite ends of the bar if they happened to be in there together, chatting with their own friends. Sean had barely said a word before he left and Libby was relieved when he'd gone, watching in silence as he slung his Barbour jacket on. He'd mumbled a 'don't wait up' to her before sending a quick text to someone and shoving his phone in his pocket, closing the back door behind him, his limp more pronounced than ever. Libby wasn't sure if he'd meant to slam it.

'Drink up. It'll help you relax,' Marion said, taking a crocheted throw from the arm of the sofa. She draped it over Libby who, after her bath, had put on clean pyjamas. She'd brought a few extra things up from the cottage, making her conviction to not move back any time soon evident, despite Sean saying they must. The farm, even though it was old-fashioned and had none of the comforts of home, suddenly seemed like the safest place to be.

'Thanks,' Libby said, staring into the mug. She squashed the teabag with the spoon.

'I know it's hard, love, but you need to stay strong.'

'Sean tries to be brave but I know when he's stressed,' Libby said, blowing on her tea. 'His knee gets worse.'

'It always has done,' Marion went on. 'When he was younger, I used to think he put his limp on for attention. I know he doesn't.'

'Tell me about his accident,' Libby said. The warm bath had made her feel unusually relaxed, as if, just for a few moments, she could switch off. 'He never talks about it.'

Marion looked uncomfortable. 'It was a long time ago,' she said, as if that was reason not to discuss it. 'Some things are best forgotten.'

'But I want to know,' Libby said, refusing to be fobbed off. 'He's my husband, after all.'

'Then maybe best he tells you himself?' Marion said, but Libby was having none of it.

'How old was he when it happened?'

Marion touched her head. 'Seventeen, if I remember rightly.'

'Had he been drinking?' Libby said with a smile. 'I've heard what those village boys were like – him, Chris, Dean, Tony and Phil. Sean told me they pretty much graduated straight out of Scouts and into the local.' Sean was still good friends with many of the guys from his youth – he'd been to school with some of them since the age of five – though not all had ended up as successful as him. But, despite taking different directions in life, they were still friends, seeing each other when they could – and they'd welcomed Libby into their community when she and Sean had got together. She couldn't have asked for more.

'No, love, he hadn't been drinking, despite the reprobates he used to hang out with.' She gave a tight smile. 'But most of them came good in the end. As good as could be expected, anyway.'

'You must be very proud of Sean,' Libby said. 'He's such a good vet, and a brilliant dad.'

Marion smiled again. 'Of course,' she said. 'I just wish Fred felt the same.' She slowly covered her mouth, as if she'd not meant to say anything.

'Oh?' Libby knew there was tension between father and son, but whenever she'd asked Sean about it, he always changed the subject. She wasn't sure if it was just healthy rivalry or something deeper.

Marion sighed, clasping her hands around her mug. 'Fred always expected Sean to do a stint in the army, as he and his grandfather and great-grandfather had done. After the military, Fred was going to hand over the farm. He'd got it all planned out. It's the way it's always been in this family.'

'The army?' Libby said. 'Sean's never mentioned that. He doesn't mind shoving his arm up a cow's behind, but I can't see him in camo gear on his belly in the mud with a rifle.' Libby managed another laugh.

'Ever since he was born, Fred had plans for him. We knew soon after that he'd be our only child.' Marion briefly touched her tummy. Libby suspected her health issues went way back. 'Fred's old-fashioned like that and believed you weren't a man until you'd served your country. But then the accident...' Marion trailed off, looking away.

'Go on,' Libby said, noticing the tears in her eyes.

Marion shook her head and sniffed. 'Sean and a couple of his mates were out baling. We'd not long switched to the big round ton bales, you know the kind? Fred was made up with the new machinery that spewed them out. He and the boys were out in the fields, collecting them up for storage. Fred used to offer his services to other local farmers too, and he was on the tractor, spike at the front, using it to lift them onto the trailer. Sean had been driving tractors and working on the farm since he was ten. He knew all there was to know.' She stopped, taking a breath and a sip of tea.

'It happened after lunch. I used to make them all sandwiches to take. It was the summer holidays and they liked the extra cash. Sean was meant to be driving the tractor with the trailer, where all the bales were stacked to take back to storage.'

Libby saw something in Marion's eyes – something that made her want to put a hand on her arm and tell her to stop, not to go over painful memories if it was hard. But there was also something compelling, even ominous, about the way she was recounting the story. Libby wanted to know everything.

'Anyway,' Marion went on, shaking her head as if to stop herself saying too much, 'there was no way the army would take him with that knee injury. That's what Fred said. That he'd be a liability. Said it was best Sean laid low, lived here with us until it all blew over.'

'So he didn't even apply to join up?'

'No, love,' Marion said. 'Not after… after everything. After the… accident. That's when… well, that's when things turned bad between Sean and his father. Sean had… well, it was just a *blip*, Fred eventually convinced himself – and me. Nothing more than stupid behaviour. Turns out he was right.' Marion gave Libby her biggest smile yet, touching her arm. 'It all turned out fine.'

'I see,' Libby said, not completely understanding. Fred had always been reserved, a bit gruff and unapproachable, though she'd always thought he had a soft spot for her, as if he approved of her.

'Anyway, I can't tell you how pleased we both were when you came into Sean's life, love,' Marion went on. 'After Natalie, you're the next best thing that's ever happened to him.'

CHAPTER THIRTY-TWO

Libby stared at the contents of the catering fridge in the barn, wondering what to chuck out first. It was a reminder of how things were, before Sasha went missing, when she'd bought ingredients, had menus planned, clients booked in. Everything normal.

'Damn,' she whispered, reaching for a dish of meat glaze that she'd saved. She stared into it, almost seeing her reflection through the clingfilm in the viscous surface of the dark liquid. Then she tipped it into the stainless-steel sink, running the tap, watching as the plum-coloured liquid swirled around.

Blood, Libby thought, as it spiralled down the plughole.

Her nerves on fire, she grabbed dish after dish, packet after packet, chucking them into the large waste bin near the stable door. She looked out at the empty space next to her car. Sean was still at work, even though it was nearly seven o'clock. Marion had agreed to have Alice stay at the farm another couple of nights, until things were more settled at home.

Libby hadn't wanted to come back to the cottage that morning but had reluctantly made her way out to the car where Sean stood, clutching their scant belongings in a few carrier bags and a holdall. She'd felt mentally frog-marched home, but they'd talked about it at length while lying in bed the night before and, ultimately, she knew Sean was right. The longer they stayed at the farm, the harder it would be to come back.

When the fridge was empty of out-of-date ingredients, Libby set to work unpacking the haul she'd collected from the supermarket earlier that afternoon. Running out of time, she hadn't had the luxury of picking and choosing local organic ingredients, and had missed the wholesalers' day earlier in the week. What she'd managed to find in the aisles would have to suffice for her next client – she'd figure out some good recipes. If she let anyone else down, word would soon spread. Her business was built on reputation and she couldn't afford to lose more work.

'Don't be hard on yourself, Lib,' Sean had said. 'Mum's in her element with Alice. You might have had to cancel some clients, but you've still got bookings for this week, right? And why not take some time out and treat yourself? Maybe get your nails done? It'll do you good.'

Libby had nodded, staring at his chest as he gently held her. 'But how will I ever look at anything in the kitchen ever again without thinking of Sasha?' she said, her voice wavering.

'Maybe have a clear-out – in the kitchen as well as your mind. Then it'll be easier to block out. It's the only way, Lib. Do you trust me?'

'I trust you,' she'd said, staring into his eyes. Sean had always been a coper, a fixer, the one who made things better. 'I really do,' she added, just so he knew.

Libby often listened to music as she cooked – David Bowie to Mozart and everything in between. She'd already tried a couple of times to construct tomorrow's menu to a backdrop of sound – at full volume and low – but it hadn't worked. Silence was equally as deafening as she made a list of the ingredients she'd forgotten to pick up earlier. The kitchen might be clean and organised, and the old ingredients consigned to the bin, but her state of mind was far from that.

She stared at the notebook she kept for inspiration, pen in hand, willing her mind to function in the way it had until a little over a week ago. She tapped the pen on the work surface, trying to decide how best to cater for the dietary requirements requested without having to compromise the starter and canapés. People with allergies or intolerances didn't like to be singled out, she'd learnt, so she always made a point of making similar dishes for everyone as far as she could. It was at times like this that she was grateful she'd frozen some vegan sauces and various other special meals for just such instances. They were perfect as a fall-back option now as she simply didn't have time to do different versions of the same meal.

It wasn't until she touched her cheek that she realised the tears were streaming down her face. She reached for a tissue, blowing and wiping, staring into space for what seemed like ages before something inside switched, making her lock up the kitchen, go back into the cottage, grab her phone, handbag and keys, and get in the car. She simply couldn't concentrate on work.

Libby headed straight to Fran's house. She knew she wouldn't mind her just turning up and she needed someone to talk to. With no parking spaces immediately outside, she drove around the block several times before finding a spot a couple of streets away. She bleeped the car locked and walked back to Fran's, almost in robotic mode, and rang the bell of the Victorian terrace. She was still fighting back the tears when the door opened, but broke down completely when Fran spread her arms wide and beckoned her inside.

CHAPTER THIRTY-THREE

'Right,' Fran said. 'Sit, eat, drink. Not necessarily in that order.' She pressed Libby down into a chair at the tiny kitchen table. 'You look so thin. When did you actually last put anything between your lips?'

Libby couldn't help the laugh – a cross between hysteria and relief. 'Says the woman with a fag hanging out of her mouth.'

'Fair point,' Fran said, flicking her ash out of the back door. 'Get this in you.' She passed across a plate of things she'd plucked from the fridge – salami, olives, cheese, as well as some crusty French bread – arranging them on a plate. 'And get this in you too,' she added, handing over a large glass of wine. 'You can stay the night.' Libby had already told her Alice was with Marion.

'Maybe I will,' Libby replied. 'Sean is… well, he'll no doubt be working late again. I don't think he can stand being around me, but I can't stand being at home alone either.'

'Which is why we'll throw some fresh linen on the spare bed and work our way through this.' She held up the bottle of wine. 'And possibly that too,' she added, pointing to another bottle in the rack.

'I love you,' Libby said. 'God knows what I'd do without you right now.'

'You don't think I've said the same about you over the years?' Fran went on, stubbing out her cigarette and gathering the food plate and wine. She ushered Libby through to her small living room, turning on the gas fire and pulling the curtains closed. 'Bollocks to the world tonight. It's just you, me and whatever misery we choose to invite. OK?'

'OK,' Libby said, grinning and falling backwards onto the large sofa. As she wiped her eyes, she couldn't help noticing that the framed photograph of Fran and Chris, her late husband, had been moved from its usual place on the mantelpiece and was now barely visible on a side table over by the window. She wondered if it was indicative of Fran finally moving on, of letting go of the only man she'd ever truly loved and, she believed, the only man who had ever truly loved her back. 'And I'm sorry,' she added. 'You don't need this.'

'I'm not keeping score, Lib, but you're way in credit in that department, so chin up and spew it out. What's going on – apart from the obvious? I know you better than you think.'

Libby smiled, knowing that was true. Back when they lived together – a pair of naive twenty-two-year-olds not long out of university, grappling with the transition from student to 'proper grown-ups', it was Libby who seemed to master the art of adulting better than Fran. She was always a shoulder to cry on, the picker-upper of the fragments of Fran's heart. 'You give it away too easily,' she'd told her after one particularly bad break-up. 'How long was it this time? Three weeks and you're telling him you love him?'

'He told me first,' Fran had sniffed. 'And I believed him.'

'I know,' Libby replied, rocking her back and forth on the bed. 'But don't listen to what men tell you, Franny. Listen to what they *show* you.'

'Apart from the obvious…?' Libby said, turning back to the present as she sipped her wine. 'It's the note. I can't get it out of my mind. It's like… my thoughts are a load of laundry that got knotted in the tumble drier. They keep spinning round, getting more and more tangled. Every time I think of Sasha, it reminds me why we went out for the meal in the first place. Then I'm back to the note again, who wrote it, and then Sasha is in my head again, and round and round it goes. I even once suspected Sash…' Libby trailed off, shaking her head.

'Lib?' Fran said after a pause. She sat forward, pouring more wine. 'You don't think…?'

The two women stared at each other. 'It's crossed my mind,' she said. 'Of *course* it has.'

'But she was… *is*… a kid,' Fran said. 'Sean wouldn't go there, would he?'

'No, no I don't think so,' Libby replied. 'I'm certain he wouldn't.' Then she fell silent, taking an olive and putting it in her mouth.

'Sounds to me like you're still overthinking this, my love. The note and Sasha are completely separate, if you want my tuppence worth.'

'I found something else,' Libby said, needing to get it off her chest. 'Don't judge, but Sean's been really secretive lately. He's glued to his phone too.'

'Found what?'

'Apart from him changing the password on his laptop?'

Fran shrugged, made a face as if that was inconsequential.

'I found a gift. A present. It was hidden away in our bedroom.'

'Lucky you,' Fran said. 'See? He's a good guy, Lib. Chris was like that… always surprising me with thoughtful little things…'

Libby waited until the tears in Fran's eyes had melted away.

'This is a bit different. It was all wrapped up and labelled "with love" in Sean's writing. It even had a kiss on it.' She choked back a sob, conscious that Fran was also tearful.

'And your problem is?'

'It was a lighter, Fran. An expensive-looking one. With an engraving.'

'Oh,' Fran said quietly, standing up. 'In that case, I'd better replenish supplies.' She went to the kitchen to fetch the other bottle of wine.

A moment later, Libby got the faint smell of cigarette smoke winding its way inside. She knew Fran would be standing at her back door, puffing out into the night. She'd tried to give up many times before but had always failed. She didn't nag her like she had in the past – the last year had been tough, after all. Tough on them all, but mainly Fran. Losing Chris had been a curveball no one was expecting. Once diagnosed, the cancer had torn through him.

'He didn't want me to see him suffer, any more than he wanted to suffer. He was the bravest person I've ever known.' Fran was with him when he passed away, and Sean only an hour before that. Sean had known Chris since school; he was one of the gang. *One of the good guys*, he'd said when Libby had first been introduced years before. While Sean had played matchmaker, it was Libby who'd actually engineered Fran and Chris meeting up. She knew they'd be perfect for each other and, when a work opportunity brought Fran to the area, it all seemed perfect. *Too perfect*, as Fran had once admitted, concerned it would end up the same as her previous relationships.

'All I want is for you to stop overanalysing everything,' Fran said when she came back in with more wine. I know things are rubbish right now – double shit – but none of it is your fault and you can't control any of it. You're a beautiful woman with a heart of gold and you've helped me through the darkest time of my life. I don't want you falling down some rabbit hole of self-indulgent misunder—'

'Did you hear that?' Libby said, straining her ears.

'No. And stop changing the subject. Just stay real, Lib. Stop worrying about that note and let the police do their job. It's a tragic situation and I hope to God they find the poor girl. I've been following it on the news. They found a shoe or something and—'

'Did they confirm it was Sasha's?' Libby said, still listening out. 'One of the guys on the search Sean organised discovered it.'

'Yes, they said it was hers,' Fran said, nodding. 'And as for all this suspicion with Sean, give the guy a break. He's a good man and you're lucky to have him. Trust me on that one. Life's too short and… and…' She sipped more wine, making no attempt to hide the tears as she broke down. 'I'm sorry, I just get so lonely and—'

'Oh, Fran,' Libby said, going over to hug her. She listened again. 'Did you lock the back door?' Libby said, turning towards the kitchen. 'I swear I heard something.'

'I definitely shut it. But the boiler makes odd noises,' Fran said, sniffing. 'It's been on its last legs for ages. Chris used to tweak it but I don't know what he did. I've been meaning to call an engineer though—'

'Hear that?' Libby said, holding up her hand. 'I'm going to check.' She stood up but halted halfway across the room. 'I'm sorry, Fran… I don't mean to be insensitive. I know you're still grieving. And I know how lonely you must feel, but it's a process and it takes time.' She paused for a moment, making a sympathetic face, before heading out to the kitchen, gasping when she saw the back door was wide open.

CHAPTER THIRTY-FOUR

Libby went back to tell Fran what she'd seen, but stopped dead in her tracks.

'*Sean…*' she said, her mouth dropping open. He was the last person she expected to be standing there, with Fran, clearly having just answered the front door, showing him inside.

Fran dabbed at her eyes with a scrunched-up tissue, trying to look normal. 'Please, come in, Sean,' she said quietly. 'And don't be silly, you're not interrupting anything. Sit down. Do you want a drink?' She looked nervous.

'What are you… what are you doing here?' Libby asked, hating the way she sounded – accusing, suspicious – but there was no reason for Sean to have called round at Fran's house, let alone unannounced. She didn't understand.

'I was driving past and saw your car outside,' he said without faltering. 'I thought you were home cooking, you see, and wanted to check everything was OK.'

'No, I don't see,' Libby said, keeping her eyes firmly on him. She watched as his jaw twitched, his eyes taking everything in. 'And I *was* at home but couldn't concentrate so I came to see Fran.' She'd wanted to add *to talk in private* but decided against it. 'Anyway, where did you see my car?'

'Just outside,' he replied vaguely, waving his arm towards the window.

'Where outside?' Libby pressed on, barely aware that Fran had slid another glass of wine into her hands.

'Here, have one too, Sean,' Fran said, far too brightly for the situation. 'You can have one drink surely?'

Sean ignored her.

'I can't remember exactly, love, but close by. What is this, the third degree?' He laughed. 'I only came to check that you were OK.'

'Yes. Yes, it is the third degree, actually. Tell me why you're here.'

'Why don't you talk about this another time, eh, Libby?' Fran said, ushering her to sit down again. 'You and Sean are both tired.'

Libby glared at her friend, turning to Sean again. 'You came to see Fran, didn't you? You had no idea I was here.' She knew her car was parked down a cul-de-sac several streets away.

Sean ran a hand down his face, giving Fran a quick look – a look that, to Libby, said a thousand words. She just didn't know what they were.

'Love, you're stressed. You need to calm down a bit, OK? I—'

'I'm not stressed, Sean. I'm perfectly calm.' Libby surprised herself by sounding just that – detached, composed, aloof, as though she were talking about someone else entirely. 'Tell me, where did you see my car?'

'I can't remember exactly but—'

'That's because you didn't see it at all, did you? You have no idea where my car is. You're lying. Why are you here, Sean? Tell me.' Libby put down her drink too heavily, sloshing some onto the coffee table, before folding her arms and squaring up to him. 'If you don't answer me, I won't be coming home.' She winced at the sound of the threat, knowing that not only did she not mean it, but it was impractical too. She couldn't just leave Alice, her business, all her things. Besides, she had nowhere else to go. And, if what she thought was true, staying with Fran hardly seemed appropriate now.

'Thanks for the drink offer, Fran, but I'd better be going,' Sean said, sighing heavily, shaking his head. 'I'm sorry, I didn't mean to interrupt your evening and cause an upset. I didn't realise Libby would…' He trailed off, looking sad.

'No problem,' Fran replied quietly, taking his untouched wine from him. 'I'll see you out.'

Libby's heart sank as Sean left the room. She sat down, listening intently as Fran and Sean stood in the hall for a few moments. But all she could hear were a few subdued words and then the front door opening and closing.

'What the hell was all that about?' Fran said, coming back in again. 'Nice display of married life there, Lib.'

Libby stared at her, mulling things over as fast as her addled mind would allow. Was she wrong about this? Did she want to risk her longest friendship, her *marriage*, over what could still be a misunderstanding? But God… Sean's initials coming up on Fran's phone, him turning up just now… The more she thought about it, the more two and two looked less like five and a lot like four. Or, she thought, *three*. As in the number of people in her relationship.

'Nothing,' she said, closing her eyes for a beat. 'It wasn't about anything. Look, it's best I go. I've only had a glass or so. I'm tired and—'

'Oh. OK, fine,' Fran said, an uncomfortable look on her face. 'God, I hope you don't think…' She trailed off, standing up when Libby did, watching as she slipped on her coat.

'No, no of course not,' Libby said quietly. 'I don't think anything any more really.' She pulled her keys from her pocket, checking she'd got her phone. Then she laughed – just a pathetic little laugh that sounded, to her, a lot like giving up. 'It's weird, you know, but for the first time in ages, I just *really* want to go home.'

*

Later, Libby sat at the desk in the study at Chestnut Cottage, staring at her computer screen. Sean was in the living room, his laptop balanced on his knee, and Alice was still with Marion. She'd caught sight of the news report he was reading about Sasha as she'd walked past, neither of them saying a word to each other as she'd shut herself away.

'It's not what you're thinking,' he'd said when she arrived home not long after him. He'd taken her by the shoulders as they crossed paths in the kitchen, looking her in the eye. 'I'm worried about you, Lib. You're not at all yourself.' He'd sighed then, as if he were about to make a confession. 'Look, Fran's your best friend. I thought she might be able to give me some advice about how to help you. That's why I stopped by her place, OK?'

'I don't believe you,' was all Libby had said, staring at him before sliding from his grip. Since then, they'd not spoken.

In the study, Libby scrolled through the pictures of symbols that had come up on her screen – everything from Arabic characters to pagan markings and Egyptian hieroglyphs. But nothing matched up with the engraving she'd seen on the lighter. Perhaps she'd entered the wrong search words. It was somehow familiar and she could have sworn she'd seen it before – she just couldn't recall where or when or in what context. She tried again, typing 'M with arrow on it' – a more succinct description, thinking it could actually just be nothing more than a stylised initial Sean had had engraved.

She thought of all the people she knew whose names began with M – Marion being the most obvious, but she had no need for an expensive lighter. She knew a Michelle in the area pretty well, another mum at Alice's playgroup, but she didn't think Sean had ever met her. But then if they were having an affair, she'd hardly be party to that information. There was Mary a couple of doors down, but surely, in her early sixties, she was too old for Sean. Then she remembered Molly Farrow, the head teacher of the local primary school, who was about their age and very attractive. Libby hadn't forgotten how she'd done a double-take at Sean when they'd first met her at an open day with Alice, in preparation for her starting school in the new year. But it was all so random, all so stabbing-in-the-dark and obsessive that she knew she'd drive herself mad if she dwelt on it any longer. She'd *already* driven herself mad, she concluded, cupping her head in her hands.

She racked her brains, biting her lip as she logged into Facebook to check Sean's friends list. But his privacy settings were tight and, despite being his friend, she wasn't able to see who was on the list. He rarely used Facebook anyway.

'This is ridiculous,' she whispered, flopping back in her chair. She thought she heard Sean moving about and listened out… but all was silent, apart from the faint sound of the TV quietly on in the other room.

'Think, think, *think*,' she said, wondering why the name Maggie suddenly meant something to her. She didn't think she knew any Maggies. Did she? 'Mags,' she said quietly several times. 'Mags, Mag, Maggie, Margaret…' It was on the tip of her tongue. '*Magpie*,' she whispered finally, feeling goosebumps. 'My little *Magpie*…' she said, digging her nails into her palms.

She'd not been prying but, soon after she and Sean had moved in together, it was natural for her to want to find places for her things alongside his. And the dresser drawer had needed a clear-out anyway – it was stuffed with old bills, greetings cards and general stuff that wasn't needed. For some reason, Sean had kept a birthday card from someone calling themselves 'Your little Magpie'. Naturally she asked him about it, wondering who it was, and Sean explained, slightly embarrassed, that it was in fact Natalie. *Magpie* was his nickname for her because she loved shiny things and always wore lots of jewellery.

'She saw something pretty and just had to have it,' he'd said, laughing maybe just a little too fondly for Libby's liking.

Libby shook her head, trying to dispel her fears. She was being stupid. As she thought about it more, she felt her shoulders relax and her stomach unknot. Sean had probably bought the lighter for Natalie years ago and just never given it to her, likely when their relationship broke down.

She breathed out a sigh of relief, thinking she should probably go into the other room and talk to him. They had things to discuss, things to work out between them. And that didn't involve her petty jealousy about some stupid gift. They needed to be a team more than ever. But, as she was about to shut down her laptop, she noticed the other window with images that had come up as a result of searching for 'M with arrow on it'.

'Oh,' she said, her fingers hovering over the mouse pad. 'Wait… that's… that's *it…*' she whispered, clicking on the first link. Suddenly, M for Magpie didn't seem quite so likely after all, and when she read the description of what the symbol meant, Libby was racking her brains for dates. For *birthday* dates. Because the M with a downwards arrow on its tail, it seemed, was the symbol for Scorpio.

CHAPTER THIRTY-FIVE

Now

'Can you tell me any reason why we might have found Sasha's blood in your living room, Mrs Randell?' DI Jones asks.

'*Blood?*' I say, horrified. I hear Claire shifting beside me. 'No… no comment,' I add.

'So you have no idea how Sasha's blood could have got there, in your living room?'

'No comment.'

'The blood was found beneath the corner of your wooden coffee table and on the tassels of your rug.'

'No comment.'

'In your statement, you say that Sasha was not at home when you returned from your meal. Is this correct?'

I feel sick – a deep, unstoppable nausea welling up from my stomach as I imagine Sasha bleeding in my living room. 'Yes. I… I mean, no comment.' My shoulders pull inwards as I pin my elbows to my sides, my fingers clasped as I try to still myself. 'I'm so sorry…' I add, trailing off.

'Sorry…?' DC McCaulay says. 'For what, exactly?'

'That… that there was blood. Something bad must have happened to Sasha. Oh God, and Alice was upstairs.' I'm waiting for them to tell me they've found a body, to show me pictures of Sasha – bleeding and lifeless, perhaps bruised and battered.

God knows how or where they found her, but I know I can't stand to look.

'You say that you went out to your kitchen barn to look for Sasha,' DI Jones continues.

'Yes.'

'Did anyone see you?'

'No… comment.' I think back, the taste of wine and seafood still in my mouth, the tang of fear in my nose as Sean barked and shouted at me from the moment we got home from the pub. I wasn't thinking straight – from the alcohol, the way Sean was suddenly acting with me, to the ever-present note and my suspicion, right down to the shock of what else happened that night. It was as much as I could do to keep upright, let alone think rationally.

No one saw you, OK? Sean had said later, his spit landing on my cheeks.

'No, no one saw me. I've told you this before,' I tell the detective, almost seeing Arn's face pop up over the wall, concerned he'll see him reflected in my eyes.

'Thing is,' DI Jones continues, 'we spoke to your neighbour, Arnold Ratcliffe, and he says he distinctly remembers seeing you outside that night and that you'd had a quick chat.'

'I must have forgotten,' I say. 'Sorry.'

'He said he'd heard shouting earlier, around a quarter to ten. And then on and off until about 11 p.m. Who was shouting, Libby?'

'I don't know… no comment.'

'Arnold also told us that when he saw you outside, you seemed very agitated. Were you agitated?'

'We couldn't find Sasha. Of course I was agitated.' My head couldn't hang any lower.

'Or were you agitated because you'd just killed Sasha?'

For a second, I can't speak. Every organ in my body turns cold, as if I'm shutting down to protect myself. Whatever he's accusing me of, I don't want to hear it. It's not true.

'Christ,' I'd said to Sean when I'd come back inside. 'Arn saw me. He'd heard noises and popped up over the wall.'

Sean had stared up at me then, with something I didn't recognise in his eyes. 'Too bloody nosy for his own good,' he'd said. His hands were wet and he was on his knees. 'Did he say anything?'

'Not much,' I replied, hugging myself. I couldn't stop shaking, wondering what else he'd seen or heard going on out there. 'This is all so wrong, Sean,' I said, going up to him. All I wanted was to be held, to have him say everything would be OK again.

'Help me,' he said, standing up. He was holding out his dripping hands, eyeing the bucket of soapy water. I picked it up and followed him, carrying it into the kitchen. 'There was food spilt everywhere,' he said, pointing at the cleared plate by the sink. 'I didn't want the rug to stain. No harm done.'

'Yes,' I'd replied. 'No harm done.'

'Good girl,' he'd said.

'No harm done,' I whisper now, my watery eyes blurring the detectives' faces.

'Please repeat what you said so the recorder can pick you up,' DI Jones says.

'I said… I said "Are we done"?'

'Far from done,' DC McCaulay says, tapping her pen.

'Your husband went to check upstairs in the cottage, to see if Sasha was there?' DI Jones goes on.

'I think so, yes. I mean, we both did. Several times. We hunted everywhere for her.'

'And made quite a mess.'

I shrug. 'Maybe. We were frantic looking for her. Thought perhaps she was playing some game. Maybe hide and seek with Alice.'

'But Alice was asleep.'

'Yes.'

'You went out driving around the village.'

'Yes,' I say. 'Why do we keep going over the same things? I've told you everything I know.'

DI Jones just stares at me as if I've not even spoken. 'Your statement says, apart from Eric Slater, a local man, you didn't encounter anyone else when you were out. Is that correct?'

'I can't really remember. I'm sorry. I didn't see Sasha though.'

I think back… I'd got the car keys in my hand and Sean had suddenly switched from angry to reassuring. *It'll be OK*, he'd said, stroking my cheek. *If you see anyone, make sure you ask them if they've seen Sasha. It could help.* I'd nodded, knowing he was right. But when I came back, everything had changed.

'Perhaps you didn't see Sasha in the village because she was in the boot of your car. Is that correct, Libby?' DI Jones says calmly.

'*What?* No!' Thin, bitter bile coats the back of my tongue as I fight the retch. 'No… no comment.'

'Libby, if you wish to have more legal advice…' I hear Claire say, but I can't even find the courage to turn to her, to accept what she's offering.

'Did your husband come with you in the car?' DI Jones continues.

'No, he didn't. He stayed home with Alice and also in case Sasha came back.' I stop. Swallowing. The Land Rover wasn't there when I got back.

'I'm confused, so perhaps you can help me out here, Libby. Is that OK?'

I nod.

'I'll reiterate – in your statement, you say that you didn't see anyone apart from Eric Slater when you went out in the car. Correct?'

I give the tiniest of nods.

'So why would your husband, Sean Randell, categorically say in his most recent statement that you told him you'd encountered *two* people when you went out in the car?'

'I don't know. No comment.' I had no idea Sean had made another statement, let alone one that contradicted mine.

No need to say a word about it, love. You didn't mean to hit the car... It makes no difference... I'd nodded frantically, so grateful he was on my side. We'd got each other's backs. We just wanted everything to be normal again.

'Where did you encounter Eric Slater?' DI Jones asks.

I sigh, picking at my fingers. 'I saw him when I was driving along Drover's Way. I stopped to ask if he'd seen Sasha.'

Behind my eyelids I see Sean's face, mouthing instructions at me before I left, his eyes saying one thing, his lips another – yet the words coming out meaning something entirely different.

'Eric the Elf we call him,' I continue, surprising myself with half a smile. 'He's eighty-two. He was out walking Maisy, his dog. He's as fit as any fifty-year-old. He'll tell you I was alone. He hadn't seen Sasha either.'

'Did you see anyone else?'

I stare at the tabletop – just a wooden laminate thing, grimy at the edges where people like me have put their sweaty hands or their despairing heads.

No need to say a word about it, love...

'I'd forgotten that I saw Cath, too,' I say to the detective, almost hearing Sean yelling at me for the betrayal. 'It's all been so... upsetting. I don't know what I'm thinking half the time. Cath runs the post office.'

'For fuck's sake, Lib,' he'd said, grabbing me by the shoulders after I'd got back. 'I give you one job to do, one bloody job...'

I'd felt my brain ache inside my skull when he'd shaken me – enough to make me lose my bearings for a moment. Feel the dull thud of reality.

'I'm so sorry,' I'd said to him, the tears starting again. 'I did what you said and went looking for Sasha. I didn't mean to hit that car. If I'd known I'd be driving around looking for a dead girl, I wouldn't have had any wine.'

He'd dug his fingers into my upper arms then – strong fingers used to dealing with big animals. Animals way bigger than me. 'You don't know she's dead,' he'd said to me, looking me squarely in the eye. 'Repeat after me: *we don't know Sasha is dead*.'

'We don't know Sasha is dead,' I'd whispered, tears dribbling onto my lip, getting on my tongue. All I'd wanted to do was bury my face against his shoulder, have him wrap his strong arms around me. Instead, he shoved me away, paced about again as I stared at the space where Sasha had been sitting when we'd last seen her. I swear I still saw her there, hunched over her books, flicking through TV channels as she puzzled over maths questions – the indentations in the sofa cushions marking her place, as if she was coming back at any moment.

'But Cath hadn't seen Sasha either,' I tell the detective. 'No one had.'

'OK, thank you.' DI Jones shows his file to the other detective, pointing at something. She nods. 'We also found traces of Sasha's blood in your car, Libby,' DI Jones continues, his face as calm as if he was commenting on the weather. 'In the boot. Can you explain this?'

Claire leans in. 'Libby, I don't want to keep interrupting, but do you recall what we said before you came into interview, how you should deal with it?'

I shake my head. I don't remember. I touch the tips of my fingers together – nothing. No feeling. I press my thumbs into my thighs, but they're not there either. I bring my hand to my mouth, trying to find my lips, but they've also gone. Even the thoughts in my mind are turning to white noise, as if I'm fading from life, have never even existed.

Maybe it's the same place Sasha has gone. Somewhere peaceful. Solitary. Safe.

'Can you explain why traces of Sasha's blood were found in your car?' DI Jones repeats.

'No,' I say, remembering the shock when they took my VW away a few days ago. 'There can't be. It's impossible.' Numbness everywhere. 'No comment.' I touch my forehead as the detectives' faces swim in and out of focus, my solicitor's words buzzing between my ears as she asks again if I want further legal advice, Sean's angry words lashing out at me.

'It's not looking good, is it?' DI Jones says, giving me that impatient stare – his legs spread, arms folded. 'Why don't you just tell us what happened, Libby?'

It's not looking good…

They were Sean's words that night, too. I'd have thought it was obvious that things weren't looking good, but I liked the way he took control. He's always been capable in a crisis. Like when my waters broke early when I was pregnant and we had to rush to hospital. Of course I'd done the first-time-mum routine of packing my bag two months before my due date – spare nightie plus the one I wanted to give birth in, a comfortable outfit to wear home, toiletries, snacks, baby clothes and nappy-changing kit… the list went on. I'd likely only be in for a night, yet managed to fill a large holdall.

In the end, I turned up at hospital with a carrier bag containing milk and bread from the corner shop and nothing for the baby. Still, at least Sean made good use of the milk, swigging it down while he waited – which wasn't for long, as it turned out. I was already nine centimetres dilated and wanting to push when the Land Rover rumbled up at A & E, Sean having fled the practice to answer my panicked call. He was with me in ten minutes – collecting me from the back room at the little shop two villages away as I huffed and panted my way through yet another contraction.

Later, when I'd held Alice against my breast, the midwife said I must have a high pain threshold to not know I'd been in labour for the last twelve hours.

'I have a high pain threshold…' I say now, feeling the damp patches under my armpits, a trickle of sweat running down my back.

'Libby, I'll ask again,' Claire says. 'Would you like some more legal advice, seeing as the interview is taking a different turn now? Some things you're saying are not making sense.' Claire leans in close. I smell her perfume – setting my nose alight, reminding me there's a world outside of this small room. A world that I want to see again.

'Yes, please,' I say, finally looking at her. She's the only person on my side. The only one who can help me.

'OK,' DI McCaulay says clearly. 'We'll take a short break. It's 9.43 p.m.'

Then I hear an electronic beep as the recording device is switched off.

CHAPTER THIRTY-SIX

Before

'You'll realise one day,' Jan said to Libby as the two of them sat opposite each other in Jan's living room. 'When Alice is older, wanting to go out and do her own thing.' She shook her head slowly. 'A part of you wants to stop them, wrap them up and lock them away so nothing bad can ever happen, but another part of you wants to release them into the wild, like a beautiful butterfly you've set free, watching them fly.'

'Oh, Jan…' Libby said. Her tea had virtually gone cold as she'd listened to Jan talk about Sasha, but she sipped it anyway, not wanting to appear rude.

'And she was so beautiful,' Jan went on. '*Is* so beautiful,' she added through a sob. 'Though I'm not sure Matt always realised that.'

'How come?'

'He's a boy. A teenage boy. What do you expect? When he'd passed his driving test, things changed between him and Sash. They've been sweethearts since the age of thirteen, and at school together since they were five. He's one of her oldest friends as well as her first and only boyfriend.'

'So why did things change?'

'He started going out with his mates more, for a start. When he got the car, they were always badgering him for lifts. I was worried he was drinking and driving. There's a pub on the edge of town, a bit of a dive to be honest, and they don't check ID. I told Sash not to get in his car if he'd had a drink, but love trumps sense.' Jan shrugged resignedly.

Libby nodded.

'Then Sash saw him hanging out with another girl a couple of months ago. She knew she'd got the hots for him, and she wondered if Matt had for her. They were flirting at college, spending their lunch breaks together when he could have been with Sasha. And he used to help this girl with her coursework when Sasha needed help too. It didn't seem fair. Matt's a bright lad, despite how I'm making him sound. He swore to Sash she was just a friend, but even so, Sasha felt sidelined and hurt, as if she wasn't the most important thing to him any more.

'Then, when Matt went round to this girl's house one evening after college, Sash ended things with him. He swore it was only to fix her bike, but he ended up staying late. Matt's the kind of lad who'll do anything for anyone. Soft as butter and he can't say no. But really, I think he only does it to make himself feel good. Self-esteem issues, I reckon.'

'Sounds like it,' Libby said, remembering a few things Sasha had said.

'Stupid thing is, Sasha's bike has had a puncture for ages. She never mentioned it to Matt, didn't like to take advantage of his kindness. Instead, she just bore the hurt of his behaviour. What he believed was *good* behaviour. Anyway, a couple of weeks later, they got back together of course. Matt talked her round as he always does.'

Libby listened to Jan, knowing she needed to vent, that she likely didn't have anyone else to unload on. There was no sign of Phil. Libby had called round on a whim on the way back from the market. Something – *guilt*, perhaps – had taken her home via Little Radwell with fresh flowers.

'I think Sash is prone to overreact when it comes to relationship issues, given what's happened between Phil and me. It's bound to have affected her, even though she's older now.'

Libby didn't know what to say. She watched as Jan knelt beside the coffee table, arranging her scented candles and taking an incense stick from its packet. She clicked the green plastic lighter a few times, trying to get a flame, but it only emitted a couple of sparks. In the end, she reached for a box of matches on the mantelpiece, lighting each of the candles. A plume of blue-grey smoke twisted up from the incense as it glowed orange at its tip.

'These help calm me,' Jan said, dropping the lighter in the waste basket beside the fireplace. She'd managed to put on some proper clothes today – just tracksuit bottoms and a sweatshirt – but her hair was still unkempt and her face even thinner than last time.

'They smell nice,' Libby said. 'And I'm sorry to hear about you and Phil, Jan,' she added. 'It's hard enough anyway, let alone at a time like this.'

'Sash saw things going down the pan between me and her dad and I think that's why things turned sour with Matt. Plus Matt's the possessive type. Double standards, or what?' Jan rolled her eyes. 'But it made her question things, what's right and wrong. She's got high moral standards has our Sash. Doesn't like to see people get away with things or watch others get hurt. I just wish she could apply that to herself.' She stared out of the front window, her shoulders up around her ears, the knuckles of her left hand white from the clenched fist she was making. 'I'm looking out for them cops,' she said. 'There's always someone coming and going.'

'It's good they're keeping you updated.'

'I'm at the point where I don't care if it's bad news or good news any more,' Jan said. 'Is that awful of me? I just want *any* news. Then I can deal with it whichever way I have to.' She shook her head. 'Not knowing is the hardest thing of all.'

'I understand,' Libby said.

'I want to show you something.' Jan went into another room, returning with a couple of photo albums. 'I dug these out the other night when I couldn't sleep. The cops wanted me to check photos on my phone, see if I could find pictures of the things Sasha was wearing when she went missing. But you know what it's like when you go on a crawl down memory lane. I ended up going right back to when she was a baby.'

'I hope it was a help, Jan, to look at your beautiful girl.' Libby put a hand on her arm as she sat down next to her. 'They'll find her soon, I feel sure of it.'

Libby suddenly swung round, convinced Sean was behind her.

Everything's going to be OK...

'This was her on her thirteenth birthday, look,' Jan said, sharing the album between them. 'That's Matt next to her. Cheeky, grin, eh?'

'Yes indeed,' Libby said. 'And look at Sash's dimple. It's just the same now.'

'That was her first ever disco. In the village hall. She felt right grown-up, I can tell you. Phil got her a DJ and everything. Just the chap who plays a couple of local pubs and that, but Sash was made up. Phil even hired a smoke machine and some flashing lights.'

'So sweet,' Libby says. 'Look at her, all made up and her hair done, looking as if she's going on eighteen.'

'I know,' Jan said, flipping back through the pages. 'Here's another birthday, look, though that was a few years before, combined with Phil's and Hallowe'en. Phil did her witch make-up. He was into amateur dramatics back then. Used to help out at the local society doing costumes and stuff, scenery and the like.' There was something wistful in Jan's voice.

'Looks like a fun party,' Libby said. 'Apple bobbing and everything.'

'We had a few complaints from some of the parents though,' she said, managing a laugh. 'Phil did a "pin the tail on the pheasant" game, instead of a donkey. As ever, he'd brought home several brace from work but decided to use one of the dead birds at the party, blindfolding the kids and getting them to attach the tail feathers back onto the thing. It was hanging by its neck. Quite gory.' Jan rolled her eyes fondly. Libby could tell talking was helping. She'd made the right call to drop in.

'Well, no major harm done if grown-ups were there too, I suppose,' Libby said, flipping through the album. 'Is this a family holiday?'

'Norfolk,' Jan said. 'Look how little Nathan is there. Barely walking.'

'How's he coping with all this? I know he and Sash are close.'

Jan shook her head. 'Not well. He refuses to talk about it. He's gone to school as normal since Sash… since she went, and he hangs out at his mates' houses afterwards. It's as though he's trying to find excuses not to come home. Nathan likes going to Phil's cottage on the estate sometimes,' she added. 'Thing is, he's only eleven, and too young to leave while Phil's working, so he's been feeling rejected when Phil sends him back here.'

'I'm sorry,' Libby said, not knowing what else to say. 'You've got so much going on.'

'He thinks I'm up to no good, you know,' Jan said. 'Phil. But he's got it all wrong. Yes, we've had our problems over the years. God knows we have… but he thinks I'm seeing someone else. It's a mess.'

Libby stared at Jan, swallowing hard. She hadn't denied it exactly, and Phil's suspicions must have come from somewhere. Up close, Libby could see the fine, downy hairs on Jan's face covering her gaunt and sunken cheeks. She was an attractive woman but the recent stress had taken its toll.

'Come with me,' Jan said, suddenly rising. 'Upstairs.'

Glad of the reprieve, Libby followed Jan up the staircase. At the top, they turned right and went into a bedroom.

'She talks about you very fondly, you know,' Jan said. 'Almost as if you're an aunt or big sister.' She paused, wiping a finger under her eye. 'Or another mother,' she added with a regretful look. 'And every *other mother* should know where her *other daughter* sleeps.' She smiled, touching Libby's arm.

'It's a lovely room,' Libby said, looking around. 'She's a good girl. We chatted a lot while we were working.' Libby wondered if it was the right time to bring up her concerns about Sasha's eating but, on balance, she thought it best not mention it – as ever, Sean's voice guiding her in her head.

Jan suddenly tensed at the sound of the landline ringing downstairs.

'Oh, just a moment,' she said, turning and dashing off. 'It might be news,' she called from the stairs.

Alone, Libby looked at the items on Sasha's dressing table. Her make-up, bits of jewellery lying about – just cheap, colourful stuff – as well as a few trinkets, coins, nail varnishes and some receipts. She trailed her hand over the end of the bed as she went to the bookshelves, turning her head sideways to look at the titles. Sasha was into romantic novels, it seemed, so Libby pulled out one with a bookmark, flicking through it, wondering if it was the last book Sasha had read.

Then she went over to Sasha's bedside table, still hearing Jan's voice on the phone downstairs. Slowly she opened the little drawer, discovering a couple of old phone chargers, a few pens, hand cream, several birthday cards. She leafed through the cards, seeing they were mostly from friends, with one from Matt. On the other side of the room the wardrobe door was slightly ajar. Libby went over and eased it open slowly, trailing her hand across familiar garments – things she'd seen Sasha in. When she was working, she asked her to wear plain black trousers or a skirt and a white top. She always looked smart. Libby smiled when she saw a couple of dresses at one end of the wardrobe – clearly saved for sentimental reasons. They were little party dresses that looked as though they'd fit a four- or five-year-old – one in pale pink with sequins, the other in peach velvet with a lacy high neck.

Libby froze, catching her breath as she spotted something stuffed at the back of the wardrobe, behind the shoes and other crammed-in clothes. It only caught her eye because she thought she recognised it – a navy sweater that was clearly way too big for Sasha. She pulled the garment out, holding it up in front of her. It was a man's sweater, and she instantly recognised the label in the collar, plus the slightly frayed right cuff and the mended hole on the shoulder. The hole that *she'd* darned a year or so ago. She'd occasionally wondered what had happened to the jumper but Sean had told her that he must have left it at a client's place while on a house visit. She'd believed him. Why wouldn't she?

She listened out again. Jan was finishing the call, hanging up the phone, making her way back upstairs. Libby stood there, stunned, before quickly shoving the sweater back where she'd found it. She closed the wardrobe doors and went back to where she'd been standing.

'News?' she asked when Jan came in.

'No, no…' she said quietly. 'Just a friend calling to see how I am.'

Libby nodded, her mouth burning with questions, but she didn't want to worry the poor woman even more by telling her that her daughter clearly harboured strong enough feelings for Sean to have his sweater hidden away. Though what concerned her most was how she'd got it. Either she'd taken it from the cottage when she'd been babysitting or, worse, Sean had given it to her. She imagined Sasha wearing it in bed, snuggling up in it as she read her romance novels, breathing in his scent, waiting for the next chance they'd have to be together.

'I come in here every night,' Jan said, tears welling in her eyes. 'Sit on her bed, talk to her in the hope she can hear me, say a little prayer. I'm hoping somehow it will help.'

'I… I'm sure it will,' Libby replied.

'Did you see this?' Jan went over to the windowsill and plucked a photo frame from a group of others. 'Sash loved taking pictures, though this is a rare one of her. She mainly takes nature shots and gets the best ones printed out.'

Libby took the glossy white frame from Jan, looking at the selfie of Sasha and Matt. It looked as though they'd gone for a walk somewhere; Sasha's was hair blowing everywhere, Matt was wearing a beanie hat. They were both laughing, pretty scenery behind them. 'She looks so happy,' Libby said, about to pass it back. And then she saw Sasha's necklace – a little pendant on a silver chain. She'd never seen her wearing it before.

'Here,' Libby said, finally passing the photo back, her stomach knotting and churning. She turned away, forcing the image of the pendant from her mind – the *Scorpio* pendant – trying not to believe the worst as she followed Jan back downstairs: that the person her husband was having an affair with was a missing seventeen-year-old girl.

CHAPTER THIRTY-SEVEN

Libby stared at Sean. Sean stared at Libby. Home didn't seem like home any more, especially with Alice spending more time at the farm since they'd moved back to the cottage. Marion still thought it best until things settled down. And this afternoon, things were far from settled.

Sean glanced at his watch. 'Three o'clock, you say?'

Libby nodded. 'That's what he said.' She felt like drumming her fingers on the table while glaring at Sean, but resisted. How could her husband – her beautiful, gorgeous, funny, caring, kind and selfless man – turn into a virtual stranger overnight? If anyone had asked her several weeks ago if she thought her feelings towards him would ever change, she'd have said a big fat no. Or, actually, *yes* – in that she could only fall *more* in love with him. But now, she wasn't so sure. She had seen a completely different side of him and her feelings were adrift.

Or perhaps she'd seen a different side of herself.

'He's late, then,' Sean said, making a show of standing up before refilling the kettle. 'There's only so much tea you can drink.'

'You're not going to tell me, are you?'

Sean swung round, his hand on the kettle.

'About why you went to Fran's the other night.' Libby folded her arms.

'Oh Christ, not that again.'

'But it's always "not that again", isn't it? You never want to talk about anything. You just go into emotional lockdown, hoping these things will go away. If you'd just talked more, put my mind at rest, then we wouldn't have needed to go out for a bloody make-up meal and Sasha wouldn't be—'

'Missing.'

'Yes. Then Sasha wouldn't be missing.'

'So you're saying it's my fault? That I have complete control over nutters who choose to leave notes on your car? How, exactly, am I supposed to prove I'm innocent?' He shook his head while grabbing their mugs, swilling them out under the tap. 'None of this is my fault, Libby.'

She stared at his broad back as he waited for the kettle to boil. The same back she'd seen in that navy sweater stuffed in Sasha's wardrobe yesterday – the back that she'd traced her fingers over countless times, making him shudder in a way no one else could. None of it made sense. Sean and a young girl – their *babysitter*, a schoolkid, his mate's daughter. Surely that kind of thing only happened in the news or in bad movies that made you want to switch over. None of it had a place in her life.

Except, somehow, it did.

'I can't wait around much longer,' Sean said, putting two more cups of tea on the table. 'I've a farm visit to make.'

Libby nodded. All they knew was that DI Jones wanted to have yet another informal chat with them. She wasn't sure what more they could tell him. They'd cooperated willingly throughout the investigation, and yet it felt, somehow, as though they were now in the spotlight. The ones under suspicion.

'I think we need to wait for him, however late he is,' Libby said. 'I mean, it doesn't look good if you're not here. I've got things to do too but—'

'I know, I know,' Sean said, sitting down again. 'You're right.'

'And I've no idea how I'm going to cope serving fourteen people on my own tomorrow. It's not as though I can call on Sasha to help.' Libby hung her head.

'You'll manage somehow,' Sean replied, peering out of the kitchen window as a car cruised past. 'Just make sure you don't serve up the wrong dish or something careless.'

'I should probably just cancel the event,' she said, touching her temple. 'It's all such a mess. But then we've got the final payment on the kitchen build falling due soon, not to mention other bills.'

'Don't think about that now,' Sean said, standing up. He went to the front window, one knee on the window seat, staring up and down the lane. 'Where the hell is he?'

Libby screwed up her eyes, her mind swimming with everything – coping with tomorrow's dinner party alone, dealing with the police, Sasha's face the last time she saw her, jealousy, neglecting her daughter… It was all overwhelming.

'Thing is,' Libby remembered Sasha saying to her as they were setting the table for a dinner party around a month ago. 'It's not as though I've done anything wrong.'

'So why does Matt give you all this grief?' Libby had asked, going round with the glasses, polishing each one. It was a large house with important guests, and Libby had ordered several special flower arrangements for the table. It was going to look stunning.

'Dunno,' she'd replied, wistfully. 'He's like, always accusing me of things with other boys. Saying I'm looking at them and stuff. But I'm not. He's the one being all lovey-dovey with that girl. If I say anything, he calls me jealous and crazy. It hurts, you know?'

Oh, believe me, I know, Libby had wanted to say – the way her ex, David, had treated her suddenly on her mind – but she kept quiet. 'That sounds unfair,' she'd said instead. 'Have you told him you don't like it?'

'Yes, but he believes what he wants to believe.' Sasha had dropped some cutlery then, bent down to pick it up before washing it, but Libby hadn't failed to notice the tears in her eyes.

'Hey,' she'd said, going up and taking her hands. 'Leave that a moment. We've got time.' Libby put her arms around her, noticing how thin she felt. She rubbed her back, concerned that her ribs were prominent, her waist tiny. She pulled away slightly and tipped up Sasha's chin. Tears were streaming down her face.

'It's just I'm so scared I'll lose him. I love him to bits. He's even talked about getting married in the future so why does he do this?'

'Honest answer, love, is I don't know,' Libby replied, pulling out a dining chair each for them. 'But it's probably his own insecurities surfacing, rather than anything you're doing wrong. People do that. What hurts them most, the things they're scared of, they sometimes push out onto other people.'

'So you think he's cheating on *me*?' Sasha said, wiping her face on the tissue Libby had given her.

'No, not necessarily. But he may have some worries about *you* leaving him. So he might say these things out of fear, to protect himself maybe.' Libby felt out of her depth.

Sasha thought about this, giving a little nod. 'That makes sense,' she said, shaking her head and rolling her eyes. She thought for a while longer, staring down at the dining table, biting her lip. 'I hate growing up,' she said. 'I don't want to be a proper adult. I've seen what they do to each other.'

'Your mum and dad?' Libby hadn't wanted to pry but it wasn't the first time Sasha had mentioned their troubles.

'They've been together forever,' Sasha said, sniffing. 'Like from when they were only a few years older than me and Matt. How can you be with someone so long then, several decades later, decide that you hate them? Wouldn't you have known during that time? I don't want to have that happen to me.'

'People change over the years,' she said. 'The person you fall in love with isn't always the same person a long time later. Surely if your mum and dad don't get along, then it's best they part ways?'

'But they *do* get along,' Sasha said. 'I mean, they do love each other. But it's Dad…' She hung her head again. 'He's always accusing Mum of things. It's so wrong. I've overheard stuff. *Seen* stuff.'

'Well, like I said, maybe your dad's got insecurities that he doesn't know how to deal with and he takes it out on your mum?'

'It's just…' She stared at Libby as though she wanted to say something else, as though whatever it was, was stuck deep inside her. Her face betrayed more worry than a young girl should have. 'Yeah,' she said, wiping her nose, shaking her head. 'It'll probably all work out fine.'

'You're right, though,' Libby went on. 'It *is* hard being an adult, and we do get things wrong sometimes. But just because your parents are going through a hard time, it doesn't mean it'll be the same for you and Matt, OK? You're young and you've got so much life ahead of you.'

They'd shared a warm hug then, ending in a laugh when Libby accidentally sent more cutlery onto the floor.

'I got it,' Sasha said, smiling and bending down to pick it up.

So much life ahead of you…

*

'He's here,' Sean said. 'And you're crying. You need to wipe your face.'

Libby lifted her head from the table to find her cheeks wet with tears.

'Go and clean yourself up. I'll see him in.'

She nodded and hurried upstairs before DI Jones came in. As she passed the window, she caught sight of him. A different officer was with him this time – another woman, but older than the last PC. And this one wasn't wearing uniform either.

'Please, come in,' she heard Sean saying downstairs as she leant over the basin in the bathroom. She felt light-headed as her shoulders heaved up and down in time with her short, sharp gasps. She stared at herself in the mirror, listening to the detectives' muffled voices punctuated intermittently by Sean's monosyllabic responses. Her eyes were dull and sunken in their sockets, the grey circles beneath even more pronounced. She ran the tap and leant down, splashing warm water on her face. She closed her eyes, wishing that she was underwater, drowning, slipping away into a peaceful place where none of this nightmare existed.

Because, as things stood, she was drowning anyway.

She dabbed at her face with a towel and quickly fixed her hair, smoothing down the crumpled top she was wearing, wondering if she should change. She looked a state. But then she heard Sean calling up to her.

'Coming...' she called back. As she went downstairs, she heard their voices getting louder and, at one point, she thought she heard the detective laugh, as though Sean had made some kind of joke. She couldn't imagine what.

'Hello,' she said, glancing nervously at DI Jones then at the woman standing next to him. Sean came up to her, draping his arm around her and pulling her close.

'It's OK, love,' he said, kissing the top of her head. Libby looked up at him, wondering why his mood had suddenly changed. 'My wife is finding this particularly hard,' he explained. 'As you know, she worked with Sasha. They were close.' He kissed her head again.

'Well, I—'

'This is DC McCaulay,' Sean said, interrupting and pulling a chair out at the kitchen table for Libby. 'We've just had a brief word but DI Jones would like a quick chat with you now, Lib. I'll be in the courtyard loading up the Land Rover if you need me. I've got an important call-out to make.' Sean headed off, stopping in the doorway to give Libby a look over his shoulder, making a reassuring face. At least, she *hoped* it was reassuring.

'Is there news?' she said after Sean had closed the back door behind him. Her heart was still thumping.

'We need to take your car for forensic examination,' DI Jones said, ignoring her question and getting straight to the point.

'What?' Libby said, sitting forward. 'My car – why?' She wished Sean was still with her.

'Mainly routine,' he continued. 'You took a taxi on the night Sasha disappeared, yes?'

'Yes.'

'As your car was here at the house all evening, we will now be including it in our investigation. We have the necessary paperwork.'

'I… OK… but I need it for work,' she said, touching her forehead. 'And taking Alice to playgroup and her swimming class. Will it take long?'

'All depends,' the detective replied. 'But we'll keep you updated.'

'Are you taking the Land Rover, too?' Logistics were going to be a nightmare. 'Sean's a vet. How will he do his job?'

'Your husband just mentioned his vehicle was in the garage for repairs at the time Sasha went missing. We'll need to confirm this, of course, but there'll be no need to take both cars for now. So you can relax a little.'

Libby's eyes widened, almost to bursting point. She swallowed, thinking, weighing up what Sean would want her to say.

'I see,' she said quietly. 'Yes, yes, you're right. That's fine, then, if we still have one car between us.'

She clasped her hands in her lap, her eyes unable to settle on anything for more than a second. In her head, she heard herself screaming hysterically, remembering how she'd tried to snatch Sean's keys from his hand after they'd arrived home from the pub that night.

'Don't be an idiot,' she'd snapped at him. 'You've had way too much to drink. You can't do this!' She was choked up with tears, pacing about, covering her face. 'Just sit down and let's think.' She remembered how much she was shaking, how her head thrummed from the stress of it all, how it gradually dawned on her that things would never be the same again. How the Land Rover, for most of the evening, was parked right outside the cottage.

CHAPTER THIRTY-EIGHT

It was a rare moment – Dan and Alice sitting at the kitchen table together. Alice was colouring, her little tongue winding its way around her lips as she concentrated. Libby had fetched her from Marion's earlier, not wanting to be without her for yet another afternoon and evening. Libby felt as though she'd hardly seen her daughter these last couple of weeks. It was time to get things back to normal as far as possible. Besides, it wasn't Dan's night to stay – though he'd called his dad and asked to come over a day early – and Libby thought it was a good opportunity for half-brother and sister to have some time together. She wondered if things were tense between his mum and him.

'Dan, you do some colouring,' Alice said, sliding her box of felt pens closer to him. 'Help me with this tree and the birds.'

Libby took a large pot from the oven, lifting the lid and stirring the contents. She'd made enough bourguignon to last several days. She added some more red wine and another handful of herbs, stirring in some French mustard as an afterthought. She put it back in the oven and closed the door again. For the first time in what seemed like a lifetime, she felt a few tendrils of warmth spreading through her as she heard Alice and Dan chattering behind her.

They'd always got on well, with Dan harbouring none of the resentment that his mother bore about Sean having another child. Dan was thrilled to have a little half-sister, though as far as they were all concerned, there was nothing 'half' about it. It was a level playing field and they were both treated equally. It's just that Dan was only with them thirty per cent of the time. She knew Sean wished it could be more and, even with this limited access, Natalie still made things difficult. But she didn't think this was one of those times – Dan had chosen to come over early of his own accord, though they'd likely soon feel the brunt of Natalie's annoyance. She didn't like being rejected.

'Only if you help me with chemistry,' Dan said, lunging in for a tickle. Alice squealed, hunching her shoulders.

'OK,' she said, leaning over to him.

'Whoa, no...' Dan said kindly. 'No purple pen on my schoolbooks.'

When Libby glanced round from the sink, she saw that Dan had slid his books aside and was colouring in some birds for Alice. She smiled and sighed at the same time. If only this was a normal evening, if only it wasn't marred by everything else. She shuddered, closing her eyes as she dried her hands.

'Right, I've just got to pop out to the barn kitchen to get something,' she said, though the kids weren't listening. Libby grabbed the key and went across the courtyard, letting herself in, opening the stainless-steel door of the catering fridge-freezer – each side lockable, though she never bothered. With only her working there and occasionally Sasha, there was no need. Besides, the stable door to the barn was secure.

'Celeriac...' she said to herself, scanning the shelves. Everything was ordered properly and in line with hygiene rules. She was extremely careful and proud of her high standards. 'I swear there's one here somewhere.' She moved a couple of things aside to eventually reveal the gnarly root vegetable. She pulled it out, closing the door behind her. As an afterthought, she opened the freezer, wanting to put a specially made sauce in the fridge to defrost for tomorrow. Everything was meticulously labelled, with prepared dishes even having colour-coded lids just to be thorough, though the sticker on this container had fallen off. She picked the label off the shelf, checking when she'd frozen it. It was still well within date. Libby took a new label and marked it with today's date – the date of defrosting. She left it in the fridge and locked up the kitchen again, heading across the courtyard and into the boot room.

'Doesn't your mummy love you, then?' she overheard Alice say, just as she was about to go back into the kitchen. She stopped, her hand reaching out for the latch, but decided to wait for Dan's response. The door was ajar – enough to hear the conversation, but not wide enough for them to see her.

'Good question, Alice,' Dan said. 'Mums can be funny things, right?'

'Yeah,' Alice replied in a voice that Libby knew she was putting on to sound more grown up in front of her big brother. 'Mine's funny too.'

Silence for a moment, then the sound of Alice slurping on her drink. Libby closed her eyes briefly.

'Why is your mummy funny?' she pressed on. 'Does she cry a lot, like mine?'

'I've never seen my mum cry,' Dan said with a laugh.

More silence and the sound of felt pens scrubbing over the paper.

'Pass the green, please,' Alice said.

'Why does yours cry, Ali?' Dan asked.

Libby felt herself bristling, wanting to burst in and change the subject. But then, she also wanted to hear what Alice had to say.

'She must be sad, mustn't she?' Alice continued slowly, clearly not really knowing.

'Mmm,' Dan went on.

Thinking their chat was fizzling out, that it meant nothing in particular, Libby was about to go back in. But she suddenly froze again.

'Your mummy's scary,' Alice said.

Dan laughed loudly. 'Depends who you ask,' he said in a tone that Libby knew would go straight over Alice's head. 'She's all right really.'

'She was the bad lady in my dream except it wasn't a dream and she was in my house and she shouldn't have been cos Sasha was babysitting not her and I was going to tell on her but then I didn't as I was too scared so I just hid with Mr Flumps and we made a tent under the duvet until she went away.'

Libby held her breath as she listened out for Dan's response. Whatever Alice was talking about had come spewing out in a quick-fire stream.

'Sounds scary,' Dan said, clearly not paying much attention. 'But I've got to learn the periodic table for a test as well as write up an experiment, so why don't you do the colouring now?'

'No, I want you to help, Dan.' Alice made a whiny noise. 'What's a speriment?'

'Shhh,' Dan said.

'Doesn't your mummy like our daddy any more?' Alice pressed on.

'No,' Dan said, sighing. He was a patient lad, but Libby knew that a switch would soon flick and he'd either end up leaving the room for somewhere more peaceful or he'd snap at Alice. Then Libby heard the thud-thud as Alice swung her legs, kicking her chair. She knew it meant she was agitated.

'Hey, guys,' Libby said, striding back into the kitchen. As expected, Dan was leaning over his books, glasses on. 'I found it.' She held up the celeriac, her hands shaking. But Alice jumped, letting out a high-pitched scream, making Libby drop the vegetable. They all watched as it fell to the tiles, as if in slow motion, splitting clean in two.

*

'How did Alice seem to you earlier?' Libby asked Dan. Alice was upstairs in her room playing and, after eating dinner, she and

Dan were in the living room watching TV. Dan was sprawled on the sofa but, since *that night*, Libby had refused to sit on it. She either perched on the window seat or, as now, sat in the small armchair beside the fire. Sean hadn't come home yet and Libby was conscious he was late.

'Talkative,' Dan said, laughing, his almost-broken voice squeaking high then low as his eyes stayed fixed on the screen.

'I wasn't eavesdropping exactly,' Libby went on, 'but I couldn't help hearing Alice talking about your mum earlier.'

'Yeah,' Dan said, scraping out his yoghurt pot. 'She said something. I dunno, I wasn't really paying attention.'

'I think Alice was… was concerned about…' Libby wasn't sure whether to mention it or not, but however much Sean wanted to protect Natalie, the more she thought about it, the more she realised it could change everything about that night, what they told the police. 'I was just wondering if your mum had come round here several Fridays ago, Dan?'

'Maybe. I'm not sure,' Dan said. His attention stayed firmly on the TV. 'Can't really remember, soz.'

Libby reached for the remote and turned down the volume. 'Can you have a think? It's quite important.'

'*Hey*, it was just getting to the good bit.' He held out his hand for the remote, making a silly, pleading face.

'It was the nineteenth of October, Dan. Is there any way you can check what you were doing that night? It might remind you of where your mum was?' Libby kept hold of the remote control.

'Hang on,' Dan said resignedly, going off to the kitchen and returning with his school bag. He pulled out his phone and checked his messages. 'The nineteenth?'

Libby nodded.

'I stopped over at my mate's house. I've got texts here arranging it. We played *World of Warcraft* most of the night, watched a movie. Don't tell Mum but it was an eighteen.' He pulled a face then, knowing Libby wouldn't mind.

'Where does your friend live, Dan?'

'Oh, just round the corner. He's in Great Lyne too. Tom's place is on…' He paused, looking at the ceiling. 'What's it called? That last lane off Drover's Way. Mum was annoyed at having to drive me out here at short notice, that's all I can remember. Said it was Friday night and she wanted a drink and had better things to do than to be driving me around.'

'What time did she drop you off?'

'About eight, I think. Knowing her, she'll have not wasted the journey and gone into The Falconer's for a quick one before she went home. Between you and me, I think there's a guy who goes in there that she likes. She's always going on dates and stuff.'

'I see, thanks, Dan. That's helpful.'

He held his hand out again for the remote control but pulled back, suddenly looking worried. 'This won't get Mum into trouble, will it? That I've told you? I mean, I don't know for sure if she went in the pub or came here or went to Timbuktu for that matter. I'm just going by what she usually does if she drops me off at Tom's.'

'No, no, don't worry, it's fine.' Libby smiled, her mind racing. She wished Sean would hurry up and get home. 'Here,' she said, passing over the remote. 'Carry on with your show, love. I'm going to tuck Alice in.'

Dan smiled and turned the volume up again while Libby went through to the kitchen. But, instead of attending to Alice, she poured herself a small drink and picked up her phone. 'Hi,' she said, when Sean's voicemail kicked in. 'It's me. I've no idea where you are but you need to come home immediately.'

CHAPTER THIRTY-NINE

Libby stared at the note through teary eyes, the words blurry as she pondered what to do with it. Last night, she'd decided to get rid of it, but couldn't. Not yet.

The *second* note.

I'm warning you again about your husband. He's having an affair.

'Alice,' she called out from the study. She had to get Alice to Marion's so she could get on with food preparations. 'Are you ready, darling?'

'Coming, Mummy,' was the response from upstairs.

Libby held the paper between shaking hands, leaning on her desk, then hid it under some papers, vowing to destroy it later. She hadn't been thinking straight, and no good would come of showing Sean. A second note wasn't going to make him confess anything, especially as he'd probably realise right away that she'd faked it.

'There's a good girl,' Libby said, after she'd bounced downstairs, her toy dog tucked under her arm. 'You taking Mr Flumps?'

'Yes,' Alice said, hugging him to her chest. 'He saves me from the baddies.'

Libby crouched down, halting her daughter in her tracks. 'What baddies, Alice?'

Alice tugged on her hair, twiddling it between her fingers while still clutching her toy. 'The baddy that made Sasha go to the angels,' she said, matter-of-factly. 'Where are the angels, Mummy? Are they really in the sky?' Alice glanced up at the ceiling.

Libby paused, looking lovingly at her daughter – her bright blue eyes reflecting innocence. 'I, um, I think so, yes. Here, look at you. You've got toothpaste round your mouth.' Libby took a tissue from her pocket and wiped Alice's lips. She shied away, pulling a face and squirming.

'Will Sasha come back from the angels?'

'I don't know, darling,' Libby said, reaching for Alice's pink coat. She slipped it on her daughter, zipping it up. 'But I really wish she would.'

*

Libby strapped Alice into the car seat in the hire car – much smaller than her VW estate, but Sean said it was all he could get locally at short notice.

'Where have you been?' Libby had said to him last night when he'd finally arrived home. She'd already put Alice to bed and had gone into the study to deal with some bills, but she'd got distracted. When she couldn't concentrate, she went and sat in the kitchen, waiting for him, her anger welling up as the minutes passed.

'Sorting out a car for you,' he said at the door, waving someone off as they drove away.

'Who was that?'

'Andy from the garage. OK? He and his mate helped me out getting the car back here.'

'Don't talk to me about the bloody garage, Sean Randell,' Libby said. 'What were you even *thinking*?'

'It's fine,' he said. 'Andy's cool about all that. I thought you'd be pleased to have a car, not berate me for it.'

Libby shook her head. 'Thanks, sorry. Of course I'm grateful.' She peered out of the front kitchen window. 'But you know what

I'm talking about. You lied to the police about where the Land Rover was that night.'

'It's the little blue Ford outside,' he said, ignoring her comment. 'Will it do you for a few days? I got a child seat in it for Alice. It's all Andy had to rent out right now and I wanted to give him the business. Besides, Crossroads Garage is local and they've always been good to me.'

'Oh yes, they're being good to you all right, covering up.' Libby turned and scowled at him. 'Just how good do you think they'll be when the police come knocking on their door asking questions about when the Land Rover was in for repairs?'

'Trust me, OK?' Sean said, taking her by the shoulders. 'It's sorted. And you really have no choice.'

Libby slumped down at the kitchen table, holding her head in her hands. 'I do trust you…' The words burned up her throat. 'All this is just so… I don't like it,' she said. 'I don't like it one bit. None of this is right.'

'Look,' Sean said, pulling up a chair beside her. 'I don't know how many times I've told you, but I need you to be strong. For our family. For you. For *us*.'

'Is there an *us* any more, Sean? Answer honestly.'

He opened his mouth but Libby put her finger over his lips.

'I don't want to hear it. I really don't…' She'd got up then and gone to her desk in the little study, putting on a brave face as she passed Dan, who was still engrossed in the TV. She sat staring at the piece of paper she'd carelessly left on her desk, eventually hiding it under a file, deciding she would throw it on the fire when everyone had gone to bed.

*

A potato rolled off the stainless-steel worktop and onto the floor. Libby swore under her breath and bent down to pick it up, chucking it in the waste bin. It was mid-morning and Alice had been up at Marion's a couple of hours, so she wanted to cram in as much preparation for tomorrow night's dinner as she could. Anything to distract herself from what was going on, especially as the police had been an unnerving presence in the village over the last twenty-four hours.

She continued peeling the potatoes, ready to boil them up to make the black garlic gnocchi. It was one of the dishes on the menu that could be made in advance and cooked on-site in the client's kitchen. She held back the tears as she worked, the sudden switch of music from a fast, powerful tempo to something moving and wistful making her doubly emotional.

Normally she'd be enlisting Sasha's help right about now – to make sure all the cutlery and crockery was counted out, all of it clean. It was her job, too, to pack the plastic storage crates with the items they'd need – the correct number and type of wine glasses, coordinating napkins, table decorations, place cards as the hostess had instructed, the red wines plus making sure the whites were chilling in the fridge along with any champagne, place mats, tablecloths… the list was long. Libby had most things that were required for an 'at home' dinner, but occasionally needed to hire stuff herself if the event was bigger.

Either way, not having Sasha flitting in and out between the kitchen and her car, checking off the list, was unsettling. No, it was *tragic*. She had so much to do between now and tomorrow evening when, in reality, she didn't want to do anything – let alone be around happy people tomorrow night celebrating at the birthday dinner.

'Knock, knock,' a voice said at the kitchen door – a familiar voice that instantly set Libby's nerves on edge, even before she saw who it was.

'Oh…' Libby glanced up. 'Natalie.'

'No, don't stop what you're doing,' she said, stepping into the kitchen. Even though it was fresh outside, Libby had the top half of the stable door open while the stock pot simmered on the stove. The reduction was a long process to get the full flavour for the artichoke and truffle risotto and, even with the extractor, the kitchen soon got steamy and warm.

Libby put down the knife. She didn't trust herself not to cut her finger with Natalie looming over her. 'Do come right on in,' she said as she came up close.

'If you're going to take that tone, I may as well get down to it.'

Libby felt her heart rate kick up another notch, her mouth go dry. She opened her mouth but didn't get a chance to speak.

'Stop filling my son's head with shit,' Natalie spat out.

'*What?* I—'

'A simple enough request, I would have thought. Even for a woman stupid enough to steal my husband.'

'Natal—'

'Dan is vulnerable. He doesn't need you and your spoilt child filling his head with rubbish, OK?'

'I really don't know what you're talking about, Natalie,' Libby said, angry that her cheeks decided to colour up even though she'd done nothing wrong. 'Let's stay calm. Why do you say Dan is vulnerable?' Libby had never once sensed that Dan wasn't settled, competent and stable – in and out of school. Sure, he'd had the occasional teenage mood, had lost money and items of school uniform once or twice, and occasionally forgotten to do his homework, but he was a kind boy who loved his family. She'd never have labelled him vulnerable.

'About that girl,' Natalie said. 'The one who's disappeared.'

'Sasha?' Libby said as she rinsed her hands under the tap. She dried them and stood squarely facing her husband's ex-wife, only the narrow work bench separating them. 'What about her?'

'He had a thing for her, of course. Why do you think he was always hanging around here when she was working for you in your…' Natalie glanced around, turning up her nose. 'In your shed?'

'What are you talking about?' Libby couldn't help the incredulous expression.

'It's true. You ask Sean. The poor boy was lovesick. Making me drop him off in case she was here.'

'I had no idea,' Libby said, though she couldn't recall many instances when Dan had been dropped off without prior arrangement. In fact, Natalie often changed the court-ordered arrangements at the last minute to suit her, with Sean complying to keep the peace. What she was saying didn't make sense.

'Parenting instincts come more naturally to some, I suppose,' she went on. 'And don't ever think you'll be my boy's mother.' Natalie looked her up and down. 'That's mine and Sean's job to parent him. It will bond us for the rest of our lives.'

'Yes, yes, I know that and I'd never try to—'

'So what I suggest, Libby, is that you don't quiz my son about my whereabouts, you don't allow your four-year-old daughter to bad-mouth me to Dan, and you mind your own fucking business about where I am, where I've been and who I see. OK?'

Libby stood frozen, reeling. 'Wow,' she said finally, quietly. 'That's a lot of anger you've got packed up there, Natalie.' Libby went round to the other side of the work island and faced her full on. Her body was shaking from the inside out, but she didn't care. 'Look, I know you hate me. And I know you hate that Sean left you, and he and I got together. I know you also hate that we're blissfully happy together. Plus you hate that we have a daughter – you always wanted a girl, didn't you? – and I know, too, that you hate that we live in the type of house you've always coveted. You also hate that Dan actually really likes coming here and spending time with us, as a *family*, while you're left bitter and alone. I get that.'

Libby took a step closer, aware that Natalie was a good few inches taller than her, especially in the heeled boots she was wearing. But with that ridiculous pink bag slung over her arm and the mortification that would come from breaking a nail or tearing her designer blouse, Libby didn't feel in the least bit threatened. In fact, right now, she'd love nothing more than a scrap with her and to pull her stupid hair extensions clean off her head.

'But Dan is a good lad, Natalie. He's honest, hard-working as much as you could expect at his age, he's liked by his mates, he adores his little sister and gets on great with his dad. He likes coming here because… well, he *likes* it. I've never seen any evidence of him having a crush on Sasha. In fact, I don't even recall him encountering her, let alone hanging around when she's here. What *I* think, Natalie, is that you're trying to cover something up. Hiding behind an innocent boy.'

Natalie opened her mouth to protest, but Libby raised her hand, halting her.

'I think if anyone's got a thing for anyone, it's you for Sean. You can't let go, can you? You can't stand the thought that he's happier with me – a normal woman who gets the occasional spot on her chin, doesn't have time to get her hair done as often as she would like, is guilty of buying clothes in Primark or Tesco, sometimes feeds her daughter spaghetti on toast, and who hasn't had the chance to paint her toenails in living memory. But you know what? Sean loves me. And he's done with loving you. So what I suggest is that you be a better mother to your son, keep your nose out of our business and stop leaving stupid notes on my car. OK? No good will come of it.'

Libby stepped back and took hold of the worktop to steady herself. Her chest heaved up and down, the adrenalin firing through her making her breathless. She felt better for saying what she'd said, but also terrified of the repercussions. She knew Sean was protective of Natalie and she only hoped it was because of their shared responsibility – Dan – and nothing more.

Natalie's smile grew – exposing brilliant white teeth behind her full, pink lips. 'Poor Seany,' she said, looking her up and down.

'What *was* he thinking?' She swished back her hair with her free hand, pushing back her shoulders, her lips blooming into a pout. 'You're *so* not his type. Trust me on that one. I know him way better than you ever will. I know what he's *like*.'

That was all it took. Libby reached out, and before she could stop herself, she'd shoved Natalie in the middle of her chest, sending her staggering backwards. She bumped against the refrigerator but quickly regained her balance, her face betraying little shock.

'I know you were here that night,' Libby said, spit flying from her mouth. 'When Sasha went missing. I know you were in my house. What were you doing here, Natalie? What did you *do*, more to the point?'

Natalie just stared at her, pulling her car keys from her bag. She shook her head, making a pitying face. 'I'm going now, Libby. You know I could go straight to the police and file an assault complaint. But you're just not worth it. You're really not.' She gave a brief glance back over her shoulder before she left, her ankles wobbling in her heels as she strode over the courtyard cobbles.

CHAPTER FORTY

Libby leant against the worktop for what seemed like hours. Head down, cradled in her arms, the potatoes she'd already peeled browning in the colander. *Fuck*, she shouted in her head. *Fuck, fuck, fuck*.

She stood up, going over to the radio and thumping the off button too hard. The scene with Natalie had been made all the more surreal with Mozart orchestrating a dramatic backdrop. She stared at the food she'd set out ready to prepare: the beetroot to braise for the scallop starter, the cauliflower to puree to go with the lamb, the aubergine to smoke as an accompaniment to the cod, and the honey she was going to steep with orange blossom for one of the desserts. With several choices for each course, the menu was ambitious. More ambitious than she was able to cope with right now. As things stood, even picking up a takeaway on the way to her clients' house would be more than she could manage.

There was nothing for it but to pack up the kitchen for the afternoon and take a break. Perhaps she'd come back to it later, perhaps she wouldn't. All she wanted was to crawl into bed and stare at the ceiling, accept that her business would go down the pan. With everything put back in the fridge, Libby turned off the lights and locked up the barn.

She walked across the yard and went into the boot room, going on through to the kitchen. It was only lunchtime but she didn't care – a drink would calm her nerves, perhaps provide a solution, but as soon as she set foot inside, she sensed something was wrong.

A noise. Someone crying – coming from the living room.

It sounded like a man.

Slowly, quietly, Libby crept through the hallway. She hesitated outside the door, hearing only sighs now and someone clearing their throat. It didn't sound like Sean. With her hand on her phone, in case she needed to dial for help, Libby slowly opened the door and peered round it.

'Oh my God, *Phil*,' she said, exhaling with relief. 'You scared the daylights out of me.'

'Libby,' he said, standing up from the sofa. 'I… I'm *so* sorry. I know I shouldn't be here but the back door was open and—'

'Hey,' she said, holding up her hands. 'It's OK. I totally understand. Jan has done exactly the same thing, if it makes you feel any better. It's OK, honestly.' Either way, she had no energy left to argue.

'Thank you,' Phil replied. 'That means a lot.'

Libby gave a little nod. 'You take as long as you need.'

Phil looked solemn, sitting down again.

'It's natural that you want to feel close to where Sasha last was at a time like this.'

Phil frowned briefly, staring at the floor, touching his forehead. 'Yes, yes you're right. It's… it's important for me.'

Libby disappeared back to the kitchen to give Phil some space, but returned shortly with two mugs of tea. 'Here,' she said. 'Drink this.'

'Thanks, Libby.' Phil didn't look at her as he took the mug.

'Can I ask you an odd question?' Libby said, still shaking from her outburst with Natalie. Part of her wondered if she would go to the police, just to spite her and have her arrested or cautioned or whatever they do for shoving someone. She would no doubt twist what actually happened into something far more dramatic.

'Of course,' Phil said, still not making eye contact.

'Does Sasha know Dan, Sean's son by his first wife, do you know?' Libby knew Phil had met Dan a couple of times in the past when he'd been on shoots with his dad. He'd also earned some pocket money as a beater and loved being part of the group, working together as a team, flags to hand for flushing the birds out of the woods.

Dan had often come home exhilarated during those autumn and winter months, full of stories about how he'd had to push through the undergrowth, how the spent shot had rained down on him when he'd reached the crest of a hill and the guns were firing high over their heads, how he'd been given game pie for lunch and got to pick some of the birds to bring home. Libby remembered his rosy cheeks too, knowing that Sean would have given him a few sips of port from his hip flask as they'd stood waiting around for instructions, often in the sheeting rain. She knew it was all part of the day, part of the camaraderie.

Phil looked thoughtful but his expression gave nothing away.

'Has Sasha ever been on a shoot, perhaps? Is that how they know each other?' As under-keeper, it was Phil's job to organise the beaters.

'No, not our Sash,' Phil answered immediately, almost mustering a smile. 'You wouldn't catch her dead... doing that.'

They both fell silent for a moment, Phil visibly fighting back more tears.

'I'm sorry, I... I didn't mean to pry. I just wondered if that's how she knew Dan.'

'I don't think she knows Sean's lad. They're different ages, aren't they? Though it's not outside the realms of possibility, I suppose.'

Libby thought about this, concluding it was probably Natalie stirring or covering her own tracks for whatever reason. 'Yes, you're right, it's unlikely.'

'Sean's been organising another search,' Phil said. His mug was clamped between his hands – rough hands that shook as he brought the tea to his mouth. 'We're probably on a hiding to nothing but that shoe...' He dropped his head. 'She's out there somewhere, I feel sure of it. The first search covered the estate ground and the area between here and Little Radwell in case she'd walked home, somehow got lost or had an accident. This time, I said we should head further east and search between here and the Dentons' farm. There are a few old buildings and copses along the way that warrant a look.'

It was clear from his expression that Phil thought the expedition would prove fruitless but, as a father, he couldn't just do nothing.

'Haven't the police already scoured that area?' Libby asked, wondering why Sean hadn't mentioned the search.

'Of course,' Phil said. 'But no one knows the land like us. They could have missed something vital. All the lads are coming, even Eric. We'll get the dogs on it too, and use the radios to stay in touch. It's all thanks to Sean this is happening.'

'I see,' Libby said, going cold inside. 'Let's hope it turns something up.' She hadn't wanted to say *Sasha* because, after all this time, that would probably have meant finding a body.

Phil reached out and touched her arm, sliding it down to her hand and gripping it, meshing his fingers with hers. 'Thanks, Libby. I know this has been hard for you too, because—'

'Oh, hello Sean…' Libby said, suddenly turning as she caught sight of him standing in the doorway. Her cheeks flushed as he stared at them, Phil's hand still entwined with hers.

Libby quickly pulled away, standing up and going over to him. 'How come you're home?' she said, giving him a kiss. Sean didn't respond.

'Phil,' Sean said. 'How are you doing?' He cleared his throat.

'I'd like to say bearing up, but that would be lying,' Phil said, also standing. 'I'll be out of your way now. Sorry to have disturbed you.'

'No problem,' Sean said, giving him a wary look. 'Will you be up to coming on the search tomorrow or would you rather leave it to us? There should be a good turnout.'

'I'll be there,' Phil said. 'It's my girl. My *baby*...' He covered his face before making an apology and heading for the front door.

Libby let Sean show him out, thinking it was best. After everything, she didn't want Sean to get the wrong impression about what he'd just stumbled in on. She had enough problems as it was.

CHAPTER FORTY-ONE

Now

I'm taken back to the interview room with Claire. I'm shaking, my legs feeling as though they'll give way at any moment. Before the door is shut, I turn back, taking a look at the other rooms leading off the corridor, wondering who is behind the closed doors – drunk drivers, people arrested for disturbing the peace, a domestic violence perpetrator, a drugs dealer.

A murderer.

'I didn't do it,' I'd told Claire when we were alone. 'I did not kill Sasha.' I'd covered my face, rocking in my chair, unable to take in what the solicitor was saying, the advice she was giving me, asking if I wanted to make a statement for her to read out. Nothing was sinking in. Nothing was making sense.

We sit down again.

'This interview is being recorded,' the detective says after the beep from the device. She states the time. 'My name is DC Ellen McCaulay and the other people present in the room are…'

She pauses, allowing DI Jones to identify himself, along with my solicitor, who again states her name and reason for being here. Finally, I say my name and date of birth.

'Thank you,' the officer says. 'Libby, we've had a break now in order for you to take legal advice, but there are a few things we'd like you to explain further, if that's OK with you.'

Slowly I look up. Why does she sound different, as though she's suddenly on my side? As though we're friends having a coffee? I don't understand why her voice is now calm and kind, with none of the previous accusing tone.

'OK,' I say, head hanging low again.

'Before you begin,' Claire says, clearing her throat. 'My client has made a signed statement that I'd like to read out.'

'Go ahead,' DI Jones says.

Claire clears her throat. '"I, Elizabeth Mary Randell, wish to state for the record that on Saturday, sixth of October, thirteen days before Sasha Long's disappearance, Sasha was working with me on a dinner party event. When she was loading up my car with items, she accidentally dropped a box containing wine glasses while trying to put them in the boot of my Volkswagen estate. She picked up and rested the box in the boot, unwrapping several glasses to check for breakages. Sasha then cut her finger on a broken glass and blood dropped onto the carpet of my car as well as getting on the paper protecting the glasses. This paper later got strewn around my boot. I witnessed all of the above and went to fetch a plaster for Sasha and applied it as it was bleeding badly. Signed Elizabeth Randell".' Claire then passes my statement to DI Jones.

'Thank you,' he says, glancing at it and sliding it into the file. 'You didn't think to tell us this before?'

I don't reply.

'OK, Libby,' he continues. 'Putting aside forensic evidence for now, we're still a bit confused about the timings on the night you went out for a meal with Sean. We'd really like it if you could help us understand. And we do realise that this is stressful for you, that things might feel muddled.'

DI Jones's voice doesn't sound like him any more either. Gone is the gruffness, the blank face as I dare to meet his eye. Instead, he's sitting there, leaning forward on his forearms with almost a smile on his face, as if he's telling me that if I just clear this up, I'll be able to go home. Back to my daughter. Back to my life.

'I know, I'm sorry. Things may have got muddled. We'd both had wine and…' I trail off, hearing Sean's voice in my head, seeing his hand rise up above my head. 'I'll do my best to help.'

'If you can quickly recap how things went for you and Sean at the pub when you ate your meal? Were you getting on OK or were things a bit strained, would you say?'

'A bit of both,' I say, wishing I'd said 'no comment'. But that hadn't done me any good so far. 'I felt wretched about accusing him of… of having an affair. I got annoyed when he received some texts and calls. We were supposed to be spending time together. It just got out of hand. It wasn't anything like the nice evening I'd imagined. And it was all my fault.'

'Who do you think was texting and calling your husband, Libby?'

I shrug, staring at the floor. 'I don't know.'

'Is Sean close to his mother?' DI Jones goes on, his voice still encouraging, as if I just need to say the right thing and then all this will be over.

'Yes,' I say. 'They're close.'

'How would you describe your relationship with Marion Randell?' DC McCaulay asks.

'She's…' I pause, thinking. Anything about Marion is hard to describe, almost as if she has a tough shell around her – protecting her, never allowing anyone in. 'She'd do anything for us. I know she felt wretched that she couldn't babysit that night.'

DC McCaulay makes notes, looking up periodically.

'She's a good mother-in-law,' I continue. 'She adores Alice, and Sean too, of course.' I smile. 'She coddles him a bit, if I'm honest. As if she's, I dunno, stuck in the past. As if he's still a little boy. I don't think she's got much in the way of a relationship with Fred, her husband, so she pours all her love into Sean and Alice.'

A chill runs through me as I hear my own voice, saying stuff that I've internalised for so long.

'It can feel a bit stifling, to be honest. As though everything has to have Marion's approval. Does that make sense?' Perhaps it's therapy I need, not a police interview. 'She's had some health issues over the years, though she never likes to talk about that. She puts on a brave face, so I try to be understanding.'

'Did your husband tell you who was calling and texting him when you were out for dinner?' McCaulay continues.

'He said it was his mother,' I say. 'But I didn't believe him.'

I hear Claire fidgeting beside me, uncrossing and crossing her legs, clearing her throat.

'Why couldn't Marion babysit for you that night? She normally does, doesn't she?' DI Jones asks.

'She had a church meeting, but Sasha was free so it was no big deal.'

'What was Marion's church meeting for, do you know?' DI Jones asks. 'And where was it?'

I shrug. 'Flower rotas or something,' I say. 'At St Andrew's, our local church. Marion is always organising something.' I stare at the wall behind the detective, unable to look him in the eye. 'It's almost as though she needs to be in control of everything. Because she once wasn't,' I add, thinking out loud. Then Sean's accident is on my mind, the pain etched on Marion's face as she described how helpless she felt, how she should have been there for her son, done something to prevent it. But she still couldn't bring herself to tell me exactly what had happened.

'And if the meeting had been cancelled, would Marion tell you?'

'Well of course,' I say, without even having to think. 'She'd have been round to babysit like a shot.'

'Marion's meeting *was* cancelled, Libby. Do you think that's why she was calling your husband when you were out for a meal?'

I stare at DI Jones, not knowing what to say. 'No comment,' I say, coughing as something catches in my throat. 'Please may I have some water?'

'Can you tell us how you left things at home when you went out for your meal, Libby?' DC McCaulay asks, turning in her chair. She pours me a cup from the machine next to her, sliding it across the table.

'Thank you,' I say, gulping it down, wiping my mouth with the back of my hand. 'What do you mean, how I left things?'

'You know, was the television on, what was Sasha doing, where was Alice… that kind of thing.'

'Um… well Sasha was sitting on the sofa with her books spread around her. Alice was in bed, though I'm sure she'd have come down a couple of times. She likes Sasha. The TV was on, yes, and Sean had lit the fire earlier. Sash would always keep it going.'

'What do you burn on the fire, Libby?' DI Jones asks.

I pause, twirling the plastic cup between my fingers. 'Logs,' I say. 'Occasionally coal.'

'Do you tend to throw rubbish on the fire?'

'No,' I say. 'I recycle as much as I can.' I crunch the cup until it makes a cracking sound.

Cracking and popping, just like the logs on the fire – sparks spitting out against the guard…

'Christ, oh Christ *no*…' I'd yelled to Sean after we'd got back home that Friday night. My hands covered my mouth as deep, painful screams came up my throat, cutting like razor blades. I didn't care, I *wanted* to feel pain as I stared at the contents of Sasha's backpack lying everywhere – tipped out in what must have been a frenzy.

'Shut *up*, Libby,' Sean had boomed at me. 'Let me think.'

'Think? *Think*?' I'd said, hyperventilating as I walked away, walked back again, unable to take my eyes off the mess. The plate of food was upturned on the floor, some of it spilt on the wooden coffee table – an ochre-coloured sauce mixed up with chicken and rice – some on the rug too. The fork was a few feet away, lying in front of the hearth. Sasha's glass of water was still beside her college books, a little crescent of lip balm imprinted around the rim where she'd sipped. It seemed the only thing left of her, the only thing to mark that she was ever here…

'Libby?' DC McCaulay says, making me snap back to the present. 'Can you answer the question?'

'Sorry?'

'Did you or Sean put anything on the fire that night apart from logs or coal, either before or after you went to the pub?'

I squeeze harder on the plastic cup, the sides almost meeting in the middle as I think back again…

'No, oh no, no, *no*…' I'd cried a hundred times until Sean had to slap me again.

'Stop, don't touch anything!' he'd boomed as I reached out for the pen lying on the floor beside Sasha's backpack.

'How did this *happen*?' I'd said, pointing at everything. 'It *can't* have done…'

'No comment,' I say to DC McCaulay now, looking her in the eye. 'I would never put plastic on the fire.'

'OK, Libby, thank you. Though I didn't specify plastic. Can you explain further?'

I crunch the cup even harder, hearing the loud crack as it finally splits – reminding me of how I felt that night – torn in two…

'Sean, you *can't*,' I'd said to him, grabbing his hand. '*Don't…*'

He'd yanked his arm from my grip, doing it anyway, stoking the glowing embers despite my protests – the hottest part of the fire. Then he chucked on a couple more logs. 'Everything will be OK, Libby.'

'*What?*' I'd cried. 'You can't honestly mean that. You're mad. *Crazy*. I'm calling the police.' I'd reached for my phone then, but Sean grabbed it from me.

'Libby, stop. We don't need to call them yet.' Sweat glistened on his top lip and his cheeks were flushed. The flames licked around the fresh logs, cracking and popping in the grate…

'No, no I'm sorry, I can't explain,' I reply to the detective, putting the plastic cup down. 'I can't explain anything any more,' I whisper, staring at the ceiling. 'I trusted him, you know. I really, *really* trusted him.'

'I understand this is hard for you, Libby,' she continues, her voice still soft. 'Can you tell us who it is you trusted?'

I can't help the tears rolling down my cheeks as I remember how Sean had taken me into the kitchen, talked to me, calmed me, told me everything would be OK over and over again until I'd believed him. I'd nodded, pressed my face against his chest as he'd held me, knowing he'd make everything better.

'Sean,' I say, wiping my face. 'I trusted Sean.'

CHAPTER FORTY-TWO

Before

Libby woke before it was light. She'd slept fitfully and knew Sean had too – each of them tossing and turning, their backs to each other, sleeping as far apart on the bed as space would allow. She got up to use the bathroom, washed her face, saw the gaunt woman staring back at her in the mirror above the sink. The woman she'd come to hate.

'Sean,' she whispered, climbing back into bed. 'Are you awake?' She pressed herself against him, feeling his warmth against her chilled body. He groaned, turning slightly before slinging back the duvet and wrenching himself away from her. He sat up.

'I have to get up. We're starting the search early. Phil and the others will be up at the gatehouse soon.'

'It's not even light.'

'It will be by seven. That's when we're meeting.' Without looking at her or saying anything else, Sean went into the bathroom. A moment later, Libby heard the shower running, the steamy scent of familiar body wash seeping out under the door. When he came back, a towel slung low on his hips, Libby was already dressed, having thrown on some old jeans and Sean's sweatshirt that she'd found lying over the back of the chair. Her hair hung down her back in a messy ponytail. She didn't care what she looked like, didn't care if she'd washed or not.

'Where are you searching?' she asked, sitting on the bed, watching as Sean stepped into his underpants, pulling on his socks. He opened the wardrobe, yanking out a pair of dark-green trousers, the ones he often wore when out on a shoot, followed by a clean T-shirt and a dark fleece top. He sat down on the bed beside her.

'Near where Sasha's shoe was found. They want to cover ground east of that, towards the Dentons' place. I'm not so sure. I went out yesterday, to do a recce, and I'm going to tell them to go west. I'll cover the eastern fields in the Land Rover, probably with Eric and a couple of others. There's a track all the way up.' Sean's voice was devoid of emotion. 'If there's anything of hers still out there, they'll find it.'

Libby nodded. 'Fine,' she replied. 'I'll make some coffee.' She went downstairs, listening outside Alice's door for a moment, her heart melting at the sound of her soft breathing – the only thing keeping her going right now.

She put some coffee beans in the machine, topped up the water and pressed a couple of buttons.

'Natalie was here that night, you know,' she said, turning when Sean came up behind her. 'I'm convinced of it.'

'What are you talking about?' Sean replied, running a glass of water and gulping it down.

'Why are you trying to protect her?' Libby hated that their exchange was so terse and stilted, every word measured. As though they weren't a team any more. She looked at his back as he stared out of the window, wanting nothing more than to slide her hands onto his shoulders, rest her head on him.

'You've never liked her, have you?' Sean shook his head. 'There was no reason for Natalie to be here. It wasn't my weekend with Dan.'

'She was in the village dropping Dan at Tom's house. I'm certain it's the reason why Alice was scared. She's as good as told me that Natalie was here. And then there was the bracelet I found. Why would she call round, Sean?' Libby said, her tone more accusatory than she intended. 'What did she want? Think about it… what did she *do*?'

'Jealousy is an ugly trait, Libby,' he replied. 'And it's more than I can handle right now. I've got a search to lead and—'

'I don't understand why you're protecting her.'

Sean grabbed a mug from the shelf and put it under the machine. While it was filling, he came up close to Libby, taking her by the shoulders. 'Listen, Natalie was not here while we were out. Only Alice and Sasha were in this house. Got it?' His grip tightened.

Libby stared up at him, barely recognising her own husband. 'Yes,' she whispered, shrinking away.

She went to the window seat and curled up on it, tucking her legs beneath her, watching as Sean downed his coffee before heading to the back hall to lace up his boots. He returned wearing his Barbour jacket and cap, holding a long walking stick – his favourite one with the silver top. As he came past, he hesitated, and Libby wasn't sure if he was about to pull her into his arms, or hit her. That was how little she felt she knew him any more. His mouth opened to say something but then closed again and, a moment later, Libby heard the front door open and bang shut, followed by a rush of cold morning air into the kitchen.

She watched out of the window as he unlocked the Land Rover, got in and drove away. And then she sobbed for what seemed like hours. It was only when she felt a warm hand on hers, only when Alice whispered, 'What's wrong, Mummy?' that she stopped crying, wiping her face on the sleeve of Sean's old sweatshirt.

'Oh, sweetie, Mummy's just a bit sad,' she said, giving Alice a hug. 'But I'll be OK. Sometimes grown-ups cry too, you know.'

Alice looked concerned. 'Is it because Sasha has gone to see Jesus for a little while, Mummy? Is that why you're sad?'

Libby stared at her daughter, nodding. 'Yes, sweetheart, yes. That's why I'm sad.'

*

Mozart's Symphony No. 41 filled the kitchen as Libby worked on the remaining courses for tonight's dinner party. She peeled bulb after bulb of garlic, chopping the cloves finely and setting them aside. She simmered russet potatoes, smashing them up with flour, kneading and shaping them into little garlic and truffle oil-infused balls ready for later. She braised tiny turnips to go with the scallops, spatchcocked the woodpigeon, mixed up an anchovy dressing to drizzle over the Atlantic cod, and melted a pan of rich, dark chocolate to go in the salted caramel dessert.

Then she stopped, standing motionless, head down with her hands leaning on the work surface.

Sasha has gone to see Jesus for a little while…

Libby wiped her hands and went to the stable door, leaning out over the bottom half, sucking in the cool air. She wasn't sure if it was the heat in the kitchen or her short, sharp breaths that were making her feel light-headed. She bent her head down low, trying to get some blood back to her brain. When she thought how much she had to do before tonight, she wanted to weep again. Her mind was all over the place, what with Sean out searching with a dozen or so others, all with one purpose: to bring Sasha home.

'Christ knows what we'll find,' Sean had said last night as they were trying to fall asleep. Libby hadn't responded and Sean hadn't elaborated – each of them locked in their own thoughts.

'Finding Sasha's shoe is the only thing keeping attention on the area, you realise,' Libby had said an hour or so later when they were still both awake.

'I know,' Sean said quietly, almost regretfully.

'It's made everyone think she's still out there, in the fields or woods, somewhere local.'

'You heard what the detective said last time we saw him, Lib. He said it doesn't mean anything of the sort and they're broadening their enquiries. Yes, it's Sasha's shoe but she could have been bundled into a car and driven off anywhere. It doesn't indicate she's still in the area at all.'

Libby had sighed heavily, trying to get to sleep but failing.

'Fuck everything to *hell*,' Libby screamed into the courtyard, the tea towel knotted in her hands.

'You OK over there, Libby?' Arn's head popped up over the wall.

'Oh, God yes, yes, I'm so sorry for the bad language, Arn. Had a bit of a rubbish morning and I forgot myself for a moment.' She wiped her eyes, hoping he wouldn't see her tear-stained face from that distance. 'Just a few problems in the kitchen but nothing I can't sort,' she added, forcing a smile.

'Wish I could help, love,' he said, 'but I find microwaving a ready-made curry a challenge.' He held up a pair of secateurs. 'Just off to trim a few things back in the garden while the weather's fine,' he added. 'Hope you get it sorted.' And he ducked down again, his whistling getting fainter as he disappeared up his garden.

After a few deep breaths, Libby went back inside. When she searched in the freezer, she finally found what she was looking for. 'Useless labels,' she said, picking up yet another sticker from the shelf underneath the tub of sauce. But, when she opened it, it wasn't the one she was looking for, which meant she'd have to make another dip for the little chicken skewer canapés. She thought she'd had one in stock, was looking for ways to save time.

Libby took the haunch of venison from the fridge, ready to bone and marinade, thumping it down on the large chopping board. Her hand shook as she chose a knife from the block, selecting the sharpest she had. It wasn't an easy job and, in hindsight, she wished she'd asked the butcher to do it for her. But she'd wanted to learn, wanted to get the bone and offcuts into a stock straight away.

She washed her hands, tying back her hair to keep it out of her eyes. She splashed water on her face, soothing her puffy skin, and caught sight of herself in the little mirror by the stable door. She knew she looked a state – there were even more stains down the front of Sean's sweatshirt now. She'd somehow have to find time to shower and change before tonight.

As she manhandled the haunch, digging her fingers into the reddy-purple flesh to turn it over, the last few weeks flashed through her mind. A cruel gallery of images and uncontrollable thoughts played out in fast-forward as she slid the knife into the meat, letting the path of the hip bone guide her. Somehow, she knew it all fitted together – she just wasn't sure how.

And right at the core of everything was Sean – her lovely, kind, loyal man. But, as she hacked at the meat, cutting deeper and deeper into the flesh, pushing the knife around the bone, loosening it, all she could see was him with another woman – a faceless woman whom, for some reason, she blamed for everything else that had happened.

Libby's tears dropped onto the dark meat as she cried, her shoulders jerking in time with her sobs. Through blurry eyes, she managed to pull and ease away the large bone at the top of the haunch, dropping it in a big pan for the stock.

'Ow!' she cried as the knife suddenly slipped from the shank. Blood oozed out of her forefinger as she ran it under the tap; she squeezed it inside a paper towel to stop the flow. She didn't want to contaminate the meat so managed to unwrap the finger and apply a blue plaster with one hand. Everything felt so hopeless, so futile.

As she carried on working, she imagined Sean out with the beaters, his limp getting steadily worse as he trudged the fields, leading them west over the rise and down towards the stream – a possible shortcut home for Sasha that night. Then she pictured him in the Land Rover with Eric, scouring the lower-lying ground as he headed towards the Dentons' place. They owned most of that area and it was well marked with tracks, though Sean would be in and out of the driver's seat opening and closing gates. But he was familiar with the area, and it was also where, according to Marion, he'd had his accident all those years ago.

Libby lifted her shoulder, wiping her face on her sleeve, sniffing back the tears as best she could. She would not give up, she would not cancel tonight, and she would trust Sean that everything would be OK. She simply had no choice.

'Mrs Randell,' came a deep voice at the stable door, startling her.

Libby whipped her head up, the knife blade pressing against the bone, her fingers digging into the meat to steady it.

'Detective?' she said quietly, wondering what news he'd come to deliver. Then it dawned on her. *Natalie.*

DI Jones unlatched the bottom door and stepped inside, followed by a female uniformed officer she didn't recognise. 'Please put down the knife and step away from the worktop,' he instructed.

'What? I've got a dinner party later and—'

'Please do as instructed,' he said.

Libby put down the knife and walked away from the work surface. She shivered, staring at each of the officers in turn. 'I know this is Natalie's doing,' she said, rolling her eyes and trying to stop her voice from failing. 'I know it was wrong of me, but you have to understand that she blows everything out of proportion. Whatever she's told you, it was honestly just a tiny shove. She wasn't hurt and—'

'Mrs Elizabeth Randell, I am arresting you on suspicion of the murder of Sasha Long. You do not have to say anything, but it may harm your defence if you do not mention, when questioned, something that you later rely on in court. Anything you do say may be given in evidence,' DI Jones said, his arms folded as the female officer approached Libby, producing a pair of handcuffs.

'Hold out your wrists, please,' she said.

'*What?* I… but… no… *no*… I don't know what you're talking about!' Libby's head swam and her entire body shook as she felt the cold metal snap around her wrists.

'You'll be coming with us now, Mrs Randell,' the officer said, less sternly. 'Do you have any shoes?'

Libby stared down at her bare feet, not even certain what shoes were any more, let alone where she'd find any.

'Here, look, put these on,' DI Jones said, pointing to a pair of Crocs by the door. They were her old gardening shoes.

'The gas…' she mumbled, looking back over her shoulder to the stove. The officer went over to it, studying the knobs for a moment before turning off the burner. Libby cast an eye over the discarded ingredients on the worktop before being led outside. And that's when she saw the police car in the yard, parked across the gateway.

'Mind your head,' the PC said, opening the rear door of the vehicle, the sound of Mozart still ringing in Libby's ears. As DI Jones turned the car around and pulled out onto the lane, the familiar village scene suddenly looked like an alien landscape. Libby nervously lifted her hands to her mouth, biting on her nails. And all she could taste was blood.

CHAPTER FORTY-THREE

Now

I screw up my eyes as I step out onto the street, shielding my face with my arm as I stumble down the ramp. People walk past me, barely giving me a glance – the woman in jeans and a dirty sweatshirt. The woman who hasn't washed or eaten properly in what feels like days. The woman whose hair is tangled and greasy, whose face is puffy and tear-stained. The woman with blood under her nails.

There's a bus stop to my left and a rack of bicycles. Neither are any use to me for getting back to Great Lyne. A taxi is on its way.

'You're free to go,' DI Jones had said earlier this morning. At least, I think it was this morning. It could have been in the night for all I knew. I was flat on my back on the bunk, shivering, with only the thin blanket covering me, drifting in and out of a fitful sleep filled with dreams that I weren't sure were nightmares or real life.

I sat bolt upright, my head throbbing.

'What?'

'You're free to go,' he repeated. 'We're releasing you under investigation,' he added, as if I knew what that meant.

'Free?'

'For now,' he added, his face deadpan.

I swung my legs over the side of the bunk, slipping my feet into my Crocs. A uniformed officer came into the custody cell just as DI Jones left, striding off down the corridor with his hands pushed into his jeans pockets, his head down.

'Come with me,' the PC said, as another officer joined her. They escorted me back to the custody sergeant's desk – a different officer on duty now – and went through the process of booking me out of custody.

'Are you sure?' I said, too tired, too raw, too emotional to even feel happy about being set free. 'You're letting me go?'

'Unless you want to stay a while longer,' the sergeant said, his face spreading with lines, his teeth exposed. He produced a plastic bag with my belongings in: a couple of tissues, a small bag of Haribo, my house keys and my belt. 'Sign here,' he said, saying something over his shoulder to another officer. Something about doughnuts.

'OK,' I said, my hand shaking as I scrawled my name. Then he asked me how I was getting home and I said I didn't know. Though I didn't tell him that I wasn't sure where home was any more. He asked if I wanted him to call anyone.

'Sean,' I'd said, watching as he dialled the number on file, not even asking me who Sean was. It went straight to voicemail. 'Can you try Fran, my friend?' But as he was dialling, I asked him to stop. If hers went to voicemail too, my mind would connect the dots. I couldn't take that right now. 'It's OK,' I said. 'I just want to go home.' Then he'd called me a taxi.

I walk to the edge of the pavement as the black-and-white car pulls up, the driver winding down the passenger window, peering out at me. 'Taxi for Randell?' he calls out and I nod, getting in the back. I give him my address, trying to blank out the disappointment that Sean isn't waiting for me, pulling me into his arms, taking me home and making everything OK again. I have no idea where he is.

'Is it OK to grab my card when I get back?' I ask, shuddering as I remember paying the taxi that night. 'I don't have my purse.'

'Course, love,' he says, giving me a look in the rear-view mirror as if to say, *Don't worry, I pick up from here all the time...*

I buckle up my belt, hugging my arms around me, feeling light-headed and unreal as the taxi pulls away and drives off. There's not much traffic as we head north back through the city.

'What time is it?' I ask him, and he tells me it's twenty past twelve. Then I ask him what day it is and, after another few glances in the rear-view mirror, he tells me it's Sunday.

'Sunday?'

The driver nods, a knowing smile on his face.

Twenty-four hours, I think. Twenty-four hours of being apart. Being alone. Being separated. Being terrified. Being grilled and brought to my knees. Being abandoned. Being, strangely, the most at peace with my thoughts in three weeks. And probably the safest.

No one could touch me in there. I couldn't even harm myself.

Half an hour later, the taxi slows as we enter Great Lyne – the stone urns of autumnal flowers beside the village name sign flashing purple and yellow in the sunshine. It's a beautiful day, but not one that matches my mood. Or maybe it does. Maybe it's over now. Maybe life can go back to normal and Sean and I can pretend none of this ever happened. Pick up from that Friday evening as we prepare to go out for dinner, each of us looking at the other, Sean saying, 'Shall we stay home instead?' and me nodding, wrapping my arms around him before kicking off my heels, ordering a takeaway, cancelling our reservation. Cancelling our babysitter.

A few familiar faces – two women and a man, standing on the village green chatting, dogs on leads – stare at me as the taxi slowly passes. Almost the same scene as yesterday playing out but in reverse. Tongues will be wagging again. Gossip will be rife.

'Just there on the left,' I say, leaning forward, pointing. 'The thatched place,' I add, even though most in our lane are. He slows and pulls up outside, the engine running.

'Twenty-seven fifty, please, love,' he says, swinging round, one arm on the passenger seat.

I nod. 'Give me a moment,' I say, getting out of the car. The air smells fresh and clean, sweet in the sunshine, as if the village has been laundered since I've been gone. With shaking hands, I unlock the front door to my home and step inside. All the lights are off and the house feels cold.

'Hello?' I call out, though I already sense no one will reply. 'Sean?' I pause in the hallway, listening at the bottom of the stairs. 'Sean, it's me. Are you home?'

Nothing.

I go into the kitchen and find my bag on a chair. I take out my purse and go back to the taxi, paying on my card. My hand shakes as I push it into the machine, trying to remember my PIN through the fog in my brain. 'Thank you,' I say and the driver nods before driving off up the lane. As I head back inside, I hear the crunch of his gears as he turns around.

The house is just as I left it: my cardigan draped over a kitchen chair, a couple of mugs and the breakfast things left beside the sink, Alice's colouring book open on the table with a few felt pens beside it, a couple of the caps left off. There's a small pile of washing on the floor in front of the washing machine and another pile of clean laundry dumped on the window seat from when I didn't have time to fold it yesterday morning. I was intent on getting into the barn kitchen to prepare for last night's meal.

'Oh *God*,' I say, thinking of my clients, imagining them calling my mobile over and over when five o'clock, the time I was meant to arrive to set up, came and went. I go to my bag and pull out my phone, checking the screen. The battery is dead so I plug it into the cable next to the kettle and leave it to charge, heading for the back door and out to the barn. Both doors are unlocked – my house left vulnerable and everything ripe for the taking. I didn't even think to lock up when I was taken away yesterday, and Sean was probably too preoccupied with the search, then with trying to get me out of custody.

The hire car is still in the courtyard, just where I left it, but there's no sign of Sean's Land Rover. There's a strange smell in the barn kitchen – somewhere between delicious and disgusting as I see the half-butchered haunch of venison still on the chopping board. Blood has stained the wood, dark and dry, and a single fly walks across it. The contents of the big stock pot on the stove are cold and grey, the translucent onions floating in a skim of dirty froth and fat. A few fat carrots and sprigs of soggy herbs are stuck around the edge, the large bones protruding out of the soup. Everything is fit for the bin.

'Libby?' I hear someone call. 'Is that you?'

I whip around, half expecting to see DI Jones and another officer standing there, ready to arrest me, to take me away again. But there's no one. When I poke my head around the barn door, I see Arn's face over the wall.

'Everything OK?' he asks, looking me up and down.

'Yes, thank you,' I say automatically, though I know I look the opposite of OK. *Released under investigation…* echoes around my head as Arn tells me about his daffodil bulbs and how he's been pruning shrubs.

'Really?' I say. 'That's good,' I add, wishing he would go away. 'They'll be pretty in the spring.' I turn to shut the door.

'Couldn't help noticing the police car here yesterday,' he says. 'Everything all right? I didn't see any lights on in your cottage overnight either. I tried to call you and Sean but couldn't get through.'

Arn. Ever the good neighbour.

'Yes, yes it's all fine, Arn. Thank you. It was just to do with the investigation,' I add. 'There's no more news.' Which, as far as I'm concerned, is true. DI Jones never revealed they'd found a body, and the supposed evidence they had against me was, apparently, not enough to charge me with. I could have told them that at the beginning. I *did* tell them that at the beginning.

But what's more disturbing is that Arn didn't see any lights on in the cottage. Where was Sean? I shake my head, forcing out the nagging thoughts – not of *where* he was, so much as who he was *with*.

With the meat and food in the barn disposed of, I go back inside the cottage and check my phone. There's enough charge in it now to last a while and all I want to do is get to the farm, to fetch Alice. Before I leave, I call Sean but it goes straight to voicemail – and there are no messages from him, either, which is unusual. I'd have thought he'd have at least updated me on the search yesterday, before he realised I'd been arrested.

I get into the hire car and drive out of the courtyard, turning left up towards Marion and Fred's farm. The route takes me past the area where Sean and the others would have been yesterday – past the eastern gatehouse of the big estate. I imagine them all tramping across the dewy fields, their boots wet and muddy, shots of hot breath in the cold morning air, the gun dogs scampering about eagerly – running off at the slightest scent, before turning back to their masters, tails wagging, tongues lolling, silky ears flapping.

I slow down as I pass the open gateway where Sean would have parked. It leads into a small, flat area where, on a shoot, the beaters congregate early in the morning, getting into their gear – their sturdy dark-green trousers and jackets, tweed hats – as they sip from hip flasks and munch on snacks ready for the off. The area is empty, of course, though there are fresh tyre tracks in the mud, possibly from yesterday. I pull over, stopping in the gateway, almost hoping to see Sean's Land Rover still parked there, that perhaps he got a lift to the pub afterwards because he didn't want to have to drive later.

And then I see it, lying on the ground where the gateway opens up into the field. Sean's stick – longer than most walking sticks and perfectly straight apart from the top third, which is gnarly and twisted right up to the embossed silver top. He'd fallen in love with it the moment he saw it in the artisan's workshop. I'd secretly told the sales person to reserve it, that I'd be back to collect and pay for it the next day. It hadn't been long until Sean's birthday.

And here it is, lying in the mud. Discarded.

I go and fetch it.

'Sean?' I call out, knowing that if the Land Rover isn't here, then he's unlikely to be either. 'Sean, are you here?' There's nothing but the sound of the wind in the trees and the flapping of a couple of pheasants as they fly, almost vertically upwards, out of the thicket, their long tail feathers billowing behind them.

I take one last glance around before putting the walking stick in the boot and heading off.

It's when I'm passing through Chalwell, driving past the Old Fox pub, that I spot a couple of cars I recognise – Phil's estate Jeep, Tony's once-white van, plus Dean's wife's car, which he's obviously borrowed.

The shooting crowd are inside.

There's no sign of Sean's Land Rover, but he may have left it at Fred and Marion's – *again* – and got a lift down if he wanted a pint or two, perhaps ordering a Sunday roast with a couple of the guys. Though with me being arrested, I can't imagine him doing that.

I pull into the car park, knowing it's worth checking before I head to the farm. And someone may have news from the search.

As I get out of the car, I look at where Sean and I stood several weeks ago as he phoned for the taxi after our meal. My insides knot as I head for the door, opening the latch to be confronted by a warm, beery smell. The fire is blazing in the inglenook, and the flagstoned area is crowded with locals, most of whom I recognise.

And then I spot Sean's usual group standing at the far end of the bar, but not before they've spotted me. It's almost as if the entire pub falls silent as I walk inside – a lamb to the slaughter without realising it. I manage a small smile before I realise that every one of the group is glaring at me, their faces sour, their eyes bitter. News travels fast.

CHAPTER FORTY-FOUR

I stumble as I approach the men. A couple of them turn their backs on me, while another ignores me. Two of them, Dean and Tony, face me squarely, their expressions blank. Sitting behind them, I see Eric in his usual spot on a stool at the end of the bar, leaning over a spread-out newspaper.

'Hello,' I say, feeling small next to these giants of men. 'Is Sean here?'

'Nope,' Dean says, taking a sip of his pint.

'And neither should you be,' Tony says, edging me out of their group with his shoulder.

I lower my head, giving a small nod, and walk around them, approaching Eric. He lays down the pen he's holding.

'Eight down,' he says, pointing to the crossword puzzle. 'Missing,' he adds, looking directly at me. 'Four letters, second one is W.' Eric stares at me over the rim of his glass as he drinks.

'Erm…' I lean forward to take a look but my eyes glaze over. 'I'm not sure,' I say, aware that the others are staring at me, their eyes burning into my back. 'I'm not good at crosswords.'

'Do you want a drink, love?' Eric asks. 'Look like you could use one.'

'No, no thanks,' I say, relieved he's being friendly. I could easily knock back a couple of shots to steady my nerves, but on an empty stomach it would wipe me out. 'I was just wondering if you'd seen Sean today. And if the search turned anything up yesterday?'

Someone makes a noise behind me – a cross between a growl and a laugh.

'I've not seen Sean since yesterday,' he says, scratching his nose and clearing his throat. 'Sorry, love.' He turns back to the crossword, tapping his pen on the bar. 'Missing, missing, missing...' he mutters to himself.

'Did you and Sean search out near the Dentons' place?'

Eric looks up again, giving a loud smoker's cough. 'No, no, love. Sean and Phil went up that way, towards the big feed store on the crest of Cotton Hill, but didn't turn nothing up as far as I know. I went with the others, past Blake's Hill and over the rise. Covered a good few miles between us. We found a couple of things, a glove and a belt, but no one knows if they belong to the lass. The police have them.'

I nod, thinking.

'It's like the land harbours everything,' Eric says, coughing again. 'Layer upon layer of history trampled into the earth. Keeper of all secrets.'

'Oh... I—'

'Every time someone takes a step out there, they're leaving their mark one way or another. Hiding things.'

'I see,' I reply, unsure what Eric is trying to tell me.

'That man of yours, he's a good man, Libby. I've known him since he was born. I remember young Marion being pregnant, ripe as a peach. You won't believe it, lass, but I had a thing for her back in the day.' He coughs out a chuckle.

I force a smile, just wanting to go. Someone knocks into me from behind and then I feel wetness down the back of my leg. I doubt it was accidental.

'She's not well, you know,' Eric says, the look in his eyes turning serious.

'Marion? I know she's had a few health problems but—'

'I found her lying on the ground earlier that night, you know. Before I saw you out in your car looking for the lass. Remember?'

'On the *ground*?' I say, shocked.

Eric nods, sipping his pint. 'She'd just come out of your cottage. I helped her up, of course, but she wasn't herself. I wanted to call an ambulance but she wasn't having any of it. She said she just wanted to go home, insisting that she was fine to drive her car. She was deathly pale, sweating, clutching her side. And then, just after you stopped to speak to me, I saw her again, driving Sean back home. She really shouldn't have been behind the wheel if—'

'Oh *God*, why didn't you tell me any of this when I saw you that night, Eric?' My mind races, wondering what this means. *Knowing* what this means.

'Marion swore me to secrecy,' he says, with a look of regret. 'Like I said, I always had a thing for her, would do anything to make her happy.' Eric shakes his head. 'But ever since, it's been playing on my mind. She's a one for suffering in silence, is our Marion, but I can't stand the thought of it any more. Look out for her, will you, love?' he says, tears collecting in his eyes. 'Make sure she's OK?'

'Of course, of *course* I will,' I reply, planning to do exactly that, though not necessarily for the reasons Eric has in mind.

Marion was inside our cottage that night…

'I'll go up and see her right now,' I say, my voice shaking.

Eric nods. 'And remember, lass, what happens on the land, stays on the land. It's lore around here. Unspoken, but lore nonetheless.' Eric taps the side of his nose again and grins, exposing his yellowing teeth, a couple of them missing. 'They don't call me Eric the Elf for nothing now, do they?' He wipes away a tear in the corner of his eye.

'No, no I guess they don't,' I say, returning his smile as best I can.

'But sometimes,' Eric goes on, 'sometimes, the land whispers back. You remember that, too, and keep your ears open. Listen to what this place is telling you. It's wiser than any of us. Even me,' he says, breaking into a chesty laugh again.

'Thank you, Eric,' I say, touching his arm, just wanting to get up to the farm. 'By the way,' I add, leaning over and pointing at the crossword. 'Eight down is AWOL.'

And, as I turn to go, I see that Phil has come into the bar and has been standing right behind me all this time. I squeeze past him and the others, head down, willing myself not to stumble again as I push through the crowded bar. He tries to block my way, looking as though he wants to talk to me, but I ignore him, just keep on going.

'Leave it, mate,' I hear someone say. 'Come on, let's go out for a smoke.'

I rush for the door, running across the car park to my car. I fumble with the keys in the ignition – just managing to hold back the sobs before I drive off.

'Marion?' I call out at the back door, still shaken by what Eric told me. All I want is to scoop Alice up and take her home – but not before speaking to Marion. When I push the door to the boot room it's open, so I go in. 'Hello, anyone home?' The lights are off and the kitchen feels chilly, as if its soul has been removed. I look around. Everything is neat and tidy as usual. I carry on to the long hallway with the big staircase off, calling upstairs and listening out for the creaking floorboards.

Nothing.

In the living room, it's the same – the hearth empty of its usual coal fire, the newspaper folded up neatly on the small wooden table, the sofas with their flower-covered cushions plumped and unoccupied. One of Alice's dolls lies, half dressed, on the floor.

'Hello?' I call out again. They must be out on the farm.

Then I hear giggling.

'Alice?' I say, flinging open the door to the dining room that's only ever used at Christmas. A musty smell greets me, as does emptiness. There's no one in the stark room with its pink carpet, green velvet curtains and polished table – a tarnished silver candelabra sitting in the middle.

I close the door again and open the only other room off the hallway – Fred's study. I shove it open, almost frantic that Alice has been left alone but, when I go in, I see her sitting cross-legged on the floor opposite her granddad, who's in his chair, leaning forward, each of them with broad smiles on their faces. Neither of them notices me in the doorway.

'Oh no, Granddad, not again,' Alice squeals, clapping. 'You did get on a ladder and have to go all the way to the beginning again.' My little girl half rolls on her side with laughter, swishing back her hair as she bounces up and down with approval. 'Go on, go back to the square here, Granddad.'

'You're a hard taskmaster,' Fred tells her in a silly voice. A voice I've never heard before. 'And an expert at snakes and ladders. I bet you beat all your friends at playgroup.'

'We play catch and I always win,' Alice says, chewing on her finger. 'And we do skipping races, but I don't do playing this game with them. This is just for when I'm here with you and Nanny.'

Fred chuckles then looks up, catching sight of me in the doorway.

'Libby,' he says, nodding, half standing. He flicks his eyes to Alice, slowly shaking his head, as if I need telling not to say anything in front of my daughter.

'Mummy!' Alice squeals when she sees me. She leaps up off the floor and runs over to me, almost tripping on a pile of paperwork that Fred has left lying about. 'Mummy, Mummy, *Mummy*...'

She hurls herself against my legs, hugging me tightly. 'Pick me up, pick me up,' she says in a voice she knows will win me over.

I bend down, my hands underneath her armpits as she stiffens, hauling her up onto my hip. 'Oh, my darling,' I say, whispering into her hair, pressing her against me. 'I'm so sorry, Mummy had to go away for a little bit.'

'That's OK, don't be sad,' she says. 'Nanny let me make brownies and Granddad took me on the tractor.' I feel her little body tense with excitement around me.

'That's good,' I say, trying to sound enthusiastic. 'Do you know where Nanny and Daddy are, sweetie?'

'No, but Nanny said I can live here if I want and that I can feed the hens with her every day. Can I, Mummy?' she says in a pleading voice.

I give her a squeeze. 'Well, we'll see,' I say to humour her. 'Fred, do you know where Sean is?'

'Best you ask Marion about that,' he says, glancing at Alice. 'She's out on the farm somewhere. Said she had some kind of work to do.' Fred wipes his big hands down his face, shaking his head. 'She… well, she had that *look* in her eyes again, Libby.' He half stands up, an almost helpless look about him.

'Alice, you stay with Granddad and finish your game. I'll be back soon and we'll go home, OK?' I glance at Fred, nodding. He's obviously worried about Marion too.

My daughter makes a noise halfway between approval and disappointment as I leave, closing the study door before heading through the kitchen and out into the yard. I start with the usual places – the potting shed where Marion likes to spend time, tending to her seedlings in the spring or clearing out and planning for the next season in the autumn. But she's not there. Neither is she in the outbuilding at the back of the kitchen, where she stores the feed for the hens and other birds she keeps.

'Marion?' I call out. 'Are you here?'

I go up towards the pond and the henhouse, checking all around, knowing how, apart from doing the smaller jobs she's still capable of, she likes to just walk the land, just *be* in nature.

Keeper of all secrets... I hear Eric's voice say in my head.

'Hello, Marion?'

There's nothing in the henhouse but a few hens – their broody clucking somehow comforting, along with the smell of the wood shavings and chopped straw scattered about. I head on, further out towards the big barn where Fred keeps his machinery, mainly managed now by the three lads from the village he employs full-time. He has other seasonal workers come in to help when needed.

But the barn is empty, apart from several tractors, the combine and other equipment needed to run a farm of this size. I continue round behind the barn to an area that's rarely used, apart from storing the trailers and, sometimes, the big round bales wrapped in black plastic. I check several brick buildings including the old pigsty, some in disrepair, others being used for storage, all the while calling out for Marion.

There's no sign of her.

The last building I come to is the game store – a low brick structure with a tiled roof and concrete floor and, from what I can recall when Sean first showed me round the farm, several old freezers at the back for longer-term storage. It only gets used during the winter months, and it doesn't look as though anyone has been up here for a while. Fred hasn't done any shoots so far this year, though it's still early in the season.

'Marion?' I call out, about to turn round and give up, deciding to phone Sean again. I'll be checking with the hospitals if I can't contact him soon.

I freeze.

Someone is singing.

A soft but intense song on repeat. Someone chanting the same words to a soulless tune, over and over. It's coming from inside the game store.

'Hello?' I say, approaching the door. I pull it open, waiting for my eyes to adjust to the dim light. 'Oh…' I say, gripping the door frame when I see her.

Marion has a mop in hand and is frantically sloshing soapy water all over the painted concrete floor.

'Marion, are you OK?' I ask. But she doesn't look up – she just carries on, dipping the grey mop head in the bucket over and over without wringing it out, sluicing water onto the floor. Tears stream down her face as she keeps on singing in time with the mopping action. It doesn't look as though there's anything to clean up.

I go up to her, careful not to slip in the soapy water that's spreading around her. I reach out, putting my hand on her arm, her hair falling from its knot, her cheeks red and blotchy from crying.

'Marion, stop,' I say gently. 'What are you doing? Why are you crying?'

'*Hush little baby, don't say a word…*'

'Please, Marion. Stop for a moment. Talk to me.'

She gives a quick glance up, her glassy eyes looking straight through me, as though I'm not there.

'*Mama's gonna buy you a mockingbird…*'

She dunks the mop in the bucket again, not even watching what she's doing. Just mopping the same spot over and over. The game store reeks of disinfectant.

'Marion,' I say more firmly. 'Please stop. I'm worried about you. Let's talk.' I take her arm again, with a stronger grip this time.

'*And if that mockingbird don't sing…*'

'OK, come on. Enough now.' I feel her arm straining against mine as she tries to carry on, but I manage to pull the mop from her grip, putting it back in the big metal bucket. 'What are you doing out here? Tell me why you're crying?'

My eyes scan around the inside of the store. I've only been up here once before, when Sean brought me up to show me the dead game, how it was hung and matured before being butchered. The louvred windows had cast an eerie light over the carcasses hanging from the hooks – the deer to one side, the pheasants, partridge and rabbits to another.

I'd shuddered at the dead animals. Seeing them pre-butchering, their heads, eyes, fur and limbs all still attached, had somehow brought home their provenance, knowing that by eating them, I was part of the kill too. Marion often made and served game pies and stews and, indeed, moving to the area had made me think more about my menus and incorporating locally sourced ingredients. And, ultimately, that's what it was: food. The way the locals did things. Though the game larder made it seem much closer to death… to *murder*.

'Mama's gonna buy you a diamond ring…'

'Marion, please…' I glance about, looking for somewhere to sit. But apart from the stone slab against one wall for laying out meat, or the old chest freezers, there are only a couple of plastic tubs to sit on. And they don't look comfortable.

'Shall we go outside, get some fresh air?' I ask, putting my arm around her shoulder. The smell is unpleasant.

'No,' she says, stopping singing. Her lips are thin and dry, pale like the rest of her face. She doesn't look well. 'I can't leave. I need to clean up.'

'Where is Sean?' I ask, trying to guide her outside, but she refuses to move.

'They took him,' she says, matter-of-factly.

'*Took* him? Who took him?'

Marion stares at me. 'The police, of course. They took him away in handcuffs yesterday.'

CHAPTER FORTY-FIVE

I reach out for the wall, steadying myself. Sean *arrested*?

Marion starts singing again, taking hold of the mop. I slide the bucket out of her way with my foot, but it hits an uneven bit of floor and tips over, browny-green water spilling all around our feet. The mop clatters to the floor.

'Come and stand over here,' I say, taking her arm, leading her out of the mess. 'Your feet will get wet.' I guide her over to the freezer, trying not to shake, but it's cool in the game store, even colder than outside – though my shivering isn't just from the temperature. I go to lean against the old freezer and that's when Marion explodes.

'No! Don't touch that! Get *away*!' Her fists come up and she starts thumping me, tears streaming down her face as she pulls at me, tearing at my clothes. I grab her wrists, suddenly realising how frail she's become – almost brittle.

'Marion, stop, please. Tell me, what do you mean, the police took Sean?' I look her directly in the eye.

'They took him. They *arrested* him. That's what… what I was told. It's terrible. They said you'd gone too, but now you're back. Where's Sean? Where's my boy? Oh…' She sobs again, barely making sense.

'Who told you this, Marion?'

'His friend told me,' she said. 'It happened while he was out searching for Sasha. When he was trying to *help*.'

'Marion…' I bow my head, thinking. Sean must have been arrested the same time as me, then. All that time and he was likely in the next custody cell, perhaps in the interview room next to me. I shake my head, steadying myself on the freezer lid again. And that's when I see the hair – a few blond strands trapped in the seal.

I scream, unable to take my eyes off it.

'Oh *God*,' I whisper, backing away. 'No… no, please God, no…' My eyes are saucer-wide, fixing on Marion's face then back to the freezer again. I don't understand.

'Libby, don't,' she says, more in control now as I dare to take a step towards the freezer again. I need to know. As I reach out to the stainless-steel lid, Marion snaps her arm across mine, batting me away. 'Don't interfere with stuff you know nothing about. This doesn't concern you.'

'Marion, it concerns me greatly,' I say, my voice barely working. 'Let me look in there,' I say, reaching out for the handle again.

She shoves me hard, putting herself between me and the freezer. I stumble backwards, tripping against one of the two big plastic tubs, but manage to stay upright. 'What the hell's going on, Marion?'

'It's all sorted. All dealt with. Let me clean up,' she says, humming again, reaching for the mop.

'What is it you need to clean up?' I say, trying to stay calm. I'm speaking like I'd speak to Alice – coaxing, cajoling. She won't tell me anything if she thinks I'm against her.

She stops, leaning on the mop. 'It was so messy in here,' she says, eyeing the freezer. 'And it keeps… *leaking*.' She turns up her nose, shuddering.

'Leaking?'

'And if that diamond ring turns brass…'

'Marion, why is the freezer leaking? What's in it?'

'Mama's gonna buy you a looking glass…'

It's as if she's in a trance again, her thin body rigid, her arms gripping the mop as she swishes it back and forth in the spilt water.

Slowly I edge towards the freezer, reaching out for the handle, one eye on Marion in case she lunges at me again. I pull with one hand, but the lid doesn't give. I step closer and use two hands, trying to break the rubber suction seal. I try again and again, getting my weight behind it and, on the final pull, it suddenly gives, opening six inches or so.

I stop, staring, blinking, my eyes smarting. Vile fumes fill the air around me, making my open mouth snap shut, my eyes screw up tight, never wanting to open them again.

'Oh… *God…*'

I drop the lid down again, recoiling, screaming, covering my face. I double up, retching at the sight of what was once Sasha's face, leering up from beneath the foam and congealed fat. Parts of her head have come away – amorphous lumps of *stuff* with one piece attached to the edge of the freezer by a clump of blond hair, floating in some kind of liquid.

'No… no, *nooo*!' I scream over and over, unable to hold back the vomit. My stomach twists and clenches as I spew watery bile out onto the floor. There's nothing in me to come up, but still I retch. I wipe my mouth on the back of my hand, sweat pouring out of me.

'What have you *done*?'

Marion's face shows no emotion.

I retch again, my nose still filled with the stink of the freezer contents. There was nothing frozen about it – I can still feel the heat of whatever decomposition is taking place in there.

'I think the lye must have eaten some of the freezer too,' Marion says flatly. 'It's leaking. That's why I need to keep cleaning. Sean told me I must.'

'Sean…? I… I don't understand. Why is Sasha even *here*?' I cover my face again but all I see is that night – catching sight of myself in the mirror in my dress and boots, putting on my coat, my lipstick, smiling to myself that by the end of the evening things between Sean and me would be OK again. I'd gone downstairs to greet Sasha, asked if she'd got everything she wanted, told her there was some food in the fridge, then the taxi had hooted…

'Sean said it wouldn't take long, but it's been three weeks now. I keep adding more crystals, more water.' Marion points to the two big plastic tubs.

'Sodium hydroxide?' I whisper, looking at the labelling – big orange and black warning signs. *Danger… Corrosive…* plus a large cross and a person's hand with liquid dripping onto it, making a hole.

'Fred uses it to make the soda wheat feed for the cows. Not our cows any more, of course, but the local farmers buy our wheat once he treats it with the caustic soda. It's good for them, see. Helps with digestion. There's a special way of doing it, mind, and Fred's is the best.'

'Digestion?' I say, retching again. I'll never be able to unsee the fatty mess in the freezer. 'Oh, Sasha, no, dear *God…*'

'It's digesting her too,' Marion says, her voice thin and cold. 'But it's taking too long. Sean said it really needed heat, though it will work eventually. Water and lye. A good old-fashioned solution. Sean knows his chemistry.'

'*Sean…* oh God. But I don't understand why Sasha is even here at the farm. Marion, tell me, what's going on? And why are you involved with this?' I can't take it all in, the implications, how Sasha has ended up in the game freezer. After *everything*.

Marion begins mopping again, covering the same spot over and over. 'I only stopped by that night because I saw Natalie's car outside your place,' she says, glancing up at me, almost a smile on her face. 'I'd found Natalie's bracelet down the back of my sofa and popped it in my bag for when I next saw her. I'd gone to the church meeting at the vicar's house and, on the way, spotted Natalie at yours. But when I got to the vicarage, the meeting had been cancelled and no one had bothered to tell me.

So I drove back, hoping to catch Natalie to give her the bracelet, but it turned out she'd already left. I felt so bad not being able to babysit, I thought I'd call in anyway, see if Alice was OK, if Sasha was coping. I'd nothing else to do.'

The expression on Marion's face tells me she's being truthful, that she'd wanted to help. She must have dropped the bracelet while she was there.

'Go on,' I say, drawing closer. Anything to get further away from the freezer.

'Sasha was doing her homework when she let me in, but I could tell she was upset.'

That figures, I think, remembering. She'd seemed different when Sean and I went out, her mood low.

'I knew she'd been crying,' Marion goes on, leaning on the mop. She stares out of one of the louvre windows, the sunlight casting slatted shadows over the stone slab.

'Crying?'

'Well, she was *still* crying,' Marion goes on. 'I asked her what was wrong and she said that Dan's mother had upset her, calling her stupid, that kind of thing. She was trying to brush it off but I could see she was distressed.'

'Natalie upset Sasha?' I take another step away from the freezer. 'Why was she even there?' Alice was right, then. Natalie *was* in our house.

'Apparently Dan had left one of his schoolbooks there and she insisted that Sasha find it. You know how Natalie can be. Impatient, demanding.'

I nod.

'Dan wasn't there, of course, and Sasha did her best to find the book, but Natalie gave her a hard time. The thing is, it was the final straw for Sasha. She… she told me she'd already got a load on her mind, that she was upset anyway.'

I remember thinking the same as we left for our evening out. The taxi was outside and I was talking to her while Sean was doing something in the kitchen. I'd told him to hurry up.

'While I was there, I went upstairs to check on Alice. It sounded as though Natalie had caused quite a commotion. The poor lamb was hiding under her duvet with Mr Flumps. I calmed her down, read her a story.'

'I'm glad you were there, Marion,' I say. 'Did… did Sean know you'd come round?'

'Yes,' Marion says, pushing the mop again. 'I phoned him soon after. And sent lots of texts. I didn't want to disturb your meal, but didn't know what else to do. I had to… Well, things had happened, Libby. *Bad* things.'

'Marion, *what*? What happened?' I take both her wrists in my hands.

'Sit down,' she says, pointing to the two big tubs of caustic soda. I nod, leading her over. 'I don't feel well,' she says. 'I'm a bit light-headed.'

We sit down, our knees pressed close, our hands clasped tightly. And Marion begins to talk.

CHAPTER FORTY-SIX

'So many tears for a young girl, it broke my heart,' Marion says, pulling a handkerchief from under the frayed cuff of her sweater. She blows her nose. 'Plus I wasn't about to leave her in that state in charge of Alice. I wanted to know that she'd calmed down, could be responsible.'

'Thank you, Marion.'

'But I should never have asked her what else was wrong. Should never have *pried*, but how could I not? She was so upset and she knows… *knew*… who I was: Sean's mother. She couldn't help herself, all those feelings towards him bottled up. It all just came tumbling out.'

'Sean and *Sasha*,' I whisper, resigned to what I suspected all along. My head drops; I hate myself for doubting Fran, even for doubting Natalie. 'But she's a kid. How *could* he?' I barely have any tears left to cry, especially when I recall the look Sean gave Sasha as we left. He thought I hadn't noticed but I had – a last, longing gaze over his shoulder as we went out for the evening.

Marion looks puzzled for a moment, frowning, but continues anyway. 'After I'd settled Alice, I went and sat down in the living room. Sasha was even more emotional, telling me everything she knew. She just spilt it all out as though she couldn't contain herself, as if it was somehow *my* fault. And I didn't like what I was hearing. I didn't like it one bit.' Marion shakes her head, bites her lip, deep in thought, as though she's back there. 'I thought it was all in the past.'

'I can imagine, Marion. I'm so sorry. Sorry for the both of us. Him being with Sasha… it's unforgivable. So *much* of this is unforgivable.'

Marion looks at me as if she doesn't understand. 'She only found out by accident, you know. It's strange how these things stay buried for so long then resurface when no one's looking. Old secrets playing out.'

Eric's words flash through my mind again: *Keeper of all secrets…*

'Such a huge thing for a young girl to harbour,' Marion continues. 'But it was what she'd *done* about it that I didn't like. I haven't spent nearly twenty-five years covering this up for nothing, you know.' She wiped her face on her sleeve. 'And Fred… oh, *Fred…*' More tears come.

'I… I don't understand. Marion?' That's when I realise we're talking about different things. 'What secrets?'

'It wasn't an accident, love. Sean's leg,' she says, sniffing.

I make a face, wiping my own tears away. 'What do you mean?'

'It was his father. *He* did it.' Marion shook her head. 'He went for Sean with a shovel all those years ago. It was the nearest thing he could find in the barn. He was relentless, hitting him over and over, trying to beat it out of him. His leg took the worst of it, but, dear God, he almost killed him. For many years after, Fred wouldn't speak to his son. And Sean took a long while to recover physically, but more so emotionally. Though I doubt he ever has really.

'But you know what?' she went on. 'He never said a word against his father, telling the doctors he'd had an accident instead of the truth. Of course I felt wretched that I did nothing to protect Sean, that I was as terrified as he was. And anyway, I felt very differently about it all. He's my *son*. But Fred is old school, Libby. It's just his way. You'll never change people like him.'

'I… I still don't understand. What's this got to do with Sasha being so upset?'

'She *knew*, Libby. Sasha knew the secret. And… oh…' Marion buries her face in her hands, the tears coming hot and fast. 'First his marriage to Natalie broke down, and then I thought you'd leave him too… I couldn't risk it going wrong again, the family being torn apart. It's all been so perfect and I just wanted to keep it that way.' She sniffs, blowing her nose again. 'For Sean. He's been through so much and needs a good woman in his life. But it was for Fred too. I've been stuck in the middle for all these years.'

'What secret did Sasha know, Marion?' I'm freezing again, my entire body shaking as I sit holding my mother-in-law's hands, trying to push the image of what I saw in the freezer from my mind.

'I'm afraid I lost it, Libby. I'm not proud that I shouted at Sasha. It's the last thing the young lass needed after Natalie had laid into her. She was upset enough as it was. But when Sasha told me that she'd left a note on your car, trying to warn you, I just saw red. Sean is with *you*, and she was going to ruin everything. Your family, Libby. I was trying to protect your *family*.'

I shake my head, hardly able to believe it was Sasha who left the note. 'But why would she admit to her affair with Sean? Why would she tell me?' And then it dawns on me. 'She wanted to split us up so she could have him for herself…'

Marion pauses for a moment. 'No… *no*… what are you talking about? That's not how it is. Sasha wasn't having an affair with Sean. For God's sake, if only it were that simple.' She squeezes my hand. 'I tried to calm her down. She was pacing about, crying one minute and getting angry the next, going on about how her little brother would be devastated if their parents split up for good, how she needed to protect him too because he was still young, that she had to save their family unit. It was awful.'

'Oh, Marion…' I imagine the scene playing out as Sean and I were eating our crab claws, tearing into the focaccia, sipping on red wine.

'When she'd calmed down, I asked her if she'd eaten. She looked so thin, so pale. She said she hadn't been able to stomach food for days, so I went to the kitchen to heat something up for her.' Marion bows her head. 'Sasha told me you always put something special in the fridge for her because…' She chokes back a sob. 'Because of her nut allergy. She told me specifically which meal she could eat. I told her to leave it to me.'

I nod, barely listening, wondering if what I gave her – the chicken in a creamy turmeric sauce, her favourite – is now decomposing in the freezer along with the rest of her.

'But I did something terrible, Libby. It was as though I wasn't myself, as if someone else had taken over my thoughts. This voice in my head told me everything would be OK if only Sasha wouldn't tell the secret. *Couldn't* tell the secret.'

'What are you saying, Marion,' I whisper, grabbing her by the shoulders. 'Tell me!'

'I heated up a meal for her, even making her a cup of tea, and brought it in on a tray. It looked very similar to the food you'd labelled and left for her, but… but the one I gave her was a chicken satay. She didn't even eat much of it. Hardly anything really. Just a few mouthfuls before she got upset again, hysterical almost, saying she was going to tell you everything, that you deserved to know the truth.'

'About Sean having an affair?'

Marion nods.

So it *is* true. I close my eyes.

'Then, after another mouthful or two, Sasha slammed the tray down on the table and was pulling odd faces. She went bright red, standing up and lurching towards me. I didn't know what to do. Then she started throwing stuff around – her backpack, almost as though she was looking for something, but making a terrible mess too. I was scared by what I'd done, Libby. Can you understand that? I was really scared and instantly regretted it. She'd *trusted* me. I didn't mean to push her, but she came at me, spluttering with her eyes bulging and her arms flailing.'

I cover my mouth as Marion tells me her story, matching everything up with what Sean and I found when we got back from the pub – each of us caught up in our own problems, completely unprepared for what we would discover after the taxi dropped us back.

I'll never forget the sight of Sasha's contorted face when I went into the living room, staring up at the ceiling as she lay sprawled on the floor.

Dead.

'She fell, Libby. Sasha dropped to the ground and hit her head on the corner of the coffee table. And I just watched her.' Marion sobs, choking back more tears. 'Her mouth was so huge and her eyes… they were just gone. Taken over by all this… *face*.' Marion gestures her hands around her own face. 'It was as if her features had grown to twice their size. Her hand was reaching out to something on the floor – some kind of medication in a tube, so I grabbed it away from her. There was blood coming from her temple and by now her skin was covered in this… this *rash*. It was awful to watch but I was doing it to protect Sean, to protect *both* of you. I couldn't have her ruining everything.'

'*Shit*,' I hear myself saying, though it doesn't sound like my voice any more. I imagine Sasha trying to get to her EpiPen – the EpiPen that Sean threw on the fire, knowing that Marion's fingerprints would have been on it. 'Christ, *no*.' I think back, my hand over my mouth, racking my brains. I remember what Sean said to me – how he'd blamed me from the moment he saw Sasha's dead eyes staring up at us. And I'd believed him, blaming myself too. He said that I must have given Sasha the wrong meal and she'd had a massive and fatal anaphylactic reaction. I just didn't know *how* it had happened. I'm always so careful. I remember him going into the kitchen as soon as we got back, leaving me to discover Sasha's body. He must have disposed of the nut-free meal, protecting his mother.

'Marion, what colour was the lid on the food you heated up?'

'It was red. Yes, yes, I'm certain of that. A glass dish with a red plastic lid and a "chicken satay" label on it. The other dish in the fridge, the one you'd labelled for Sasha, had a green lid. It said "nut-free".'

Sasha knows to avoid anything that doesn't have a green lid on it. Vegetarian, vegan, gluten-free, nut-free… they all have their own colours. And, because she didn't heat up her own meal, she wouldn't have known it contained nuts. I *did* leave out the correct meal; it just didn't get eaten.

'As soon as it happened, I phoned Sean in a panic,' Marion continues, her face crumpled from worry. 'I was absolutely frantic. I didn't know what else to do. I instantly regretted what I'd done, that I'd killed her, but I knew Sean would understand why, that I was trying to stop everything coming out. It all happened so quickly. And her *face*… I just can't get it out of my mind.'

'No, me neither, Marion,' I say, thinking of the puffy, disintegrating remains in the game freezer. Sick rises up my throat again.

'Sean didn't answer his phone, so I called over and over. Then I sent text messages asking him to call me back. I wasn't sure if he even had phone reception in the pub and I didn't want to disturb you both, but this was… well, it was an emergency. I should have called for an ambulance, but after what I'd done, I was just too scared. Sean finally called me back from the pub toilets and I confessed everything. I told him that Sasha *knew*, that she'd intended on telling you everything, Libby. He said he'd take care of it all, that I should go home immediately, that he'd come back right away. He said Alice would be fine left alone for fifteen minutes. I hated leaving her but I'd told him she was finally asleep.'

I shake my head, cradling it in my hands. 'Oh *God*,' I whisper, thinking back over Sean's plan. It was riddled with holes from the start, though not so much a plan, I'm now realising, but a *set-up*. He knew Sasha was dead before we even left the pub, had had just enough time to concoct a story, putting the blame on me. Sean convinced me everything would be OK if I just did as he said, went along with him. But why?

'*What* did Sasha know, Marion? What was she going to tell me?'

Marion stares at me, blank-faced, ignoring my question. 'Sean told me to deny ever being at the cottage, and that if Alice had heard anything, she wouldn't know what had been going on, that the word of a confused and sleepy child wouldn't count anyway. But now it all just seems so *wrong*, Libby. Sasha is *dead* and I killed her. I feel so wretched, but I acted on impulse. And since then, I've had to keep...' She stares over at the freezer. 'I've had to keep yet *another* secret.' She sighs, crossing her chest. 'I just can't do it any more.'

Marion clutches at my hands again, desperate. 'Sean's been coming up here when he can, adding more of this stuff to... to make it, to make *her*, go away.' She taps the caustic soda tubs, a familiar sight on the farm, usually stored under lock and key. 'And now he's been arrested, when it should have been *me*.' She lets out another sob. 'I've been a fool, lived my life as a lie, all for nothing. I can't let it all be in vain.'

'Secrets are only secrets if you keep them, Marion,' I say, clasping her hands tightly.

Everything will be OK...

Sean's words after he'd hit me. It was the shock of finding Sasha, seeing her swollen and lifeless body, my subsequent hysteria that had made him do it. He'd panicked, needed me to shut up while he figured out what to do.

'Sean, *no*,' I'd said, my face smarting. 'We have to call the police. Our babysitter is *dead*.'

He'd stared at me, hatred in his eyes. 'This is *your* doing, Libby,' he'd said coldly. 'And I'm not prepared to have my life ruined over it. My career and family destroyed because of your carelessness – or, worse, your *jealousy*.' He'd paced about, occasionally stopping to stare at Sasha lying in the mess – the spilt food, the contents of her backpack strewn about, blood on the rug, her skin red and blotchy. 'I will sort it out. I will clean it all up and make it go away, but you have to do *exactly* as I say. Do you understand?'

Fear had made me believe him. Made me believe that I had killed her, that I'd left the wrong food out, knowing full well she had a severe nut allergy. 'The police will think you planned it, Libby, that you thought the note was about Sasha, that you were convinced she was having an affair with me. That you had a grudge. That you wanted her dead.'

My head – shaking and disbelieving – finally turned into a frantic nod. I knew he was right, not even caring if he was telling the truth about any affair or not. That was the least of my concerns.

'Do you want Alice to be without a mother while you spend the next twenty years in prison?' he'd said, pacing about, agitated.

Sitting silently on the window seat, the curtains pulled closed behind me, tears had poured down my face, my head shaking slowly. 'No,' I'd sobbed. 'No, I don't.'

'Then do you trust me?'

I'd nodded, not knowing what else to do. I felt trapped. No way out.

As time ticked on, Sean convinced me that he would take Sasha far away, get rid of her where no one would ever find her, somewhere peaceful, a decent burial. He said he'd leave a few of her things in another part of the countryside so that the police would think she'd wandered off, that something bad had happened to her. After a while the investigation would be scaled down, he'd said, and her body would never be found. 'It'll all blow over. Before you know it, Sasha will just be another teenage runaway,' he'd told me. 'I know the land well enough.'

Keeper of all secrets, I can almost hear him saying.

CHAPTER FORTY-SEVEN

'I can't believe he brought her *here*,' I say to Marion, knowing that he'd hauled Sasha into the Land Rover while I was out driving around the village, pretending to search for her. Marion must have driven him home, leaving Sean's contaminated vehicle up at the farm to clean. 'Whatever you did, he shouldn't have left you to deal with… all *this*.' Part of me wants to give her a hug, while the greater part of me wants to thump her. 'What the hell are we going to do now?' My mind is all over the place – Sean's voice still filling my thoughts, ordering me what to do, terrifying me into complying, controlling me. 'We… we need to get rid of…' I glance at the freezer.

Marion is suddenly on her feet. 'He's my *son*, Libby.' She looks at me, imploring me. 'And I still need to protect him. I'm going to confess everything to the police – tell them that I came to your cottage that night and I was angry,' she continues. 'That I shoved Sasha and that she hit her head. I'll tell them it was an accident, that it was all my fault and I panicked and brought her body up here. She's only small, after all.' She stands tall and straight. 'I can't have my son take the blame for this, not after everything. I've kept his secret safe for so many years, Libby. I'm not giving up now.'

'*What* secret?' I yell, getting up close to her and grabbing her again. But she looks right through me, her lips tight together. 'But they found blood in the boot of *my* car,' I whisper, my hand coming up to my head. It was true that Sasha had cut her hand. 'They'll never believe you.'

'Then I'll tell the police I used your car, that I took it without you knowing. It's an estate, after all, and the boot is bigger than mine. It makes sense. Plus I drove it not so long ago, remember? I'll make them believe me,' she says, suddenly animated and more like her controlled self again.

'No, this is madness. You can't do this. I won't let you.' I clutch my head, thinking. 'We need to tell them that Sean covered everything up, that he brought Sasha's body up here. It's time for the truth, Marion.' It hurts to betray Sean, but then he didn't hesitate to do the same to me. I just don't understand why.

Marion stops me, grabbing my wrists. 'Libby, you know I've been ill. The truth is, it's worse than I've been letting on. They thought I was in remission, but this last six months, it's come back. It's much worse now.' Marion holds her stomach. 'I might seem OK much of the time but it got in my liver, then my lungs. They thought they'd got it out all those years ago.' She shakes her head. 'I'm a fighter, Libby, but I also know when I'm beaten.'

I stand up, going over to her. 'Oh, *Marion*, I know you've had health issues, but… but you've got… *cancer*?'

She nods.

'I'm so, *so* sorry. I had no idea.' All this time she's been taking care of Alice while dealing with her illness, going to hospital appointments alone, and no doubt taking countless pills, having treatments.

'They found it just after Sean was born,' she says. 'I had a hysterectomy and was given the all-clear. But I knew I'd never have more children. Three years ago, I found out it had come back. They offered me chemo but I couldn't put myself through all that again. I opted for some radiotherapy, hoping that combined with medication would do the trick.' Marion smiles. 'But now it's in my bones too. It's the end of the line, Libby. I can't fight any more.'

'Oh, Marion,' I say, reaching out to give her a hug. But she ducks away, almost as if she's infectious.

'I've already called the police, Libby – not long before you arrived. They'll be here soon. Please. I can't change everything, but I can change *some* things. Let me put this right. I'll take the blame for everything, including covering everything up.'

I stare intently at her and, for a second, there's a flash of understanding between us. That, since she couldn't save Sean from harm all those years ago, from the wrath of his father because of whatever it was he'd done, she's been trying to save everything and every*one* ever since. Keeping his secret safe – so safe that she won't even tell me.

'Go to Alice,' Marion says. 'Go and get your beautiful daughter and go home. Hold her close and don't ever let go,' she adds. 'Not for a long while, anyway. Enjoy your life, whether that's with or without Sean. I have no control over that now. But talk to him. And maybe, just *maybe*, he'll talk back. But whatever happens, you will both always be Alice's parents. Love your daughter. Love her so much it hurts. And then, when it comes time to let her go, you know that whatever she does, whoever she is, however she chooses to live her life, promise you will always still love her, just as I have Sean. A mother's love can set free too, you know.'

My skin prickles as more tears well up. 'Marion…' I say, glancing out of the slatted window, listening out for cars. I don't understand what she's saying. 'I can't let you—'

'No,' she says, holding up her hands again. 'Go. Just do as I say and everything will be OK.'

Everything will be OK…

I nod, my eyes wide, one ear listening out for sirens.

'Sasha was not at your house when you came home from the pub.' She takes me by the shoulders, shaking me slightly. I give her a little nod. 'She'd gone missing and you don't know what happened. I've got less than six months to live, Libby. Let me do this. Please.'

I stare at her, wondering if Sean knows she's dying. I suspect he doesn't. Marion wouldn't do that to him.

I break down in tears again. 'Thank you, Marion,' I say, closing my eyes as she pushes me towards the door. When she picks up the mop, starts humming the nursery rhyme again, I give one last glance back then I turn and run – run as fast as I can back down to my little girl, back to the sweet scent of her hair, the softness of her skin, the depth of her sparkling blue eyes and the chatter of her constant questions.

'Oh, Alice,' I say, tears blurring my vision as I charge across the uneven ground to the farmhouse. 'Oh, *Sean*,' I sob, hardly able to take in what he's done. While I want nothing more than for him to hold me, for Alice to be pressed between us, I know I can't stand to face him. His betrayal is unspeakable and, right now, as the breath burns in and out of my lungs, I never want to see him again. All I want is to hold my daughter, to protect her. *Like Marion protected Sean all this time*, I think as I stumble across the courtyard – though I still don't know what from.

'*Alice…*' I call out, gasping for breath as I rush in through the back door. 'Alice, get your stuff, we need to go.' I charge through to Fred's study just in time to see them packing up the game of snakes and ladders. Alice turns suddenly, her surprised face changing into a grin when she sees me.

'Can we have fish fingers for tea, Mummy?' she asks, sliding the game onto a shelf.

'Yes, yes anything,' I say, scooping her up. I'm about to say something to Fred, my eyes locking with his as he sits, reclining in his armchair, but I stop. I just want to go, have time alone with my daughter before I face more police questions, which I know I will. Besides, I don't want Alice in the presence of a man who assaulted his own son, whatever the reason.

'Put your coat on,' I say to Alice in the kitchen, sliding her arms into her little jacket. I grab her backpack off the table and scoop her up, running out to the car, my hands shaking as I buckle her up in her car seat. I get in the driver's side, fumbling to get the keys in the ignition at the same time as dialling Fran's number, pinning my phone to my ear with my shoulder. Reversing the car round, I drive off up the bumpy track to the lane, praying that Fran picks up. Either way, I'm heading to hers. Either way, I can't go home.

'*Fran*,' I say, choking up the second I hear her voice. 'It's me… thank *God*…' I glance both ways along the lane as I pull out, catching sight of two marked police cars with flashing lights coming the other way. They don't take any notice of me as they scream past, don't slow down as they swing down the farm track.

'*Yes, yes of course*,' I hear Fran say when I ask her if we can come over, if we can stay for a while. She senses my urgency, doesn't ask questions. After I hang up, after I've dropped the phone from relief, tears stream down my face so that I can hardly see to drive.

EPILOGUE

Yesterday

It was first light and there was a chill in the air. The group of men met in the usual gateway, the one just past the eastern gatehouse of the estate. The first rays of sunshine bled between the trees, highlighting the honey stone of the building with flecks of gold. It was virtually silent – as though the land was still sleeping, with only the sound of the men's low voices and birdsong audible. A pheasant flapped out of a nearby thicket.

Sean raised his arms, holding his carved walking stick as though it was a shotgun, closing one eye and tracking the path of the bird with the imaginary barrel. He made a shooting sound and recoiled, as if he'd fired.

'For another day,' Phil said, treading from one foot to the other.

'Yeah,' Sean replied, looking at him, leaning the stick against the back of the Land Rover. He made a sympathetic face, patted Phil's shoulder. 'Everything will be OK,' he said, giving a nod.

Phil nodded in return.

'Right,' Sean called out to the group. 'You four head up towards Blake's Hill,' he said, gesturing to some of the men. 'But track along the brook first, taking in the area around the silos too.' Then he gave further instructions to the others. 'Phil and I will head out towards the Dentons' land, covering the lower areas first, including where it adjoins the estate near the patch of woodland with the pheasant-rearing nets.'

They all nodded, a couple raising their hands to show they'd understood.

'We'll check the maize areas too,' he continued. 'No one's been up there yet and Christ knows what ground the police have covered. Not much, by all accounts.'

There was a rumble of agreement as the dozen or so men nodded, shaking their tweed-capped heads, before the groups set off – some on foot, spaniels running to heel, and several others in their vehicles.

'Hop in,' Sean said, pointing to his Land Rover. 'We'll take mine.'

Phil nodded and opened the door, shoving aside things on the seat, including Sean's Barbour jacket and a flask of coffee. 'Someone's birthday?' he said, moving the gift bag. His face betrayed no expression. He wasn't in the mood for jokes.

'Yeah,' Sean said, glancing at him and starting the engine.

The Land Rover bumped off and they drove in silence along the lane, slowing at a gateway as a car came the other way. Sean sprayed the windscreen with water, smearing it for a moment until it cleared, squinting into the sun.

'I saw her, you know,' he said, gripping the steering wheel. 'Sasha.'

Phil's head whipped round. '*What?*'

Sean raised a hand. 'No, no, I don't mean since she went missing. It was five days before that, on the Monday. I saw her standing at the bus stop in Great Lyne, the one just opposite our place. It was early in the morning.'

'What was she doing there?' Phil said, frowning. 'She always gets the bus from our village.'

'She'd walked to Great Lyne, apparently, and was waiting to get to college. That's what she told me as I was de-icing the car. I'd waved to her and she came over. She didn't look happy. I was on my way to work so ended up giving her a lift into town as the bus was late. She took some coaxing to get in.'

'But why was she in your village?'

Sean swallowed drily as he remembered having exactly the same conversation with Sasha, asking her why she wasn't leaving for college from her usual stop. She'd been vague with him to start – terse and curt – and was shaking and visibly upset. Despite this, she'd wanted to talk.

'Because she *knew*, Phil,' Sean replied, giving him a glance. 'She was troubled about it. *Very* troubled, and didn't look well, as though she hadn't eaten properly in days.'

'Christ,' Phil said, resting his elbow on the door ledge, staring out at the countryside. 'I had no idea.'

'I drove her to college and calmed her down, convincing her she'd got it all wrong. By the time I dropped her off, she promised me she wouldn't say anything. But it turned out she already had,' Sean said, his knuckles turning white as he gripped the steering wheel. 'She'd left a note on Libby's car.' He gave Phil another look.

Phil sighed heavily, shaking his head. '*Shit...*'

Of course, Sean hadn't been able to tell any of this to Libby. And now he couldn't tell everything to Phil – what they'd found when they got back to the cottage that night.

A mile or so further on, Sean slowed again, pulling over into a gateway. But this time there was no car coming. He turned off the engine.

'Don't you need to take the track up ahead? Loop back round to where the Dentons' land meets the footpath from Great Lyne? It's a route Sash may have taken for a short cut,' Phil said.

'Yes,' Sean said. 'We'll go there. But look.' He pointed across the field, currently lying as grass. A tractor shed and a couple of barns sat squat over to one side, up against a wooded area. 'I remember when all that was planted,' Sean said. 'The saplings were only so high, about the same as us.'

'How time passes,' Phil said, staring out at the mature wood.

Sean nodded. 'Come on,' he said. He beckoned Phil out of the vehicle, pointing up to the barns.

Phil hesitated. 'No, Sean. Why would you want to?'

'I've never been back since. Haven't been able to. But now... well now, things feel different. As though I *need* to.'

Phil shook his head. 'OK,' he said, sighing and getting out of the Land Rover.

Sean gathered his jacket from the seat, slinging it on before he got out of the car. The two men climbed over the five-bar gate, jumping down the other side, their breath clouds of white in the cold morning air. They walked over the uneven ground towards the barns in silence, each of them thinking of times past – long hot summers on the land when Fred would employ them, paying them each ten pounds for the day to drive tractors, cart bales, unload them into the Dutch barns. In the winter, when the land was frozen hard, they'd still be out here. Up to no good on their bikes, pedalling fast between the villages to see their mates, sneaking off with whatever bottles of alcohol they could nick without being found out.

They were just lads. *Good* lads.

'It was here, wasn't it?' Phil said as they drew close to the red-brick building. 'It's looking a bit worse for wear now.'

'No, it was this barn. The stone one. Not something I'm likely to forget.' Sean stopped for a moment, one hand on his hip, the other clutching his jacket around him. 'It wants tearing down.'

'Looks as though it'll fall down before long.'

Sean stared up the steep incline to the north side of the field. The incline he claimed the round bale had rolled down, flattening him in its path, badly bruising and smashing up his right knee. No one ever questioned his story, why his injuries didn't quite match up to his version of events. Things were different in those days. Boys mucking about on a farm – tractors, machinery. Accidents happened all the time.

Sean went closer, right up to the flaking wooden door of the barn. It was half hanging off its hinges. He stood, peering into the darkness, his skin prickling with goosebumps as Phil came up behind him.

'Hooky, bread and cheese,' Phil said, laughing. The first laugh Sean had heard from him in three weeks. 'And some weed if we could get it.'

'The good old days,' Sean added, turning to find Phil close, his eyes filled with tears.

Sean stepped inside the barn, brushing cobwebs off his face. His eyes gradually grew accustomed to the dim light, his nose catching the smell of rotting hay, of rats, of ancient oil from the rusting quad bike. There was a pile of tools stacked in one corner: rakes, picks, forks and shovels. They were virtually as old as the building. Sean swallowed and screwed up his eyes as he remembered…

'Dad, no, *don't*!' he'd cried, tears streaming down his face. His young cheeks burned pink from embarrassment. 'Da-*ad*!' he'd wailed, shielding his head with his arms. He'd tried to save himself, pushing himself back on his bottom along the floor, trying to escape his father's wrath. Fred loomed over him, shovel in hand, grabbed from the stack of tools when he realised why Sean wasn't out working.

'*No son of mine…*' he'd roared, raising the shovel, bringing it down on Sean over and over, smashing him wherever he could. His rage was unstoppable.

Sean had screamed and yelled, trying to stand up and run away, but every time he did, his father knocked him down again.

'It still smells of blood in here,' Sean whispered, swallowing, opening his eyes. He was shaking. A tear rolled down his cheek, and, at close range, he saw the same on Phil's face. He stopped, turning his ear to the doorway, thinking he'd heard something – a car perhaps.

'I've got something for you,' Sean continued, thinking he'd imagined the noise. He slipped his hand inside his Barbour, pulling out a black and gold gift bag. 'Happy birthday,' he said. 'For next week. I didn't know when…' He lowered his head. 'I just thought today would be a good day to give it to you.'

Sean listened out again.

Phil nodded, drawing closer. 'Thank you,' he smiled, his voice wavering.

'Go on, open it, you silly bugger.'

Phil took a small packet out of the bag and pulled off the paper, dropping it on the ground. He opened the box inside, staring at the lighter before taking it out. He turned it round in his big hands, running his thumb over the engraving.

'Thank you,' he said quietly. 'It's beautiful.'

Sean drew closer and wrapped his arms around him, closing his eyes when Phil reciprocated. He felt Phil's warm breath on his neck. 'I'm glad you like it,' he said, listening out again. He swore he heard voices, that they were getting nearer.

'I'm sorry I didn't do anything back then,' Phil whispered, 'after your father found us together. I'll never forgive myself. I was a coward. I ran away, almost knocking your mum over as I fled.'

Sean shook his head. 'It's history now,' he said. 'Secrets buried in the land.'

He put his finger under Phil's chin, tilting his face close. And then he kissed him, each man seventeen again, their attraction undeniable as they lost themselves in the moment – reliving everything from the past as well as enjoying what they had now.

'She saw us, you know. Sasha,' Sean said, pulling away, their faces still close. 'It was one night several months ago when I dropped you home after we'd been to the pub. She told me she'd seen us kissing in the Land Rover, after Matt had brought her home. We were too careless.'

'Oh, *Sash*,' Phil said, resting his forehead against Sean's.

'She was upset, said she didn't know what to do, that she was angry as hell you were cheating on her mum. Then she decided to keep it a secret, not tell a soul. That's why the sweater I gave you went missing. Sasha was trying to hide any evidence from her mum. She just wanted you and Jan back together.'

Sean stroked his head as Phil let out a sob. 'Oh my poor beautiful girl.'

'But then she started watching us, getting more and more suspicious. When she saw us together several more times, watching and waiting to catch us out, she realised it wasn't just a one-off. *I know you love each other*, she told me.'

'And what did you say?'

'I told her she was right, that we did love each other, that we had done since we were teenagers but that sometimes people couldn't always be together.'

'Christ, I should never have hidden this from her, *or* from Jan. We should never have hidden it from *anyone*.'

Sean nodded, hanging his head. 'But Phil, right from the start when my father caught us, we were told it was wrong, that *we* were wrong. We didn't know any different back then, and *he* certainly didn't… and then… and then Mum tried to make everything OK, introducing Natalie to me, virtually forcing us to get married, to be "normal" for my father's sake. And that's just the way it stayed for so long… oh God, it's all such a mess… If only things had been different…'

'Don't cry,' Phil said, hugging Sean close.

The two men looked at each other, drawing in for another kiss – but Sean suddenly stopped, catching sight of four police officers standing in the barn doorway, silhouetted against the morning light.

'Sean Randell?' one of them said loudly, approaching.

Phil swung round, their arms still entwined.

Sean froze. He didn't recognise the officer. 'Yes?' he said, his mouth suddenly dry.

'I am arresting you on suspicion of the murder of Sasha Long. You do not have to say anything…'

The police officer's voice faded into the background, obliterated by the ringing in Sean's ears as he realised what was happening, as the other officers came up and surrounded him, snapping cold metal cuffs around his wrists. Everything seemed in slow motion.

'What the *hell*…?' he heard Phil say, the horrified expression on his face boring a hole into Sean's heart.

Phil backed away, while Sean's eyes implored him, begged him to see the truth – that by covering everything up, by protecting his mother, he was also protecting *them*. Keeping their secret safe.

'Phil, no… It's… it's not what you think, I swear…' he heard himself say, hating the look of agony and betrayal on Phil's face. 'Honestly, please believe me,' he said, his voice failing as Phil backed away, his eyes flicking between Sean and the police officers as they drew around him. 'Phil, no, you have to listen to me, please… Everything will be—'

And the last thing Sean remembered before he went down, before the world went black, was Phil's fist against his jaw.

A LETTER FROM SAM

Dear Reader,

I do hope you enjoyed reading *Date Night* and that it kept you gripped all the way to the end. I really loved writing this one – and not least because of the beautiful Cotswolds setting. Meantime, I'm already planning my next novel, so if you'd like to read more books by me, then it would be great if you could take a few seconds to sign up below to get all the latest news about my forthcoming titles.

www.bookouture.com/samantha-hayes

One of the questions I get asked most is 'Where do you get your ideas from?' and it's a really tough one to answer. For me, weaving a finished book is an organic process, with ideas coming from many sources (before and during writing), and not least my imagination. For *Date Night*, the seed of an idea began when I read a woman's cry for help after she'd been sent an anonymous note stating that her husband was having an affair. It was sadly one of many similar public posts on a forum about relationship break-ups – with the common denominator being that once the trust between two people is destroyed, there's a tough journey ahead.

For some time, I'd wanted to write a book set in this beautiful area of the Cotswolds, becoming utterly convinced of this after I spent a weekend there, staying at an idyllic village pub/B & B early in the writing process. Wandering around the pretty lanes, it seemed that the very fabric of the ancient buildings were steeped in history – and potential mystery – and I wanted to capture the tranquillity and beauty of the area, but with the horror of a terrible crime rocking the close-knit community.

Before I began writing, I already had several of the main characters developing in my mind – Libby and Sean especially, a hard-working couple who have always pulled together as a team. But what if things weren't as perfect as they seemed? What if one of them had a secret? What if that secret came out and their lives unravelled? Sasha's disappearance was integral to this evolving picture, adding to Libby's shock and upset after receiving the note. All I needed was a way to tie the two threads together.

What I love most about writing psychological thrillers is that nothing is ever quite as it seems. People in 'real life' don't fall into neat categories, and neither should they in fiction. It's all too easy to make assumptions about people (often based around our own experiences) and I wanted to challenge that notion. What Marion did to Sasha was horrific – and indeed Sean attempting a cover-up – but the terrible crime mother and son committed was ultimately based on fear – a fear that had been socially instilled in Marion and Fred, and similarly in Sean since he was a teenager when all he'd done was be true to himself and his feelings.

The severe prejudice of his father drove Sean to live most of his life as a lie, though the essence of Sean as a whole person, who he intrinsically was, could never be extinguished. It was taking this theme of 'all is not what it seems' that provided me with the inspiration to gradually unpack the truth through Libby's ordeal after she was arrested – how the story she and Sean had spun to the police, to their family and friends, was so very far from reality. Similar to the way Sean had been forced, through no fault of his own, to live his life as a lie.

So that's a glimpse of how ideas develop for me And how *Date Night* came about. If you enjoyed reading it as much as I loved writing it, I'd be so thrilled if you wrote a quick online review. Feedback from readers is invaluable to authors and I love reading your thoughts on my books – as do other readers!

Finally, it would be great if you joined me over on Facebook, Twitter or Instagram, and my website has details of all my other books, plus a little bit more about me and how I came to be an author.

Until next time, happy reading and I can't wait to share another book with you.

Sam x

samanthahayesauthor

 @samhayes

 @samanthahayes.author

www.samanthahayes.co.uk

ACKNOWLEDGEMENTS

Behind every book there's a brilliant team and, as always, my huge thanks go to my amazing editor Jessie Botterill, who makes every book shine. Couldn't do it without you, Jessie! Of course, my sincere thanks and gratitude go to all the brilliant people at Bookouture – it's a pleasure to be part of such a supportive team – staff and fellow Bookouture authors alike. Massive thanks, too, to Kim Nash and Noelle Holten for their tireless work – and always with a smile on their faces!

Big love and thanks to Oli Munson, my agent, for 'having my back' and similarly everyone at A.M. Heath. Thanks muchly for all your hard work.

I'd like to say a very special thank you to all the bloggers and reviewers who read and review not just my books, but thousands of others, helping to spread the word about stories they love. I really do appreciate every review, tweet, follow, share and general shout-out.

Finally, thanks to you, my amazing readers, for taking the time to read my book and getting to know my characters. I hope they keep you entertained and that you'll join me in my next one!

And, as ever, much love to my dear family, Ben, Polly and Lucy, Avril and Paul, Graham and Marina, and Joe, who have been so utterly supportive and kind this last year. It means so much. xxx